Under His Protectio

The White Rose Trilogy
Book One

Stacy Von Haegert

Dragon Crest Publishing

Nashville, TN

Under His Protection
Book One: The White Rose Trilogy
by Stacy Von Haegert

Cover Art:
Dawne Dominique of from DusktilDawne Designs
Edited by: Laura Ranger

Published in the United States of America
Worldwide Electronic & Digital Rights
Worldwide English Language Print Rights

CONTENTS

I	1
II	23
III	49
IV	93
V	101
VI	115
VII	131
VIII	155
IX	167
X	187
XI	201
XII	221
XIII	237
XIV	251
XV	259
XVI	289
Preview	293
About Stacy Von Haegert	301

I

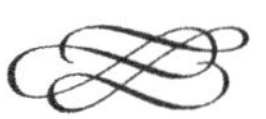

LONDON

Alexander felt the wind precede the expected blow, a split second before the blond man's fist drove into his jaw. A moment later, his attacker came into focus from where Alex now lay on the floor. Nothing like good fisticuffs to start the evening. Alex hooked his left leg behind the man's calf and with a twist, brought him down.

The man hit the ground as if he had been hurled from the sky. He quickly righted himself, much faster than expected for a fellow well into his cups and flew at Alex. Unable to avoid the charge, they collided with bone-crunching solidness and rolled.

A high-pitched scream rang out amongst the rough sounds of chairs being pushed back and excited exclamations of eager patrons, men ready for more lively entertainment. Alex rationed, between blows, the scream had probably come from the busty redhead who had just seconds ago been sitting in the lap of the man who was now trying to smash in his ribs. He could understand her concern, though it was more likely due to the possible loss of income rather than feigned care for her potential client. Men tended to forget their lustful pursuits when they had a broken nose after all, and to her credit, she had worked all her charms on the young blond man for the better part of two hours.

Alex smiled as his fist found its mark on the man's mouth again. He decided to consider it a lesson he was providing the girl. She should have kept her ass on the quiet viscount's lap instead of trading up for the wealthy, arrogant American.

A tankard of ale doused the feuding men and Alex was dragged backward forcefully. He hoped like hell someone on his side of the evening's debacle was putting forth the brute force effort. He was swung to his feet.

He spun to see who had removed him. A mixture of relief and remorse took hold when his eyes met the Earl of Kennington's scowl. Alex spat blood out the side of his mouth and adjusted his cravat.

"Time to go, old chap," Thomas, Alex's lifelong friend said in what was becoming a familiar, and equally annoying, chastising tone.

Alex felt a brief pang of guilt for his best friend. Thomas had been winning all night, and now, before the count of ten, they both would be escorted out.

Across the room, another man hauled the American to his feet. He angrily wiped the back of his hand across his busted lip. "Tomorrow at dawn, Hyde Park!"

Alexander inclined his head, just enough to be considered rude. "I shan't be late."

Thomas all but shoved him out of the club's side doors just as two burly doormen marched in their direction. Alex waved them off. "I will have my man bring around the necessary funds in the morning."

The men followed Alex and Thomas outside. Once they were in the black of the alleyway and cut off from all commotion inside, one of the men addressed them. "We know you're good for it, Your Grace, and we normally wouldn't ask ye to leave, but The Queen is pushing these new town orders. Has a blasted guard at every pub." The man's brows twisted uncomfortably on his face, as he glanced at his comrade. "We can't be losing our living, ye know."

Alex reached into his coat pocket and tossed a bag of coins at the man. "I know. This should cover what I have destroyed, and as I said, I will have my man bring more in the morning."

He turned on his heels and strode to the waiting carriage, which bore the Kennington family crest proudly on the door. Thomas's driver hurried down from the rig to get the door.

"Well, that is bloody damn great," Thomas said. "A duel at dawn over a game of Loo. Mayhap, next time you can beat someone senseless over getting the best shade tree at the park."

Alex shrugged and swung into the carriage. Thomas climbed in with an exasperated snort and sat across from him.

"He was cheating," Alex growled.

"It was only a game," Thomas reminded him. "And I believe calling someone a…what was it?" He paused for dramatic consideration. "Oh yes, 'a slave-trading halfwit'." The earl donned his best droll expression. "That is rather provoking."

Thomas chuckled, unable to maintain the serious inclination that Alex was better known for, but his mirth faded into an awkward silence as the rolling carriage made its way onto Oxford Street. The somber mood in the rig closely matched the closed shops that lined the lane. They would be bustling again in four hours' time; about the time Alex would be putting a bullet in an obnoxious American.

After a spell, Alex pulled his fixated stare from the window and ventured a glance at his companion. Thomas's face was void of cheer. In its place was… *Was that pity?* Alexander studied his best friend closely.

"Alex, I know it has been hard…"

Alex rolled his head back and stared at the ceiling. "Do not start, Thomas. And, for the love of God, do not ever allow your face to assume that expression around me again."

Thomas closed his mouth and looked down at his boots. "I guess I should thank you," he said after a few moments. "Since you have developed your fighting skills so effectively, I have learned everything one should know about being a man's second. Why, I think I shall write a book."

The earl lifted his gaze and smiled. Alex shook his head, unable to maintain his ill-temper. Thomas had that way about him. A way of lightening even the darkest of moods.

The earl was a big man—taller than Alex's six-foot frame—and quite intimidating. Until he smiled. When the corners of the earl's lips curved up, his whole face beamed. It was absolutely contagious. Alex hated it.

"Will there ever come a day when you might allow me to just brood in peace?"

Thomas laughed. "No."

THE CARRIAGE ARRIVED at Westington Manor. Alex jumped out in hopes of avoiding further conversation. Before he could get away, Thomas stuck his head out the door and declared, "You are the bloody Duke of Ravenswood now. Best start acting the part."

Alex turned back and glared at his friend. "Thank you for the reminder. Now pray, excuse me, for I need to rest before I kill someone in a few hours."

"I will meet you at six." Thomas tapped the roof and the coach rolled on.

Samson met Alex at the door and took his jacket without inquiring as to the evening's affairs, or to his master's disheveled appearance. Alex appreciated his butler's stoic silence. The man had worked for the family for thirty years. The household's first rule was, do not ask. The second, do not gossip.

Alex entered the study, snagged a decanter of brandy as he passed the bar and poured himself a glass before plopping down in his favorite chair and lifting his long legs onto the footstool. He set the bottle on the side table and sunk back into the supple leather. Swirling the liquor in his glass, he watched the brilliant dance that played out between the golden liquid and the transparent crystal. Round and round it moved as long as there was a human hand to incite it. Once he stopped, gravity would regain control and drag the brandy back down the edges of the glass.

Alex swirled the beverage again as if he expected a different outcome. Almost hopeful that the amber hues would defy their fate and continue to spin, filling the interior of the glass with bewitching color. It did not happen.

He sighed and lifted the crystal to his lips. At least it was a consistent disappointment, much as his life had become. No one could label him misleading, and brandy would always surrender to gravity. On that note, he tipped back the glass and closed his eyes, allowing the sweet warmth of the alcohol to soothe his throat.

After a few blissful seconds in numbing darkness, Alex opened his eyes. A pair of glowing gold ones peered out at him from the shadows cast on the far side of the room.

"Ah, Malikite. Come." The eyes moved up a good three feet before the muzzle of the black wolf came into view. Alex laughed and patted his thigh. "You bloody well would rattle someone's bones."

Malikite padded forward and nuzzled his hand. The half-Collie, half-wolf had been a gift Alexander's father had brought him back from Ireland two years prior. Despite the original owner's insistence that there was indeed Collie in the beast, the half-breed looked as if it were the walking definition of a wolf. Because of that, Alex had to be careful where he took the dog in public. He preferred to keep Malikite in the country but his prolonged, self-indulgent, stint in London had meant bringing the unusual pet with him. The half-breed did not do well in the kennels with the other hounds at Alex's country estate. The dog was a loner, just like his master. He was also the last gift Alex's father had ever given him, and the last living connection he had to the late Duke of Ravenswood.

On that sobering memory, Alex drained his glass and reached to refill it. His father had been dead four months now. He ran his fingers through the animal's thick coat, drawing a tail wag. Malikite's stealthy eyes softened as he relaxed into his master's familiar touch.

Alex tilted his head into the high-back chair. He really needed to get his act together, the rational part of him mused. Duels at dawn had to desist. However, the other part of him, the irrational and metaphorical devil side, insisted the man he had fought tonight was a blatantly arrogant bloke and deserved to be put in his place.

And, he had been cheating. Alex continued to mentally list off distasteful attributes the blond gentleman possessed. He was clearly an outsider. Just like Alexander's half-brother, Henry.

Even though his best man, Hobbs', investigations turned up nothing, Alex knew Henry was responsible for his father's death. But Alex could not interrogate him if he could not find him. His brother had vanished without a trace. The man was like some kind of elusive water creature, always disappearing into the depths just before discovery.

Alex stood and placed his glass down forcefully on the table, hard enough to make the dog flinch. He needed to get to bed. Going over where his deplorable brother might, or might not be, would only keep him refilling his glass and staying up until the sun was high in the sky. No, Henry was not going to rob him of another night's sleep.

Alex patted Malikite's head, as a way of an apology, and headed for the door. He desperately needed to maim something, and if it could not be his half-brother, it might as well be that pompous American fool.

Unable to sleep, Greyland had abandoned her bed and sought refuge in the library with hopes that a good book might ease her troubled mind. She glanced up at the grandfather clock and sighed. Literature, for the first time in her life, was failing her.

Try as she might to lose herself in a good story, thoughts of her father's parting conversation with her eldest brother, Perkin, still plagued her. She had overheard, conveniently from outside her father's half-closed parlor door, that her father wished all three of his children to find respectable spouses. "With luck," Richard Kingston had added in a confident tone, "you will all be married off within a year."

A year! Greyland felt her blood-pressure rising anew just thinking back on his preposterous challenge. How on earth could she find a respectable man, a man she could grow to love, a man that loved her, and cats, and long walks, and swimming at night, and plays, and lemon-cakes, and—

She snapped the book closed, irritated. She could do a lot in a short amount of time but finding her dream match within the confines of a year was just unheard of! And why the sudden hurry to send them off? Up until arriving in England, it seemed to Greyland that her father preferred she never leave the family.

She had left no stone unturned in her relentless questioning of Perkin. After their father left for Ireland, she had stalked him at every turn, peppering him with her assumptions, willful denial, and finally, absolute refusal. Completely unaffected, a Perkin trait, her insufferable brother had simply assured her 'it was time'.

"Greyland, we all must play our part," he had said. "We cannot live our entire lives under the same roof. I know father has always shown you special considerations..." He had looked down at her like one might consider a wounded duck that knew not of his afflictions. Greyland had wanted to stomp on his foot.

His foot's only saving grace was that he had thought to smile, a sympathetic older brother smile that always managed to calm her and continued. "You know father will always be here for you and support your decisions." He leaned in and kissed the top of her head. "It is time."

Marriage. Within a year? She shook her head, causing curls to loosen from their braids and fall around her face. The task was daunting, but it certainly had a few merits.

Greyland tapped her lips contemplatively and felt them curve into a half-smile below her finger. She would get to spend time in London, a city bursting with potential for a love match. She was beyond lucky that her father did not subscribe to arranged marriages. She would be free to choose. And she was eager to indulge in all the hoopla surrounding the many balls and plays, masquerades, and dreamy walks in the parks. Those aspects thrilled the hopeless romantic side of her nature.

It would be nice to settle in one place for a while. Her father had kept them traveling for the past three years, everywhere from Budapest to Brazil. The voyage was exciting and made Greyland feel most worldly. Why, it was as if she had lived a hundred lives in her mere nineteen-years.

However—a big however, and odd for her personality—what she craved now was a sort of stillness. Granted, she still wanted events to clutter her days and evenings; she needed activity. But now that their traveling was done, she yearned for a slowing down of sorts. Time to relax and immerse herself in a culture and its people. London seemed like the perfect place to have her 'proverbial cake' and eat it too.

Greyland stood and walked over to the bookshelf. She nudged a leather-bound copy of *The Divine Comedy* over and fit her book snuggly back into the pristine row of beautifully gilded, stamped, hand-sewn and branded literature. One nagging thought still bothered her. *Why now?* What was so important about this year that all three Kingston siblings must be married off? Granted, she always felt like her father secretly groomed his children for something different than their peer's parental expectations, and she had always wondered, for what? In a world where gently born men and women were obligated to align themselves for advancement and foster every relationship like a grand business adventure, her father had not pushed acquaintances on any of his offspring.

Greyland had always thought this was just an eccentric side to her handsome father that only made him more appealing to others. "Richard Kingston cannot be bothered with the mundane task of entertaining the newest Duke off the boat to America," Greyland had once heard a woman say at a party when they lived in New Orleans.

Was that the case? She was now beginning to wonder if it was less about her father not caring, and more, that he cared too much. Perhaps that Duke was not good enough in Richard Kingston's eyes.

That thought brought a familiar smile to her lips. She knew two things for certain, and the first of those two things was that her father loved his children dearly. The second was that her father was a very sought after and impressive man, to say the least, with business connections around the world. Greyland marveled at his vast demographic outreach. She could not even remember how many nobles and lords she had met, including kings and queens. Another queen would join that impressive list tomorrow night when Greyland would be introduced to England's newly crowned Queen.

The front door opened and closed, jarring Greyland from her considerations. She heard faint murmurs being exchanged down the hall between the butler, Ocman, and her two older brothers. She looked at the clock again. Just after two A.M. They were home early tonight.

Greyland smiled and headed towards the library doors. Edward would regale her with some colorful account of their adventures out this evening. He could always be counted on to cheer her up and clear her mind of anxiety.

She paused midstride when Perkin's voice sliced the quiet like a knife. "I will fix this…this…*mess* you have once again, placed yourself squarely in." Her oldest brother said hotly. "What were you thinking, challenging the Duke of Ravenswood to a duel?"

When her brothers rounded the corner toward the library, Greyland instinctually bolted back into the room, leaped behind the sofa, and smashed herself against its back. They would never continue this conversation in her presence. As a little sister, she had learned a long time ago what it took to get information in the Kingston household.

A duel? Her heart rate picked up. Edward had a temper. Father had always said it was the Irish side of him, but never had he tried to harm anyone with anything other than his fist.

Edward sighed. "I told you in the coach it was not one of my better moments, but I do not need you to fix anything."

"You were cheating, Edward. I saw you lift that card."

"I am not going to lie. I was bored and just wanted a little sport. He is obviously not accustomed to losing. Ever."

"He is obviously not used to being cheated," Perkin scolded. "The man's a bloody legend."

Edward flung his body onto the sofa with such force that it moved off the rug a good four inches. Greyland had to cover her mouth to suppress a yelp when the well-made Louis XV collided with her cheek.

"Why did you have to bait him so?" Perkin demanded. "We have only been in the country for three weeks. Everyone has told us about the Hamilton family's darker side, and how influential they are."

Edward huffed. "He took it too far with that 'slave-trading' remark."

"You took it too far by being...well, you. Dammit, Edward! We must not forget our purpose here. And I cannot have a dead brother when father returns from Ireland tomorrow." Perkin was pacing, she could tell by the way his voice floated around the room. Then, with what Greyland imagined to be a dismissive wave of his hand, he said, "Go see what the cook has left in the kitchen. I will be in there with wine in a few."

As soon as Edward left Greyland heard Perkin stride across the room. He cursed as he poured the wine. In the moment of silence that followed, a strange little pop resonated. Like the unstopping of a medicine cork.

Greyland peeked around the sofa. Perkin's attention was thankfully on what he was doing, so he did not notice her. He deposited three drops of liquid into a wine glass and returned the small vial to its hiding place behind an old vase. He then exited the library.

Greyland scurried to retrieve the vial. She turned it in her hand and made out the familiar script of their family physician.

A sleeping draught. With that amount, he would be out for half the day.

Greyland returned to her chamber. Eventually, she heard approaching steps, followed by a loud crash from the hallway and some cursing.

She tiptoed to her door. Perkin spoke in a quiet tone. "Thank you, I can manage from here?"

"Yes, sir," came Ocman's deep bass reply.

Greyland grinned, picturing the scene playing out on the other side of her door. Ocman could probably carry both men at the same time. He was the largest man she had ever seen and dark as midnight. He had been their butler for as long as she could remember, and she loved him dearly. Ocman was the one who rescued her kitten from a tree when she was five, snuck her sweetmeats from the cook and of course, held her hand while she cried when her mother had passed away.

Unlike other Southern men, her father did not believe in slaves—a radical idea for a family in New Orleans. And Ocman was not just an employee to her family; he was family.

Greyland pressed her ear to the wooden door.

"And," her brother persisted, "I will need to be leaving by six. But do not bother trying to wake Edward as he is in need of his slumber."

Greyland sank back against the door, her mind racing.

God's bones! Perkin was going instead!

Once they entered the park, Alexander and Thomas slowed their horses to a walk. The mist cleared on the south side of the river, exposing what would inevitably be a lovely spring day. Daisies fought for supremacy over the dew-laden grass that stretched like the thickest of French rugs across the park. The ever-sprawling patchwork blanket of flowers only thinned when it met the consuming shade of the ancient oaks that guarded the edge of the perimeter like well-trained soldiers.

Alex couldn't wait to get back to the country. Maybe, after he shot the impertinent American, he would retire to one of his estates for a while. At least until this new scandal died down.

"Well, if things do not go our way," Thomas commented, interrupting his thoughts, "It will be a pretty morning to end one's life."

"I have no intention of depriving you of a happy spring day, Thomas. My only concern is that the whole of London's bon ton will turn out right over that hill, expecting to see a duel. I wish the bloody American had not publicly announced our fight last night."

"Yes, the mysterious Duke of Ravenswood is again up to no good." Thomas spread his large hands as if manifesting a newspaper. "It will be in every rag from London to Belfast. They probably printed it last night."

Alexander stiffened. His notorious family tree had surely done a spectacular job of giving their name that reputation. "Perhaps I will end up dead and tomorrows' headline can read, 'Menacing Lord Finally Ends His Terror on Barstools Across the City.'" He smirked. "How much have I paid out in damages over the last month?"

"More than most men pay their mistresses," Thomas said as he chuckled and drew his coveted dapple-grey stallion closer to Alex's horse. "However, you cannot go getting killed." He reached out and patted Alex roughly on the shoulder. "Not only would my favorite establishments lose their design budget, but think of all the mothers with eligible daughters? You really must not rob them of your existence." Thomas's smile widened, showing how much this particular line of teasing pleased him.

"Ah Thomas, I knew you would find a way to make death sound inviting."

Just ahead, the bushes moved, and in a blink, a scrawny boy slid out from his hiding place. The horses snorted and sidestepped hotly.

"By God, boy, take care! Do you have a death wish?" Thomas glared as he fought to control his horse.

"No, me lords. I have a message. Will you come with me?"

Alexander stared pointedly at the child. "Who has need of us?" The boy kept his eyes trained on the ground. "The man you are to duel with, me lord."

Alex and Thomas regarded each other a moment before Alex waved his hand to continue. The boy disappeared as quickly as he had emerged. The two men dismounted and led the horses through the thick brush only to uncover a secluded clearing. The boy turned and nodded to a man sitting under a tree before scurrying off.

The man stood with the grace and swagger of a cat, then proceeded towards them. "Good day, gentlemen." He flashed a lazy smile as he casually ducked under a low hanging limb, artfully dangling a wine glass from his fingertips.

"And whom may we be addressing?" Alex queried.

"I am Perkin Kingston, and I believe we are to engage in a duel this morn." The man had an even tenor voice with an unusual drawl to it that left each word hanging effortlessly in the air after he spoke. Certainly, a voice the devil might affect to lure women into his bed. This was the accent all the bon ton ladies went crazy for, or so Alex recalled one of them twittering on about it at Lady Boswell's soiree last week. A Southern gentleman if you will.

That thought brought Alex up short as he focused in on the man's face. Sure enough, this Perkin fellow had been the companion of the man he had brawled with last night. Upon closer inspection, they were clearly related.

"Seems we have a slight problem then, sir," Alex said. "I have no grievance with you." He glanced around, making a deliberate show of searching out his would-be opponent. He found only the chestnut mare belonging to the man, and what appeared to be a picnic blanket spread out with enough food to feed a king's traveling party.

"I am very sorry to disappoint you, but I fear it is only me today." The man continued to smile as he gestured back to his noted offerings. "Care for some wine? Or something to eat?"

"Yes," Thomas said.

"No," Alex shot back, giving Thomas a warning glare.

Perkin strode to his horse, clearly choosing to ignore Alexander in favor of Thomas. He retrieved two glasses from a saddlebag and returned with one for each man. He handed each a glass after pouring the golden white. Alex could not help but notice the blond man's exceedingly handsome features when presented with his own glass, which he begrudgingly accepted. This, Perkin, carried himself with the same aplomb as Alex's brawling companion, who had been all too aware of his own physical blessings last night. *Smug bastard!*

"Pray tell, why would I accept a drink from someone clearly aligned with the man I am supposed to shoot?" Alexander asked dryly. "Are you offering to take his place?"

Perkin Kingston cocked his head back and laughed heartily, and to Alex's surprise, it sounded genuine. He honestly found the idea humorous. The blond man leveled his gaze back on Alex, a gleam in his eyes. "I would truly like to avoid that and offer my brother's sincere apology instead, Your Grace. You see, he was well into his cups, and is still quite young and foolish," Perkin intoned, nodding reasonably. "I daresay he will regret his actions when he awakes. He is currently under the influence of a sleeping draught. I drugged him with it, last night."

So, this was the brother. The resemblance was acute, although the man from last night had been shorter than the one who stood before him now. Still, they both carried the same self-assured attitude, though Perkin's was decidedly more authoritative. The man who delivered the punishing blows at White's was more muscular, compared with the lean form of his brother who was every bit of six-foot-four.

Alex assumed Perkin's presence here today meant only one thing, his reputation for being a deadly shot preceded him and Kingston feared for his brother's life. *Wise.*

Alex could not blame him, and deep down felt envious of the brotherly intervention. It must be nice to have family that one actually liked.

Perkin continued, and Alex found himself intrigued yet again by the man's unusual accent. Every syllable seemed to receive individual attention and drew on forever with natural undercurrents that oozed charm and familiarity. He was beginning to see why the ladies appreciated it so. This man would be on everyone's dance card this season. Alex briefly glanced down, looking for a wedding ring on Kingston's finger. There was none. This might bode well for Alex, after all. Perhaps, instead of killing him, he would offer Perkin Kingston up to the eager young maidens and their bloodthirsty mothers.

"I was hoping to acquire your friendship, instead of sending you to your grave," Perkin supplied with a grin, effectively snapping Alexander out of his studious ponderings.

Thomas spewed his wine.

Like hell! Was the man actually giving insult while asking for friendship in the same breath? Who in God's name did this bloke think he was? No one ever spoke to Alexander Hamilton like that.

He stared at Perkin Kingston's patient smile, remembering why he had enjoyed the fight with his brother so much last night. "Friends? I believe I require a less cryptic explanation."

Thomas wiped his mouth clean with his jacket sleeve. "This is becoming a most interesting duel."

"The man who challenged you…" Perkin paused, casually swirling the wine in his glass. "He is my younger brother, as I just stated. Do you have any brothers?"

"I do," Alex admitted through clenched teeth, ready to knock his own best friend off his horse if he continued to find this spectacle entertaining. "Unfortunately." He added, angling the last word in Thomas's direction.

"Then you know how annoying they are. Mine would bait a bear if he thought it would give for good sport. Not the brains of the family, yet still, family." A stillness edged Perkin's features. "I know who you are because my father and your father were business partners, and if I am not overstepping my mark, they were also friends. My brother does not know any of this and thinks we are in England to find a suitable husband for our younger sister."

Alex suddenly felt lightheaded, but his mind forced the blond man's words to take shape. *Friends? Business partners?* Perhaps he was still asleep. This had to be some sort of strange dream. Maybe he had a concussion.

"My father is dead," Alex said. "I am sure I know all his business dealings and, of course, his friends. What exactly are you about, Kingston?"

"I am very sorry for your loss," Perkin said respectfully. "Yet your father's passing is the reason we are here. I am not at liberty to discuss this further with you. I have already said too much, but my brother's outrageous antics last night have made me act in haste. My father returns later today from Ireland. Your uncle accompanies him. If my father were to hear that I let you kill Edward, he might see fit to kill me, and, though selfish on my part, I prefer to remain among the living. Father will be requesting an audience with you when he returns, and I am positive he will want you still drawing air into your lungs. So, you see, it is a win-win, for both of us."

Before Alexander could speak, a black figure stole into the clearing. Perkin's horse shied and bolted. Neither Thomas's nor Alex's stallions stirred, for they were well acquainted with the family pet.

"Holy mother of God!" Perkin lunged backward as the animal moved closer. "Is that a wolf?"

Thomas doubled over in laughter at Mr. Kingston's expression.

"Malikite, come!" Alexander commanded, quickly dismounting. "Samson must have had us followed." He shook his head, still trying to make sense of the American's story.

"Does your family not also collect strange pets, same as Alexander?" Thomas asked Perkin, barely able to sit his own horse now due to his unbridled merriment.

"We have a rather fat house cat." Perkin grinned in obvious relief that he might not be dismembered on this day. "I am sorry to not have formally acquainted myself with you, my lord," he said to Thomas. "Not very becoming of me."

"Understandable, with the looming duel and all." Thomas waved a hand as a way of explaining the events as a whole. "I am Thomas Whitfield, Earl of Kennington." The two men shook hands.

Alexander knelt beside the dog and patted his head, all the while fighting to digest everything that Perkin Kingston just proclaimed. Suddenly, his pride seemed overindulgent in this new light. His uncle was coming to town? His father had a secret involvement with an American family?

The sound of thundering hooves trampling over the earth brought Alex's mind right back to the present. All three men jerked their heads toward the intrusion. A bay steed burst through the bush carrying a wild-eyed girl. Her beautifully carved slender legs were exposed up to her knees and she was missing one of her slippers.

The horse immediately sensed the wolf and reared straight up. Surprisingly, the bareback rider managed to hug tight to the beast's neck and stayed on. As the front hooves made contact with the ground—and before the horse could rise in protest again—the girl catapulted off the side and unsuccessfully grabbed for the reins. The mare bolted away.

"Damn!" she said, simply annoyed, as if she had lost a shilling rather than a thoroughbred.

"What on earth?" Perkin's previous calm appearance all but shattered into a thousand pieces in front of them.

"Is that a wolf?" The girl's sites fixated on Malikite, a glint in her bright eyes, her breathing coming hard, causing her small breasts to rise and fall, threatening to escape a much-too-slack bodice.

Alex stared. Who on earth had helped this poor woman dress? Clearly a dressing-maid with a vengeance. Unless the young lady before them was newly escaped from the asylum. Which might explain the entry.

The girl was completely disheveled. A twig dangled from her raven-black curls. Windblown pink cheeks decorated her milk-white skin, and a bead of perspiration highlighted her cupid-bow lips. Her eyes were like the palest green of the sea, and they raged as wild as a developing storm. Never in his wildest dreams had he ever thought a woman could be this...*inspiring. Captivating. Alive!* She had to be from the asylum, Alex concluded. Someone's daughter or young bride that had lost her wits and had to be committed.

Still, she was magnificent, albeit, likely touched in the head. Alexander felt a stir in his fawn-colored pants. He tried to retrieve his thoughts from their rapid downward descent. He could have any woman in London and had turned down half of them in the past month alone due to a lack of interest. Now here he was, the Duke of Ravenswood, in the middle of the park getting brought to life by a lunatic. Gone completely was the conundrum of the previous conversation with Perkin Kingston. The issue at hand now may well be his own dwindling sanity.

"It is a pet," Perkin answered her. "What are you doing here? Where is your chaperone?" A slight panic was rising in the American's voice with each new question. "My word, your dress!"

He grabbed the girl's shoulders and forced her around, moving his own body between her and the other two men while his hands went to work fastening the buttons on the back of her gown, though not before gifting Alex and Thomas a glance at her delicate, ivory back. Alex shut his eyes and tried to think about the hideous mole with its wiry hairs on old Lady Dodger's third chin.

"If we're pointing out obvious problems, where was her saddle?" Thomas interjected.

Perkin rounded. The exasperated look on his face spoke volumes about his experience with this little spitfire.

The 'spitfire' spoke first. "Pray, excuse my appearance," she implored Perkin, not them. "But I overheard you and Edward talking last night and I just had to stop you." She continued to prattle off as if no one else were in attendance. "I overslept, and Churchill woke me by licking my face. Rotten cat. I did not want to alert Ocman, and I had no time to ring the maid. Oh, the stable boy was more of a hindrance than a help, really, so I decided I would make better time if I just did it myself. I could not bother properly outfitting Zanity with a saddle. She always bloats up her middle when I try to tighten the girth. She really is a pain of a beast, that one. I do want to pick out my next horse myself when father gets back and trust me, I will want to check its stubbornness first-hand by grooming the animal before purchasing just any—"

"Greyland," Perkin interrupted, frustration coloring his voice.

"I know you always talk about the merits of each horse as if it is some kind of fancy racing rig," she said, waving her hand in an exasperated fashion, "but I think you overlook the most important parts, such as temperament and one's ability to saddle a mare in a timely fashion when one's brother is trying to get himself killed." She nodded her lovely head in conclusion. "These things are really more important, don't you agree? Oh, and not killing the rider when a mere wolf appears on the path."

Perkin Kingston seemed to be at a loss for words. Finally, he took the young lady by the elbow in what appeared to be a means to secretly steady himself, or mayhap a place to put his hands—other than around her neck, that is. "We will discuss this back at the manor."

She begged forgiveness with her eyes. Tears threatened to break the thick barricade of her lashes. Her bottom lip quivered, and to his horror, Alexander's heart flipped upside-down.

Kingston embraced the girl in a silencing hug and then turned back to Alex and Thomas. "Did I mention how annoying little sisters can be?"

His sister... Alex mentally breathed a sigh of unexpected relief.

"Annoying? I'm only trying to help." Her sweet soprano held the same silky tones as her brother.

"By getting yourself killed?" Perkin asked.

"My lady," Alex hedged, hoping to break up the siblings squabble, "I am Alexander Hamilton, Duke of Ravenswood. This is my friend, Thomas Whitfield, Earl of Kennington." Both men offered a slight bow. "I would not have my face to be one that brings fear to your mind. There will be no duel, thanks to your brother."

Her eyebrows arched, and something akin to amusement played in her eyes. Alex did not know exactly how to interpret the look, but a blush had spread from her chest to her cheeks. He knew exactly how to interpret that.

"My apologies for the delay in introductions," Perkin said, breaking the sudden silence. "This is Miss Kingston, my sister."

Alexander inclined his head. "Quite understandable. It is a pleasure, Lady Kingston."

"Now, pray excuse me, gentlemen, but I must escort my lovely sister home." Perkin retrieved his horse, and before she could protest, grabbed the lady around the waist. With no effort at all, he hoisted her upon the steed. "Sidesaddle," he said sternly.

"Should you come across a spooked bay mare," Perkin said as he swung up behind his sister on the saddle, "will you be so kind as to return her to our manor on Chelsey Lane?"

Alex had never met a man more naturally confident, other than himself. He had to admire Perkin Kingston for that. Even more, he respected how quickly he recovered from the hailstorm that was his sister.

"Of course. We shall keep a lookout on our way back into town," Thomas assured them, a bit too eagerly.

Alex turned his head to the side and looked over at his best friend as it dawned on him this was the longest The Earl of Kennington had ever gone without talking.

Interesting, Alex mused.

He looked back to Miss Kingston. This little woman was either going to take London by storm or burn it down.

Miss Kingston spoke up. "Will you be attending the ball tonight, my lords?"

"Will you be attending, my lady?" Alexander responded.

"I shall."

"Then you must save me a dance, for we too, will be in attendance." His grin met its mark as her eyes widened with controlled delight.

"I shall love to introduce you to my betrothed," Thomas added.

Miss Kingston smiled. "I will look forward to meeting her."

"See you this evening, gentlemen." Perkin regarded Alex with sincerity. "I beg your forgiveness. I will have Edward make a public apology if it pleases you?"

Alex nodded. "I will require an apology from him, only to assure me that it will not happen again, but I daresay, he need not embarrass himself with it being public. I know how impulsive young men can be."

"Thank you. It shall be done." Perkin spurred his horse on and the pair dashed off.

Miss Kingston turned and called out over her shoulder, "Feel free to keep the mare, should you find her."

II

Greyland sat while her dressing maid tried, with gritted teeth, to coax her unruly curls into something that did not resemble a beaver's dam. She smiled when the young stylist scrunched her nose, twisted her mouth, and murmured a little curse.

The maid sighed, almost defeated. "I do not know, Miss Greyland. We might need to try a different approach. Perhaps if I leave a little of it down?"

"I trust whatever you do will look just splendid, Elise."

The maid took a large breath and dove back into the mass, twisting here and there.

Despite the tugging at her scalp and the occasional grunt that sounded like Elise was wrestling a piano up a flight of stairs, Greyland was blissfully in her own head. She could not stop thinking about Alexander Hamilton, the much-too perfect gentleman she had met earlier that day. Alexander Hamilton, with his full lips that curled into a downright, scandalous smile. Alexander Hamilton, and those intense blue eyes; deep pools worthy of drowning in. Alexander Hamilton, with a voice so cool and smooth, it sounded like a creek ambling over river stones. Alexander Hamilton, and the curious way he tilted his head when he addressed her: *Alexander Hamilton...*

She sighed.

Elise stepped back and exhaled. "There. I think we may have something." She held up a mirror for Greyland's inspection.

"Oh, it is beautiful."

Elise had swept up the curls on both sides, leaving just a few well-placed ringlets cascading down her back.

"Now for the dress," Elise declared.

Greyland had chosen an off-the-shoulder peach silk gown for tonight's ball. Seed pearls lined the corset's bust and trailed down the back along the lacing. The bottom of the gown shirred up, revealing a deep purple lace and silk underskirt. Elise helped Greyland step into it.

"Do you think it is too…" Greyland twisted her mouth, considering. "Colorful?"

"Not in the least," the tawny-haired maid replied over Greyland's shoulder as she fastened the many buttons at the gowns back. After what had to be the hundredth button, she paused and stepped back, scrutinizing her work. "One last detail."

Elise plucked a purple ribbon from the vanity and deftly wound it through Greyland's hair. She stepped to the side.

"My, my, you are the picture of beauty."

Greyland turned to face the mirror and beamed. "Elise! You are a Godsend. It is…well, it is just perfect!"

"Grey?" Edwards's voice called out from just beyond her sitting room doors. "Time to head downstairs."

She hugged Elise and ran to the door.

"Oh!" He exclaimed when he saw her. "You have never, well I mean to say, I have never seen you so…organized."

She laughed and took her brother's arm. "I shall take that as a compliment."

"You know, I have never been good with them." He grinned down at her.

It was a complete lie, but she let him have his excuse. Edward was as silver-tongued as they came. Her brother was such a charmer that his reputation literally could proceed him into a room. Greyland could never recall a time when two things in life were not certain; cats liked cream, and women loved Edward Kingston.

She smiled to herself as he led her down the stairs and to the waiting carriage. Tonight was the start of a grand adventure. She could just feel it.

GREY SQUEALED with joy and threw her arms around her father, as soon as they climbed into the carriage. "Father!" She nestled into his familiar embrace.

Richard Kingston chuckled and hugged her back. "Now, let me have a look at this dress." He gently nudged her back toward her seat across from him.

Greyland folded her hands in her lap and playfully tossed her chin from side to side in regal fashion. When no one in the rig made a sound, she froze and looked at each one of the men of her family in turn. They all wore similar expressions, if not varied per individual.

Perkin looked pleased, as if he actually thought he might get through the night without a scandal. Edward was grinning, in typical Edward fashion, genuinely appreciating his sister's ability to make him laugh. Then Greyland's eyes landed on her father's. What shone back in his steel-grey orbs made a lump form in her throat. *Pride.* His face said everything she needed to hear. He was proud of her.

"Just one more small matter with that lovely dress, dear." He reached into his jacket's front pocket and pulled out a small box. "It needs a little something else."

"Oh daddy," she exclaimed, even before her fingers could lift the box's delicate lid and lift the diamond necklace. "It is wonderful!"

"It was your mother's. I gave it to her on the day you were born, sunshine."

Greyland felt the sting of gathering tears building behind her lashes. Not tonight, she scolded her emotions. She refused to enter the palace like a puffy-eyed child. Nor would she risk smudging the rose-powered-blush Elise had dotted lightly on her cheeks. By sheer will, she stiffened her chin and her resolve, and kept the unwanted tears at bay. She smiled. "I will wear it with all the honor she did."

"What did you give mother on the day I was born?" Edward asked, effectively refocusing the conversation back to where it normally stayed—on him.

"You did not bless the world," Perkin stated dryly. "Your arrival was more in line with introducing the Bubonic Plague to humanity."

The carriage erupted in laughter. Only one passerby heard the resounding sound of Edward's boot landing squarely on Perkin's shin as the carriage rolled down the lane.

ALEXANDER SURVEYED THE CROWD. Any minute now, half the bon ton would be inquiring as to why he had not carried out the duel this morning. He also realized that every virgin in the city—and some from the country—were in attendance tonight.

And as usual, all seemed to be staring at him as he entered the palace ballroom.

"Thomas and I will fend off the really hideous ogres," Bella said with a grin.

"You are too kind." Alex smiled down at the auburn-haired beauty by his side. "Thomas definitely snagged himself a gem in you, my lady."

His friend truly was a lucky man. Bella was bright, funny, and quite easy on the eyes. But what Alex admired most was her loyalty to Thomas, and everyone she called a friend. It was such a refreshing quality to find in a city drowning in cattiness and greed.

New arrivals were being announced. Attention being diverted to the ballrooms grand entrance, Alex found himself looking around the room more closely for familiar faces. Faces that did not produce the strong desire to throw himself into the Thames.

The men, largely composed of lords and gentlemen of parliament, mulled around the edges of the grand ballroom, some eager for the night to be over, but the large majority sizing up every face that passed them. And then there were the ladies. Alex was sure London could support at least three impoverished countries on the sum of money spent just on dresses and jewels in this room tonight. It was an extravagance he had been raised with, but one he had never admired. Sure, he enjoyed the feel of a finely cut suit across his shoulders and a saddle that fit his horse like a glove, but he did not need those things to make others envious.

Everything Alex had was because he specifically wanted it. Acquiring possessions and people for the sheer extent of 'having' had never been his fancy, which was precisely why he was still unmarried. Until he found a woman that brought him as much joy as racing a fast rig at dusk or winning the best hand at White's, he would continue to live his life, as he always had, on his terms.

Bella patted his arm and turned to address Lady Martinson. Alex pulled a watch from his jacket pocket and groaned. He would not be able to leave for at least three more hours. The only thing that had brought him out tonight was his curiosity about Richard Kingston. Well, that was not entirely true. There was one other noteworthy topic concerning tonight. The wild, raven-haired beauty Alex had met earlier that day. The interesting fact she also happened to be Mr. Kingston's daughter was just an added perk in his investigation.

In the hours leading up to the ball, Alex and Thomas had searched every document in Alexander's father's study for information on the Kingston family. They found nothing.

"Who are these people and what do they have to do with my

father?" Alex had asked Thomas while pacing the study when they had returned from the park.

"The carpet is close to retaliating if you do not at least slow to a stroll," Thomas responded.

"And that sister..." Alex continued his relentless strides around the large room.

"She was a sight to behold, to be sure. I daresay she may be one of the most beautiful women I have ever laid eyes on, and I believe her brother said she was looking for a husband." Thomas raised one brow as he spoke.

"And how do you believe she not only rode the horse without a saddle but stayed on its back when it reared?" Alex shook his head. "And the dismount! I have never seen anything like it." He rubbed the stubble on his jaw. "She has obviously had extensive and unorthodox instruction."

Thomas grinned. "She did not even blink or swoon from meeting the notorious Duke of Ravenswood. Whatever man takes her to the altar will have his work cut out. Hey, do you not need an heir and a spare?"

Alex stopped mid-stride and stared at his friend. "I do not need a wife, but you are right about one thing. It will take a very patient man to deal with that one, regardless of how bloody comely she is." He tried to shake off the image that had been running around his mind since parting ways with Greyland Kingston; green eyes, porcelain skin...the way the sun wrapped blue ribbons of light through her midnight hair. Damn it!

"The whole family is odd," Alex concluded. "What kind of father, or brother, for that matter, would let that kind of disobedience occur in their family? Why, the girl is a liability to a respectable name! What if someone with a gossip's tongue had seen her? She and her family would be ruined." He glanced at the clock. "I intend to put this puzzle together tonight."

Thomas looked at him in earnest. "Please promise me you will keep your fists to yourself this evening. I am bloody tired of rising early to be your deuced second."

"I will make no such promises," Alex stated flatly.

After Thomas quit the room, Alex sat down at his desk and penned a quick letter to his uncle. He rang for a footman and instructed him to carry it to Derrick's townhouse. He had not spoken with his uncle since his father's burial. The brothers, being ages apart, had never been close. Derrick was only seven when Alex was born. However, if Perkin Kingston was right, his father had trusted Derrick enough to involve him in something. Something he had chosen not to share with his own son.

Alexander needed answers and his uncle was the best person with whom to start. He hoped Derrick might be in attendance tonight, but it was unlikely. His uncle disliked events such as this one, as much as all Ravenswood men. That just meant Alex would have to settle for the second-best source of information—the Kingston's themselves.

The Americans had not made a formal debut. Tonight, would be their first, and what a debut it would be, considering it was taking place at the palace under a direct invitation from The Queen.

"Lord Ravenswood!" A grating voice forcefully dragged him from his thoughts and back to the chaos of the ball. Lady Primrose scurried over, practically knocking people out of her path and dragging a mousey looking girl in her wake.

"I have got this one." Bella pushed forward, and Alex sought refuge behind a pillar.

"Sorry, Lady Primrose. I just sent Lord Ravenswood off to procure me a glass of punch," he heard Bella say, intercepting the would-be match-maker. "As you can see, Lord Kennington was too busy with the baron to notice my parched throat. Alexander, always the gentleman, came to my rescue."

From his hiding spot, Alex observed Lady Primrose's narrowed gaze. "Ah, well, that is just like you to busy not one, but two of the Bons ton's best men?" She stared down her nose for a long second before turning on her heels and dramatically stomping off, dragging the unwilling participant towards her next victim, the Viscount of Essingburg.

When all was clear, Alexander returned to Bella and Thomas who had finished his greeting with the baron. Suddenly, the crowd around them went quiet. Alex followed the collective eyes of the room.

In the receiving line was a man that could only be described as the ghost of Edward IV, the twelfth Plantagenet King, and first Yorkist King to rule England. The man approached, as if he had just stepped out of a painting. Although much older than Edward of York would have lived to be, still, the resemblance was uncanny. A straight-as-an-arrow spine, blond hair highlighted by streaks of grey, sparkling eyes, and an ancient Roman profile. All the characteristics that marked him as a bred-in-the-bone aristocrat and the spitting image of the striking White Rose lineage.

The announcer broke the silence: "Mr. Richard Kingston, of America, and his sons, Perkin Kingston, Edward Kingston, and daughter, Greyland Kingston."

PERKIN GRABBED Greyland's hand and squeezed, but the reassuring gesture did nothing to stop her knees from waging war with each other. She hoped no one could tell. Surely four petticoats were enough to hide her jittery limbs. No matter how many times she faced a crowd, she always felt uneasy upon first introductions. Something about the way people sized up her family. Their eyes seemed to ask a myriad of questions—questions that never manifested onto their tongues. Greyland often wanted to just voice the issue directly: Is there something off-putting about us?

She had spent countless hours observing people enter rooms over the years and rarely did they receive the scrutiny that Greyland, her brothers and father did. She asked Perkin once if he noticed it, the looks. He replied that people were inherently curious, and then, in typical Perkin fashion, dismissed the topic as quickly as it had been brought up.

Greyland ventured a glance at each of her family members. If they were nervous, it surely did not show. Her father was smiling graciously as he accepted the first introduction. Edward's eyes were already scanning the room, taking stock of the female occupancy, and Perkin just looked like he always did, the embodiment of a prince. The one thing none of the men in her family lacked was confidence.

She pulled her shoulders back a bit more, smiled until it hurt, and tried to muster up a quarter of their mettle. Reprieve was too small a word to describe her relief when a smiling man rushed up and enthusiastically shook her father's hand, drawing the room's quizzical eyes to the gesture. Greyland exhaled, breathing in what felt like her first breath of air since stepping inside the palace.

Her father waved them forward to meet the man, Lord Melbrooke, The Queen's chief advisor. After brief introductions, the ballroom descended on them. The advancing crowd parted her from her family.

She was introduced to a Lady Burgsworth, followed by Lord Wittingham, who kissed her hand. She smiled shyly and looked about the room, seeking reassurance from her father, Perkin, Edward, *anyone familiar*. The press of curious faces surrounded her. Greyland's temperature begin to rise with every new hand presented to her. Not being very tall, she was quickly swallowed up by a sea of colorful fabrics and shimmering jewels. Polite, but inquisitive voices chirped in her ears. "Where was she residing? How long had she been in London? Had she been to Hyde Park yet? Would she like to go tomorrow?"

Greyland nodded and smiled, terrified of missing someone's question. The bodice of her dress suddenly became too tight, like a boa constrictor snuggling up to a rat. She was feeling overwhelmed. A cool masculine voice stroked the back of her neck and she turned quickly, too quickly, as she nearly smashed into Lord Ravenswood. She breathed a sigh of relief.

"Miss Kingston." He bowed over her hand and paused, then glanced up with a mischievous grin. "No gloves?"

The Duke turned her hand over in his much larger one, exposing her palm, and then did the unthinkable. He placed a kiss on the inside of her wrist. The action sent a slow burn up her arm that spread like wildfire throughout her body. She turned crimson and her left knee once again started a fight with her right.

"Lord Ravenswood, how—"

He took her arm and hooked it neatly over his. Without further explanation, or apparent care to what anyone else thought, he walked her out of the crowd and across the ballroom to the less populated, and refreshingly oxygenated, side of the room. It was a bold and high-handed gesture. It read indisputably one way, and one way only: claimed. For some utterly unfathomable reason, it did not bother Greyland in the least. He was providing her relief from the pressuring crowd. He was offering her *stillness...*

"Lord Ravenswood, thank you. It was a bit overwhelming over there," she confessed.

"Yes, you and your family seem to be tonight's shiny new bauble."

"I felt as if we might be tonight's main course."

He tilted his head and smiled. Surely, she thought, there had to be a law in place that forbade one's mouth to look so devilish.

"Miss Kingston, may I have the honor of taking the first dance this evening?" His voice was clear and strong, completely controlled. The effect it had on her was astounding. Greyland willed herself to stay focused.

"I would like that very—"

"Lord Ravenswood! There you are." The bubble encasing them burst and the noise of the ballroom once again filled the hall.

A pretty blonde laced her arm through Lord Ravenswood's. "I was hoping you would not forget our dance this evening," she said, stroking his jacket sleeve like a white cat on black trousers. Then, seemingly taking notice of Greyland, shot a disapproving glare in her direction. "Is this the American?"

Lord Ravenswood gently removed the lady's arm from his and attempted to speak. Greyland was quicker.

"I am Greyland Kingston. And as you can tell by my third eye, I am clearly the American. Or maybe you were able to discern that from the announcement of it a mere ten minutes ago. Either way," she could no more stop her words than she could make Lord Ravenswood unattractive. "I was born in America, even though I have traveled most of the world and can trace my family line back to England and Ireland, as early as the thirteen hundred's. How far back does your family tree go in jolly-old England, Lady…?" Greyland pasted the most insincere smile she could muster on her face. "I am sorry, who are you again?" She left the smile, as tight as Louisiana mud in the August sun, in place for the gaping woman, who was turning a very unattractive shade of pale.

"Thomas!" the Duke said after the long and perfectly awkward pause.

Greyland turned to see the Earl of Kennington approaching, accompanied by a pretty auburn-haired woman. She hoped they had not overheard her un-ladylike rebuttal. However, based on their thinly concealed smirks, they had.

"Ah, Miss Kingston," began the other woman, completely ignoring the rude blonde who was still in the apparent throes of recovery, "You are even more beautiful than Thomas and Alexander said." She smiled sincerely. "It is a pleasure to make your acquaintance."

The, now seething blonde huffed, shot Lord Ravenswood a hateful look and stalked away.

ALEXANDER ALMOST FORGOT how to speak after witnessing one of the best direct cuts he had ever heard anyone deliver. How he dreaded crossing paths with Lady Chatsworth later that evening. Greyland

Kingston was a sight to behold, indeed. She had the poise of a high-born lady, but a tongue as sharp as a blade. She might just be the most exhilarating woman he had ever met. The sudden thought gave him an alarming pause.

He managed to locate his own tongue to make the appropriate introductions between Miss Kingston and Bella. He and Thomas then watched as the ladies became fast friends. Alex would never understand how women did that. Before he could reassert himself into their conversation, Bella was leading Miss Kingston off to acquaint her with 'better peers'. It took less than five minutes for both women to agree Lady Chatsworth would not be counted among these.

"Go on," Alex said. "Say it and be done with it." He did not need to lay eyes on the earl to know he was staring at him, amused.

Thomas shrugged "Well, it is easy to see that you like her. Who would not?"

A trumpet sounded. The Queen and her newest courter, the prince, were announced. All eyes watched as they made their way through the ballroom to the two gleaming thrones under The Queen's banners. The line of well-wishers formed. Through the crowd, Alexander observed Miss Kingston greeting her two brothers and father. Lord Melbrooke moved himself to the front of the line with the Kingston family in tow.

"Well, look at that," Thomas exclaimed under his breath. "They are getting the first introductions!"

To the shock of the crowd, The Queen rose and embraced Richard Kingston. The prince stood beside her and smiled, shaking Kingston's hand. Ladies' fans rose to obscure gossiping mouths like quail taking flight from a bush. An announcer introduced the rest of the Kingston family. After a few moments, The Queen waved off the line of guests and motioned for the band to play the first waltz of the evening. Then, completely skipping protocol, The Queen took to the floor with Richard Kingston.

"Can you believe this..." Thomas started to say, but Alex was already afoot, pushing around the edge of the dance floor.

He could just make out through the thickening crowd—everyone vying for the best view—that Miss Kingston and her brothers were still talking with the prince. Good, he hoped to procure the first dance.

Alex brushed past the last standing obstacle just as the prince reached for Miss Kingston's hand. She nodded her dainty head, blushed politely, and accepted his waiting proposal. Alex froze in place as irritation climbed up his spine, one vertebra at a time.

"Have you ever seen such a sight?" a woman near him proclaimed, as the prince escorted Miss Kingston to the dance floor.

"These people must be very important," another female answered. "They are all so marvelous to look upon. I hope one asks me for a dance."

A third lady chimed in. "Rumor has it they are descendants of nobility, which must be why The Queen knows them so well. Oh my, this is so exciting!"

Alexander spied Bella and Thomas joining the others on the dance floor out of his peripheral. However, he found his focus solely fixated on one exquisite creature whirling lithely about with the prince. She was mesmerizing.

A man's brash voice came from somewhere in the audience. "What I wouldn't give to have that chit warm my bed."

Alexander turned, pinning the ogling bastard with a glare. "Mind your tongue!" A surge of anger overcame him.

"Lord Ravenswood." The man wisely took a step back. "I did not realize you had first dibs."

Alexander fought his rising desire to punch the other lord square in the nose. Instead, he said through clenched teeth, "The young lady is here as a special guest. I am quite certain The Queen would have you treat Miss Kingston with the utmost respect." He added menacingly, "As would I."

The man mumbled an apology and quickly marched off as the next song began.

A country dance. Alex turned back to the dance floor in search of

Miss Kingston but once again, found her in the arms of another would-be suitor. Jealousy hit him smack center in the chest. He surveyed the ballroom and realized, to his shock, and equal parts horror, that nearly every man in attendance was staring at the young debutante.

"Everything all right?" Thomas asked.

"You are going to have to be quicker," Bella teased, placing a gloved hand on his forearm. "That lady's feet will not leave the dance floor tonight."

Miss Kingston smiled as she gracefully spun by in another lord's clutches. "We shall see about that."

Alexander made for the floor. He practically jumped in front of the approaching Lovingston twins who also raced to claim a dance.

"Miss Kingston."

She smiled. "Lord Ravenswood."

"I believe I have the next dance," he said as the music faded.

"I will have to take your word for that, Your Grace, as I have misplaced my dance card." She glanced over to the orchestra. "I wonder what we shall have. I do wish for another waltz."

"I would like that very much." He looked towards the band, which had ceased playing for the moment. "But I fear we shall have to wait a few more dances before they play—"

"My dear friends, and loyal subjects," The Queen said before pausing politely for all eyes to turn to her. "As many of you know, the Prince and I are great admirers of the arts, dance in particular." Another well placed pause. "During my conversation with my special guest tonight, Mr. Kingston, he has informed me his children are very well versed in a great many different dances. I was overjoyed when he told me of the most recent dance they have added to their extensive repertoire."

Miss Kingston's hand shot out and took hold of his. It was a simple action. Reactive. However, it would be viewed as most improper by the leering eyes of the bon ton. Alex stealthily slid his arm under hers. It gave the appearance of him escorting her and allowed her to keep touching him.

He glanced down at her. Miss Kingston's brows were pinched, and her lips were drawn tight. *She was nervous.*

An irrational protectiveness consumed him. This brave little dove had a fragile side. He drew her in closer to his side and held her there snugly. He cared not if anyone thought them linked. He rather liked the idea. She relaxed immediately into his touch, and Alex felt some invisible string inside him snap. In that second, she had undone him.

The Queen smiled at Richard Kingston and continued. "Everyone loves the fluidity of the slow waltz with its gentle rise and fall, and swing and sway. And..." She gave a half-smile, "we all love the proximity to one's partner."

Laughter and agreeing nods bobbed around them. The innuendo was daring but had hit its mark perfectly. Curious eyes begin to cast sideways glances at prospective dance partners from every corner of the ballroom. After this speech, more than a few couples would be meeting in the gardens for a midnight tryst. The thought of Miss Kingston doing such a thing with one of these adoring men almost blinded Alex with white-hot rage, followed by an altogether different sensation of a much more primal nature.

Alex self-consciously lowered his other hand to just above his belt. He desperately sought a distraction, other than the one standing much too near him. He considered what crops might be best to plant on Esterton estate next fall.

The Queen continued, "When it was first introduced to polite society, many thought it scandalous." Women began to blush, and fans rose. "Well, my friends, the slow waltz has a much faster sister, the Viennese waltz."

Little gasps buzzed around the crowd. Alex glanced down at Miss Kingston, who chewed ever so lightly on her bottom lip.

Dear Heavenly Lord, he thought miserably. *She must stop that at once.*

"I would be truly honored if Greyland and Perkin Kingston would demonstrate this beautiful dance for us," added The Queen.

Silence enveloped the ballroom as Perkin emerged from the crowd. The other dancers cleared the floor. Kingston extended his hand to his sister from across the large ballroom. It was not a request.

She let go of Alexander's hand and stepped toward her brother. When she reached him, Perkin gestured to the band.

They took to their dance frame as the music seeped into the space, its melody descending slowly at first, drifting around in the edges of the ballroom in measured control. Then, as if watching a lightning storm form, a piano rang out brightly, joining with the violins as the tempo accelerated. A cello layered itself into the texture of the song and the energy of the music climbed to a thunderous peak, enveloping the still dancers. Higher and fuller, the sound rose. Just when it seemed too late, the pair of dancers took flight.

Seamlessly becoming the fourth layer of music, they moved with unbounded grace across the marble floor, hitting every beat with expert timing. The crowd hung like fog. Their very souls affixed to the two dancers moving as one. The music intensified and the dancers' bodies matched it as if they themselves were the instruments being played. Faster and faster went the crescendo until Perkin moved his hands to Greyland's waist and lifted her off the ground. He kept up with the driving tempo, twirling beneath her. Greyland let go and threw her hands gracefully behind her. She tipped her head back and surrendered all control to her partner.

The song crashed down around them, and Perkin lowered her delicately back to the ground. Directing their movement into a more controlled cadence, he danced the last fading notes into a dip. Some of Miss Kingston's hair had come loose during the frenzy of the dance. Glossy black curls kissed the polished white marble as Perkin bent and held her there.

The crowd held its breath as the wafting violins trailed off into the night. The dancers remained still, frozen in time until the ballroom was again, soundless. Then carefully, as if bringing a sculpture to life, Perkin straightened, lifting Miss Kingston out of the suspended hold. It could not have been executed better. Alexander was in awe.

The Queen rose from her chair with tears in her eyes, clapping excitedly. A roar of explosive applause followed suit.

Miss Kingston's chest rose and fell in delicate timing as she looked to her brother. He grinned approvingly and nodded before grabbing her hand for a bow.

GREYLAND REMAINED motionless as The Queen and the prince met them on the floor. Perkin squeezed her hand as they approached. It was the signal for her to curtsey.

"Oh, you have to teach me," The Queen gushed.

"We would be most honored," Perkin replied humbly.

Lord Melbrooke, her father, and Edward approached them now.

Her father beamed proudly. "Very well done, children."

"I have never seen dancing with such emotion and control," Lord Melbrooke added.

Greyland curtsied again beside Perkin.

The prince turned to Richard. "You have a beautiful family. One I can only assume now will be even more popular." He dipped his chin in Greyland's direction. "I would keep an eye on your lovely daughter here," he added. Greyland feared she might swoon on the spot from the bold compliment.

Richard smiled and inclined his head. "By the end of the season, there will not be a blond hair left on my grey head."

They all laughed and Greyland began to feel her blood pressure returning to normal. After a few more well-wishers joined their party to admire and congratulate them, Greyland excused herself.

"I thought you might be thirsty, madam."

The man she was hoping to see approached her, two glasses of punch in his hands.

"Thank you, Lord Ravenswood." She downed the drink. "Is there anything stronger?"

"Would you like a glass of wine?

"Yes, right after a glass of brandy," she replied judicially.

He arched a brow. She eyed him, waiting for him to chastise her the way her brothers would, or rather, the way Perkin would. Edward would just tell her where the best hedgerows were located around the grounds, for expelling said alcohol should she partake too heavily. Not that she ever had. It was no fair that men got such allowances while women were expected to be perfect dolls. *Rubbish!*

Lord Ravenswood took her by the arm and led her to a small settee. "If you will rest your feet right over here, I will procure a glass from the other room."

She took a seat, now skeptical. There were only two types of men that would indulge her in this: rakes and Edward. Considering Edward was a rake, she amended that down to just one type of man and studied Lord Ravenswood, as he cut a straight line across the ballroom. With his broad shoulders, thick wavy hair, long legs, and straight as a rod spine, he sure looked every bit the rake. *Was he, though?* Or was she guilty of the very thing she hated most; compartmentalizing people into tidy safe boxes society thought they fit best in.

She watched as Lord Ravenswood stopped briefly to address Miss Herst. Greyland strained to hear their conversation. His tone seemed tense.

The pretty auburn-haired woman nodded to Alexander before continuing her path to where Greyland sat. "Miss Kingston, that was quite possibly the most wonderful display of skill I have ever seen."

"I was beside myself with nerves, but thank you," she confessed. "Please, call me Greyland."

Miss Herst took a seat beside her. "Only if you will call me Bella." Greyland nodded enthusiastically, unable to keep her happiness hidden. She really liked Miss Herst...*Bella.*

Bella smiled warmly. "If you were nervous, it certainly did not show. Where did you learn to dance like that?"

"Yes, indeed," a husky voice interrupted them. "Where did you learn to move like that?"

Greyland looked up to see the outline of a man leaning against the pillar to their right. The shadow cast by the stone structure kept him well concealed.

"Lord Ashlown, Your Grace!" Bella said. "I did not know you were in town."

"Oh, I could not resist this, and what a reward I have been given for my attendance."

He stepped into the light and Greyland felt the atmosphere around them shift. The man was uncomfortably handsome. He was tall, broad-shouldered, and dressed in solid black from his cravat to his high-polished boots. His dark, shoulder-length hair was the color of coal. He wore it loose but brushed sleekly back from his chiseled face. The effect was both cavalier and purposeful. This was not a man to be trifled with.

"I could not help but notice this diamond that sparkled so brightly for us tonight," Lord Ashlown purred—the sound like velvet over sharp steel.

"Miss Kingston, this is London's other notorious Duke, His Grace, Lord Ashlown."

"Ah, Miss Kingston," he smiled. The smile did not reach his eyes. "You were just about to tell us where you had learned to dance...So. Very. Well."

"I..." Greyland felt oddly entranced by his stare, like a serpent to a flute. "That particular dance was learned in Vienna."

"Interesting." He studied her closely, any closer and he might as well be undressing her publicly. "I love a well-traveled lady." He extended his arm. "Would you care to show me personally?"

"That is not an option." Lord Ravenswood's voice was ice.

Lord Ashlown's hold on Greyland snapped in two. Her eyes shot up the towering block of rigid stone that was the Duke of Ravenswood. If silence could be categorized, his was murderous.

"Lord Ravenswood, what an unexpected disappointment to see you," Lord Ashlown replied unenthusiastically. "I think the lady can decide for herself with whom she would like to dance."

Lord Ravenswood handed Bella the two glasses he was holding and in one swift movement, snatched Greyland from the chair. He fixed his eyes on Lord Ashlown. "I will forgive you those inappropriate words with Miss Kingston just this once, but you will not seek her out again!"

Before Lord Ashlown could counter, Lord Ravenswood escorted her—or perhaps dragged her would be more accurate a description—to the dance floor. Greyland was not sure what exactly happened, but as they passed the Earl of Kennington, Lord Ravenswood motioned his head toward Bella. "You will need to remove your fiancée from that filth."

"Was just on my way." The earl looked every bit the Viking as he thundered towards Lord Ashlown. Greyland found herself actually fearing for the other Duke's striking face.

When they reached the edge of the floor, Lord Ravenswood pulled Greyland into a dance hold. His eyes were so sharp she thought they might cut glass. "You should not have further conversations with that man. He is a known scoundrel."

The sternness in his tone irritated her. She was not a child. How dare he presume to lecture her? She had only just met him.

"I am inclined to agree with Lord Ashlown. Whom I converse with is of my own free will." She pulled herself to her full height...all of five-foot-two. The music began, and before she realized she was moving, Lord Ravenswood was whisking her about the ballroom.

"Then I shall convey to your father my warning when I meet with him."

She tried to pull back, aghast, but he held her tight. "I believe the waltz is meant to be danced close." A pleased smile splayed across his full lips.

"Pray tell, what meeting are you talking about with my father, Lord Ravenswood?"

"Your brother informed me of it this morning before you made your jaw-dropping appearance."

Jaw-dropping? Greyland flushed at the blunt acknowledgment as to what he may, or may not, have been thinking when her horse came crashing through the brush earlier that day.

She reminded herself to stay focused. There would be time to obsess over his words later in the privacy of her own room where she would replay them a hundred times in her head.

"I know not what it is about, and please, call me Alex."

"Does that mean we are friends?"

"Yes."

"Well then, as a friend, I would appreciate it if you do not speak of Lord Ashlown to my father."

"Will you stay clear of him?"

"No."

He looked down at her consideringly. It occurred to her the man had likely never heard that word spoken to him before. "Are you always this difficult?" he inquired.

"Quite. Just ask my brothers."

He turned her with ease, and when they were once again face-to-face, he said, "Then we are at an impasse, my dear."

Greyland decided it best to let the subject drop for now. If she had learned anything living with headstrong men, it was that one must apply a different tactic later, when they had forgotten what they might disagree with. "You are very good, my lord. Alex," she tested the name on her tongue. The informality sent a shiver of rebellion through her body. "Your rhythm is perfect."

"You have no earthly idea how good my rhythm can be." If she had not caught the double meaning, the smirk on his handsome face would have tipped her off. *And he knew it,* she realized. He continued on, as if he had not just placed the wickedest of images in a young lady's innocent head. "However, I believe you are the expert. How long have you danced, Miss Kingston?"

"I have danced ever since I can remember." She willed the blush burning up her chest to cease. "My mother used to dance around the house with my father."

"Sounds like a lovely childhood." The music ended and he, with an approving incline of his head, led her off the floor.

"I would love to hear more about your past," the Duke said formally now that they were in earshot of others. "May I call on you tomorrow?"

"I would like that very much." She tried to sound just as prim and unaffected as he did, despite her inner child doing somersaults.

Thomas and Bella waited for them along the wall with proffered glasses in hand. Greyland thanked them and turned her glass up. She emptied the sweet wine in three swallows. Both men's jaws dropped open, but to their noble pedigree's credit, they recovered before anyone else noticed.

Bella laughed. "Greyland, we are going to be great friends."

"THERE YOU ARE!" Edward, completely in his element at tonight's event, danced towards them. "My lovely sister." He swung her into a hug. "Why did you not choose me for that magnificent Viennese waltz? You know I am the better dancer." He grinned mischievously.

Greyland giggled. "I knew nothing of the dance. You will have to talk to father about that."

He feigned seriousness. "Oh, trust me, I will."

"Edward, this is Lord Kennington, Lady Herst, and Lord Ravenswood." Greyland emphasized the last name with a pointed stare at her brother. "The man you were supposed to shoot."

Edward smiled and extended a hand to Alexander. If Greyland did not know the two men had engaged in a barroom brawl less than twenty-four hours before, she would not be able to discern it now. "I do believe I owe you an overdue apology, Your Grace," her brother said sincerely.

Alexander accepted the handshake. "I owe you one, as well, for the whole 'slave' remark. Very unfair."

"I see everyone has made amends," Perkin interjected, walking up. He flashed a card to Edward, who like a child, snatched it from his hand.

"Well, well, little sister, you are very popular," Edward exclaimed upon examining the card.

Greyland reached for it, but Edward held it above his head. "What is that Edward? Let me see." She hopped on one foot and stretched as high as she could, to no avail.

Perkin plucked the card from Edward and handed it over to her. She quickly scanned the writing. It was a list of names.

"I do not understand. These are some of the men I danced with tonight, but—"

"These are twelve men that wish to call upon you tomorrow."

Out of the corner of her eye, she glimpsed the hard set to Lord Ravenswood's jaw. His shoulders appeared to grow tighter in his pristinely cut jacket.

"Oh!" Greyland flushed. "Lord Ravenswood asked to call on me as well." She looked over the names again. "His name is not on here." She looked up and immediately felt embarrassed, talking about him as if he were not standing right there.

"Splendid!" Edward clapped his hands together. "We shall add him to the list." He turned to Perkin. "She will be married by the end of summer at this rate."

"Edward!" She gasped, mortified.

"What?"

Perkin regarded Alexander with a steady, unreadable expression. "Lord Ravenswood, may we talk?" he asked, after more pleasantries had passed between the group.

"Of course." Alexander followed Perkin out onto the terrace.

"I am not a man to mince words so I will get right to the point." Perkin stopped once they were well enough away from any eavesdroppers. "If your intentions with my sister tomorrow are in any way an attempt to uncover what I shared with you this morning…" His eyes relayed the rest. Family came first to this man. Despite his relaxed charm, underneath it all, he was a man who should not be crossed.

"I admit, my concern regarding your father and mine is of utmost importance to me," Alex responded honestly. "However, my interests with Greyland are of a different sort of curiosity altogether. I find her most unique."

"You are on a first-name basis with her now?"

"Yes, and she with me."

"Well then," Kingston regarded him without a trace of emotion, "good luck." He lifted his glass in a toast. "May the best man win."

"Indeed." Alex clinked his glass to Perkin's. *Challenge accepted.*

A different tenor voice called out from the terrace doors. "Your Grace." Both men turned.

Perkin smiled. "Father!"

Alexander locked eyes with the elegant older man strolling up to them. "Mr. Kingston."

"Call me Richard." He dipped his chin respectfully. "I hear you are calling on my princess tomorrow?"

It was one sentence, one small term of endearment from a father in regard to his daughter, and it told Alexander all he needed to know about this man's affections. Alex chose his next words carefully. "That would be my wish. Do you think she can find the time?"

"Oh, I believe she will make the time. But first, I will need to meet with you in private. We have much to discuss. Can you come by tomorrow at say, one o'clock?" The Kingston monarch regarded him closely.

"I believe that will be a fine time." As badly as Alex wanted to demand his answers now, he knew this was not the place. Plus, there was the new predicament he found himself in. The predicament that was Greyland Kingston.

"Good then." Richard Kingston grinned before turning to survey the gardens, his hands moving to clasp behind his back, thoughtfully.

"If we see eye to eye, then you may call upon my daughter." The older gentleman turned back and inclined his head ever so slightly. "Until tomorrow, Lord Ravenswood."

LORD MELBROOKE EXHALED a large smoke ring into the black of night. Less than a stone's throw away, under the lantern light that lined the circular drive, footmen scurried about fetching carriages for their departing guests. "I had a very interesting conversation with someone today."

"And?" his companion asked, concealed by the shadows of the palace's high walls.

The pair paused for a moment as they spied Lord Ravenswood enter the courtyard, locate his own rig, and leave.

"Seems The Queen is being taken advantage of," Melbrooke said. He inhaled another puff of the cheroot and exhaled slowly. "I knew she was too young to handle the responsibilities of her court."

"Who is taking advantage of her, and who told you this?"

"Never mind who informed me, for now. Just understand, I wish you to keep a close eye on the new Kingston family." Melbrooke dropped the cheroot and snuffed it out on the pavers with the heel of his boot.

"I thought you said The Queen told you they were dear family friends?"

"She did, but it is my understanding they have other reasons for returning. I intend to flush out those reasons before they can upset the crown."

"Upset the crown? But how?" The other man grew noticeably more anxious.

Melbrooke squared off with his companion. "Let us just say that if rumors prove true, their lineage goes further back than The Queen's right to the throne."

The man cursed into the night. "How is that possible?"

Lord Melbrooke glared into the night. "The correct baby was not killed a very long time ago."

III

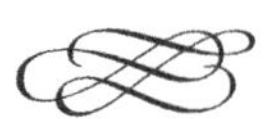

Alexander sat in the Kingston's large parlor waiting for Richard. The manor was impressive—as big as his own. The marquee outside bore the Kingston name, so the family clearly owned it. He had only been in the room a few minutes, admiring the eclectic artwork, before he heard a familiar voice making his goodbyes. Alexander jumped to his feet and headed to the hall.

"Lord Ashlown." Alexander's fingers curled into fists.

"Ah, Lord Ravenswood. Just when I was having a pleasant day..."

"I thought I told you to stay away from Miss Kingston."

"Yes, well here is the problem with your drab attempts at a threat; I do not care," he said simply. "Plus, I was invited here today by the family. I am a Duke, you know. Everyone wants me to marry their daughter." His lips curved up on both sides, his version of a smile...if crocodiles could smile, that is. "And I must admit," Ashlown continued, "this conquest has many admirable qualities for a man such as myself."

Alexander crossed the room in three strides. Before he could get his hands around the man's throat, Perkin's voice called out from the study. "Lord Ravenswood, good day. My father would like to see you now."

Alexander calmed his twitching palms but kept his sights glued to Lord Ashlown. He would be damned if this odious man married Greyland.

"Stay out of my way," Alex growled, "or I will make you a head shorter." He followed Perkin into the other room.

Richard Kingston sat behind a large carved desk. It had clearly been made in another part of the world, for Alexander could not place the type of wood. *Teak?* A tribal etching ran up the legs. It was a truly magnificent piece and immediately filled Alexander with a score of questions. Questions such as where had Richard Kingston's desk been made? Who the hell were these people? How did they know the newly appointed Queen? How did they know of his father? How did the young lady of the house know how to tighten a blasted girth strap on a horse?

The older man stood. "Lord Ravenswood, care for a glass of sherry?"

"Yes, please, though I would appreciate it if you would address me by my Christian name."

Richard nodded and turned to Perkin. "I would like to speak with Alexander alone."

Perkin bowed gracefully, then strolled from the room. Richard poured two glasses of sherry from the sideboard table before returning to the desk and handing Alex one. They both took their respected seats.

Alexander unleashed his concerns. "Not to overstep my place, but Lord Ashlown is a womanizing, wicked man that you should keep a close eye on around Miss Kingston." Alex knew he should stop now. He had given his unsolicited opinion, and that should be the end of it. However, his mouth had plans that his brain had not thought out. "He cannot be trusted and is not suited for her."

Richard Kingston's brows rose in what Alex interpreted as controlled amusement. "I thank you for your advice, but I have given my daughter carte blanche to choose her own path. I trust her judgment." The older gentleman made a deliberate study of Alex's reaction.

Alexander schooled his features and waited. As much as he wanted to push to his feet, to lay down the law, and demand that Richard Kingston see reason, he knew that would not go over well with this particular father. After another long moment of silence, Kingston resumed the narrative. "I dare say, I am curious as to what harm you think he would do to her?"

Alex was taken aback, seldom had anyone questioned him outright, much less, dismissed his concerns. He certainly had never met a man who would let his daughter—or son for that matter—choose his or her own spouse. It was completely unheard of. In fact, it was so peculiar that Alex would be less shocked if a prancing unicorn carrying a woodland nymph had charged into the room singing Christmas carols.

He quickly reconfigured his tangled thoughts. Perhaps reason would make a better case. "Ashlown is a Lord of the Realm, I daresay his word would mean more than Greyland's, should they ever be caught in a compromising position." He paused, trying to get a read on Kingston's thoughts. It was useless. The man had a card-face that was impenetrable at the moment. "I do not proclaim to know how it is in America, but here a man's word is above that of a woman, even one as elevated as Miss Kingston."

Richard drew in a deep breath, letting emotion factor back into the conversation. "It is the same in America. For now, you will just have to trust that Lord Ashlown and I have an...understanding. He is aware of how much harm would befall him if he were to cross me. Even without a title of my own."

"I did not mean to insinuate—"

Richard held up a silencing hand. "I know you are just thinking of my daughter's well-being. No need to explain. Let us begin our business and you let me worry over Greyland. For now." He smiled and sat down at his desk. "Lord knows, it will be some other man's job before I wish it to be," he mumbled, almost plaintively.

After an hour's time, Alexander felt a little of the previous day's weight dropping from his shoulders. He liked Richard Kingston immensely, and his family's connections in the trade market with

Ireland, England, and America made sense. Alex was unaware of how successful the business had been. His father kept those ledger books separate, which explained why his solicitor failed to provide them with the others after his father's passing. Instead, they had been sent to Richard.

Apparently, the two families had been involved in business dealings for the past three generations. Richard assumed Alex would continue with the inherited partnership. Alexander, to his own amazement, welcomed the idea. The only question that still plagued him was why he had never known. His father trusted Richard Kingston over his own son with the business ledgers—what else had he trusted this man with?

Richard informed him that during the often-turbulent relationship between the countries the families had kept the business as quiet as possible. Alex understood this respectful explanation as a polite way of skirting over the illegal aspects of the company. His family had not earned its name by playing by the rules. Although Alex had known his father to have been a just man, he was no saint. His father was ruthless in the things he desired and let very little deter him. The Ravenswood name was built on power, wealth, and cleverness.

Richard also assured Alex that all the same information would be confirmed by his uncle Derrick upon his arrival to town later that evening. Derrick had been unexpectedly called away yesterday, soon after he had arrived in London. That explained why Alex had not received a return message from him yet.

After one last glass of sherry, Richard leaned across the desk. "I believe you also came here to call on my daughter?"

"Yes." Alex sat forward in his chair, ready to stand. "Now that we are in agreement, I would like that very much."

Richard Kingston's eyes turned quizzical. "Forgive me the probably obtuse question, but, why? What is it you find so agreeable about my Greyland?"

Alexander shifted. He was so drawn to the young beauty that he had not stopped to scrutinize the snare he might be stepping into. "Your daughter is a very beautiful, intriguing young woman," he answered honestly. "I would be a fool not to acquaint myself with her."

Richard held him with that unflappable focus he seemed to be able to call upon at will. "I am only curious because your father spoke of you often, so I feel as if I know you a bit," he explained. "That being said your father seemed to think you had very little interest in marriage."

Alex thought a moment, then said, "That would have been true, as I have lived my life on a very strict set of tracks. However, I would have to say that my biggest lack of interest regarding marriage has to do entirely with having not yet crossed paths with the right young woman. Miss Kingston has, more or less..." Alex felt himself smile as he contemplated her. "...derailed me."

Richard considered him quietly, as he might look over a horse, he was debating the purchase of at auction.

"I need you to know something about my daughter. If you have not figured it out already. Greyland is not like most young ladies. I have given her many liberties and have not held her back in anything. Nor have I ruled her with a heavy hand. Maybe, looking back, I should have provided more structure, but after her mother had passed...Well, it is hard being a father to a little girl with no female influence to guide her."

Alex felt his chest constricting in on his lungs at the familiar loss. "I am very sorry to hear about your late wife." Richard nodded, acknowledging the sentiment. Alex resumed his train of thought, "I have only just met your daughter, but I can see that she measures up to everything you described of her. She is head-strong, indulged, whimsical, unpredictable, and willful."

Alex realized his pragmatic list of characteristics might sound a bit *too* pragmatic. "A certain type of man might find those traits unbecoming. Rather," he rushed, choosing his next words with better care. "A certain man might not be up for the challenge." *Still rubbish!*

"You see," giving up, Alex spread his hands and exhaled. "I am the sort of man who wants a marriage that feels like riding a fast horse down untested trails; a wife that intrigues me the same way a new hand at the card table does. I am not looking for a proper, composed and biddable bride to just sire my sons and play her part."

The words coming out of his mouth were as shocking to Alex as he imagined they sounded to Richard Kingston. Alex had laid bare more of himself in these last three minutes than he had to anyone in his whole life. Might as well keep going.

"Sir, I would never want to change your daughter. Maybe help guide her, should our friendship grow. Her zest for life is refreshing, her spontaneity a gift, and her humor unrivaled." Alex shook his head. "I find myself drawn to her in a way that can only be described as… authentic."

Richard Kingston smiled a smile that reached all the way into his hairline. He stood suddenly and held out his hand. "Well then," the older gentleman said as Alex stood, taking his proffered handshake. "Let us go find my daughter."

ALEX WAS BEING LED down an impressively large hall towards the back garden. He once again took note of the lack of traditional English décor. In place of thick floor-to-ceiling curtains pooling on the floors of each window, were shutters; plantation shutters, he believed they were called. A very Caribbean and Southern America style that served a practical need for wind-flow in their much warmer climate.

In lieu of delicate knickknacks adorning side tables and desk—a favorite amongst the older ladies—were books of all sizes, shapes, and subjects; with these were journals and ready to use quills on nearly every available surface of every passing room. An Oriental rug ran the length of the hall they were currently traveling down. Various tribal masks decorated the walls and ornate furniture, not entirely French, lined them.

Alex recalled The Queen's mention of the Kingston's travels abroad. This house reflected that. It was not a manor house decorated to simply impress, but a home filled with memories. A practical place that reflected the needs of the family and a collection of experiences. There was not a stick of furniture in this house that did not beg a conversation to start up about its existence.

Alex was impressed, and even more curious than he had been yesterday. He was just about to inquire how Richard Kingston knew The Queen when a loud commotion from outside interrupted the calm.

They opened the French doors to see Greyland, knee-deep in a large fountain, trying frantically to retrieve something. A large black man also stood in the water attempting to keep hold of a very fat, very wet, and very irate cat. A serving girl stood squealing from the water's edge, holding out her arms to the lady of the house.

"I have it. Here, take the second one." Greyland thrust something small into the girl's hands and then plunged both arms back into the water.

"I can't hold this beast much longer, Miss Greyland," the man yelled.

Richard and Alexander ran towards the motley crew. "Ocman, give me the damn cat before you bleed to death!" Richard shouted.

"Miss Kingston!" Alexander jumped into the fountain just as Greyland stood up and thrust a wet flailing baby bird into his hands.

As soon as her eyes met his, she gasped.

"Lord Ravenswood!"

Alexander handed the bird to the serving girl, gaping up at him. He secured Greyland by the arm and helped her out of the fountain. Her gown slipped down over one shoulder, exposing the most kissable skin he had ever seen. He held her for longer than she needed to reorientate herself on dry land. Long enough to realize he was the one in over his head.

Richard's voice broke Alex's hold, literally and figuratively. "Greyland, dear, please go and get out of that wet dress. Alexander will wait here for you to return."

"Indeed, before you catch a cold." Alex could not keep the amusement from his tone. Never in his life had he dreamt of a day when he would witness a lady sacrificing her fashion for a bird. Thrilled, he let out a delighted chuckle that earned him an inquisitive look from her lovely green eyes.

"We were just about to have tea when the branch broke under Churchill's weight and toppled him. His would-be snacks fell out of the nest and into the pond. I very well could not let the poor things die."

"Of course not," he concurred, no more able to stop the smile from forming on his face than he could stop the sun from shining above their heads.

Greyland tossed her glossy curls back with one last glance over her shoulder, gifting him with her angelic profile. "I shall be right back." She nodded officially.

A silence followed in her wake, a calm settling in after a storm; a storm with perfect skin, wild dancing eyes, and a penchant for saving small helpless wildlife.

Once she rounded the double French doors, Richard chuckled softly. "I believe 'zest' was the word you used."

GREYLAND RETURNED to the garden in a dry, mint-green gown. Lord Ravenswood and her father were conversing. The men faced in the opposite direction from which she approached. This gave her time to set to memory the way Alexander's fine-cut britches clung to his muscular legs. The man really was much too attractive. He was tall, about Edward's height, but his deep olive complexion and dark chocolate hair was a stark contrast to her brother's fair hair and lighter coloring.

He must have heard her approaching, for he turned his head and smiled, reminding her that the front view of him was just as appealing as the backside. His blue eyes, surrounded by thick dark lashes, caught the light and sparkled like cresting waves on the Atlantic.

"Ah, sunshine," her father called. "Much better, darling. I will leave you to get to know Lord Ravenswood, and," he moved his eyes towards Ocman sitting on a bench under a shade tree, "Ocman will continue to act as chaperon." He shook Alexander's hand and retreated to the house.

"Your father is a very upstanding man," Alexander said when the doors closed behind her father. "I can tell he loves you very much."

"My father and my brothers are everything to me." She glanced in the direction of the gardens. "Care to take a walk?" Her eyes bounced back to Alex.

"Yes. That would be lovely."

Ocman rose and followed, mindful to keep pace a good way behind them. Her acting chaperon must be tired by now. The poor man had been overseeing her conversations all morning. She only had to remind him twice to keep a little more distance from them. It was very hard to get these men to open up to her with his imposing figure looming. Well, all except for Lord Ashlown, who seemed to blatantly disregard the fact that anyone else was alive outside of Greyland and himself.

"You are having a busy day," Alexander stated, more than asked.

"That might be an understatement." She reached out a hand to lazily brush the soft petals of an azalea bush. She noted the way his eyes followed her fingers as she did so. It made her feel...*admired.*

"Surely, you like all the attention?" he queried. "Do not most young ladies?"

"Oh, I do not know how most ladies feel, however, I am beginning to feel a little like a horse at auction."

Alexander stopped abruptly and faced her, tilting his head to one side. "I had the exact same thought a mere ten minutes ago in your father's study," he said. Then, suddenly concerned, added, "I hope I do not make you feel that way. That would not be my intent at all."

Greyland felt her cheeks brighten. "No, no. Not you. It is just a bit much. I can hardly keep the names straight, much less remember the days they wish to call." She put the back of her hand to her forehead and sighed dramatically. "It is all *so* exhausting."

Warmth enveloped her when Alexander smirked in response to her earnest acting skills. "I completely understand. I have been dodging would-be suitors for years. Yet today, here I am." He grinned. "One more among your many admirers."

Greyland hung spellbound by the man's honesty.

"So, you are an admirer?" Mentally, she kicked herself for the question. Perkin had cautioned her about being too bold.

"How could I not be, Greyland?" He reached out and took her hand, igniting tiny fires once again on her every nerve ending.

Do not blush, Greyland Kingston, she said to herself as she fought to control her traitorous body. "Tell me, why was Lord Ashlown here?"

"He was...Perkin thought..." Just like that the butterflies in her stomach caught fire, turned into little raisins of ash mid-flight, and crumbled into the wind. She decided meeting the inquisition head-on was the best course of action. "He was here to call on me. I had no idea until this morning, when Perkin told me he would be one of the twelve...now, thirteen suiters..." She trailed off. She was rambling now.

"I see." He let go of her hand and stepped back, taking some of the air with him. "I told your father of the man's reputation. Hopefully, he will not be received again."

She tried for indifference. "I am not sure why it matters to you. Do you, yourself, not also hold a rather...interesting reputation?" She watched his mouth set in a grim line. *So much for indifference.*

"It is not so much my reputation, as it is my families' enthusiastic past pursuits of deplorable action and questionable taste," he stated pragmatically. "I have had my share of turmoil, but I assure you, I am nothing compared to Lord Ashlown. He is a very dark man." A shadow fell across his eyes, "Lastly, it matters because I wish to know you better. During which time, I would prefer you to remain pure, should I choose to ask for your hand."

"*Remain pure!*" The dormant butterflies in the pit of her stomach rose from the dead and manifested into tiny fire-breathing dragons. "Should you *choose?*" Her hand twitched at her side. "I, will be the one choosing, Lord Ravenswood." She squared her shoulders up with his. "And, what I choose to do, or not do, with my body is entirely up to me."

He narrowed his eyes.

Ocman charged up. "All is fine." Greyland stopped his advancement, though she rather fancied the visual of seeing her chaperon plow over Lord Ravenswood at this very moment. Instead, she plastered a tight smile to her lips. "Lord Ravenswood was just leaving. Please show Lord Lovingston in. Whichever Lovingston twin is here first."

Damn him! she thought furiously. She would not be bullied, no matter how attractive the blasted man was.

"I will see myself out," Lord Ravenswood said stiffly, inclining his regal head down to her. "I am sorry for my blunt honesty, but you have no idea what that vile creature is capable of. You are a courageous woman, Miss Kingston, but even you are no match for the likes of Lord Ashlown."

Before she could reply, he turned and stalked off.

Greyland's limbs turned to mush as all her mustered adrenaline slithered to her toes and dissolved on the ground at her feet.

"What century does he think we live in?" she scoffed, shaking her head. "Is Lord Ashlown going to club me over the head and drag me back to his cave?"

"Perhaps a small break is advisable?" Ocman offered, bringing to her attention she was thinking out loud.

She stopped her mental pacing. "I am fine," she assured him, as much as she did for herself. "All is fine," she repeated, forcing herself to smile when she heard her father announcing the next suitor. She tried, to no avail, to forget Lord Presumptuous' remarks.

JEREMY LOVINGSTON WAS A VERY PRETTY, young man. Every word rolled off his tongue as if they were a recited sonnet. She wondered if they were. Greyland had given up trying to cross-compare his every sentence with the great poets of the past. If he were passing off others' words as his own, she was not the historical aficionado to spot it. She decided to focus on his manners, but again she found herself overly scrutinizing them. They were too perfect, as polished as the finest of silver. And his pedigree, this one she did not have to decipher as he was quite proud of it and gladly brought it into conversation—twice—and was better than The Queen's Spaniel bitches.

All in all, he was absolutely fetching and utterly boring. Greyland glanced repeatedly toward the house. Surely it was time for the next and final gentleman caller.

"Would you like that, Miss Kingston?"

Drat, caught woolgathering!

She absentmindedly reached a reassuring hand out and placed it atop his. He jolted upright. She pulled her hand back, suddenly afraid of how he might have taken the gesture. He seized it back awkwardly.

Oh dear, an unrehearsed handholding.

His regard bounced from their clasped hands to her eyes. *Oh no,* he was taking the gesture precisely wrong. "Would you do me the honor of a picnic in the park tomorrow?" he asked again, desperation seeping from his soft brown eyes the same way sweat now coated his clammy palm.

Greyland did not want to crush his spirits, but she really did not wish to prolong his pain either. He seemed so fragile and young, especially compared to another demanding, but definitely not insecure, lord who had set her blood boiling just an hour ago.

Lord Lovingston was a sweet man, but he was not right for her, nor she for him. He needed a woman who would swoon at his compliments and watered-down conversation. Someone who would play the role of dutiful wife and never give the bon ton anything scandalous to talk of. This man needed to be loved for whom he had so carefully crafted himself to be. She inwardly sighed because she was none of those things, and she could not love a man that forced himself into a pre-set role.

She squeezed his hand. "I would—"

"Miss Greyland, you have another guest." Ocman's announcement saved her just in time.

She leapt to her feet, probably a tad too enthusiastically. Lovingston frowned and cast a wilted look down at his sharply polished Hessians. "My lord," she continued, "I will speak to my father and send word. Thank you so very much for your delightful conversation."

Rising, he beamed up at her, then bade her farewell. She smiled back warmly, just not too warmly...she hoped. *Gods teeth,* would this day ever end? Any more time spent stroking the sensitive egos of the bon ton dandies and her face might freeze this way, forever stuck in contrived compliance.

The second of the identical Lovingston twins, William, was announced from the doorway, cueing Greyland to repeat the role of an over-joyed, besotted young lady.

The brothers exchanged a heated look as they passed each other on the lawn.

After the Baron finished his best efforts at swooning over her, Greyland gave her goodbye and wearily headed upstairs to rest before it was time to sup.

Edward met her at the top of the steps. "Well, who did you like?" He asked, fresh as a daisy. "More specifically, who did you hate?"

"Really Edward?" She passed him and continued into her room. "You are worse than a girl."

"Sure, sure." Edward gave her his best attempt at a puppy face from her doorway. "Did they give you all their best lines?" He continued into her bedroom and flopped down on the bed before propping himself up on one elbow. "Do tell me at least one of them used my favorite, 'Your skin is like alabaster. Your leeches must work overtime.'"

She laughed. "Are you sure you are the older one? Very well." Deciding there was no avoiding him, she sat down at her vanity and began to brush out the ends of her hair, careful not to upset the ringlets. She watched him from the mirror as she began. "They were all nice. Lord Ravenswood would be the most attractive, if only he was not so overbearing." She rolled her eyes.

"What do you mean, 'overbearing'?" Edward's brow creased. All levity gone.

"That is the look." She wagged her comb at him. "It was as if he were an older brother, or worse—father."

"Well, in that case, I like him all the more. You need someone who will look after you. We know how careless you can be. And to think," he added reflectively, "I almost killed the man."

"Me? Careless? As I recall, it was you who challenged him to a duel the day before yesterday."

Her brother gave her his classic what-can-I-say-it-must-run-in-the-family, expression. "Minor details." He smirked and rose from the bed. "I am glad you like him, though." He headed for the door. "Because he is coming to dinner tonight."

ALEXANDER TURNED the corner into his study and found his uncle relaxed behind his desk, the chair swiveled towards the fireplace.

"Derrick."

The salt and pepper haired man turned with a slight start, seemingly lost in thought. He grinned but made no attempts to rise, which only served in reminding Alex why he really did not care for his uncle. Derrick Hamilton, quite simply, was a pain in the ass. A handsome man, like all the men of his line. But unlike the others, Derrick seemed to have a natural repellant to him, much like the stripe down a skunk's back. Which, after further consideration, would explain why he had remained unmarried. No potential father-in-law wanted to put up with him. And since he would likely never ascend to the title of Duke of Ravenswood—not without stepping over two coffins first—it made aligning with him even less appealing.

"Alexander, we need to talk."

"I have heard. Care to give me back my chair?"

Derrick rose reluctantly and repositioned himself across from the desk. "I will get to the questions you likely have first." Derrick reached over and poured himself a brandy. "I have been overseeing all interest on the Irish side of the business."

"Why do you suppose father never saw fit to tell me this?" Alexander poured his own glass of spirits and took a seat.

"Perhaps he did not think you would care." Derrick picked a piece of invisible lint off his jacket sleeve and held it out for inspection, rolling it between his thumb and middle finger. "You never had a mind for business, after all."

Alexander stiffened. "Excuse me?"

"Which I admire." His uncle looked up earnestly. "I would prefer to spend my time consorting with women and gaming as well. But someone had to keep the family coffers filled. How else could you enjoy your plush lifestyle?" He smiled.

"Careful, uncle," Alex said, staring at the man across the desk from him. "The line you are walking is held together by my name and title. You would serve yourself well to remember that."

Derrick considered him carefully. "Forgive me, Your Grace."

Alex took a long swallow of his brandy. He and Derrick had never been close, but they were family, and despite all his own reservations regarding his uncle, his father had obviously trusted him. Though he was beginning to wonder why.

Filling the family coffers...

Alexander mulled over the insolent remark. He had overseen the running of three family estates for the better part of five years, all of which had flourished under his guidance. He was far from some entitled Duke's son out gallivanting across the country, whoring his inheritance away. Granted, he led a fulfilled lifestyle, just not the type his uncle had described. Still, the words had hit their mark, clearly Derrick's intention, casting a shadow of doubt.

Derrick changed the subject. "So, tell me about the Kingston children. More importantly, the young lady. Is she as striking as I have heard?"

Alexander bristled at the inquiry. "She is. She is also stubborn. And I fear she has a tendency to get into trouble."

"Interesting."

"Why do you care?" Alex asked, his hackles lifting.

Derrick crossed his legs, getting more comfortable in his chair, "If she is as pretty as you say, then I plan on bonding our families together. For the business, of course."

Bile rose in Alex's throat. *Jesus Christ!* Was there not a man in England looking to press his suit on this woman? He downed the last of his glass and tried to not show the revulsion he felt. Derrick was a Hamilton, after all. Competition ran through his veins like rainwater through a downspout.

"She is very hard-headed," he said, by way of dismissal. "I do not think you would be overjoyed trying to keep her in line."

"I do not give a rat's arse about her personality, Alex." A wicked grin touched on his uncle's lips. "As for keeping her in line, that is what whips are for."

Alex felt an urge to stab his uncle with the fire poker... repeatedly. "I would take care with that tongue of yours. Greyland's father and brothers are extraordinarily protective. If they heard you mutter such interest—"

"Why Alexander!" A smirk slithered onto Derrick's face. "You have designs on her; already addressing her by her Christian name?"

"Yes!" Alex snapped, abandoning the ruse. "So please keep your filthy mind off what may be mine."

"What *may* be yours..." Derrick laced his fingers together. "Have no fear nephew. I will stay clear. For the moment." His uncle stood. "However, if you do not have her secured in a month, all bets are off."

Alex rolled his eyes. "Thank you for the, oh-so-gracious, head start."

"Of course," Derrick said brusquely and headed for the door. He paused upon reaching it and turned around. "Oh, on another subject you will dislike, I heard Henry was in Hampshire."

Alexander's brows shot up. "He is still in the country?"

"That is the rumor."

"I will put Hobbs on it tomorrow, see if he can find out anything."

"Do not do anything rash, nephew," Derick warned. "We do not have any proof that he was the one who put the bullet in my brother."

Alex felt his fists balling. "I know it was him, and that is all there is to it."

Derrick nodded, considering. "I think knowing where, and what he is about, is a good start. To know, not to act. For now."

"Yes," Alex bit out through clenched teeth. "To know."

DISBELIEF WAS TOO small a word to describe the emotion that swamped Greyland when she discovered her father invited Lord Ashlown and Lord Ravenswood to the same dinner party. Now here she was, an hour later, still confused, and annoyed. Why would her father invite both men? Surely, he knew they hated each other. Neither

Duke seemed to be well-versed in the art of caring to hide their distaste for the other one. Was this to be a test? Or entertainment? *And, for who...*them or her? She exhaled a tiny huff of frustration. "Why?"

"Why what, sister?" Perkin, walking beside her, asked.

Drat. Well, there was no avoiding the question now that she had spoken it out loud. "Why do you think father invited Lord Ashlown and Lord Ravenswood tonight?"

"For the same reason he invited Lord Kennington, Miss Herst, and Lord Effington." Perkin glanced down at her. "It is our first dinner party in London. He has selected peers that hold similar power in parliament. Granted, Miss Herst is a polite gesture done for Lord Kennington, but still, of status. You like her, do you not?"

"Yes, very much so." Greyland chewed over the politics. She should have known it was that simple. Her father only entertained in small groups of like-minded people that ranked on par with each other. Tomorrow night he might have a completely different set of men over for dinner. And Greyland would be no more the wiser regarding their political or business agendas at the beginning of the evening as she would be at the end.

It was the way it had always been. Since Greyland was old enough to have a memory, her father had entertained, near weekly, these types of dinners. Richard Kingston would shuffle the men off to the smoking-room after dinner where they would get down to business. In fact, the whole evening was centered solely on that smoking room. The large pocket doors would shut, allowing Greyland and the other ladies to make small talk over lemon cakes in the receiving parlor until the men emerged.

Greyland had never questioned anything about it—until now; now that two men that were actively courting her were down the hall, seated around their dining table, likely growling at one another while waiting on her. Perkin's words chimed in her ears again: *Peers that hold a similar power in parliament.* That made sense, being that both men were dukes. Still though, Lord Ravenswood and Lord Ashlown could not be considered 'like-minded'. *Surely not.*

"All the gentlemen here tonight lean strongly in the same

direction, at parliament." Perkin seemed to read her mind. "They may have nothing in common outside of that, but that is of no concern for tonight's purpose."

"So, tonight's dinner is strictly business?" she asked, trying to not sound naïve. Or disappointed.

"It is also to place you in a controlled atmosphere so that father can see how both suitors fair, having to share the same space with one another." One side of Perkin's mouth tipped like a scale weighted with irony. "Like two lions placed in the same cage."

Grayland cut her eyes up to her brother. "I am not sure how I feel about being the proverbial bait."

"Oh pish!" Perkin scoffed. "At least you do not have to sit next to Lord Effington. I swear the man's only ambition in life is to become ever more spherical in shape."

Her brother paused and looked down at her. "Greyland..." he used his quiet voice, the one that strongly recommended she listen. "Normally, this is the time when I would tell you to mind yourself with care." A wayward smile tugged at his lips, and he carefully caught a loose curl at Greyland's cheek and tucked it behind her ear. "Tonight, just be yourself."

Everyone rose when she and Perkin stepped through the double doors. "So sorry to keep you all waiting," Perkin apologized as he escorted Greyland into the room. "I had a last-minute correspondence I needed to get off this evening."

"I think we have all been in those shoes," Lord Ravenswood said understandingly, as he reached and pulled out Greyland's chair.

Alexander smiled warmly at her. Greyland felt her frustration regarding their earlier conversation subside. In part, due to that swoon-worthy smile, and the exhausting memory of the monotonous time spent with the oh-so predictable Lovingston duo. At least neither of them were in attendance tonight. She was not sure the muscles in her jaw, required to focus a smile all night, could take it.

Greyland smiled demurely back up at Lord Ravenswood as he pushed her chair in neatly. She almost felt bad for him now. Not only had she dismissed his deep-seated concerns mere hours ago, but he was now also having to endure the presence of his bitter rival. The man must be made of a strong constitution to take this much abuse in a day. And then, one must not forget, there was the unfortunate beating he had endured at the hands of her brother the day before that. A tinge of purple on his jaw could still be seen in the candlelight, reminding her of the poor man's first impression of the Kingston family.

No sooner had Greyland started mentally counting off every reason why Lord Ravenswood should run screaming from the room, did Lord Ashlown incline his head in her direction. "The view is worth all the wait in the world." He smiled radiantly from where he sat across the table from her.

Greyland saw out of her peripheral a muscle in Alexander's jaw jump. Ashlown, on the other hand, appeared as if he had not a care in the world. This was going to be a very long night indeed.

AN HOUR LATER, and Greyland was glad her father had invited Bella. However, Lord Ashlown was so overwhelmingly engaging, he left little time for the two women to chat, much less to acquaint herself with the other ten guests.

"Tell me more about Louisiana," Lord Ashlown implored, his tone thick and blatantly sensual.

"Oh, it is magical!" Greyland could not control her exuberant response. "Spanish moss drapes the ancient oak trees like a warm cloak individually gifted to each branch. The branches—in seeming thanks—spread out their huge inviting arms as if begging for a hug. And, it is much warmer there than here." She sawed into a piece of lamb on her plate as she continued. "The Gulf's temperature is ideal for swimming," she finished, taking a bite.

No one picked up the conversation where she left off. Greyland was suddenly aware of her own chewing as the silence stretched on. She swallowed, then dared to lift her head, scanning the room. To her utter dread, all eyes were still glued on her, waiting for her to continue.

She looked down, frowning into her plate. She had gone and done it again; run off on a tangent like a small child finally asked to speak. This was clearly not how a lady of London should describe something. *Too much fanciful description,* she mused, pushing a pea with her fork and hoping someone would take pity and talk, thus filling the empty void.

The silence stretched on. It irked her. She felt her embarrassment receding and conviction taking over. *The hell with proper.*

She picked up Alexander's glass of wine that was beside her water and took a deep drink before continuing. "The trees speak of a knowledge that seems to go back to the beginning of time…" She trailed off, allowing herself the indulgence of getting lost in her memories. Perkin had requested she be herself, after all.

"I miss the trees the most," she said wistfully. "England's trees are lovely too, of course, and maybe it is the climate that makes the subtle differences. However, the trees back home just hold a sort of magic. A charm. It is as if each live oak hides its own mystery." She smiled. "A story that only *it* knows."

To her surprise, it was Lord Ravenswood's voice that cleared beside her. *Probably to request his wine glass back.* She inwardly cringed at her own audacity.

"I know exactly what you mean," he agreed. "I have found that the trees in parts of Italy hold an endearing charm that is all their own. Their foliage challenges others to dare rise above their glory."

"Why Alexander," Bella said, a smile hidden in her words. "I did not know you were such an admirer of flora and fauna and their apparent attitudes?" She flashed a dimpled grin before popping a fig into her mouth. The guests all laughed.

Alexander returned Bella's grin and then repositioned himself in his chair so that he fully faced Greyland. "I have never met someone who speaks so much from the heart." He stared at her in contemplation.

Greyland felt her skin heating under his intense observation of her person. Just before she was sure the room would see the exacting effect the man held over her, he turned back, addressing the rest of the table. "Miss Kingston has eloquently tapped into my own thoughts regarding the simple and precious sides of life. I wish more people spoke their mind in such a way instead of the mindless prattle I am often forced to listen to." Alex shook his head, reflecting with a chuckle. "A man could really care less what hairstyle is of the latest fashion."

"Here, here!" Thomas roared, raising his glass for a toast and gesturing to the two ladies at the table. "To intelligent woman that do not prattle on."

Greyland drank in the compliment, beaming as she joined in the toast. "Yes," Lord Ravenswood said from beside her so that only her ears could hear amongst the clinking of glasses. "To intelligent women." His words were low and even. They smoldered like a fuse burning towards gunpowder. "Especially the ones that will blatantly steal a man's wine."

He winked.

RICHARD JOINED Alex by the hearth after they had retired to the smoking-room, leaving Bella and Greyland in the main parlor. "So, Alexander, your father told me you represent the Whig party in Parliament?"

"I do."

"I believe Perkin might have already told you before we left America that I was a congressman for my state of Louisiana." He paused a moment. "I am an Abolitionist."

"Oh?" Alexander was shocked into momentary silence. He had heard of this anti-slavery group and how dangerous it was to be aligned with them. "Is that not rather a risky side to lean toward in Louisiana?"

"Your father said you were quite familiar with global matters of state," Richard replied.

"I would be dishonoring my country if I did not keep a close eye on foreign policies."

Richard smiled approvingly. "Neither of our sides are house majorities. However, with new leadership in place, your side is more readily accepted. I fear my country has an uphill battle still on its hands." His expression grew more solemn. "I fear a great struggle ahead."

"I believe you are right," Alexander concurred. "Change is inevitable. But likewise, never met without struggle and great sacrifice. I can only imagine how delicate the situation becomes being on the opposing side to your state."

"Indeed." It was one word, but it carried the weight of a whole country.

Alex felt a touch of tension lodge itself between his shoulder blades at the thought of just how dangerous it might have been for the Kingston's. Particularly for a young, unwed girl whose father might be considered a radical. The fact that Greyland was late in making her debut suddenly made more sense. Her father was afraid of not finding suitable matches in their home country, which called to mind a sudden, and very important question. "Do you plan on returning?"

Richard regarded him for a long minute. "It is not safe for us there —not yet anyway."

"Is England where you plan to call home now?"

"My family ancestry goes back a long way here. While it is not the country of my, or my children's birth." Richard's gaze flickered down to the blazing fire in the hearth. "England's blood runs deep in our veins."

"If you do not mind me asking, is that how you know The Queen?"

The older man smiled. "I admire your directness." He took a sip from his glass of sherry. "Yes. The Queen's family and my own have been aligned for the past two-hundred years."

Alexander raised an inquisitive eyebrow.

"The Queen shares our beliefs," Richard answered Alexander's unvoiced question. "I have been waiting a long time for her to take the throne." He smiled the smile of a man that knew better than to tip his hand too soon. "But that is a story for another day."

Lord Ashlown sauntered over just then. "I believe the ladies are in need of our company in the main parlor," he addressed only Richard. "We have been summoned."

"Well then," Richard said, nodding. "We must not keep them waiting."

MISS KINGSTON SAT at the large pianoforte with her eyes closed, playing a melodic piece. Alex took the opportunity to admire her. Long black eyelashes swept her lightly rouged cheeks. The crown of her head tilted ever so slightly, elongating her slender neck, and creating kissable divots just above her clavicle. His eyes followed a thin shimmering necklace down her milky flesh. It came to rest at the apex of two perfectly rounded breasts that pushed the boundaries of her tight bodice.

Alex had never been jealous of anything in his whole life...but that necklace. He wanted to be the gold chain that caressed her bare skin.

Applause lilted through the hall when Greyland finished her piece, pulling Alex forcefully from his wayward thought progression. "Bravo!" Lord Ashlown cooed and stepped forward.

Alexander felt his teeth grind together when the arrogant bastard had the audacity to smirk at him before helping Greyland rise from the instrument.

"She is not an invalid," Alex growled under his breath.

Lord Effington cocked his head in Alexander's direction. Expression came hard to a man like Effington, but enough of the ridges of his face tightened around his double chin and bug-eyes to show that he was puzzled by the exclamation. "My lord?"

Alex forced a smile and inclined his head. "My apologies," he offered. "Excuse me." He turned and quit the room.

Once in the hall leading to the gardens, Alex chastised himself for letting Lord Ashlown rile him so. He simply needed to keep his anger in check. That, or, just knock the bloke senseless and be done with it.

Alex's animosity with the other duke spanned years, going back to when the two had been adversaries at Cambridge. One always tried to outdo the other, in literally everything. Somewhere along the road, it had taken a darker turn and they had resorted to more violent means of competition. Ashlown shot Alexander in a duel, waylaying him in bed for a month. Alex, in turn, stole the other lord's favorite mistress. Ashlown was then obligated to spread gossip that Alex had various male troubles. So, Alex all but bankrupted the pompous ass in a game of cards. It was a well-played rivalry as far as rivalries go.

Alex pushed through the double doors and walked out into the courtyard. Closing his eyes, he turned his face up to the moonlight. None of those memories were why he feared Greyland in the other lord's presence now. Ashlown had a much darker side to him.

Alexander had once watched Ashlown beat a banker near to death. It had taken four men to pull him off the other man. The banker later succumbed to head trauma, reportedly given to him when he was thrown from his horse. Considering the man was newly released from the hospital following the severe beating obtained by the irate lord, it was unlikely he had taken up horse riding so soon.

As disturbing as the vacant look in Lord Ashlown's eyes was that day on the street, when he repeatedly bashed the other man's head in, nothing could have prepared Alex for what the duke did next.

It was an unusually warm night in early May some years back when Alex witnessed Lord Ashlown escorting a pretty young woman from the Cork and Cow tavern. The same girl was found in a field, not far from the town watering hole the next morning, raped and beaten to death. Somehow Ashlown concocted a solid alibi; not that it was hard to do, being a duke. Alexander was not as convinced as his peers.

Over the years that question had nagged him. Was Ashlown capable of an act so heinous as to turn his fist on a woman and take her against her will. While the man was known to violence, the one thing he never lacked was female attention. Still, the mere idea that he could have committed the deed was enough to make Alex leery of him around Greyland. If his lifetime rival was merely a cad, so be it. But if he were a rapist and murderer…

Out of the corner of his eye, Alex detected movement. He turned quickly and saw a wisp of dark hair sail by the side of the house. He knew exactly who it was. He made his way towards the figure in the shadows and stopped short.

Before him, poised high, as if presented on a serving tray, was the most delicious derriere he had ever seen. The owner of said derriere was bent over at the waist and reaching for something in the rose bushes. All he would have to do was reach both hands out in order to grab hold of her round little bottom.

Alex bit the inside of his mouth, but it was too late to stop the rapid hedonistic descent his mind was tumbling down. He folded his arms and dug the heels of his boots into the soft grass, trying to cage the urges surging through his blood. He cleared his throat.

Greyland squeaked, whirled around, and leaped back into the

thorny rose bushes. Alex lunged for her, snatching her in the opposite direction; perhaps a little too hard for the force of his gallant effort now sent her crashing forward into his chest.

This is decidedly bad, he thought just before her scent wrapped around him. *Honeysuckle and...* He leaned forward and inhaled slowly, his senses trying to identify the other intoxicating aroma. *Storm clouds...* The smell that wafted in on the breeze just before it rained. That exciting blend of life-giving sustenance and possible danger.

And then he felt her. Soft, inviting curves pressing against his much harder, contrasting edges. A wave of hunger swept over him.

Do not look down, Alex instructed himself.

She tilted her head, bringing her doe eyes up to meet his. *Damn it!* He pushed her away, an attempt to save her. Or at least give her a head start. But apparently, he had once again used too much force. With cat-like reflexes, Alex reached out and caught hold of her before she could fall. All was well and good except that she was back in his arms.

He steadied her in his hold. "I am sorry. I do not seem to know my own strength around you."

She stared at his cravat, her breathing coming hard against his chest. "Do you know your strength around other ladies?"

"Yes."

"Oh."

"Greyland?" She looked up, those emerald eyes shining in the moonlight. He nearly forgot how to form words. "Can you forgive me?" Alex could not find the strength required to release her, so he continued talking, or at least making words. "I mean, for the way I just manhandled you about in your own garden?"

Greyland laughed. "I suppose you can be forgiven, Lord Ravenswood. Plus..." she said, smiling impishly, "I sort of fancy being the first to test your lack of strength."

Alex moved his hands from her shoulders to her dainty wrists, circling them. He could feel her heartbeat; it was quicker than it should be. *Good!* "You really have no idea the weight of that statement, Greyland."

"At least you caught me after you accidentally thrust me."

"I should not be thrusting you anywhere." He released her and took a healthy step back, casting his eyes to the night sky. "No one should even contemplate thrusting you." Alex ran a hand through his hair and sighed. "What I mean is…" He forced himself to look back down at her. "What are you doing out here all by yourself?"

"Churchill got out, and since he has been behaving so naughtily, I have been trying to keep him in after dark. He ran this way, and I was trying to catch the little rascal." She began surveying the flora again, set right back to her original task as if she had never been close to danger, or had any idea how close Alex was to dropping to one knee.

"I will look for your cat," Alex said. It was now proven that the last thing he needed was her ass in the air in pursuit of the blasted cat. "You need to go inside before you catch a cold."

She bobbed her delicate chin. "Indeed. I did promise to sing for Lord Ashlown."

Alexander's fingers balled into fists at his side. He suddenly pictured Lord Ashlown in the same scenario that he was presently residing in. There was no way Ashlown would have been able to deny his desires. Hell, Alex's decorum was only slightly higher than that of a barbarian himself.

Unwanted images assaulted him. Lord Ashlown's hands on her; his body stretched out long across Greyland's on the grass; his hard mouth covering hers... Alex felt his stomach sink and bile rise in his throat.

"On second thought," he said, taking Greyland's arm and wrapping it snugly around his own. "We will have a servant look for the blasted cat." He grinned down at her. "I suddenly feel in need of a song."

GREYLAND LAY awake in her bed, replaying in her head every moment she had shared with Alexander over the past two days. She smiled, remembering how genuinely pleased he had seemed to be conversing with her at the dinner table. And then there was his speech! For that was truly what it was. He proclaimed her, 'unlike most women' and commended her on being unique. Greyland was sure she had never received a more heartfelt compliment in her whole life.

She rolled over on her back grinning stupidly. She was getting to her favorite memory of the Duke of Ravenswood. The one of him holding her tightly. Despite the privacy of her own chamber, she felt her cheeks heating anew. The way he yanked her to him was downright scandalous. Why, if her brothers had seen him; they would have demanded a wedding by the week's end.

Greyland pulled a pillow to her face and screamed into it. She was as giddy as a schoolgirl. Something she had never truly experienced before. She was becoming absolutely smitten with the dashing, Dark Duke, and according to his own words, she was having a similar effect on him.

Greyland tried to pull to mind the exact phrasing he had used. *She caused him to forget his own strength...* Something like that. The conversation was disjointed, and her heart had been racing, so she may have gotten that wrong, but he definitely implied she made him feel different than all the other women.

All the other women...

The blood drained from her cheeks as quickly as it had filled. This was a man that was used to having women in his arms. What if this was just a typical evening for him? Alexander, according to all the rumors, took his pleasures regularly. She had Perkin to thank for that knowledge. *Damn him.*

Greyland rolled onto her side, her fingers going instinctively to her lips where she began to worry them to the point of pain. She immediately withdrew her hand and scolded herself for the horrible bad habit. Her mother had always been able to tell when Greyland was concerned, for her lips would bear the burden. She wished her mother was here now to tell her to stop picking her lips. And that Alexander Hamilton was not a total rake.

Would she? Tell her that the duke was interested in her, and not just looking for his next conquest? Greyland sighed and reached for the broken-spined book on her nightstand. These were the times she missed her mother the most, when the world felt too big and her paths too varied. Times when only another woman could bring clarity and solace.

Greyland ran her hand along the books worn and gilded surface. The diary was the last gift from her mother. She carefully opened it and turned the yellowing pages until she came across the words she sought. Her mother had written three poems—one for each of the children at their births—and Greyland had transcribed them into the diary after her mother's death. She smiled, as she read the lines written for Perkin:

May these tiny hands become strong with all the strength of a humble farmer, but may their touch remain light with all the grace of a king.

Her mother must have been a fortuneteller. Perkin was solid as a rock and never did anything without expert poise. It had to be a gift from God. How else could he be so perfect?

Next, she read Edward's:

There will be two types of people that will enter your life, those who care for you, and those who do not. May you learn from them both, forever bending with the wind and reaching for the stars.

It was uncanny how accurate the woman had been. Like Greyland, Edward was more impulsive. And unlike Perkin, Edward usually failed to choose the right direction. It was as if his life was meant to be tested.

Greyland closed the book, a lone tear rising to blur the vision of her left eye. A nagging voice inside her forced it back open. Swiping the tear away she turned the pages to find the poem about her:

May you always dance, sing and share with the world. For problems of your present will be mere skipping stones across the river of your life tomorrow.

Greyland lifted her gaze to the ceiling, pondering over the familiar script. It was curious to her that when she read her brother's quotes, they seemed so accurate. Little foretold musings, *or blessings,* her mother had bestowed upon them, as if she had known they would grow so exactly into their individual poems. By contrast, Greyland could not analyze the lines written about herself. She was not sure how the words were meant to describe or guide her, other than to encourage a little girl that worried her lips too much not to fret.

Greyland folded the beloved book softly and hugged it to her chest. If that was all it was supposed to mean, then that was all that mattered, because one thing was certain…

An angel was watching over her.

ALEXANDER CRESTED the hill and slowed Socrates to a walk. There, in the middle of the field where he was told to meet the Kingston men for a day of sport, were two individuals engaged in a rather heated fencing match. He recognized Thomas, Bella, and Edward right away. Thomas and Bella were a welcomed surprise, and the sight of Bella gave Alex hope that perhaps Lady Kingston would be there as well.

Surely, Thomas had mentioned the invitation last night and Alex had just forgotten. Truth be told, much of the evening had gone a bit foggy after his garden run-in with Greyland. The extra pour of brandy when he had gotten home, followed by a lack of sleep, certainly did not help the old memory bank today.

Alex pulled off his kidskin riding gloves, remembering how he laid awake hours, unable to shake the succulent visions that Greyland Kingston planted in his head. When Alex finally had fallen asleep his dreams were plagued by nightmares of his mother. It was the same reoccurring dream he suffered his entire life. He could not reach her, and she appeared so helpless and terrified as her fingers disappeared for the last time under the water's lethal pull.

Alex had tried ridding himself of the imagery all morning, but nothing seemed to shake the dreaded memory. It was his hope that meeting up with the Kingston's now might shake his dreary mood. A healthy dose of competition usually did the trick, after all.

He leapt off the stallion and led him toward the others who were too engrossed in the sparring match to notice his approach. Squinting into the sun, Alex was able to discern that Perkin looked to be one of the fighters. There were only so many men of that distinguished height. His opponent, however, was quite short...unusually short for a man, actually. *Perhaps a jockey friend of the family's.*

All three of the onlookers excitedly heckled the two swordsmen. Alex scanned the surrounding tree area for Greyland. All he spied were their tied horses. If she were to be attending today, she was likely still at the house getting dressed. Alex did not know much about the details of ladies readying themselves, but he imagined a head of hair like Greyland's took extra time.

He felt himself grin thinking about her unruly locks and how they always managed to find a way to escape any configuration thrust upon them. The style of Miss Kingston's hair when she arrived in a room would not be the same style seen exiting it. Simply put, the hair was wild and free-spirited, exactly like its owner.

The sudden realization that he was contemplating the up-do of Miss Kingston's hair made Alex nearly falter a step. What on earth had gotten into him? He shook his head and turned his attention to the match.

The fencers did not wield typical rapiers, but rather turn-of-the-century swords—or at least something fashioned to look that way. Moreover, they were not applying 'proper' English fencing technique. Instead, they skillfully danced all over in more of a Spanish style.

"She is doing great!" Bella squealed.

"She?" Alex exclaimed, shocked.

Perkin's opponent paused just a fraction of a second too long, allowing Perkin to get in the move he needed to disarm his competitor. Edward and Bella objected loudly.

Alex peered closer and noticed a midnight-black curl of hair escaping Perkin's opponent's fencing hood. The loose shirt and trousers, coupled with the round bottom of the fencer, caused Alex's mouth to fall open. The fencer was Greyland!

"Good match, sis," Perkin praised.

Miss Kingston removed the hood, releasing a mass of tumbling hair. "I got distracted." She nodded with a smile toward Alex.

"That is the difference between women and men," Edward teased.

Greyland slapped him hard on the rump with the dull side of her sword.

"Ouch! Damn it, Greyland!"

Alexander finally found his tongue. "Miss Kingston, you never fail to impress."

"Thank you, Your Grace. Do you play with swords?"

Everyone burst out laughing.

"What?" She looked around, baffled. "What did I say?"

Thomas snorted. "Oh, he can wield a sword, all right."

"Thomas!" Bella scolded her husband-to-be, but she too, could not contain her amusement.

Still perplexed, Greyland turned to Perkin for an explanation. Her brother covered her ears. "Such talk is not appropriate for a young lady." He tried to sound stern, but the effect pointless.

"I am sure Lord Ravenswood's sword gets played with regularly," Edward barked out, now doubled over with laughter.

"I do," Alex said, replying to the original question and trying not to grin, too big. "But I daresay, not in the same form as you and Perkin." Being the gentleman, he was, Alex shifted the taboo subject matter. "Where did you learn that style of fencing?"

Perkin, Edward, and Greyland shared a collective glance, some fashion of silent sibling confirmation before Perkin began to explain,

"We have had lessons since we were children. However, a professional instructor did not teach us this style."

"Oh, go on and tell him," Edward encouraged. He then added before anyone could rob him of the story, "We learned from a pirate."

Bella gasped. "A real pirate? Where does one meet a real pirate?"

Perkin raised his hand to ward off the onslaught of questioning. "First of all, this is never to reach father's ears." He eyed them all, one by one. "Understood?"

Like a bunch of schoolchildren, everyone nodded eagerly.

"We met a Spanish pirate in the south of Spain who made the mistake of losing a bet with Edward. In order to pay his debt, he taught Edward and myself the skill. Of course, our nosy sister got wind of our secret meeting and followed us. She threatened to tell father if we did not let her learn, too."

Greyland smiled in triumph.

Perkin continued. "I need not go into the reasons why Richard Kingston should not know that his two adolescent sons sought adventure in the corrupt parts of town by placing bets with known thugs." He raised a warning brow to his audience. "Nor that they endangered their young sister's life by allowing her in the company of men that take their pleasure in killing others."

Greyland's lip curved up on one side. "Oh, do not be so dramatic. Ernesto was a big teddy bear."

Bella exclaimed, "My word, Greyland, most men of eight and forty have not seen so much life! I have to admit, I am extremely envious." She considered Greyland approvingly as if the other woman were a rare piece of artwork.

"Even more amazing is that your father allows you to fence! Period!" Bella exclaimed. "Such an open mind in a world where men still see women as cattle ready for trade." She smirked in Thomas's direction. "Maybe I should marry *him*!"

Thomas, never one to miss a quip, immediately clutched his heart and silently faked his own death. Bella, in accordance, threw her hand to her forehead as if she might swoon. To which Thomas miraculously regained his life and dramatically swooped Bella up in his arms, swearing not to ever treat her or their unborn children as livestock.

Everyone roared. Alex took hold of Greyland's hand during the communal laughter. She smiled up at him happily. "Care to take a walk with me, Miss Kingston?" he asked.

TWO SWANS SOARED in from above as Alex and Greyland strolled around the nearby lake. The pair landed on the water's glassy surface with a dancer's grace. Barely disturbing the last remains of the morning's low hanging fog, they seamlessly merged their beauty into the day. The gentle wake of their arrival created a small wave that rolled and lapped at the bank's tall grass. The water parted in black silken ribbons for them. *As if it were nothing at all,* Alex mused. *As if it were everything.*

He looked down at Greyland's small hand, still resting in his much larger one. Was she the reason he was suddenly finding poetry in waterfowl? He nearly barked out a laugh when he heard Thomas, a few paces behind, comment to Bella that he wished he had his bow and arrow. Alex did chuckle when he heard Bella slap his best friend's arm hard enough to make the pair of swans' drift closer to the center of the lake.

Alex peered down at Greyland. "So, I never had the chance to ask you last night. How were the Lovingston twins? Do I have stiff competition?"

She smiled mischievously, keeping her gaze set straight ahead on the path. "I would say you have an enormous amount of competition, Lord Ravenswood."

"Why Miss Kingston, you do know how to wound a man's pride."

She squeezed his hand reassuringly. "Not the Duke of

Ravenswood?" Her rosy lips formed a small O shape. "I thought your pride was impervious to harm?"

"I dare say my ego has undergone quite the testing the last few days," he admitted.

They walked a few more paces in contemplative silence. "I do feel I have done you an injustice, Alexander." Greyland canted her head and looked up at him. "You are a proper gentleman, and I should not have been so harsh with you yesterday afternoon. I feel simply awful for how I spoke to you."

"Oh, really? So, you admit you were wrong?"

"Of course not."

Alexander chuckled. "Well then, I accept your apologies for whatever offense you believe you have dealt me."

She rolled her eyes. "I am sure you did not mean to demean me, my lord, by thinking I could so easily fall prey to a man."

Alex stopped short. With more force than he had intended, he turned her to face him. "I do not think you are wanton. On the contrary." He locked his eyes on hers. "I do not trust other men with you." She stared back at him, her big green eyes never breaking hold with his. "Greyland, tell me you understand my reasons?

She nodded, her gaze drifting down to where their hands joined. "I do."

"Now please," Alex said, and grinned as they resumed their walk, "let us move on to another topic before we end up right back where we were yesterday, with you bringing me to the verge of jealousy."

"Jealousy? I had no idea the illustrious Dark Duke could suffer such an emotion," she teased. "However, I suppose you are correct. I would not want to ruin the day." She looked straight ahead as if contemplating a less controversial topic. "Will you be attending Perkin's class tomorrow at the palace?"

Earlier that morning, Alexander received his invitation to learn the Viennese waltz. The missive from The Queen herself had only added to his curiosity regarding the Kingston's and the crown. "I would not miss it for the world."

Greyland beamed beside him.

"The invitation listed both you and Perkin as the instructors," he hedged. "Have you taught this dance before?"

"I have, but Perkin is the better teacher," Greyland confessed. "I am really just going to help attend him and to demonstrate when needed."

"Well, I am sure we will all learn a great deal just by observing you," Alex commended her, and to his sudden realization, he meant it. He could not recall the last compliment he had paid a woman that was a hundred percent accurate. Granted, he never lied to any of them. Rather, it was more that he never felt *passionate* about most praise. All of Alexander's acknowledgements were done out of politeness and customary accolades. He was an English gentleman, after all. Or, he mentally added, to achieve something completely selfish. *He was also a man.*

"That is very kind," she said and smiled, pulling him out of his own thoughts.

"It is true. Thus far, I have seen you ride a horse like, if not better than, most men. Dance with more skill and grace than anyone I have ever witnessed." He held up his hand to begin ticking off his fingers. "Deliver a direct cut like no other, rescue helpless wildlife, offer the most poetic descriptions of nature, and even fight a man with a sword. Alex smiled down at her. "Oh and let us not forget how you dismissed me from your company yesterday, as no one has ever dared before."

Alex wanted to kiss the blush that bloomed to life on her cheeks. "You have been paying close attention," she said, modestly.

He smirked. "It would be very hard not to notice." He glanced over his shoulder to check on Thomas and Bella. The swans on the shoreline held the pair's attention.

"Your life has been quite adventurous and unconventional thus far, Greyland." He paused and cocked his head to one side to get a better read on her expression. "What kind of future do you envision for yourself?"

"Children." The word came out resoundingly, as assured as cannon fire. "I want children and a home filled with love, and animals, and

Christmas trees, and everything simple." She threw her arms out from her sides and spun in place, completely carefree.

Alexander laughed. "Children and Christmas trees?" he questioned. "Not, more adventure?"

The smile faded in alarming degrees from her eyes "Did I say something wrong?" He mentally kicked himself.

She peered up at him from beneath the shelter of her lashes and shook her head. "Not at all. I have had a wonderful and fortunate life thus far, yes. It is just..." She paused and exhaled. "I want stillness. I want time to lie in the grass and waste away the day. Time to stop... running." She glanced down as if she had just said too much and bit her lower lip.

The last action was too much for Alex to withstand. He leaned forward and cradled her face with both hands. She tilted her chin up bravely as he bent closer. His lips hovered just over the top of hers. He would not rush this. Slowly he breathed her in. That marvelous mix of honeysuckle and storm clouds that were distinctly, Greyland. He threaded one hand around the nape of her neck and squeezed ever so slightly. She instinctively opened her mouth to him, giving him access to take as he pleased. And take, he did.

His eyes closed as his senses raced to keep up with the spiraling emotions that threatened to consume his soul. She tasted of cloves and her lips felt like silk. A coil deep inside him tightened to the point of snapping. He ran his fingers through her hair and pulled her body to his, deepening the kiss. He trailed his hands from her face to her back and down to the small of her waist.

The fencing clothes did nothing to hide her delicate curves. In fact, the absence of a restricting bodice alluded to all kinds of truths about her perfect shape. She was the most stunning woman he ever beheld, and he was within a scant second of taking her right here and now.

Alexander's eyes burned with a need that was frightening. The power he radiated with was almost tangible. Greyland's body warred between the desire to submit or to flee. There was really no middle ground. She felt like she had willingly walked into the lair of a dragon. This was nothing like the kisses in her dreams.

And she had been kissed before! At least she thought she had. Now Timothy Johnson's innocent peck behind the barn all those years ago felt...*childish.* There was nothing childish about Alexander Hamilton, and this kiss.

He stepped back just in time, for the hardening of his manhood pressed against her stomach. She knew how much restraint it must have taken him to retract. He looked to be in a great deal of pain. Her own traitorous body could no more have parted from his than she could part the Red Sea.

Still tasting him on her lips, she felt her tongue dart out to inadvertently lick them. Alexander's attention sharpened. Greyland was unsure if she should step toward him or run for the hills.

Words finally formed on those wonderfully full lips of his, and his gaze turned marginally softer. "Lady Kingston?"

"Yes."

"I would like to give you stillness."

She swallowed hard. "What can I give *you?*"

"You."

"Oh."

He looked down at her, a sea of emotion raging in his eyes. "I know we barely know each other, but Greyland, I have never..." His voice faltered. It implored her to reach out and touch his chest, encouragingly. "I have never felt this alive, scared, and determined before. You do something to me. And it is something that, now that I know it exists, I cannot live without."

He took a hasty step away and ran a hand through his hair. "Damn it!" he half growled, one hand landing with pointed frustration on his hip. "I cannot stand the thought of anyone else at your side." His eyes implored hers. "Does any of that make sense?"

Greyland bridged the space between them wordlessly and reached up on to her tippy toes. "I do not wish anyone else to have you either." She placed a tender kiss on his jaw.

"Marry me," he whispered.

Greyland's heart skipped a beat.

"I swear to give you children and Christmas trees," he rushed. "We can have as many as you want." His arms came around her waist as if he feared she might try and bolt away.

Her head spun so fast she was glad Alex had a hold of her. Gentlemen that Greyland had known much longer had asked for her hand in marriage, and she had turned them all down. She shut her eyes to steady her emotions. All she saw was him; around her, beside her, above her, and within her. The flutter inside only confirmed this man had to be the one.

"Children, and Christmas trees?" she heard herself ask.

"Both, either...whatever you desire."

"Yes." She hurried the word out before she could rethink it. Her gaze climbed his chest to find his storm-blue eyes. They searched hers, desperate and with a vulnerability that nearly tore her heart in two. "Yes," she heard herself confirm.

"Yes, what?" Bella asked from behind Alexander.

Greyland jumped like she had been shot. Alexander did not even budge. The man was a conundrum. He was solid and brave. Fearless and honest. And yet, gentle and poetic. He noticed details that most men did not. He searched out his life, boldly plotting its course. He had an adventurer's soul and a warrior's pride. He was the most beautiful person she had ever met. And he wanted her, in all her unusualness, despite all her unusualness.

Greyland suddenly wanted to cry. Alex seemed to sense her emotions were getting the better of her and kept his back to the advancing couple, effectively shielding Greyland from view and granting her the time needed to compose herself. She swiped away a tear and donned a ready smile.

Greyland stepped to the side to greet Bella and Thomas. "I am glad *we* are the ones coming to find you," Thomas said, brow arched. "You do know those Kingston's have swords, Alexander?

"Thomas," Alex returned, still not removing his eyes from Greyland's. "I have an urgent need to speak with Richard Kingston."

"I should suppose so." Thomas eyed the two.

"Thomas," Alex quipped, finally glancing at the intruding couple. "Do not look so surprised. You were right, for once."

"Father will be gone until tomorrow," Greyland offered, still trying to wrap her mind around what was happening in her world. "He has a meeting in Essex. He will be joining us for the Hastings' mask, though."

"Can you wait that long?" Bella asked with a little grin.

Alexander turned completely and assumed the perfect ducal deposition, hands behind his back, a beacon of seriousness. Greyland had to giggle.

"I am just messing about," Bella laughed, holding up her hands in surrender. "Now come, join the fun. We are moving on to bow and arrow, then pistols, and last, rifles." She said, excitedly, "Did you know those swords have been in the Kingston family since Queen Mary's reign?"

"You do not say?" Alex shot a quizzical brow in Greyland's direction and smiled. "It seems you and your family have many interesting stories. I cannot wait to hear every single one of them."

ALEXANDER DANCED up to his front steps. It was a combination of little moments over the past three days that made up a whole unwavering emotion. *Happiness.* And more peculiar than that was the thought that it could be prolonged, unlike a fleeting sensation of joy gifted to a man in passing minutes. What Greyland offered him was a lifetime of sustained beatitude.

To be sure, Alexander was not such a smitten fool that he did not recognize there would be struggles. He had observed, all too clearly, the woman of his heart's desire came with challenges. She was impulsive, free-thinking, and unpredictable. Three traits that were, not only dangerous given the wrong situation but, frowned upon in a society that expected its women to be biddable and steady.

Luckily for Alex, he admired his intended for everything that the hoity-toity bon ton might find displeasing. He found Miss Kingston exhilarating, passionate, intelligent, and desirable beyond reason. He was also a man who loved a good challenge.

Alexander grinned as he took the last step to his city residence. Greyland Kingston would definitely keep him on his toes and there would be many a disagreement between them, he was sure. However, the idea of how those arguments could be concluded caused the front of his trousers to tighten.

Samson opened the door and Alex breezed past, humming. He paid no attention to the bewildered look on his butler's face. He took the stairs two at a time, looking down as he went and nearly collided with Lady Chatsworth.

"Lady Chatsworth!"

Lady Chatsworth's eyebrows shot up to her hairline at his unexpected presence. "Lord Ravenswood!" Her hair was unpinned, where it had clearly once been tidy, and her dress looked to be in a state of perplexed contemplation as to how it should be worn. "I was just leaving." She made to rush past him.

Alex grabbed her arm before she could get off the landing. "What are you doing in my house?"

"I was, er, I was—"

"She was visiting me, Alex."

Alexander turned to see Derrick, adjusting his shirt from a guest bedroom doorway.

"Derrick." Alexander's mood soured further. The last thing he needed was someone spotting a half-dressed woman leaving his residence now that he had just proposed to Miss Kingston. "I would prefer you keep your company at your own townhouse."

"Since when?"

"Since now."

"Keep your hat on. I was simply waiting for you when Lady Chats…" His uncle turned his attention to the blushing woman. "I am sorry, dear. What was your name again?"

"Chatsworth," Alexander supplied for her. "The lady's name is Chatsworth."

Lady Chatsworth turned and ran down the stairs.

"See you tomorrow, love," Derrick called after her, smirking.

She glanced back with a hesitant grin before taking her coat from Samson and hurrying out the door.

Alexander scowled. "You are unbelievable."

"Oh, come now. Half the damn bon ton has had that one and if you had been here when she came to call on you earlier, you would have too—or *again,* as I recall?"

"Past. That is in the past now."

"Oh, really?" Derrick looked amused. "Did you convince the Kingston chit to marry you then?"

"Yes, as a matter of fact, I did."

Derrick's face dropped all levity.

Alex brushed past him. "But I have not sealed the deal. I still need to speak to her father tomorrow, so keep your mouth shut."

"I had no idea you were serious. I thought a mere romp in the hay was all you really needed?"

"Oh, I want a lifetime of romps in the hay with Miss Kingston." Alex continued down the hallway, stopping only when he reached his bedroom door. He turned. "And Derrick, I will only ask you kindly once more. Never talk about—or even *think* about—my betrothed in such a fashion again. Do I make myself clear?"

"Crystal."

The sarcasm practically dripped from his uncle's voice like pond scum off a stick. Alex turned the doorknob, choosing to ignore the deliberate baiting.

"I cannot wait to meet your intended at The Queen's dancing instruction tomorrow," Derrick added.

Alex exhaled, counting to ten before responding. "You are attending?"

Derrick grinned. "Oh, I am coming undone with anticipation, nephew."

IV

Greyland and Perkin finished their two-hour private lesson with The Queen and the prince. It had gone splendidly. She now wondered why the idea of teaching half the bon ton frightened her. Instructing The Queen of England should have felt more intimidating, but The Queen was so welcoming and complimentary that Greyland forgot all about her nerves.

Enjoying a tray of fresh fruit, smoked haddock, various fancy breads and wine, Perkin rambled on about how to teach the next group lesson as effectively as they had just taught The Queen.

Greyland tried to listen, but she could not keep from daydreaming about Alexander. The man had consumed her every thought since their first meeting. And now, he was asking for her to be *his* for eternity.

She had not told Perkin or Edward about the Duke's proposal yet, so she had to be careful with her high-flying emotions. No use being subjected to a barrage of lengthy lecturing before Alex discussed the matter with her father. Greyland shivered with giddiness. She wanted to shout her soon-to-be new name from the rooftops.

"Greyland." Perkin waved a strawberry in her face. "Are you

listening? I need you to demonstrate the woman's steps while I am showing the men."

She snapped out of her woolgathering. "Sorry. Yes, of course, whatever you need."

Her brother pushed his chair back and stood. "Good. Now let's let them in. I can hear quite a crowd gathering outside the doors."

Perkin walked to the center of the large ballroom. With a brief nod of his head to the posted footmen, the gesture was complete. The massive double doors were pulled open, and half of London poured in. Her brother seemed completely unfazed as he smiled and bade their guest's entrance. The lords and ladies, in return, eagerly accepted and followed him into the room like little cygnets in the wake of an elegant swan.

Perkin smiled over at her, a cue to join him where he stood. "I am Perkin Kingston, and this is my sister, Greyland Kingston." He paused for a minute to allow the crowd to quiet. "Let us start by having all of the ladies' line up on the right. Gentlemen to the left and facing your partners." He issued these orders as if he was commanding a royal army.

They scrambled to their places, eager to do as they were instructed. Greyland scanned the large room for Lord Ravenswood. Her eyes lit on his and he rewarded her with his handsome smile. He stood between Thomas and another man, who looked a lot like Alexander, only older and with salt and pepper hair. The man smiled at her, though something about his smile was off. It made the hairs on her arms stand on end. She dismissed the sensation and walked to where Perkin had instructed her to stand in front of him.

Perkin said, "This dance is very fast and requires a good understanding of frame and footwork. We do not dance in a circle, even though the steps give that appearance; instead, we dance down a line. I will begin with the men's footwork while Greyland demonstrates the women."

He held up his arms, demonstrating the hold, and began to move. "Heel, ball, ball, flat," he instructed. "Same as the waltz, only I cross my left foot in front of my right on my third step in the first half of the box—even though it looks nothing like a box." He flashed the group a winning smile and nodded to Greyland.

She demonstrated, in much the same manner, following the steps of her imaginary partner.

When she finished, Perkin took his sister into dance-frame and after briefly explaining the hold and reasons for counterbalance, he danced the pattern with Greyland. Everyone clapped.

"Any questions?" he asked.

A few mutters of consent followed by heads nodding that they understood.

"Great! Now, let us all give it a try."

The two lines moved together, and before Greyland could ascertain who was to be her first partner, Alexander slipped his arm around her waist and pulled her close.

"Like this?" he whispered, a feline smirk playing on his lips.

Reluctantly, she used her own hand to move his up to just under her shoulder blade. "A little higher, my lord—for more control." She liked this fun and flirtatious side of him immensely.

"Oh." He wagged a brow. "I do like control."

She blushed and averted her eyes. He was going to make it impossible for her to remain professional. "We both take turns with the moving force of the dance," Greyland continued, trying to keep them on task. "But yes..." She grinned, despite her best efforts not to. "You get to lead."

"I can think of many positions I would enjoy leading you into."

Dratted man!

"Lord Ravenswood, pray, pay attention," she scolded. "I have no idea what exactly that wicked smile on your face is for, but I am sure it has to do with something naughty. And I needn't remind you that I am still a maid and must not have such wanton suggestions branded on my impressionable mind." She tried to sound as much like Perkin as possible.

Alexander pulled her tighter against him and bent his head, lowering his voice to the point that it almost purred against her cheek.

"Then we shall have to make this courtship a short one so that I may start my corruption on that beautiful mind of yours."

Greyland was convinced that if Alex were to take a step away right now that she would melt onto the marble. She looked into his fervid eyes. *And he knew it!* Why, if her brothers heard him whispering such words there would be another duel. Right here. Over her swooning body in the middle of The Queen's palace. *That* would be one way to make the history books.

Perkin's voice interrupted their much too dangerous flirtation, his voice booming out over the vast room. "We will dance this pattern four times in a row with our current partners, and then I need the ladies to move down one partner to their right." The students readied themselves as he counted them off, "One, two, three..."

The dancers moved down the floor, some with more ease than others. Alexander was a natural.

Naturally, Greyland mused.

"And switch," Perkin instructed.

Greyland started for her next partner, but Alexander grabbed her hand, holding her in place. "Let me be the first to introduce you to my uncle, Derrick Hamilton, your next dance partner."

She wiped the look of surprise off her face and replaced it with a smile of acknowledgment towards the other gentleman. "My lord."

He placed a delicate but lingering kiss on her hand. It did not have nearly the same effect Alexander's had had the night of the ball, but still, she wondered if 'charming' just ran deep in this family tree. "I see my nephew forgot to mention me?"

The question had a surprising effect on her. It was as if reality slapped her right across the cheek. She had agreed to marry a man and barely knew anything about him, or his family, except for what her father mentioned. She pushed down the sudden doubt and did what she did best in awkward situations: smiled. "I knew Alexander had an uncle, but I thought you would be older."

"Only by seven years, and please, call me Derrick," he said, grinning.

Perkin's voice announced the next set. "One, two, three."

The Marquis took her into dance-frame. "Mayhap I can fill in other gaps about your soon-to-be family at the ball tonight." Whispering, he leaned in closer and said, "When there are not so many ears hanging about."

For the second time in the last few minutes, Greyland found herself taken aback. Alexander had told his uncle of his intentions to marry her. Had he told anyone else? She would hate for word to reach her father before Alex could speak formally to him.

The set ended with a suddenness that left Greyland questioning how her feet had even moved at all through the patterns.

"Well, how did I do?" Derrick asked, his lips hitching into an aplomb grin. He knew exactly how well he had done. At dancing, and at rattling her brain. Another Hamilton family trait.

"Good dancers seem to run in the family."

Derrick handed her to her next partner. "Until tonight, Miss Kingston." He bowed.

His eyes were so much like Alexander's, she could not help but compare when he stepped away, yet they held an unnerving glint that made her decidedly leery. Greyland mentally shook off the unwarranted feeling and tried to focus her attention on her new dance partner, Lord Danberry, and his sweaty palms. She was probably just jittery over the huge secret she was keeping from her family. *That had to be it.*

Lord Danberry's lips were moving. Greyland smiled and nodded, hoping it covered whatever question the rotund lord had just asked her.

"One, two, three..."

Perkin's voice rang out, and Lord Sweaty Palms stepped right on her foot.

THE HOUR FLEW BY. The crowd protested profusely when Perkin announced the dance instruction was over. Everyone wanted more and judging from his smile, her brother had enjoyed teaching them. Greyland was not surprised to hear him promising another lesson the following week to the departing guests.

Excitement returned to the room as voices swore oaths to practice and hands shot up with questions: What time would it be? What day? This was too big a matter for the elite ladies and gentlemen of the bon ton to wait on. They needed to know and plan accordingly, now. Greyland snickered as she overheard one lady suggest to her husband that they move a funeral if the day and time of the next lesson overlapped it.

As the group bombarded Perkin with questions, Greyland seized her opportunity and began to pick her way over to where Alex was standing. A tall masculine figure moved in front of her, blocking her path.

"Lord Ashlown—"

"Miss Kingston, you were astounding," he praised. "But then again, that is really nothing new."

His eyes wandered the length of her body, assessing, weighing.

"Thank you, Lord Ash—"

"Call me Dalton."

His words were not a request.

"You are very kind, Dalton. I am so glad you enjoyed yourself. You seemed to pick it up very quickly."

"I pick up everything quickly, Grey-land," he said, dragging out the syllables of her name, as if he could taste them. "Everything I set my eyes on."

Well now. Greyland was not quite sure how to follow that statement up.

He continued after a perceptible pause. "I was wondering if you might be able to give my nephew and niece a lesson sometime. They are in town for the season, and I am afraid my sister has kept them in the country far too long, for they are in want of the finer arts. It would be the highlight of their year to receive a lesson from a lady who has taught The Queen, herself."

Greyland shifted from foot to foot. "Perkin is the better teacher, I really—"

"They are only eleven and thirteen. I feel they would take to a female better than a man. Your brother is rather...intimidating."

The man had a point.

Greyland could not think of anything more innocent than teaching two children a couple of dances to further their education. "I suppose I have some time tomorrow—around two?"

"Splendid! They are staying with me. Should I send my carriage?"

"Oh, no need. I am sure my driver knows how to get to your residence."

Perkin appeared, as if by magic, at her side and cut in. "Lord Ashlown, so glad you could make it. Did you enjoy the instruction?"

Dalton inclined his head respectfully. "Very much so."

"Then I am quite pleased." Perkin took Greyland's arm by the elbow. "I am afraid I must steal my sister away to get ready for the ball tonight."

Greyland was mystified by her brother's sudden desire to hasten their leave. Had Alexander warned him about Lord Ashlown?

Did he know about the proposal?

"You know how much time women need for this sort of event." Perkin excused and pulled Greyland along. "Good day."

Forced neatly to Perkin's side, her view shifted as they turned away from Lord Ashlown and came face to face with Alexander, who sported a scowl that would likely kill baby bunnies on the spot.

"Greyland." He said her name but kept his icy stare fixed on Lord Ashlown, behind her. "May I escort you to the mask tonight?"

"I would like that immensely," she responded loud enough for Lord Ashlown to hear. She did not need a fight to break out between the two men. She also hoped to defuse any scolding from Lord Overprotective later.

"Marvelous," Perkin nodded curtly to Alex. "She will be ready by eight."

LORD MELBROOKE LIT a cigar and took a seat at his mahogany desk. "Are the festivities in the ballroom complete?"

"Yes."

"We need to act fast. The Queen is set to marry that pup in six-months' time and I cannot have any surprises before then."

"All will be taken care of. My sources are on it. Three men are returning from France in a fortnight, and two will be back from Ireland tomorrow."

"Do you think any of them know?" He puffed a smoke ring as he sat back in his chair.

"No."

"They are becoming quite popular. If what you say is true, they are a true threat to the crown."

"I have set eyes on the eldest. His every move is being tracked. Nothing will happen without my sources getting wind of it first."

Melbrooke sat up and snuffed out his cheroot. "Good. I have played this game too long to have another pretender join in."

"If they try anything, we will simply squash them as King Henry did. This time, we will make sure not to leave any children behind."

V

Alexander's carriage pulled into the Kingston's large circular drive at five minutes to eight. The moon was completely full and high in the sky on this particular evening. It illuminated the trees and lawn as if it were day and cast an almost ethereal aesthetic over the grounds.

As soon as the rig slowed to a slow roll, Alex pushed open the door and alit from it. He strolled briskly up the cobblestone steps. The double doors parted as he made his ascent.

"Good evening, Your Grace," greeted Ocman, sweeping his arm and bowing low.

Alex followed the butler into the foyer with a tip of his head. Once inside, he felt her presence before he saw her. Alexander turned and looked up the curving staircase. He nearly stopped breathing. There, poised at the top of the steps was the most exquisite image he had ever seen. *A dragon.*

Greyland donned a blood-red velvet gown that hugged her body like a leather glove. A low-cut bodice exposed her milky shoulders. Her eyes peeked through a half mask decorated with red, gold, orange, and emerald crystals, meant to resemble scales. Feathered wings, attached to the back of her dress, also held glimmering stones.

She wore long gloves past her elbows adorned with the same labyrinth of crystals. Red and orange ribbons wove through her black ringlets, resembling flames cascading down her ivory back.

Alexander watched with amazement as the lovely creature descended the stairs like smoke atop water. He should not be surprised by her choice in wardrobe, but he was. Marvelously surprised. Most of the women tonight would be fairies, Greek goddesses, or queens from days of old. Alex was fairly confident he would be the only man accompanying a dragon to the masked ball.

His blood thrilled through his veins. Greyland was a prize; a gift to be cherished. She would be on his arm, a clear warning that Miss Kingston was spoken for. And yet...Alex felt the same protective instinct start to wrap around his muscles, tight and alert, primed for a fight. He would not be able to let his guard down tonight, or anytime soon for that matter when it came to this beauty. At least, not until he had given her *his* name. Until then, every man was a predator, ready to try and steal what was his.

"Alexander, you are a wolf!" she exclaimed. "I love it."

The irony between her innocent comment, and his not-so-innocent thoughts, made him smile. And helped push down his apprehensions. He was the most feared man in this town. There was nothing to worry about. No one would dare try and take what was his.

"Greyland you are..." Alex paused, drinking her in. She, and this flawless creation of a gown were apparently too much for his dwindling vocabulary to adequately articulate. "The details on this costume are...well, simply..."

"I hope you do not address Parliament like this." Edward chuckled, breaking the spell Alex had been under. "I believe any Shakespearian verbiage will suffice to describe my sister." He jogged down the stairs after her, eyepatch covering one eye and fake parrot teetering precariously atop his shoulder.

"I do not think even Shakespeare could do her justice," Alex amended.

"Thank you." Greyland took his offered hand. "Shall we be off?"

"Arrrrrrrggg, maties. Best be leavin', b'for I make ye all walk the plank!" Edward brandished a pirate's sword and led the couple in the direction of the door.

Alexander turned. "Will we see you there?"

"Aye Aye," Edward grunted, sheathing his weapon, and waving them on.

"He likes to make an entrance by being late." Greyland grinned and kissed her brother on the cheek as she passed him.

Edward winked. "Shhh. Do not give away all my secrets."

They took the front steps, Alex being extra careful with each foot placement in case Greyland's mask was a visual hindrance. From the carriage, Thomas and Bella applauded wildly. Alex had almost forgotten they had ridden there with him.

"Bella! You are Aphrodite." Greyland said gleefully as Alex helped her into the carriage. Once inside, she addressed Thomas. "That gladiator costume is most befitting."

The girls erupted into a fit of giggles.

Alex watched as the corners of Greyland's mouth moved and she canted her head slightly to one side. He adored her bewitching accent and the way she spoke with such animation. He could spend eternity admiring all the subtleties that made this woman so spectacular.

"Where are your two handsome brothers tonight?" Bella inquired, casting Thomas an impish sideways grin. "I am certain I saw a roguish pirate in the foyer."

Thomas grasped at his heart in protest of his lady's affront.

Greyland laughed. "Captain Edward and King Perkin will be arriving later. I have no doubt Edward will use his swashbuckling ways to commandeer a dance with such a beautiful Greek goddess." To this, Bella chuckled.

"They will have to outlast me in the arena," Thomas promised, grinning wickedly at Aphrodite.

The whole rig rocked with laughter. Tonight, was going to be perfectly splendid, Alex mused.

Nothing could spoil their fun.

Once through the receiving line at the Hastings' manor, all eyes landed on the four new arrivals. Enticed by the opportunity, Alexander could not resist the chance to embarrass his best friend. He leaned into Thomas. "Your gladiator's showing."

Thomas' color dropped three shades. He pivoted in place, away from the eyes of the crowd and brought his hands down to conceal his nether regions. Alexander, Greyland, and Bella laughed.

"Why you, Alexander!" Thomas, realizing he was late to the punchline, recovered his posture and promptly punched Alex in the arm.

"Sorry, I could not resist." Alex grinned as the four made their way to the right side of the ballroom.

"Ladies." Alex motioned to two of four chairs that were nestled into a quiet alcove. With two huge potted palms flanking either side, it was the perfect spot for the four friends to chat without enticing too much attention. The fewer men filling up Miss Kingston's dance card, the better. Alex was feeling rather selfish concerning his beautiful dragon.

He and Thomas waited while Bella and Greyland got comfortable. Alex smiled. "If you will excuse us, my gladiator friend and I shall procure the refreshments."

Thomas slapped Alex on the back when they were safely out of earshot. "So, the Dark Lord is really going to settle down?"

"Keep your voice down," Alex said brusquely under his breath. "I still must ask her father, and if anyone of her other would-be suitor's catches wind of it, well..." He leaned in conspiratorially. "There would be many an early morning for you as my second."

"I do hate mornings," Thomas concurred thoughtfully and smirked, signaling a serving boy. "And I would hate to rid half of

London of its bluebloods, so I suppose I will keep quiet and be the first to congratulate you."

A woman's voice came up behind them. "Congratulate you on what, my lord?"

Both men turned to face Lady Chatsworth, batting her eyelashes.

"On my new business endeavor in the trade market," Alex replied, knowing the remark would set her back. Trade was not considered suitable work for the upper echelon of London.

She did not even blink. "Oh! how very splendid. Mayhap I can take a walk in the gardens with you to hear more?"

"I have attended tonight's ball with another, and I fear it would be rather rude of me. Surely, my uncle would be more than happy to escort you."

Alex watched as her eyes grew dark. "Very well then," she said. "Maybe a dance later?"

Gadsbudlikins! Alex silently cursed.

"I am afraid not, Lady Chatsworth. Now please excuse me for I must return to my friends."

She muttered an explicative of her own under her breath and stomped away.

Thomas chuckled a bit nervously before stating the obvious. "That one is a bit of a loose cannon, Alex."

Alexander shook his head. "I have had fleas on a hound that were easier to dismiss."

THE SERVER APPEARED with a tray of ready glasses. Alex took two, as did Thomas, and headed back to the damask-covered chairs where Greyland and Bella sat surrounded by a gaggle of enthralled men.

Of course, they are.

Alex mentally pictured chopping off all their debauched heads. He sighed.

"Is this what I am signing up for, Thomas? Constantly fending off besotted men for the rest of my life?"

"It gets easier once she is off the market, but I fear with that one, you will always be looking about for predators."

Alexander pushed through the throng of admirers and handed Greyland her wine. An excited young man, whom Alex could not remember ever having met before, piped up. "Will they play a Viennese waltz tonight so that we can all give it a try?"

Greyland smiled sweetly at the pup. "I believe they will. But I have promised *that* dance to my brother Edward when he arrives." She dismissed the young man gracefully with her eyes, sat down her glass, and placed her dainty hand in Alexander's. "This one is yours, my lord," she said, standing.

"Indeed, *she* is," Thomas said in a low tone with a grin. Alex handed off his glass to Thomas and led Greyland to the center of the ballroom.

If eyes could shoot daggers, Alex was certain there would be eighteen in his back. An old saying of his father's came to mind: *Winners are admired, but rarely liked.* Alex was used to winning. He was used to having a truly small circle of friends. What he was not used to was this all-consuming and completely foreign fear of losing something he could not imagine living without.

He stepped onto the dance floor with Greyland and drew her into his arms. The heat of her body radiated through his jacket. He had been with many women and knew the female form well, but never had one sent such unbridled desire racing down his spine. It unnerved him that other men might experience the same sensation when they were in her company. He closed his eyes, hoping that when they opened again the room would contain just the two of them.

"Are you all right, Alex?"

"I am," he said, peering into Greyland's concerned eyes. "I am just getting used to completely foreign feelings."

"I do hope they are not bad feelings?"

Their figures swayed to the music. "Not bad, just new. In time, I will adapt to having something which everyone else in the kingdom desires." He smiled down at her. "I am a very strong-willed man, after all."

She grinned. "That you are."

His gaze roamed over her slender neck and elegant shoulders and then followed the line of her bodice. "Your dress is very provocative, Miss Kingston. I do not know that I approve of other eyes being drawn to places only mine should see."

"Are you sure you are not Perkin under that mask?" She grabbed at his wolf snout playfully.

"Greyland, I assure you, I am the furthest thing from a brother you will ever know." Her cheeks deepened as he pulled her body closer.

"Oh my! Alexander!" She gasped and leaned in quickly, tilting her chin up toward his ear. "Your man part is throbbing," she whispered, distress coloring her voice. "Is that healthy?"

He chuckled at her naivety. "Perfectly hale. That is the effect you have on me, my dear." The music softened around them sooner than Alex anticipated. He willed himself to think about the effect maggots had on an impaled and rotting human head.

"Does it hurt?"

"The current state does beg for relief, but hurt, no." He could not stop the spread of his widening smile.

She pursed her lips, contemplation etching her brows. "Is there a special license one can procure to rush this whole marriage business along?"

Alexander's mouth went dry. Dear Heavenly Lord, he had found the one!

Before he could form an appropriate answer, a serving boy darted by, handed Greyland a note and sailed on. She opened and read the missive. "Seems father is still tied up and will not be able to make it tonight. He said he will be home in the morning."

"There you are!" Perkin approached, dressed as King Arthur, crown and all. "Greyland…" He stilled, mid-stride, taking in his sister's costume for, apparently, the first time. "That dress is entirely inappropriate."

Greyland and Alex both looked at each other and grinned surreptitiously.

"We were just discussing that," Alex confessed.

THE BREEZE CAUGHT and played with her loose curls, like strings dancing a marionette doll, when she stepped out onto the large veranda. Greyland removed the demi mask and closed her eyes, listening to the night speak. She could hear the gentle beating of soft wings, moths dangerously courting a nearby lantern. Further out in the garden, something was moving around the branches on a bush. Greyland tried to focus in on just that sound. The foliage could be heard bowing and then on occasion, snapping back into place. She smiled. Likely a tenacious badger.

Another sound was making its way to her ears now. The sound of leather on stone. Greyland's eyes popped open just as a man's voice stole into her silence.

"Boo!"

Despite the audible warning, she still jumped and turned quickly. It was only Derrick, Alexander's uncle. Greyland exhaled, but it came out sounding more like a nervous chortle to her own ears. "Lord Hamilton."

"Please, call me Derrick. We shall save the titles for my nephew."

"You gave me a fright. Your steps were quite light."

"I am surprised you heard them at all. Most do not." He studied her with a mix of interest and calculation.

"Do you make a habit of sneaking up on unaccompanied women?"

He smirked. "Sometimes. How else must a man learn their secrets."

"By asking them," Greyland returned.

"Ah, then where is the fun in watching them jump?"

Greyland smiled. She had spent too many hours playing hide and seek with her brothers as a child to not understand the playful thrill one got by surprising another. Too bad no one on this terrace was a child.

She watched Derrick a bit more closely. He was sharply dressed, and he took extra care with picking out his boots. Either that, or he paid someone to take extra care. Either way, it ended up being the same effect—perfection. The appearance he kept mattered a great deal to him. A far from an unusual matter in London, Greyland knew.

However, there was an extra layer to the polish on his knee-high Hessians, and a particular attention to detail paid to the knotting of his pearl-white cravat. Neither Perkin nor Alex would worry over their clothes that much, and they were two of the most particular men she knew.

She moved her observation up to his face. He wore a trimmed beard that was immaculate. The closer Greyland looked, the more obvious it became that she had never seen a better-kept beard. She had the sudden urge to sniff it. If it smelled like pomade, case closed. She would have pinpointed Alexander's uncle down as the most perfected man in London.

But, if he were a true formalist, why would he like playing games? The two did not naturally go hand in hand. Edward was silly. Edward also did not give two figs about his clothing. Perkin, on the other hand, could be roused into a more lighthearted mood, but he tended to fall decidedly on the more proper side of things. *Who was she kidding,* Perkin was the walking definition of the word 'perfectionist.'

Greyland leaned back against the terrace rail. Yes, Derrick was peculiar. He was almost as handsome as his nephew. *Almost.* She could certainly understand why this family had such a reputation with the ladies. But still, there was something about him that made her nervous, she just could not quite work out exactly what—

"Are you done?" he said, interrupting her contemplation. "Sizing me up, as it were?"

She flushed, mentally adding *'too observant'* to her notes on the man. "Forgive me, it is just that you and Alexander have such a strong resemblance," she lied. Their differences were starting to outweigh the similarities.

He smiled devilishly. "Maybe if I had met you first, it would be us walking to the altar."

A chill skated across the surface of her skin. "I fell in love with Alex for more than just his looks, my lord," Greyland said, a bit more defensive than she had intended. Derrick was about to be her family; she did not want to offend him. She smiled politely. "I believe you were going to tell me about your family tonight?"

"Ah, of course. Redirection." Derrick tipped his hat to her. "We would not want to make my nephew jealous, now would we?"

He crossed the distance between them. "But first things first." He reached out and brushed a strand of her hair back behind her ear.

The intimate gesture unnerved her. She quickly looked about for other partygoers, her hand going up to where his touch had just been. "My hair has a mind of its own," she proclaimed, nervously.

"I brought you a glass of wine." One side of his lips curled into a grin. Either he liked making her uncomfortable, or he simply did not care. "I am sure you are parched from all the dancing." He held out what she had assumed was his own glass.

"Thank you." She took a sip.

"Did you know Alex has a half-brother who he believes murdered his father?"

Greyland nearly choked.

"Forgive me," Derrick apologized. "I should know better than to bring up such a delicate subject matter with the faint of heart."

"It has nothing to do with my heart, my lord."

Sympathy filled his expression. "Ah, you did not know."

Greyland felt the proverbial punch he was delivering. She did not know. And this was Derrick's way of reminding her of that striking fact. One thing she was starting to figure out was Derrick was not socially awkward. Instead, it was entirely possible he was just cruel.

"I knew his father was murdered." She would not rise to his

prodding. Greyland straightened, lengthening her spine as much as humanly possible. "However, you are correct. I had no idea he had a brother, or that he was the suspected assailant."

She took another sip from her glass, hoping she came off nonchalant and un-wavered. How could she be expected to know everything about a man she had only met four days ago? It was absurd to think otherwise. Why, women married men all the time that they had only just met. *Except...*this was different. She was falling in love with her intended. *She should know.*

"He is only a half-brother, born of the woman whom my brother took to bed after Alexander's mother passed away," Derrick continued, matter-of-factly. "That is probably why neither your father, nor Alex, ever felt the need to mention him. Second sons never get paid the time of day. Especially bastards." His lips slanted into a mocking grin.

Greyland bristled. The verdict was signed, sealed, and delivered. This man enjoyed making her uncomfortable. She knew her father and Alex would never imply that someone's station in life was insignificant, but that was not what Derrick wanted to impart upon her. No, he wanted to sow the seed of doubt—not just about Alex, but about her family as well.

"Alex is a member of Parliament. It is my understanding he sides with our new Queen's forward thoughts on equality," Greyland countered, leveraging the sound information she did possess. There was something Derrick needed to know about her as well, and that was, *no one insulted her family!*

She squared up with him. "Surely, you do not think your nephew would judge a man merely on his birth rank?"

"Oftentimes one's political views vary greatly from their personal beliefs." Derrick's eyes studied her, longer than they should, before softening a fraction. "Alexander believes his half-brother meant his father and him ill will, and he set out to destroy them, in his hatred for being treated no better than a serving boy all his life."

He paused and looked out into the garden, almost reflectively. "I am sure Alexander never warmed to the lad anyway," he explained.

"His mother drowned trying to save the maid. Then, the very same maid slipped into his father's bed later that year, giving the Duke another son nine months later. Alexander was only four years old at the time his mother died. He watched helplessly from the shore as his mother took her last breath."

Derrick faced Greyland once more, leveling his eyes on hers. "Now surely you can understand why my nephew might harbor a strong dislike for his half-brother, under those circumstances?"

All the air left her lungs as if Derrick's words had just placed *her* underwater. She steadied herself on the rail. She pictured Alexander, a child, watching his own mother's tragic death. The thought was too much to bear. She longed to hold that child in her arms and console him. Hot tears stung her eyes. She looked away.

A soft touch grazed her cheek. "Are you feeling all right, Greyland?" Derrick asked, his voice suddenly warm and full of concern.

"I am fine."

He flipped his hand over and placed it against her jaw. "You feel hot. I am going to fetch some water. I think you have had enough wine this evening." He plucked the glass from her hand and guided her to a bench. "Please, sit here."

Before she could lift her voice to protest, he helped her to sit and then vanished.

As if he had never been there at all.

GREYLAND'S VISION came in and out of focus. Perhaps she was a touch warm. She lengthened her breathing to allow more air into her lungs. Slowly, the ground ceased moving beneath her feet. She looked up and noticed a figure coming toward her.

"Miss Kingston, how nice to finally find you," said Jeremy Lovingston. "I have been looking for you all evening. Care to take a walk?" He extended a smooth manicured hand to her.

"Just to the roses," she said, hoping a stroll would help clear her head. "His Grace's uncle is procuring a glass of water for me."

"Of course. May I say how lovely you look tonight?" The corners of his mouth turned up in an odd, almost feral sort of fashion. Greyland only remembered him smiling at her with pure innocence during their last meeting. She thought of him more as a younger brother than a suitor when he made his interest known. Something was off with him tonight. It was as if he were a completely different person than the sweet young man, she had met the other day.

"Thank you." She realized they had walked past the roses.

Greyland was just about to mention they should turn back when he spoke. "You seem much taken with Lord Ravenswood. I feel honor-bound to tell you that he has a rather dark side."

She suppressed a laugh. It was incredulous the number of attempts made to sabotage Alexander's and her happiness this evening. "I am so sorry; it must be the wine. I did not mean to laugh. All the gentlemen I have had the privilege of meeting, are quite nice. I have not yet seen anyone's dark side, and I have found Alexander to be quite charming."

She realized the moment his Christian name slipped off her tongue she had inadvertently said too much. Before she had time to amend her words, he reached out and grasped her arm, his eyes drilling into hers. "I am not asking about other men!" he bit out and seized hold of her other arm.

Greyland went rigid at the flash of teeth. She quickly took in her surroundings. To her dread, she had absentmindedly allowed herself to be led quite a way into the garden. "I did not mean to offend you," she said quickly, trying to appease him.

"I am quite drawn to you, Miss Kingston," he maintained his grip. "You are the most beautiful woman in current society, and with time, I am sure we would come to love each other. As such, it is my wish we marry."

Greyland did not laugh this time. Instinct told her that would be the worst thing she could do. Heat enveloped her, and not the kind she had experienced with Alex, but a feverish, sick heat. The earth below her spun too fast. She struggled, but his punishing hold held tight. Before she could respond, he smothered her mouth with his.

Greyland jerked back and managed to wrench one arm from his clutches. She slapped him. His eyes grew huge with shock, before hardening into round little rocks. He grabbed her wrist when she drew back to hit him again.

"I do not mean to hurt you," he hissed. "Calm down! I simply need Lady Chatsworth to stumble upon us, with a few other partygoers, by accident of course, and find you in a compromised position. Then your father will be forced to choose me. This will be made so much easier if you just comply."

Greyland felt her weight sinking toward the ground. All strength left her body and Jeremy Lovingston's face turned into a blurry mess.

VI

Alexander made haste towards the carriage. He was fairly certain if blood could be characterized into degrees, his was close to that of molten lava. *He would kill him.* If anything in his life had ever been more absolute, it was that Jeremy Lovingston would die.

Greyland's slight body hung limp in his arms as his feet pounded the flagstone pavers. His driver saw him approaching and nodded swiftly to the carriage boy who, in turn, hopped off the back of the rig and scrambled to the door.

Alex quickened his steps, his mind replaying the events leading up to now, when he had found her in the clutches of that fool. He cursed himself for not being there sooner. Alex had heard every word that whelp had said to Greyland, right before he forced himself on her.

Then, she crumpled to the ground, and Alex's world guttered to a halt. It was the last thing he recalled before his fist connected with the knave's jaw.

Thomas raced up from behind, caught Alexander's pace and slowed to a jog. "What is wrong?" he huffed. "I saw you disappear into the garden. Is she hale?"

"I do not know. I caught one of the Lovingston twins groping her by the fountain. I need you to retrieve him and bring him to my manor...*without* anyone knowing." Alex cut his eyes to his friend. "Now."

Thomas nodded, fear drowning out his normally cheerful blue eyes.

Alex growled, "I am certain it was Jeremy. Just look for the half-wit blacked out in the hibiscus bush."

He turned to his wide-eyed carriage boy, nervously twisting his hands as he awaited his orders. "Find Perkin Kingston," Alex instructed. "Tell him to collect Miss Herst and escort her to my house. Posthaste." The boy nodded. His pupils huge. "I need this done without drawing any attention from the other partygoers. Understood?"

The kid shook his shaggy head again and bolted towards the manor.

Alex turned back to Thomas and transferred Grayland's slight body into the earl's outstretched arms. He then pulled himself into the carriage and reached back for her. "Bind and gag him and put him in the stable."

Thomas wordlessly handed her up to Alex and slammed the door. "Ravenswood Manor," the earl ordered Alex's driver. "Fast!"

The carriage lurched into motion. Alex cradled Greyland in his lap and stroked her forehead, remembering how her body had gone completely limp in that cad's grip. He was sure it was not from a mere faint. *No,* Greyland was far too strong-willed for swooning, no matter how terrified she might have been.

A pain, repressed since childhood, welled up inside his chest. Alexander had not allowed himself to feel anything but blinding rage after his father's death. Anger was a far easier emotion to manage than fear. But it was not his father's memory that haunted him now.

He brushed a finger along the edge of Greyland's face, marveling at the woman who changed his world in just a few short days. "Greyland," he pleaded. "Wake up. Please wake up."

As if by command, her lashes fluttered.

"Alex?" Her voice was barely audible. It ripped his heart out.

"Yes, it is me. We are almost home."

"Your home?"

"Very soon it will be your home too."

Her lips parted, as if she was about to say more.

"Shhh. Save your strength."

She gave a passive nod and the dark curtain of her lashes sealed tight against the paleness of her cheeks. Her head, once again, became heavy in his hand. And Alex, once again promised death upon Jeremy Lovingston.

The carriage came to a halt outside his home and he lifted her out.

Samson opened the front door.

"Get my physician!"

Without hesitation, his butler relayed the message to a footman who launched himself off the front porch and sailed passed Alex.

"Is she going to be alright, Your Grace?" Samson dogged Alexander's steps into the house.

"She better be." Alex ascended the main stairs. "Others will be arriving in short order. Try and contain them down here."

Alex kicked open the door to the first bedroom and carried Greyland swiftly inside. He laid her gently atop the bed and pulled the covers over her.

Stepping back, he realized he did not know what to do next. Her recovery was out of his hands. The thought killed him. This was everything he feared accumulating into one moment. *Losing her.* How trivial it had been of him to worry he might lose her to the charms of another man. He could very well lose her to death.

Alex took off his jacket and pulled a chair up beside the bed. He placed one of Greyland's feverish hands in his and hung his head in silent prayer. Her breathing was shallow. *Too shallow.*

She shifted slightly and half-opened her eyes. Alex tried to mask the fear he knew was written across his face. He leaned in and placed a soft kiss on her closing eyelids. "I am here."

She had to survive this. Alex had spent his whole life waiting for her. He could not lose her now.

TWENTY MINUTES LATER, the Hamilton's long-time doctor rushed through the door behind Samson. Alex pushed from the chair and reluctantly let go of Greyland's hand so that the physician could move in.

"What do you know of the lady's condition?" the doctor asked, moving to the bedside.

Alexander told him the evening's exact events, leading up to him entering the bedroom with Greyland.

"Please leave me with her to assess the matter."

Alexander started to protest, but the man's keen eyes held no room for debate. He reluctantly turned and made for the door.

A commotion was stirring downstairs. Alex stepped into the hall. Loud voices, male and female, seemed to be accosting one of Alexander's servants at the base of the stairs.

Perkin and Bella had obviously arrived.

Long purposeful strides carried Alex towards the irate Southern and British accents. He was not surprised to find a jittery footman staring up at him from the second landing of the curving staircase.

"Your guests are in attendance, Your Grace," the man said timidly from under the intense focus of one looming Perkin Kingston.

Perkin's sharp stare shot directly up to Alex. "Where is she?"

"My physician is attending her now," Alexander said, but Perkin, who was already taking the stairs at nearly impossible measures, Bella close on his heels, cared not for this bit of information.

Alexander held up his hand. "He needs privacy."

"The hell he does!" Perkin snapped. "What room is she in, Alexander?"

Given any other circumstance, Alex would have taken issues with another man charging into his home and giving him orders. But Alex did not have a sister that had just been assaulted.

"Let me explain," Alex placed himself in front of Perkin. "I found her in the gardens, being taken advantage of. Or rather, the cad was attempting to do her harm," he quickly corrected.

Bella gasped.

"Alexander," Perkin said sternly, narrowing his eyes. "If you do not step out of my way, I will throw you over the railing."

Alexander stood his ground. "She passed out and it is not yet known why," he said firmly. "It may be a swoon, or she may have hit her head. The doctor must determine which so that he may treat her. I will not allow you to delay this examination. Her life could depend on it."

Perkin stood, glowering at him. Kingston was a large man and he was raging, so this would go one of two ways. Alexander had learned a long time ago to choose his fights wisely. Taking on Perkin Kingston would not be wise for any man, but Alex had to make him see reason.

"I will kill him," Greyland's brother said with a steel-plated resolve that could move armies into action.

"I will help you," Alex agreed steadily.

"Oh, Alex!" Bella's hand shot to her mouth. "He did not—"

"No, thank God!" Alex heard the relief in his own words. "The bastard was actually telling her of his plot to compromise her so that she would be forced into marriage. That is when I laid him flat. Thomas will be bringing him here for questioning in a little while."

"Greyland would not faint," Perkin said.

"I agree, but she is in and out of consciousness. I do not know if she hit her head when he let go of her, but she seemed dazed right before I struck him."

The door down the hall opened. All eyes flew to the elderly man who stepped out of it. "The lady has been drugged. She will be fine. She just needs sleep," the doctor concluded.

Perkin tried to push past Alex, but the physician's words stopped him. "She needs to rest. Quiet is the best thing for her."

"Drugged?" Bella queried. "Do you mean to say someone wanted to harm her?"

"She was not given enough to do more than knock her out. I

imagine the intent was to merely have her succumb to a state that would render her…compliant."

Alexander wanted to crush the solid wood banister beneath his hand.

Parasite! He turned to Perkin and Bella. They both reeled with the same revelations.

After the doctor issued his instructions for Greyland's care and descended the stairs, all three of them stood in silence.

Bella spoke first. "I would very much like a strong beverage at this time." She motioned to both Alex and Perkin with a bob of her head. "I think we could all use one."

She turned and headed down the stairs. "I would imagine brandy and murder are natural allies."

"IT WAS JEREMY LOVINGSTON. I do not think he intended to do anything more than have it appear as if they were in the throes of an affair. Nevertheless…" Alexander's fist tightened around his glass, "he clearly seemed prompted to accelerate his courtship with her."

"She has only just made her debut," Perkin countered. "What on earth would make him act so rashly?"

Alexander hesitated. There was no way Jeremy Lovingston could have found out Alexander had proposed. Not even Richard Kingston knew of it. His mind traveled back to what he had overheard Jeremy saying to Greyland in the garden. There was another that was supposed to walk by and see him kissing Greyland.

"Lady Chatsworth."

Bella and Perkin stared at him.

"Lovingston mentioned Lady Chatsworth." Alex explained the sudden correlation. "He mentioned her in the garden, just before he threw himself on her. In telling Greyland of his plan, he let it slip that Lady Chatsworth was supposed to stumble upon them together."

Bella's brow creased with distaste. "That is no lady, Alex. She desires you all to herself."

Her words hit him like a bullet right between the eyes. What if Lady Chatsworth had put two and two together about his and Greyland's betrothal? The blasted woman had been trying to ball-and-chain him for the last year. What if she hatched a plan benefitting herself and that stupid young buck?

Perkin eyed Alexander. "You believe him? That he and the lady in question orchestrated this together?"

"I would not have, if I had not heard the bastard with my own ears."

Perkin tapped his glass skeptically. "The rush of it all still does not make sense. Lovingston clearly executed this plan in haste. It was too sloppy. So again, I put to you, what would make him act so rashly?"

Alex took a breath. "I was going to ask your father's permission to marry your sister. My only conclusion is that somehow Lady Chatsworth and Lord Lovingston suspected this and formulated a plan to intervene. A scandal on Greyland's honor would serve to disrupt a possible engagement."

Perkin simply looked at him. "Has it? Disrupted your plans?"

Alexander stared the blond man dead in the eyes. "Not for a second."

"I AM GOING to ask you a series of questions," Alexander said, looking down at one bound and gagged Jeremy Lovingston on his stable floor.

He bent at the waist and with one hand, yanked the rag from the other lord's mouth. As if on cue, Malikite at his master's other hand leaned in on a short tether and snarled. "If I dislike the answers, you will be killed."

Jeremy bobbed his head enthusiastically, his eyes bulging with unadulterated fear.

"First, who else was in on your plot to compromise Miss Kingston?"

"Lady Chats… She said it would… It would…"

"Bloody hell, Thomas," Alex cut in. "How many times did you hit him?"

"The bounder is lucky. I went easy on him. Hand me the bucket."

Thomas grabbed Jeremy by the hair and plunged his head into the freezing water. He held it under while the man thrashed about in the mud.

"That is enough. Let's see if he can form a coherent sentence now."

Thomas reluctantly relented. Lovingston gasped for air, his mouth opening and closing, cheeks concaving and expanding again like a trout out of water.

Alexander knelt in front of him, coming eye to eye with the younger man. Malikite dropped his head between his shoulders and growled at Alex's side. "This will be easier on you, if you speak clearly. Who else knows?"

"Lady Chatsworth told me you were planning to marry Miss Kingston and suggested I lead her away from the ball," Lovingston rushed, snot bubbling out of one nostril. "She said she would bring some partygoers outside at the right moment. They would catch us locked in a kiss. Lady Chatsworth said Miss Kingston's father would force her into a marriage with me, after being ruined in the eyes of society. It was just a kiss. Please!" he pleaded. "I never wanted anything more than to have her as my wife. I am... I never meant…"

The man broke into sobs.

Perkin, who until now held back with enormous self-control, took two strides towards Jeremy, and kicked him right in the face.

Lovingston's neck snapped back with a sickening sound of splintering bone and tearing sinew. Blood spewed in various directions from differing parts of the man's head, as his body flipped completely over with the force. Alex was fairly certain their inquiry had come to an end.

They waited.

After a few seconds, Jeremy's chest heaved with a newfound breath, and he coughed up a pool of blood. And a tooth.

Thomas wrenched the whimpering fool up again and forced his head back into the icy water.

"If you are truthful, we might not kill you," Alexander explained when Thomas saw fit to release the swine. "Needless to say, this will not be a walk in the park, either. You may wish for death at some point."

Alexander released his grip on the half-breed and let Malikite lunge. He pulled back on the leash only when the animal was within a hair of Jeremy's bloodshot eyes. "Did you place the drug in her wine?"

"I do not know what you are talking about. Please..." Lovingston groveled, "I know nothing of any drugs."

Jeremy swallowed hard, his lungs working to find the air required to live. He was crying like a child now. "I promise. She told me Miss Kingston had consumed too much wine and would be easy to lure away from the ballroom. It was just a kiss. I swear. I never meant to do her harm."

This time Alexander was the one who lunged forward. "So, you thought to take advantage of a young lady who was well into her cups?" He spat. "You reasoned that forcing her into marriage with you —a man she did not want—would not be doing her harm?"

He grabbed the coward by the throat and yanked him up onto his knees. Jeremy barely had time to start to collapse under his own weight when Alexander's fist slammed into his eye socket, driving him back into the mud and muck.

"Please—" Jeremy covered his face and rolled into a ball.

Alexander, Thomas, and Perkin regarded each other for a moment. "Well, should we kill him?" Thomas asked.

They all watched Jeremy Lovingston writhing on the ground in what smelled like his own piss.

"I do not think he will be any future trouble," Perkin's voice breached the suspended consideration. "But I think we should put him to work for us. There is someone else involved. I do not believe this Lady Chatsworth is clever enough to devise this all on her own."

"I agree," Alexander leaned over Jeremy. "We are going to release you, but if you talk of this to anyone, we will hunt you down. Next time, we will not be so gentle.

"You have one week to uncover who gave Lady Chatsworth the poison," Alex instructed. "Tell her that Miss Kingston left before you could make your move and that you quit the ball to go to White's for cards. As for your wounds..." He eyed the man's bloodied face and split lip. "You got jumped and robbed on a side street before you could get there."

Thomas grabbed an arm and hoisted Lovingston up. "Do not dream of disappointing us again, old chap."

Jeremy rolled his limp head by way of answer.

Thomas released his grip, allowing the lord to once again become one with the hard ground. "Say it!"

"I agree!" Lovingston choked out.

Perkin smirked. "I daresay, the ton will be able to tell you apart from your twin now."

Alexander gestured to the stable doors. "You have a five-minute head start on Malikite. I hope for your sake, you are more fleet-of-foot than you are quick-of-mind."

GREYLAND CRACKED ONE EYELID OPEN. The room was completely black, save for a dwindling candle along the far wall that only served to cast shallow shadows over the nearest painting. She opened the other eye and attempted to adjust her body in the bed just to realize she could not feel her legs. Frightened, but groggy, she wiggled her fingers and found that her right hand was encased in someone else's grasp. As her eyes fought to adjust to the darkness, she could just make out the form of a man slumped beside her bed, head resting on the blankets. *She must be dreaming.*

In her dream, she looked down at the senseless sensation of her legs and saw what the issue was. A large wolf was sleeping across her feet. She inhaled sharply.

The man bolted upright. The beast merely lifted his large head, determined there was no cause for alarm and plopped back down across her ankles.

"You are awake! Are you hungry?"

"Alexander?" She squinted. "What are you doing in my bedchamber?"

"You are actually in my bedroom." She could hear the grin in his words.

"Alexander!" She sat upright, completely awake now and looking about the room. Now that her eyes were accustomed to the dim lighting, nothing in the room was familiar.

"Easy." He placed a hand on her shoulder coaxing her back into the bed. "You have undergone a great deal. Best to not move too quickly. Does anything hurt?"

"My head is a little sore." Her hand went to the back of her head. "Did I hit it on something?"

He turned just enough that the moonlight fell across his handsome face, showing its concern. "Greyland, the doctor speculated you would awake with a headache. He believes someone put a draught in your drink."

He smoothed a rogue tendril of hair out of her face. The soothing touch was like a balm to her soul and a vast difference from his uncle's extremely inappropriate one earlier. Alexander's words finally took hold, pulling her back from the melancholy his caress created.

"Drugged!" She tried to sit up again, but Alex's hand blocked the action once more.

Gently he eased her back onto the pillow. "We believe Jeremy

Lovingston was working with someone who wanted to take you off the marriage market." His mouth drew into a hard line.

"Why would he do that?" Her brain scrambled to review the evening's events. One by one, images of her last known memories started to take shape. She had felt extremely unwell just before Jeremy asked her to take a walk. He had snapped at her. *Scared her.* And then he had smothered her mouth with his liquor-tinged breath. Greyland shivered.

"He wanted you all for himself."

Greyland lay there, dumbfounded. She had thought of Lord Lovingston like a sweet-hearted younger brother. How could he turn into such a different man in the span of forty-eight hours? It did not make sense.

"He mentioned another." Her mind raced back through time to when she was in the garden. "The blonde woman that was curt to me at The Queen's ball. Lady Chatsworth?" Greyland looked up, hopeful.

"Yes," Alex said, folding his arms. The action illustrated the thin loose-fitting shirt he wore. Left open at the top, it exposed his tan skin and a small patch of glossy chest hairs. Greyland felt her mouth go slightly dry. She had only ever seen her brothers in such a state of undress and thought nothing of it. Seeing Alex so intimately clad created more wayward thoughts than she imagined possible.

"The two were working together." His statement pulled her out of her reverie. "Did either of them procure anything for you to eat or drink?"

Greyland shook her head. "The only person to get a glass of wine for me, other than you, was Derrick. He would not have any reason to hurt me."

Alexander's eyes narrowed. "I am going to keep you by my side until we are safely wed."

The protective oath warmed her like a crackling fire. Who would have thought the man could turn a horrible situation into something that sounded utterly delightful. She felt herself smile. "Can I get that in writing?"

The serious expression on his face shifted into a devilish smirk and he leaned over the bed to stare into her eyes. "Gladly."

The animal at the foot of her bed adjusted his large body, drawing Alexander's attention away from her gaze. "Malikite. Down!"

"He is fine." She chuckled and reached her hand to scratch his ears. "I rather like having a personal foot-warmer."

"He has never done that before. He only sleeps in my room. On the floor." He reprimanded the dog with a scowl, but Malikite only yawned. "He must like you."

Greyland smiled and looked around the room, really taking note of it for the first time. To her shock, she spied her party dress and dragon wings hung neatly on the door. She pulled the sheets tight against her thin shift, acutely conscious now of her inadequate clothing.

Alex followed her gaze to the door and grinned. "My maid helped to make you more comfortable. She let me in once you were under the covers."

Greyland felt her cheeks flush. "You have been here all night?"

"Yes."

"Oh!"

His mouth curled in amusement. "I am trying to be a gentleman, but I *have* been tempted to have a peek under that lucky goose down."

"Do my brothers know?"

His brows shot up. "I hope not!"

She laughed. "I mean, do they know I am here, and safe?"

"Yes, Perkin was here. He helped Thomas and I deal with Jeremy and then he went home to inform Edward of the evening's events."

She cringed. Her brothers were far too overprotective as it was. This would only intensify their watchfulness over her. Then the first part of Alexander's reply dawned on her.

"You dealt with Jeremy?" A sinking feeling drifted down into her stomach like a rock tossed into a creek. She was just getting to know Alexander's temperament, *but her brothers...*

"Oh Alex, you did not let Perkin hurt him, did you? Lord

Lovingston is just a stupid boy. I am sure he did not understand the gravity of what he was doing."

Alexander's jaw twitched. "That 'boy' tried to have his way with you. Stupid is too kind a word." He stated with a finality that was irrefutable. "Lovingston has been dealt with the way a man sees fit under these circumstances."

Dear Lord, they killed him!

ALEXANDER'S FACE fell as he rushed to gather Greyland in his arms. Her little frame convulsed against his chest. He pulled her tight for fear her sobs might shake right off the bed. "Greyland, darling, 'tis alright. The boy is fine. Well…" Alex lifted her trembling chin with his finger. "Rather, he is alive."

She looked up into his eyes. "It is all my fault."

"None of this is your fault!"

"If I had not laughed at him or let him walk me to the rose bushes…"

She buried her head back into his chest.

Alex drew her face up to his and held it in his hands. He placed a kiss on her cheek and then moved to her mouth. She melted into his touch, and he heard himself groan. He pulled her to him. She had let the blankets slip. He felt her breasts push into his chest, her soft shape molding to his harder one.

He practically vaulted backward off the bed. "I am sorry, but you really must regain your sheets, for I am deficient in self-discipline at the moment." He turned in place, facing the door, and sighed at his own lack of basic control. "I really would like to take you to bed the proper way, once we are man and wife."

"Alexander?"

He turned back to face her. A shy smile swept across her lips. "How long will that be again?"

"We must make it soon, for I fear you have stolen my heart," Alexander confessed, and then glanced down at the half-breed. "And my dog as well."

She snuggled down into the blankets. "We shan't have that, now."

"No, he is unreasonable when he sets his mind to something." Alexander returned to his post in the chair beside her bed.

"Just like his master." She patted the mattress. "Will you lie beside me? You need sleep, too."

He shook his head. "I would love nothing more, but I fear I must remain in the chair."

She gave him a pout and placed her head on the pillow.

He reached out and gently stroked her hair as she closed her eyes. His mother used the same technique to soothe him to sleep as a boy. Alex hoped he was doing the memory justice and that the action would ease her.

He watched as Greyland's breathing slowed. He could not take his eyes off her. *What had this sleeping beauty done to him?* He was completely under her spell. It was astounding really. Alex had never had such a deep connection to another person before.

Sure, he had loved his father deeply. Despite the man's betrayal of his mother, by taking that whore to his bed so soon after her death. And, of course, he loved Thomas like a brother, but he had only ever cared for one other person this much—*his mother.*

And she had been stolen from him before he could even really know her. He would not let anyone steal Greyland. He vowed right then and there to always keep her safe and protected. Alex would do for her what he had not been strong enough to do for his mother.

VII

Richard Kingston regarded him closely, his astute gaze taking in everything from the way Alex's hands rested atop the arms of the chair to the way his boots sat solidly on the plush Oriental rug.

"I believe your father once told me that history was one of your favorite subjects at Cambridge?" Richard turned his head to indicate Alexander's large literary collections, housed neatly on built-in bookshelves that lined the duke's walls.

"Indeed, it was."

"I am sure The Cousins' War that raged on before the Tudors ruled England was of great interest to you then?"

"The War of the Roses was my favorite time period, actually," Alexander replied, though there was a hesitance to his response that openly suggested he wondered where this turn in the conversation was going.

"You, no doubt, remember the story of the two princes in the tower and have drawn your own conclusions," Richard hedged.

"I certainly have my opinions."

It was one of history's greatest mysteries. After losing their father, Edward of York, it was said that the young princes' uncle placed both boys in the Tower of London for safety and later, they died in there of a sweating illness. The bodies were said to have been buried in the royal cemetery. Years later, King Henry Tudor—in his paranoid state —had the tombs opened, but they were empty. Some theorized, even Shakespeare alluded to the notion in one of his masterpieces, one of the boys, the younger brother, Richard, had been hidden away in secret. Richard's mother, The Queen, had feared the real intent of their ambitious uncle. She had given one son up to the tower already, so when they came for the second, she sent a serving boy into the tower instead, knowing their uncle had not seen the lad in many years and would not recognize him.

Richard nodded and then motioned toward Alexander's sidebar. "Shall we?"

Alexander stood and said, "Allow me." He walked to the bar and poured them both a drink. "I believe the Tudors had the children executed while in the tower, not their uncle."

He returned and handed one of the glasses to Richard. Alex reclaimed his seat across from the older gentleman and continued his review. "Fifteen years after the supposed death of the two boys, a man claiming to be the long-lost Prince Richard returned to English soil, under the alias of Perkin Warbeck."

Alexander paused abruptly, the sudden correlation of names dawning on him.

Richard Kingston picked up the tale. "Perkin Warbeck had the support of the entire world, save England, in his claim as the true Prince of York. He was the rightful heir to the throne. King Henry was merely an upstart. But the Tudor King had worked too hard to allow any man to take his crown. During this time, Perkin, Richard of York, married a Scottish Princess by the name of Catherine Gordon, and he fathered a son with her before Henry Tudor had him executed."

Richard leaned back in his chair and grinned. "And here we have another mystery. What happened to that baby?"

"Most believe Henry Tudor had him killed. As he should have if he wanted no true competitor to the Crown."

"My family has another version," Richard said simply.

Alexander waited.

Richard, seemingly gathering his thoughts, continued. "After Perkin's death, Henry Tudor placed the one-year-old child, Edward, named after his grandfather, with an English family he trusted. In case Scotland ever thought to wage war against England again he would have a pawn. Some years later, Henry released Catherine back to her father in Scotland. She remarried. It was said that the child she had with Perkin Warbeck had died of a sweating illness in his fifth year with the host family.

"King Henry went on to gift titles freely to those he trusted, which were few. He knighted the father who had taken in the child, rewarding him for his loyalty to England. Then a year later, Henry learned of the child's passing. He was relieved, naturally. Henry had only spared the child so as not to have his name tied to that of a baby killer. Even though—let us be clear—he would have killed him anyway when he grew older. Henry Tudor could not have another York male heir with a claim to the throne, as you already stated."

Richard hesitated, seemingly giving more thorough consideration to Alexander sitting across from him. "This is where our families met, once upon a time."

Alexander stared, speechless.

Richards's kind grey eyes seemed to understand this reaction. "I can tell this is news to you."

"I knew I was the ninth Duke of Ravenswood, an honor Queen Elizabeth had given to us, but I confess to knowing nothing before that time."

"It was not Elizabeth that gave you the title Ravenswood, she only restored it after having stripped it during the issue with Mary, Queen of Scots."

Richard pulled his long fingers down his beard to the point of his chin. "It was her grandfather, Henry VII, that bestowed the title upon your family. Because it was your ancestors that took in that baby."

Richard watched Alex process what he had just said. "The Ravenswoods were very close to the Tudor's and remained that way.

Nevertheless, the family's loyalty to their King was not greater than their love that grew for that innocent child."

Richard took another sip of his sherry. "They crafted the tale of the child dying of the sweats to throw Henry off the York scent, so to speak. The family mercifully returned the child to his mother, Catherine. She placed him with her brother's family in Ireland to be raised as their own."

Richard sat forward. "Alexander, our two families are bonded together in this secret. My family is the direct descendant of that child. The son of Perkin Warbeck and grandchild of King Edward. The last true heir of the Plantagenet reign."

Alexander stared at the man sitting across from him in utter silence.

Minutes passed. Alex knew his eyes must appear close to bursting from his head as he cataloged every detail of this story. It would be utterly unfathomable had he not, as well as half the bon ton, found Richard Kingston to be the spitting image of the long-ago King of England, Edward IV. And the names—all the men had the same names—and they all shared the same exquisite, ancient Anglo-Saxon bone structure that iconic lineage was known for. A feature that all but died once the more rotund Tudors took the Throne.

Could it really be? Why not, Alex mused. Surely most of the earth descended from royalty. Most servants in London could trace their lineage back to the ever-greedy Henry VIII. Still, this was too close to the crown. To this day, people were still divided over The War of the Roses. Towns still secretly hung white or red rose banners in back tavern rooms. Henry Tudor might have won—or stolen the Crown, depending on how one thought—but he would never live to be remembered as King Edward IV had been.

This sort of announcement could have them all in the gallows if the slanderous words got out.

This is treason against The Queen!

Richard finished Alex's thought for him as if he had read them all in subsequent order. "About The Queen. Her family has been linked to ours for almost as long. She knows all this and trusts that we have no designs on upsetting the order; I even signed a royal decree. Once she feels she has a good grasp on her new title as Queen, she will be giving us our rightful titles back." Richard smiled. "Well, not our exact titles, but I will be a duke and will receive some of my ancestral lands back."

Richard Kingston stood, a clear indication that the conversation was nearing its end. Alex followed suit.

"The dowry I am giving you is quite substantial," the older man said and smiled, his grey eyes crinkling around the edges. "You better never give me reason to question my decision to allow you into this family."

Alex inclined his head. Not only had he been given the blessing of marrying Greyland, but he was standing in a room with a direct male descendant of Edward IV, King of England. Even The Queen of England, herself could not claim royal blood this thick. Alexander's mind spun with the weight of his new knowledge. It was as if someone had just handed him a block of stone and said it was the tenth commandment...*and it was.*

A sudden irony needled into his thoughts. His family had betrayed their own King to keep this York line safe and preserve it so that standing here today was Richard, Perkin, Edward, and Greyland Kingston. No wonder Alex felt so protective over his heart's desire. Apparently, his family had been keeping her bloodline safe for the past three-hundred years.

He schooled the emotions on his face and lifted his head, taking Richard's hand in his own. "I will never give you reason for concern," he smiled, then added, "Your Grace."

GREYLAND LOOKED at the grandfather clock for what had to be the twentieth time. For an hour she had been not-so-patiently waiting for

Alexander and her father to come out from the study. It was now close to three hours since they had gone in. Samson, Alexander's tight-lipped butler, told her six times that His Grace did not wish to be disturbed for anything save the house catching on fire.

She glanced at the cold fireplace. *How long would it take to start one?* The time was twenty 'till two. She promised Lord Ashlown she would teach his niece and nephew the deuced Viennese waltz, but now she was bored enough to attempt to instruct Malikite. She could have the dog up and dancing before Alexander and her father would ever conclude their meeting.

What was taking so long?

For one dreadful moment, Greyland feared her father might be declining the proposal. Her heart sank.

Absolutely not. He would not dare!

She contemplated what sort of tantrum she was willing to engage in, should he say no. Greyland rose as soon as she heard the door squeak but it was only Samson, dutifully checking in on her again.

"Is there anything I can get you, my lady?"

"Yes, I need to borrow a carriage and a footman. I have an appointment at Lord Ashlown's townhouse."

Samson had the courtesy to blink rapidly before opening and closing his mouth. Yet no words escaped his tightly pursed lips. She wondered if he might be in the throes of his own apoplexy and immediately felt bad for shocking the poor man. After a moment he regained his composure and seemed to be silently mouthing out different, 'appropriate', answers before finding the one he thought most acceptable.

"I believe His Grace would have my head on a stick if I were to grant you that request, my lady."

She was taken aback at the image.

"I am very sure His Lordship is quite fond of your head, Samson, and would not wish to see it impaled. Now, I have promised a dance lesson to two children and will not disappoint them. If you will not assist me, then I shall be forced to walk."

She stood and drew herself to her full height and squared her shoulders. Samson wrung his hands together and wiped a bead of sweat from his brow.

"My lady, you have just suffered a great deal in the not-so-distant past. His Grace would not at all be pleased to have you leaving without his consent."

Greyland fought the urge to scream at the word 'consent,' but opted for a more convincing strategy.

She strolled toward him, gifting him with her sweetest smile. "Well, had he taken any of my requests for an audience I could have discussed it with him and not have bothered you." She reached out and thoughtfully smoothed his sleeve. The aging butler went deathly still. "I do believe he should up your wages for having put such a task on you. Why, when I am lady of the house, I will make that my first priority."

Samson took a cautious step back and looked toward the window, as if assessing how many steps it would take him to reach it and throw himself out. "My lady is too kind, but—"

"Samson!" All patience had fled her body. "Unless you choose to physically restrain me here, which I highly suggest against for your own safety, pray, move out of my way."

He threw up his hands in exasperation. "Only if I can be your humble chaperon?"

"That is not necessary, but if it brings some comfort to your conscience, then so be it."

She strolled past him and heard him scramble to keep pace behind her.

GREYLAND MADE her way out of the house to the awaiting carriage. Samson scurried around to open the door and instructed a footman to tell His Grace as to their whereabouts and to reassure him all was well.

Samson shut the door and moved to take his place beside the driver but Greyland shot her hand out the window, waving him back to her.

"Samson, will you ride inside with me?" Again, she produced her warmest smile. "I do hate to travel alone."

Before climbing in, he muttered something about his untimely demise in boiling vats of oil.

The man was so imaginative.

Greyland liked him immensely.

Samson signaled to the carriage driver, and they were off.

They had not gone far when Greyland caught sight of something black, moving so fast it appeared to be a blur, just out the right side of her window. She craned her neck to get a better look before tapping the roof of the carriage. The carriage stopped abruptly.

Before Samson could protest, she opened the door and beckoned the half-breed inside. Malikite leaped gracefully into the carriage.

She closed the door and signaled the driver to continue. Samson shook his head but said nothing. Pleased, Greyland smiled and patted the wagging and panting wolfdog.

Two minutes later, they pulled into Lord Ashlown's drive. A footman, surprised at the sight of the animal hopping out of the carriage paused for a minute before whistling for another man to corral the beast. If there was ever a time to 'pull rank', Greyland supposed dealing with a wolf would be that time.

The footman ushered Samson and Greyland toward the house.

Before entering the front door, Greyland spied the unlucky servant tasked with handling the half-breed, having a difficult time of executing his orders. He and Malikite appeared to be at odds. She rolled her eyes and called the dog to her side, then walked to the carriage house doors, where she beckoned him inside.

She heard the head-footman start to panic, his voice rising, as he protested her involvement in the matter. Greyland then heard

Samson halting his argument with something that sounded very much like, "Don't bother, you fool."

"Stay, Malikite," she said pointedly to the dog. "I shall not be long." She leaned down and scratched behind his ears. "There might be some more of that delicious ham in the deal if you are a good boy."

Malikite nuzzled at her hand before settling back onto his haunches and cocking his massive head to the side. She was almost certain the dog had nodded in agreement.

"Good." She stood and turned back to the house. "Let us dance now."

AN HOUR LATER, Perkin and Edward were sitting on either side of Alexander, observing the scene before them. "Lord Ashlown's upper lip is swelling at an astonishing rate," Edward summarized correctly.

"It should take the cut a good two days to heal, I suspect," Perkin concurred as he shot Alexander a sideways glance.

Alex sat with his arms folded high on his chest and his long legs stretched out and crossed at the ankles. He kept his sight trained on Greyland, who had just finished the last of three flawless pivots in Lord Ashlown's arms.

Inside the impressive ballroom, the children squealed with delight as Ashlown and Greyland came to a stop in front of them. The children enthusiastically tried their turn at the advanced pattern.

"It seems they are very much enjoying their lesson," Richard observed, joining the narrative. He raised an eyebrow and smiled in Alexander's general direction.

"After what happened last night," Edward said. "I am just glad Lord Ashlown was telling the truth about why he had asked Greyland here. But I did have my doubts when we arrived and found him leaning over her in the ballroom. Almost looked like something from the opera instead of a civilized waltz. I did not see the children either. Until after you planted that facer on him. I would have hated to see you kill the man in front of those two innocents."

Alexander could practically feel the deep wrinkles carving out their homes between his brows. He briefly thought of how many more age lines would emerge after his wedding. He pinched the bridge of his nose and closed his eyes, experiencing the onset of a headache. "Yes, killing men in the presence of children is not high on my list of things to accomplish."

Alex uncrossed and re-crossed his ankles. "Now, I see he has nothing to gain from holding my soon-to-be fiancée in his arms, other than unselfish love for his young niece and nephew." Sarcasm dripped from his words. "Why, anyone can see this is just a mere obligation to him. Why, he is obviously a man of honor and would never think to lure Greyland here for any other, more sinister, reasons. Like, say, ending the lesson and having a chance to be alone with her?" Alexander's arm flew out on its own accord, as if to illustrate his not-so-subtle point. He narrowed his eyes at Lord Ashlown. "No, he would never have let that thought slither into his egotistical head."

Lord Ashlown knew exactly what he was doing; Alex knew that. The man was a rake and was not above using his own family to aid in his perversities.

Alex looked from Edward to Perkin, to Richard. As the sole female in the family, Greyland had been given every liberty and had very little concept as to what the dangers of being a woman in this world could entail. Her father and brothers always kept her safe. Now he would have that job. The thought both terrified and fueled him.

"I am just glad we saw you in passing on King Street," Perkin said, shaking his head as he grinned. "I would have hated to miss the action." He looked from Alex to his sister on the dance floor. "You said she came here with your butler and your dog?"

"Yes. Samson and Malikite, *the traitorous accomplices,* are in the carriage house at the moment, which is best," Alex said. "I am irate with both of them at the moment."

Richard patted Alex on the arm. "Your staff will have to adjust to having the demands of a female influence in the house. They operate very differently, and as you have noticed, our dear girl is very persuasive. Why, I cannot tell you how many times she has landed Ocman in trouble." Kingston chuckled. "I finally gave up holding the poor man accountable. Life is just too short, and I value Ocman too much to let him go."

All four had to grin at the logic in the older Kingston's words and the mood softened notably.

The lesson came to an end, and an unashamed Lord Ashlown ushered Greyland back to her family.

"Thank you for allowing your intended to teach my niece and nephew the dance."

Alexander squeezed Greyland to his side. "The announcement shall run in the *Times* tomorrow," he said, by way of an answer.

Alexander felt Greyland's eyes jump up to his, but he held Ashlown's gaze. He noticed a moment of panic burn across his rival's visage, but the man recovered quickly as footsteps entered from across the room.

Alex turned with the rest to see two pretty women. Lord Ashlown produced a warm smile as he introduced his sisters. The smile was the first genuine emotion Alex had ever seen from his longtime rival.

The eldest sister was the mother of the dancing children. And the younger one, Alex could not help notice, gained rapid attention from both Perkin and Edward. Four days ago, she would have drawn Alexander's approval as well.

He glanced down at the woman by his side. *But that was four days ago.* Now, Greyland was the only woman he had eyes for. Even if she had given him the second-biggest fright of his life by running off to Lord Ashlown's residence without saying a word. She would definitely need to learn how to communicate her wishes better. He could not have her running all over London on whims.

However, he was now going to be her husband, and as such, her provider, protector, and teacher.

Alex grinned to himself as he considered the scolding—balanced with smothering affection—he would dole out once they were behind closed doors. Perhaps her wild impulses had a gratifying end result after all.

IN THE CARRIAGE, Malikite's large body lounged against Greyland's legs. She knew Alex was mad, and she knew she was in for an earful, but she could not help but smile at the thought of coming up with various ways to soothe Lord Grump. She would have a lifetime of soothing him since her wonderful father agreed to the match. She stifled her glee and put on her bravest face.

After he finished reprimanding Samson thoroughly, Alex climbed into the rig, seated himself across from Greyland and stared pointedly at her. She took a courageous breath and moved with cat-like speed from her seat to his. Sliding up right beside him she leaned in and kissed his jawline before softly breathing out, "I am sorry."

He froze. Greyland moved her hand to his chest and placed another kiss on his neck. He let out a shuddered breath, providing the confirmation she hoped for. *He was not that mad.*

Blindly following instinct alone, she traced kisses up to his earlobe and bit down gently. He pulled her into his lap, before she could blink, and kissed her. His strong arms held her tight to his muscled torso, proving just how overpowered she was. He smelled of leather and something sweet...*freshly shorn grass.* Her whole body awoke as he returned hot kisses along her neck. The sensation was too much. She let out a small gasp.

He breathed warm pulsing words into her ear. "Do you see now how quickly you can find yourself powerless?"

She closed her eyes and nodded as he drew her arms behind her back and held both her wrists with one hand. His other hand snaked around and explored the collar of her dress. She let her head roll back as his lips continued to ravage her neck. The heady sensation awakened parts of her body she was not aware could sweat. She released another sigh.

His free hand traveled around her collarbone and grabbed her by the nape of her neck, forcing her head back up so he could reclaim her mouth. "I could do whatever I wanted to you right now, and you would not be able to stop me." His chest rose and fell hard against hers as he spoke.

"But you would never. And I am not fighting."

He squeezed her tighter. "No, I would never hurt you on purpose, but others would, and could. You would not give any man a challenge, my sweet. Even in your most enraged state. Do you understand that? This is why, you must act with more caution."

She stilled her ragged breathing. Greyland knew he was right. With only one hand he had been able to restrain both her arms. Sure, she still had teeth and legs if she had really been in danger, but even that would have been no match against his superior strength. "I will try to be more careful," she conceded, "but I did have a chaperon and a wolf with me."

He released his tight hold on her. "You had my sixty-five-year-old butler, hardly a defense. Malikite is a far better protector, but even he is only an animal."

They both turned to look at the giant half-breed sleeping with his head propped on Greyland's abandoned seat.

When Greyland turned back to Alex, his expression was pained.

"I would die if something were to happen to you," he said. "Will you, if not for your own sake but for mine, be more careful?"

She glanced down, instantly ashamed she had caused that look in his eyes. "Yes."

"I have a house in Brighton, and I would very much like to make it our main home if you approve."

Her eyes darted back up, excitement bubbling inside her. The only thing that could have made his sentence better would have been to add children and Christmas trees.

"It is just a medium-size castle, but it is right on the ocean."

"Only medium-sized?" She teased.

"What do you say we leave right after the wedding?"

"I say…" She clapped her hands. "Why wait two weeks?"

"One might think you excited, my lady," he smiled.

"I think the word excited is too simple. I am thrilled beyond reason."

"Good." He kissed her shoulder. "Two weeks was your father's request. He does not want it to seem too rushed. Hopefully tomorrow morning, when all of London gets our announcement, I will be able to breathe again. Knowing you will not be as readily hunted. And once everyone knows of our pending nuptials, we will be allowed more private time. Like this."

His smile was downright wicked. One of his fingers pushed past the boundaries of her bodice and stroked the silkiness of her breast. "How does that sound?"

Greyland closed her eyes. "Perfect!"

Greyland practically floated from the ballroom, where she and Perkin had instructed their third lesson of the week to The Queen and the prince. The two were set to marry in six months' time, and they had asked the siblings to choreograph a waltz for their wedding dance. Greyland gleefully agreed but refused payment. The Queen insisted that her personal *modiste* design Greyland's wedding dress, at the very least.

Greyland walked away from the Grand Ballroom, taking a different way than she was used to. Perkin told her of a closer powder room to the left. She whirled in a quick spiral, giddy at the thought of seeing Alex later that night. She had not seen him in three days. He had some last-minute business dealings to attend to. She would see him in a scant three hours at the engagement party that Bella and Thomas were hosting for them.

In her dreamy state of mind, she turned by accident down the wrong hall. She overheard a familiar voice coming from a door that was ajar. Greyland froze mid-stride when she heard Lord Ashlown speak again.

"I do not like the Kingston girl marrying Lord Ravenswood, either," he said. "I wanted her for myself, but Ravenswood seems to have a tight hold on her now."

Greyland strained closer. A voice she knew she had heard before, but could not place, responded. "This family is sinking its claws in too deep for my comfort. Until we know Richard Kingston's true motives for bringing his whole family here, I cannot rest. His claim is too strong."

"I do not think the girl is involved," Ashlown said. "But I will continue to watch them all. Even if one of them is more enjoyable to observe."

"Do not lose focus just because she is comely."

Ashlown retorted smugly, "I never lose focus! Even with a woman as stunning as Miss Kingston." There was a pause. "I put three men on one of their Irish connections that just arrived in town today. The men are of the McGreggor clan, and I am curious as to why they are here. His family is one of the more dangerous in Ireland. It appears a rip in their—"

A hand cupped over Greyland's mouth from behind and pulled her against a solid wall of chest. She tensed as she was spun around.

Derrick held his finger to his lips as he removed his hand from her mouth, continuing to pull her further from the door.

Once they turned down another hall, he released her. He crossed his arms and leaned negligently against the wall. Penetrating her with his eyes, he regarded her from head to toe in a way that made her wish for a shawl. "Little lambs should not eavesdrop on the wolves' den."

"I was just walking by when I heard my name."

"What did you hear?" He stepped closer, and she hesitantly took a step back.

He smirked. "Now surely you do not fear me?" He allowed the question to linger. "Unless you have changed your mind, you will be marrying my nephew in a week's time. You can tell me anything. I will keep all of your secrets."

"I do not fear you, and I will not be changing my mind. If you must know, I heard Lord Ashlown discussing my family's reasons for being here." She did not feel she wanted to repeat the rest, especially when Derrick always made her feel like a roasted pig on a starving man's dinner table. His over-familiar appraisal of her had increased to an uncomfortable level since Alex had been away. Even though he looked much like his attractive nephew, Derrick's attitude differed vastly.

He side-stepped and moved toe to toe with her. Placing his long arms on either side of her head, he leaned into the wall at her back and whispered. "Well, dear, we know there is no harm in your family being in England. Lord Ashlown just wanted you for himself. He is likely just venting that we got to you first. Now remember, if there is anything at all you ever need, I would be more than happy to give it to you. Just say the word. You can trust me."

Derrick backed away at the sound of approaching footsteps. Greyland's tightly wound nerves relaxed a fraction when she spied Perkin striding towards them with a look of speculation on his sculpted face.

"Ah sister, there you are." He smiled, be it brief and insincere, at Derrick. "And how are you, Lord Hamilton?"

"Could not be better. I was just showing Greyland the way out. It seems she made a wrong turn."

Perkin reached for Greyland. "You are too kind. I believe I can take her the rest of the way. We shall see you tonight."

ONCE INSIDE THE safety of their carriage, Greyland bombarded Perkin with exactly what she had heard and then wasted no time throwing questions at him. Perkin remained calm, in the same irritating way her father did when he contemplated something of great importance. She let an exasperated sigh trail off her last series of inquiries and then dove back into her interrogation.

"If you do not answer me, I will be forced to kick you in your shin." She rotated her ankle which was crossed over her other leg. "Who is this dangerous family from Ireland? The McGreggors. And what is this talk about father's claim? What claim?"

Perkin regarded her once more. "You know about our history and who our forefathers were, Greyland. That is nothing new to us. It seems to be news to others, who I am guessing, see our presence as a very real obstacle regarding the passage of the Crown of England. As far as the McGreggor's are concerned, they too, are a link in our family chain. Father said he had a falling out last year with them, but he has been working out an agreement to patch things up. He has given no indication of a problem."

Perkin hesitated and she knew he was not telling her everything. "Why would anyone think we would get in the way of the crown? And why is this McGreggor 'link' here in London? Why did father not tell you about the disagreement with them when it first occurred? He tells you everything!"

He did not answer, just stared out the window. "God's teeth, Perkin, tell me!" Panic began to gnaw at her. "I am a part of this family too! And I am getting a distinct feeling that I am somehow involved. How are we connected to the McGreggor's?"

Perkin's head snapped back to face her. "The McGreggor's are from Catherine Gordon's side—cousins of hers, to be exact. Cousins that, up until last year, wanted you to marry the only male heir in their dwindling bloodline to secure the family and strengthen the lineage. And...to create a stronger claim on the Crown."

Greyland felt his words as if they had been liquefied into ice water and doused in her face. Her mind swam through quicksand. None of that was even possible, and if it were... *It would be treason!*

The back of her hand fluttered to her lips. The Queen was the rightful Queen. And Greyland was marrying for love! How dare men she had never met assume to dictate her future! She was nobody's bartering piece. Especially not in a puzzle that went back hundreds of years.

"Oh, for Christ's sake!" Her shock turned to rage, and she leveled her fury on Perkin. "What you speak of is outrageous! It is slander against The Queen and against everything we were brought up to believe."

An abrupt, sickening thought lodged itself in her head. "Was I the disagreement that transpired a year ago with the McGreggor's?"

Perkin lunged forward, his hands grabbing hold of both of hers. "Greyland, you must understand that father never wanted anything but the best for you. You know all too well that America is not stable right now and that our views differ greatly from others in the South. He wanted more for you; he wanted you to be safe. He fears an epic war is in America's future. Be it near, or far off, he wants you nowhere near when it erupts. Ireland seemed the safest answer. You would be safe."

He exhaled deeply. "It was a year ago when father realized the true motives for joining the bloodlines. He realized they sought a higher goal by securing you to their son, Colin. They would be one step closer to making their long-hidden proclamation. And if you had a son, well, surely you can see he would be the next rightful heir to the throne of England. Since neither father nor I, nor Edward, sought such a claim."

Greyland yanked her hands free and held them tight to her sides. "Why were my feelings on this never considered? And, and..." she sputtered. "It is incest!"

"Second cousins, from three hundred years ago, Greyland." Perkin did not share her appall, *clearly*. "Hell, half of Europe has crossed bloodlines in that span. Kings and queens since the dawn of time have married within the family to ensure the blood remains pure. But that is hardly the point. When father uncovered corruption in their family, along with their ambition to seize the crown, he cried off from your joining. He only wanted you safe. He never envisioned you would be used as a pawn. Six months later, they got word of father's talks with the former Duke of Ravenswood."

Her brother stopped talking abruptly. He had said too much, and he knew it. "Greyland, father had hoped you would take to his son, Alexander. The Hamilton alliance is much safer." Perkin gave a slight shake of his head. "Of course, the former Duke of Ravenswood was murdered before he could tell his son about you."

Greyland's mouth fell open. "Alexander was my intended?"

"Yes. At least that was the hope. And once you showed signs of approval, we were relieved. Well, father and I, anyway." He rolled his wrist in an annoyed fashion and Greyland knew immediately whose name he was about to speak next. "Edward still has his reservations. But that is mostly due to his stubborn pride being offended that he was kept completely in the dark regarding every bit of this."

Greyland's mind was running in a dithery circle. It was too much to process. Her brain kept clinging to the most terrifying aspects. "Perkin, do you think the McGreggor's had anything to do with the death of Alexander's father?" She forced the words over her tongue. They tasted like vinegar.

Perkin ran a hand through his dirty-blond hair. After a beat, his blue eyes reluctantly met Greyland's. "I am not sure, but my suspicions are high. If they are indeed in London, we need to get you and Alexander out of town. I am dropping you at Bella's. It is not safe for you at the house until we get to the bottom of this. I will travel to Alexander's and inform him of the current predicament."

Greyland's hands began to shake. "Perkin?"

"I will have someone bring your things," he said, ignoring her.

"Perkin!" Tears began to well up in her eyes.

"Listen to me, damn it!" he snapped.

The tears broke free, rolling silently down her cheeks.

Her brother pulled her hands together and held them tightly once again. "I know this is scary, but you have to move and think like a Kingston now." His blue eyes, as hard as marbles and just as warm, bore into hers. "You can be scared, and mad, and sad, once you are safely out of the city. Until then you must wear theses emotions like war paint. Understood?"

She tipped her head down and fixated her sights on their joined hands. "I understand."

"Right after the ball, you will leave with Alex."

She nodded wordlessly.

"And Greyland?" He called her attention back up to his face. "Tell no one!"

ALEXANDER GRABBED THE WINDOW LEDGE. His eyes shut tight against the words coming out of Perkin Kingston's mouth. Greyland was in trouble—from the same people that had likely killed his father.

Alex had already dispatched a footman to retrieve Richard and Edward. Perkin had been closed-lipped at first, preferring to wait and explain in detail what was transpiring when his father was in attendance. The blond man's resolve loosened when Alexander threatened to pummel him within an inch of his life, if he did not disclose, right then and there, what *kind* of trouble Greyland was really in. So, he had.

All of it.

Pain and doubt gripped Alex's ribcage, squeezing tightly as Perkin's words took shape. A simmering rage began to build steadily as the story unfolded. By Perkin's last sentence the anger coursing through Alex was so wild and unbridled he feared his ability to control it. Greyland had come with such a price. *How dare any man threaten what was his. Heaven help the bastard that tried to hurt her.* His blood pounded in his temples.

Perkin's voice pulled him from the all-consuming desire to punch his hand through the window.

"I think it is best if I lay all the cards on the table."

Alex whirled around.

There were more?

Perkin rushed on. "The only problem with the McGreggor clan laying claim to my sister was...you."

"Was? I believe *is* to be the correct word."

"Alexander." Perkin's voice dropped and Alex felt the hairs on his arms lift at the undercurrents of the other man's tone. "Your father knew it was my father's intent to link the two of you in marriage."

Alex's limbs grew twenty pounds heavier. He braced himself on the edge of the window seal as gravity pulled at him. "What?"

"Right before he died. There was an...agreement."

The parlor doors flung open. Alexander's eyes locked with Richard's the moment he entered. The Kingston Monarch appeared ten years older. His once vibrant eyes were now clouded with fear and anguish. Alexander felt a drumming spike of pity for the man he so richly admired.

Richards's voice finally broke the silence as he stepped into the room. "I will understand if you want to cry off from the engagement."

"Do you think so little of me?" The hurt bled from Alexander's lips before he could think to stop it. "They took my father from me, and now they seek to take Greyland!"

Richard marched forward, covering the distance of their divide in a few swift strides. He now stood an arm's length from Alex. "Of course not! But this could be a life-or-death decision for you if these men are indeed here to take back what they believe belongs to them."

Alexander sliced his hand viciously through the air. "It is life or death for her, too, damn you!"

Richard's eyes grew large.

Edward stepped farther into the room. The older man held up a hand and stilled his son's advancement. Richard dropped his gaze to the floor and shook his head. "I deserved that, and much more. But you must know that I knew not how perilous the situation would become. I was only looking out for her best interest. I did not know I was delivering up my precious little girl to the wolves." He sighed. "Greed can change people and the extent of their hunger eluded me until it was too late..." He let the last words fade into the air.

Alexander turned his head back to the window and stared into the intruding evening outside. All this time he had blamed his brother.

A rose-colored dusk shadowed the room. He closed his eyes and allowed the numbness to engulf him, for it was far better than the guilt he would deal with later. He would find Henry and beg forgiveness.

Alex finally spoke. "It is time to fix the situation before it becomes worse. Do you think they are in town with designs on taking her?"

"Yes." The quickness of Richard's response stabbed right to the core.

"Then I shall take her to Brighton after the party. I will post Bow Street Runners around the grounds during the ball. We will slip out at the end. And you will say that we have retired to France, to my house in Saint-Étienne." Alex looked at Perkin. "You will need to talk with Lord Ashlown and tell him the whole story. Point him in the direction of the McGreggor's."

Richard and Perkin nodded in agreement while Edward helped himself to a stiff brandy.

"We will be wed in a small chapel I know of along the way," Alexander continued. "Regardless of their claims, she will be my lawful wife. It is imperative you involve The Queen and her advisors and convince them that no one in your family has designs to overthrow her."

Edward walked over and handed Alex a glass. He gladly accepted.

"Share all transgressions between you and the McGreggor's with The Queen," Alexander implored Richard. "She trusts you. She will help clear this up before any more bloodshed can occur."

"Now..." Alex knocked back the drink and headed for the door, "I have an engagement party to get ready for." He paused and locked eyes with Richard as he passed.

"I will take care of her. You need not fear."

VIII

Alex finished helping Samson pack up the remains of their picnic. The poor man was not a traveler and the last two days on the road had taken their toll on the aging butler. Instead of wasting time staying in inns along the way, Samson, Alex's main driver and he had taken turns rushing through the night. They wanted to put as much distance between themselves and London as possible.

Greyland, on the other hand, handled the excursion like a seasoned professional. She never complained, not even once. Alex assumed years of travel with three men helped with this. Still, he was impressed. She did, however, grow easily bored. Just eight hours into the trip she insisted on driving the carriage to which he firmly said no.

No was either not an answer his willful fiancee was used to hearing or it was one she was used to overcoming. She changed tactics like a crafty man-of-law and proceeded to bombard them with a relentless string of questions regarding the mechanics of the rig. After thirty minutes, every man in their traveling party was out of answers to inquiries that went beyond even the most skilled carriage makers' understanding. Alex gave in and handed her the reins. The lesson went quickly, and so did Samson's lunch.

Alex chuckled as his thoughts traveled back to the night of their engagement party. The evening had gone off with nary a hitch, no guest the wiser that Alexander was about to flee town with his young future-bride in hopes of avoiding a band of power-hungry Irishmen looking to overthrow the Crown.

They had stolen away in the middle of the night immediately following the ball with two carriages, three footmen, Malikite, Socrates, and the fine dark bay Arabian mare Alex had gifted Greyland for her engagement present. His beautiful bride-to-be had bestowed on him a gift of her own. A mahogany case that held a pair of rare silver-mounted ivory inlaid pistols, their barrels engraved with his family crest. Alex had wasted no time trying out the exquisite pair the following day when they made their first stop. Greyland, in turn, had wasted no time setting a new record for the fastest anyone had ever ridden over the English countryside.

Alex felt himself smile as he handed Samson the last of the breakfast china and began making his way back to the spot where they had broken their morning fast. Another thing he would have to grow accustomed to, Alex mused as he trudged up the small hill, was having a bride that literally threw caution to the wind on a daily basis.

He reached the top of the hill and froze. The picnic blanket was all that remained in the spot where he had left Greyland to rest. Alex turned in place, frantically looking around the sprawling countryside.

"Greyland!"

A singsong laugh drifted up from the other side of the hill. Alex moved quicker than he thought possible toward the sound. As he drew near the edge of the tree line, Malikite bounded out, seemingly pleased with himself.

Alex ducked under a low-hanging limb. The branch snagged his shirtsleeve. He cursed when it tore. His inappropriate words brought forth a chorus of laughter. Alex looked up to see three ruddy-faced children, two girls and a boy. All knelt beside Greyland on the forest floor.

"Language, Lord Hamilton!" Greyland chastised.

Alex arched a brow. It had little effect. She returned her attention to whatever she held in her hands.

Alex kept himself from shouting as he delivered the next words. "You should always let me know—"

"Can we keep it?"

She dodged the scolding, lifting her head and presenting what she held to her chest. A solid white puff of a kitten.

"No."

Greyland looked genuinely taken aback at his prompt denial. Her smile wilted on her lips, and she handed the cat back to one of the three sets of disappointed eyes. The looks on their faces made him feel as if he had just run the tiny animal through with his rapier blade. He faltered a little.

Was she giving up that easily?

"It is just that..." Greyland began. *Of course not.* "I was not able to take Churchill, since he is the family cat, Edward's really, though he will not admit it." She pouted. "I thought we could buy the kitten. The children could use the extra coinage since their mother is sick and unable to work."

My word, she is good.

Alex ventured a glance at the children. They joined in Greyland's act like a well-rehearsed traveling band of gypsies enacting a roadside play. Greyland stood and ruffled the hair of the child directly in front of her before she moved to step away. As if planned, the girl thrust the animal back towards Greyland. "You can keep him, me lady. We cannot afford to feed him no more. We do not want him to die."

"Oh, for the love of God!" Alex was man enough to know when he had been outmaneuvered. "Fine. Keep the blasted cat. But do not let it mess in the carriage." He lifted his hand to wag a finger, but quickly placed it back at his side when he realized how closely he must resemble his childhood mathematics tutor.

Greyland jumped with glee and hugged the kitten to her chest again. "Oh, thank you, thank you!" She leaned in and kissed him on the cheek. "Sir George thanks you."

"Sir George?"

She turned. "Why, yes. Named after the fine young man over there who showed him to me." She gifted the small boy of the trio with a lovely smile. The boy hooked his sights on his threadbare boots to avoid showing his bright-red blush.

Alex fished two shillings from his pocket and grinned as the children's eyes grew wide. He placed the coins in the hand of the eldest. "Take this straight to your mother. Understand?" The three nodded and dashed off with their loot.

Alex took Greyland by the arm and led her back to the clearing. "Malikite will choke on all the fur, I am afraid. Maybe you should have named your cat Sir Wolf Snack."

She whirled to face him, mouth agape. "I will have you know, Lord Doom, Malikite actually licked him when I introduced them."

"Did he, now?" *Turncoat dog*. He paused as Greyland walked ahead, admiring the view. He said, "It is quite amazing how much you can accomplish in the span of a few minutes."

She glanced back over her shoulder with a sly smile. "I will be happy to show you just what one might accomplish in a shorter amount of time if you like?"

Alex's mouth went dry. She had mastered the art of flirting, almost too quickly. His mind played tug-o'-war with the possibilities.

THEY TRAVELED on for another five hours. Alex ordered the carriages to stop on the opposite side of a small brook that parted the woods from a field. On the other side of the field, a dirt road would lead into a village. He took Arnold, the strongest of the three footmen, to procure much-needed supplies from the local villagers. Greyland, Samson, his two remaining footmen, and his driver remained at their small camp.

The trip into town went smoothly but took longer than expected. He and Arnold collected a wheel of cheese, four bottles of wine, cold chicken, smoked ham, an assortment of fruit, and two loaves of freshly baked bread. This would make for their dinner, and later tonight he would allow them all to get a good night's sleep at an inn in the next village, about three more hours down the road.

They would not make it to Foxburg, where the vicar resided that would marry them, as Alex had originally hoped. Alex was not used to traveling with a party so large, its occupants so vast in experience and age. Despite the cushion-of-time he had factored into the hasty journey, they were still about half a day behind schedule.

But he would not dwell on the uncontrollables. They were still making good time. After tonight, he and Greyland would officially be man and wife. Then he could relax a fraction of a degree.

Once they finally reached Greenshire Castle, Alex planned on keeping Greyland awake the whole night in celebration of their nuptials. The thought stirred a familiar ache in his nether regions. *Yes,* he mentally concurred. She definitely needed her rest tonight.

Everything in order, he and Arnold made their way back across the field to their traveling party by the brook. The sun was just retreating behind the horizon, so they had to tread with extra care through the tall grass. They waded across the ankle-deep water of the creek and climbed up its small embankment on the other side.

And that was when they saw the oddest of sights.

There, between the two parked carriages, in the faint glow of a torch light, one of his footmen danced. Wearing what appeared to be a bonnet and an ill-fitting petticoat, the man, Michael, twirled before Alex's unblinking eyes.

Both Alex and Arnold went quiet as death when Danny, another footman, jumped down from a box and knelt at Michael's feet. Alex heard a burst of laughter from two very familiar voices: His impish, soon-to-be Duchess, and Samson. At least he assumed it was his butler, though the man never laughed, and certainly not like this.

"What, art thou ashamed of me?" shouted Danny on bended knee, in what Alex guessed was supposed to be his best

Shakespearian voice. The young man was not half-bad. Alex shook his head.

The motion caught Danny's eye and he went rigid.

Michael, unaware of the duke's presence, delivered his next line in a high-pitched voice. "No, sir. God forbid but ashamed to kiss."

Danny cleared his throat in warning.

Alexander rounded the carriage and beheld the guilty party. Even Malikite looked embarrassed. Greyland, Samson, and his driver sat on a blanket.

Alexander's eyes traveled straight to the mastermind behind the escapade. "My dear, what on earth is this all about?"

Greyland had the courtesy to look worried, but before she could say a word both footmen interceded for her.

"It was my idea, my lord," said Danny.

"Your Grace, it was my fault," added Michael. "The lady had naught to do with it."

They had known her for all of two days and she had won their loyalty, as if she were their blasted queen. Alex looked from one brave face to the next and realized that, indeed, she *did* inspire them as if she *were* their sovereign. His raven-haired, green-eyed beauty conducted herself with the enthusiasm and authority of someone of royal birth. He was once again brought face-to-face with the fact that she *was* a direct descendant of one of the most influential bloodlines to ever rule.

*But...*she was also his, and they were his servants. He paid their wages, he kept them fed; he was their benefactor.

He was jealous.

The thought brought him up short. Alex had never been jealous of anything in his whole life. He had also never won over complete strangers with just his sparkling personality. He had to give her credit where credit was due. Greyland was a beacon of light in the darkest of tunnels. Who else could get grown men to dress up as star-crossed lovers and reenact Shakespeare?

Greyland arose and confidently strode toward him. "I know this must appear unsatisfactory, but we had a bet you see..."

"Gambling?"

"We were playing a card game and a friendly wager was made," Samson spoke up. "The lady did nothing more than take a small amount of pleasure in an otherwise tiresome day, Your Grace."

"And this was your wager?" Alex spread his hand in an arching fan that swept over the motley crew. "I am guessing you two lost?" He looked pointedly at the now bashful footmen, who nodded their heads in agreement.

"*Taming of the Shrew*," admitted the quiet little soprano in front of him.

Alex covered his mouth with his fist to keep from laughing out loud. How fitting a choice for his willful little fiancée.

Alex attempted to straighten his face. He turned to address the group as a whole and mustered the stern demeanor befitting a man that could control his own household.

They all remained as silent as a tomb.

"Greyland," Alex said. "Come here."

Greyland, looking a tad bit uneasy, stepped forward.

Alex reached out for her, hooked an arm around her waist, and yanked her close.

"Well then," he said, projecting his best Shakespearian voice. "Kiss me, Kate!"

GREYLAND AWOKE SOMETIME LATER in the carriage to Alexander's gentle touch. She lay in his lap, looking up into his blue eyes. He moved the curtain back to look out the window. Greyland admired his beautifully sculpted jawline as she reminisced on their journey thus far. She had learned so much about him. For one, he was the most competitive man she had ever met. That was saying a lot, considering her two brothers were in constant competition. He was patient with her, too.

Thus far, he indulged her more than she had expected—only really putting his foot down when she asked to ride Socrates. Not willing to give up so easily, she had put forth a theory that it was not the mount, but the rider that determined the victor of a race. She knew full well it was both rider and horse that made the winning team, but she desperately wanted to ride the spirited stallion. Unfortunately, her fiancé was not incentivized to test the 'said' theory. He said Socrates was a one-man horse and that it would be too dangerous. Of course, this had made her want to ride him even more. He had a lot to learn about telling her no.

Realizing she was awake, Alex smiled down at her. "Your cat is vicious." He held out his hands, palms turned down, to reveal tiny scratches.

Greyland grinned. "I can see. Where is our ravenous mountain lion?" She looked to the seat opposite them. He was not there.

Alex glanced down to the floor of the carriage and her eyes followed his trajectory. There, at his feet, was an overcrowded Malikite asleep with a fluffy snow-white ball curled neatly on his back.

"Like I said. Savage beast."

"I take it you played with him?" she asked through her giggles.

"I do not know if I would call falling under attack play."

Greyland playfully pushed his arm as she sat up. "What, have you never had a cat before? It is how they show they like you; rather an honor for a feline to pay you any attention."

"Ah, so a feral cat has deemed me, the Duke of Ravenswood, worthy?"

"He is not feral. And it appears he has. However, I would not go shouting it from the rafters. He probably only chose you due to your close proximity to me."

Greyland adjusted herself to see out the window. "Will we be passing over a river, or by a lake anytime soon?"

Alex cocked his head in an amused fashion. "We *will* be crossing by a river. Dare I ask why?"

"Well, I know we are in a hurry, but I would very much like to go for a swim before our wedding. Rinse off the dust from the past three days."

"You wish to bathe in a river, my lady?"

"I used to swim daily on our estate in New Orleans. I have missed the water immensely since our trip to London."

When he gently shook his head, she inquired, "Do not tell me the women in England refrain from swimming?"

He looked back out his window, but the movement had too much jerk to it. She immediately felt foolish.

Christ almighty! The man's mother drowned!

"Oh Alex, I am sorry. I never meant to bring up painful memories."

"It is fine." He gave a reassuring half-smile but kept his gaze set off into the distance of the advancing night.

The carriage wheels continued to roll as if counting the passing of time. Greyland let him have his silence.

"I have tried very hard to put that dreadful day behind me, but it still gets the better of me from time to time," he confessed.

She felt the tendons in his forearm tighten where her hand rested. "I learned how to swim the week after she passed. I thought I could rewind history somehow, and the next time, save her. I practiced swimming that river every day." Alex turned back to face her.

Greyland said softly, "I am sorry for reminding you. I cannot imagine how a child could go through something so dreadful. I never meant to..." She choked on the last words, her emotions getting the better of her.

Alex cupped her face in his hands and pulled her to him. "Never be sorry for me. I have had enough pity. And never fear to be yourself around me, either. I fell in love with you for your uniqueness. You are much like her in many ways. And while I wish you to guard your hasty actions, I will never get tired of your wonderful mouth that always speaks its mind."

He drew her in for a quick kiss and then pulled back again.

"Women and men do not swim together as a rule, but I plan on breaking that one as soon as we get you home. Then you can have the ocean as your bath." His smile narrowed into a sensual smirk.

"I would not want it any other way."

"Tonight, we will sleep in a real bed. I know this quaint little tavern that has the best meat pie. We will all benefit from a good rest. And a bath."

She looked about them, suddenly alert. "Do you think it is safe to slow down for the night?"

"Yes. Anyone who wished to engage with us would have already been reported. I hired two outriders before we left. One set out ahead of us, and one rides behind. If either of them returns with information, we will have time to act."

Greyland snuggled up close to Alexander again, loving how the warmth of his body, combined with his distinctive masculine aroma, sent tiny spirals of energy bursting through her every nerve ending. He pulled her to him. One more night and she would understand just what that tantalizing sensation evolved into.

She heard herself sigh, a mixture of eagerness and fear; she really hoped she would be decent at the act of lovemaking.

ONCE INSIDE THE small bedchamber at the Fox and Hound Tavern, Greyland shrugged out of her long coat and laid it across the footboard of the bed. Alex sank down on the chair beside the fire, that had so thoughtfully been lit. He poured them both a glass of wine from the side table, then removed his jacket.

"Take off your shoes and make yourself comfortable," he said. "They will be bringing a bath up shortly."

"Oh, how wonderful. Thank you." She paused for a minute,

suddenly confused. "Will we be sharing the bed?"

"I have a room right next door," he said, grinning. "Though it pains me to say it, I cannot share a bed with you until tomorrow."

"Alex, we will be wed tomorrow. Surely you can sleep beside me tonight. Why, we have slept together in the carriage."

A knock came before Alex could respond.

"That was quick." He opened the door and beckoned the two men carrying the tub to enter. Four women followed next with buckets of water in each of their hands. Greyland's muscles began to relax just watching the steam rise from the bath as they poured the pails in.

Alex handed one of the men some coinage and then pursued them to the door.

"Are you leaving?" Greyland queried when it looked like he might follow them on out.

Alex appeared to regard the question with great consideration for a moment. "I thought you might like some privacy while you bathed."

"Surely you could just face the other way." She bent over and pulled off one of her tight slippers. The soft rug felt like a cloud beneath her foot. She quickly removed the other bothersome shoe. She had been too many days in corsets and restrictive cage shirts. Her toes suddenly begged to feel the soft carpet without the hindrance of her stockings.

With that singular goal in mind, Greyland hitched her dress up past her knees to the garters tied at her thighs and began working her silk hose loose. A moment passed before she realized the room had gone so quiet you could have heard a pin drop.

She looked up. Alex stared as if he had been cast in stone where he stood.

"Alexander, are you hale?"

He crossed the room in three long strides, placing himself directly in front of her. "I believe you require assistance with your dress."

Faster than any dressing maid Greyland had ever had, he pulled her silk blouse over her head, turned her around, and began working loose the laces of her corset.

"I have done this myself every day since we left London," she said, feeling the need to point this fact out.

His reply came in the form of a soft kiss placed perfectly in between her shoulder blades. *Oh!* He continued to trace kisses up her spine, one vertebra at a time, pausing only to move her hair over one shoulder. Her knees went weak when his hot breath lingered on the nape of her neck.

This had nothing to do with helping her. A nervous shiver raced up her spine.

"Alex?"

"Can I help you out of this?" he purred.

Her equilibrium swayed dangerously. "Please." She more begged than answered.

As if by magic, the corset and over shirt came off and were tossed on the bed. His movements slowed when the only thing left to remove was her thin cotton shift. Greyland felt goosebumps raise to the surface of her skin, though she was certain it was not from a draft.

His fingers slowly skimmed the back of the scooped material. Suddenly, the most basic of Grayland's many articles of clothing became the most coveted. She inhaled slowly as he carefully slipped the only remaining layer off her shoulders, exposing her bare back.

He let the gown hang at her waist for a long moment before gently encouraging the garment over the curve of her hips. It fell to the floor. The cool of the room prickled her bare skin, yet it did nothing to stop the slow smolder that spread throughout her insides.

She heard the floorboards squeak as he took a step back. Greyland closed her eyes and fought to avoid blushing from head to toe under his intense inspection.

"Turn around," he commanded.

She turned slowly to face him, her hands raising bashfully to cover her breasts. Her eyes locked on his. What she saw burning in them was unquestionable admiration and something that closely resembled hunger.

"Please lower your arms."

She swallowed hard and did as asked.

He stared, and finally managed, "My God. You are beautiful."

IX

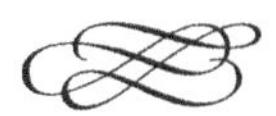

Alexander closed the door to Greyland's room and leaned back against it. He mentally willed his throbbing erection down. He could not believe he had mustered the willpower to leave her there, naked. He hoped the water in his own bath would be cold enough by now to halt his desires.

Just as Alex was deciding that he could walk without a limp, he saw Samson exiting his room further down the hall. Perfecting the mask of nothing-to-see-here, he gestured him over and instructed the butler to stand watch at Greyland's door. Even though Alex thought they were safe, he was not taking any chances.

He quickly bathed, redressed, and headed back to Greyland's room.

"Samson."

"Your Grace?"

"Go get yourself something to eat downstairs. I can manage from here."

"Yes, sir. I will keep my eyes alert to any suspicious activity."

"Thank you, Samson. Enjoy your dinner," he added before giving a quick rap on the solid wood door. "Greyland?"

"Come in."

Alex entered and found her lying on the bed in just a thin night shift. The fire and flickering bedside candle bathed her in a soft warm light. His breathing caught in his throat, and he felt the sudden urge to pinch himself. *Was he dreaming?* This beautiful creature was about to become his. *Forever.*

"You seem to have the advantage on me, my lord. For you have seen me in the flesh, but I have yet to see you."

His pulse quickened. "Are you wishing me to undress, my lady?"

She nodded and bit down on her lower lip. Alex shut his eyes, cautioning himself against falling prey to such unbecoming behavior —like deflowering his betrothed before the wedding day—but he was already unbuttoning his shirt. Who the hell was he kidding? He had never been a saint. Plus, she was hardly making honorable decisions easy at the moment.

Alex watched her watch him as he undressed. He wanted her in a way that shocked his very soul.

She kept her eyes glued to him as he removed his shirt and tossed the garment off before undoing his trousers. Not removing his eyes from hers, he noted how she eagerly followed his progress. As he began to slowly push his britches lower, her eyes widened, and he instantly grew harder.

He dropped the last article of clothing. Greyland's tongue darted out to wet her lips as she studied *every* inch of him. The appraisal was exhilarating.

Alex forced himself to stay rooted in place. She still had time to change her mind, *seconds,* really. If he took a step forward, there would be no going back from what was to come next. Her gaze scanned his body and when she bit her lip a second time, he thought he might not survive the short distance he had to travel to reach the bed.

Greyland drank him in. She was not sure she could have prepared herself for the sculpture that was Alexander Hamilton. And then he grinned. *Pure mischief.* She knew she was done for.

His chest was broad and tan. Her eyes followed his hands down the chiseled ridges to his belt. Greyland's heart almost stopped with anticipation as he slowly unbuckled it and began pulling it through the loops. Her body practically hummed in response as the leather slid free of the trousers. If she had ever held any doubts about how she would react to seeing a man naked for the first time, they were gone. She was unabashedly lustful beyond any point of reason.

His deft fingers began unbuttoning the closure to his trousers. Her eyes watched in fascination as the tip of his manhood was revealed. Button by button, inch by inch of him was unleashed until he fell free and was standing at attention in front of her unblinking eyes.

He would never fit.

All her mustered confidence skittered away.

"Greyland?" His voice broke her trance. "I do not think I can wait to be with you until tomorrow."

Her heart pounded against her chest, a mix of excitement and trepidation as he sauntered toward her.

"I told you I would never hurt you on purpose, but I have heard a lady's first time might have some discomfort."

She watched him search her eyes for understanding.

"I know. Perkin told me it would, but Edward said it would be only for a little bit. After that, women love the act."

Alex paused mid-stride and tilted his head, a gesture she had grown to love.

"Your brothers discussed such things with you?"

"You must remember, I had no female family members to talk to. I think Perkin meant to scare me off from the deed and Edward was just being honest. Regardless, I am not scared...nor am I fragile." She said this with a confidence she herself was unconvinced of. "I want to be with you tonight."

Alex moved another step to the edge of the bed and looked down into her eyes. "Let us take this slowly. And please, can you not mention your family again tonight?" He said this last with a grin.

Her eyes flitted from his blue ones back down to his massive erection. She wordlessly nodded and worried her bottom lip. Tentatively, she leaned forward and reached a curious hand out to touch his stomach. He was a rock; a warm, smooth rock. She let her hands explore his hips bones, coming to a stop just inches away from his manhood. Attentively, with just the pads of her fingers, she touched it.

It jumped.

Startled, she felt herself smile and looked up to his face. The set to his jaw was hard and his eyes had grown hooded. She could not tell if he was in pain or pleasure. Keeping her eyes on his, she traced the outline of his warm member with her fingertips.

He groaned.

A yearning within her bloomed, in perfect time, with her newfound confidence. She took him firmly in hand. He was like steel wrapped in silk. "Marvelous," she whispered.

He pulsed in her grasp, and to her disbelieving eyes, increased in size.

Before she could blink, she was pinned on her back, her night shift pulled down over her shoulders, exposing her breast.

"My turn," he said.

Alex assaulted her with tantalizing kisses that started on her neck and then descended. She ran her hands through his curls and gasped with unexpected pleasure as he cupped one breast in his hand and slid his lips around the other.

He pulled her shift further down as he continued to trail kisses along her stomach. She instinctively raised her hips. In one fluid motion, he yanked the garment over her bottom and threw it on the floor. He lowered her gently back to the pillow and resumed his seductive kisses, moving south.

Greyland squirmed under his masterful hands and arched her back.

He swept his arm around her waist, pulling her closer. She twisted and writhed under his wonderfully tortuous fingers. He placed a steadying, heavy hand on her belly and did the unthinkable; he parted her womanhood with his lips and tasted her with his tongue. She growled his name pleadingly, for what she knew not; she just knew she needed more. She felt him pull back and she dared to open her eyes.

He moved over her and positioned himself between her thighs, gently spreading her legs wide. He lowered himself to his elbows, careful not to put too much of his weight onto her.

Her breath was coming hard with anticipation.

Alex placed his forehead to hers. "On this night, I thee wed. You will be mine forever, body and soul."

Greyland lifted her eyes and locked them with his. His piercing blue orbs emanated heat as he studied her. She took in his words and repeated them.

He exhaled roughly and ravaged her with a savage kiss as his erection teased the sensitive warmth that his fingers had just recently abandoned.

Gently, he pushed into her with a patience that must have cost him greatly, for his breathing all but stopped and his heart hammered against her chest. She was surprised how willingly her body made room for the invasion. Finally, he reached what she thought might be his stopping point, for she was sure that was all she could take. And then he pushed resolutely past that threshold and sunk firmly into her.

A whimper escaped her lips.

He stilled immediately.

But the sting was over as quickly as it had developed, replaced by an aching need to have more. Greyland lifted her hips encouragingly. She wrapped her arms under his shoulders and pulled him closer. She had no idea what she was doing, but her body certainly seemed to have an idea.

He laced one of his hands behind her neck, holding the weight of her head. "I love you," he said as he began to withdraw.

"No!" Her brain was not thinking, only her body. "I mean, yes!"

He cocked his head and stared down at her. "Are you all right? I am not hurting you, am I?"

"Yes, I love you," she rasped out, frustrated with herself for even speaking. "No, do not let it be over." The muscles of her body restricted around his large shaft.

He smiled. "Oh, I am just getting started, but keep doing that."

He pushed slowly back into her, filling her to the hilt. She gasped and clung to his shoulders. His hips rotated, exploring her and then he surged forward again.

Her body caught the movement and matched his setting rhythm. It was a slow build at first, a flame burning toward oil, and then the need intensified. Greyland felt an urgency ignite within her body like she could have never imagined. Her legs wrapped around his waist, giving him full access. He took it. His hands squeezing her ass cheeks hard as he lifted her upwards and drove her into the mattress. Faster and faster, his body pumping longer and harder, and with every thrust, he claimed her completely.

Unable to keep his frantic rhythm she closed her eyes and squeezed tightly to his powerful body, holding on for dear life. Her nails dug into his back and her body began to convulse when the headboard started to crash against the wall. Her toes curled and dug into his ass cheeks and her head dropped back between her shoulders. *"My God!"*

She screamed out as her world broke apart like shards of glass tossed across an endless galaxy of blinding light.

Alex muttered some warning, or oath, right before he surged one last time and a liquid heat filled her. His breath shuddered as he continued to slowly pump into her. The effect was intoxicating and lit her nerves right back on fire. She wrapped herself around every part of him she could reach and milked the last sensations out of his body.

He collapsed, wrapped his arms tightly around her and rolled them to the side. Still firmly rooted inside her, sweat glistening his brow, he leaned in and kissed her. She continued to shudder and shake like a leaf caught in a strong wind.

Her muscles tensed around him as the last wave hit.

"Careful dear," he said. "Or you will rile me again before my heart rate has calmed."

They lay there in their mutual bliss as seconds passed into minutes. Grayland looked at her skin. *Would it forever glow like this?* she wondered. That was singlehandedly the most amazing thing she had ever experienced.

"That was nothing like horses," she finally said between breaths.

"What?"

"I have seen horses breeding. At our old estate in New Orleans. Edward said humans do it the same way."

"Oh!" Alex said, grinning. "Well, not exactly, but that position is fun, too."

"Can we try sometime?"

Alex laughed. "How did I get so lucky?"

A FRENZIED KNOCK startled Alex awake. He untangled Greyland from his body and grabbed his robe. The knock came again.

"Your Grace," Samson hissed through the thick wooden door.

Alex opened the door to his butler's ashen face. "What is wrong?"

"Riders! Heading this way from London—eight of them—all wearing the McGreggor's crest on their tartans!"

"Take the men and carriages. Head east, away from Brighton. Greyland and I will make better time with just Socrates and the mare."

Samson looked worried. "Should we not go with you? What about Lady Greyland? I…I…I just—"

"No!" Alex grabbed the sleeping kitten from the end of the bed and thrust it into Samson's hands. He opened the mahogany gun case Greyland had given him and handed one of the revolvers to Samson. "Go now! We must break up. I will take Malikite."

Samson nodded and took to the Inns' stairs.

Alex rushed to Greyland. He tossed his robe and grabbed his shirt. "Greyland, darling, get up. We need to leave...Now!"

Greyland opened her eyes and was on her feet and donning her dress before he could have counted to five. He moved behind her and assisted with the stays before quickly slipping into his trousers. He took the second revolver from the case and another pistol from his saddlebag and shoved them into his jacket.

Greyland glanced back at the bed. "Samson has the cat," Alex answered her unvoiced concern. "Come!" His free hand on her elbow, he guided her from the room.

They ran to the barn where the footmen were already readying their horses. Alex handed Greyland a short blade before tossing her up on her mare.

He mounted Socrates and they galloped out, with Malikite keeping pace beside them.

They stayed to the road as they pushed the horses harder. After a while, Malikite veered into the woods. Greyland glanced nervously at Alex. "He will keep up. He just needs to slow for a while."

Alex knew if they kept the pace, they would soon be entering the village of Foxburg, where the vicar would perform the ceremony. He would not like doing so in the middle of the night, but Alex had to make their marriage official. The McGreggor's would not dare steal a lady already married to a lord of the Realm, but an American lady without a notable husband was fair game.

As if summoned from a bad play, thundering hoofbeats could now be heard off in the near distance.

They would not make it in time.

There was no way Greyland's young mare could outrun a dozen mounts the size of Socrates and endurance trained. Still, Alex pushed the stallion harder, willing the spirited mare beside him to keep up.

The smaller Bay gave it her best effort but with every stride, she fell farther behind.

Alex pulled in hard on the reins, bringing Socrates, snorting, eyes wide with anticipation, to an abrupt halt.

Greyland slowed the mare at the same time.

Before she could speak, Alex dismounted, pulled her from the saddle, and thrust her back up onto Socrates.

"What are you doing?" Panic needled her voice.

"You said you wanted to ride him. Here is your chance. Ride as hard as you can and do not look back. He will get you to the village. From there you will take immediate sanctuary in the chapel." Alex pushed the single-shot pistol into her hands. "Just in case."

"I am not leaving you!" She set her chin in a brave line, but her bottom lip quivered.

"I demand it."

"No!"

"I will talk to them, buy them—whatever it takes, Greyland, but you must get away. I cannot protect you against all of them."

He thought she would refuse him again but when he saw the tears building in her eyes, he knew some logic had risen within her stubborn mind.

He slapped his hand on Socrates' rump and sent the horse off, clots of mud flying. "Do not look back!"

Alex watched them disappear into the night and exhaled. With the stallion's speed and strength and Greyland's light frame, they would easily outrun the riders.

He mounted Greyland's mare, turned her a couple of times in a tight circle, then squared her up on the road to face whatever uncertainty was charging their way.

THE COOL NIGHT wind slashed at Greyland's cheeks as she hunkered lower on the stallion's back. With her neck inches from his, she made herself as light as she could for the animal. He seemed to approve, moving into an even faster gallop. She let him be her eyes in the black night. She could feel Socrates's heartbeat with every long stride, and she knew he would get her to safety.

Through the whistling wind and thunderous pawing of the earth, a wolf howled close by. She knew it had to be Malikite because Socrates paid it no attention at all. They were almost there; she could see the torches.

She kept the pace as she entered the first row of shops, hoping no one would be on the road at this hour. The small chapel appeared on the next street, and she slowed to a trot as she came upon it. A stable boy sleeping outside a nearby tavern awoke at the sound of her hooves and leaped up to assist her. She brought the frothing steed to a stop at the child's awestruck feet.

He took the reins and moved to help her down, but she landed beside him before he could glance up.

"Wash him down, then feed and water him. If anyone asks, his owner is a man staying at the inn above the tavern." Greyland tossed him two silvers and ran for the chapel doors.

EIGHT STEEDS the size of Socrates bore down on Alex where he waited astride Greyland's mare on the road. He had to hold the young Bay steady as she nervously sidestepped to their thunderous approach. The eight riders drew up their mounts only a few feet from Alex.

The middle rider, who was the smallest among the group and clearly in charge, had reddish-brown hair and looked to be about Alexander's size. The other seven men were all the size of boulders. The odds of Alex making it out of this unscathed were next to impossible.

"Ravenswood," the man said. "You have something of mine. Where is she?"

Alexander involuntarily flexed his fist on the revolver at his hip. "And who may be inquiring as to my wife's whereabouts, might I ask?"

The man's mouth twisted into a grimace and his eyes darkened. "I am Colin McGreggor, son of Conner McGreggor, and the future laird." He leaned in indolently and crossed his forearms over the horn of his saddle. "And I know you are bluffing."

He motioned three of his men forward. "Search out the village. Start with the church. Drag her out if you have to—I care not for English sanctuary." He smiled wryly at Alex.

The three knights spurred their horses into a gallop toward the sleeping village.

"You are too late, Colin," Alex sneered, his tone deep and wild as he fought down the dreaded feeling crawling up his spine.

"Ah, so we are familiar now, are we? Well then, *Alexander*, I know you were to be married in that village and clearly, one of you is not there yet. So, the chit is still a maid waiting on a husband, and that man will be me. Be she willing or not."

Three of the men beside him chuckled. "She won't be no maid come morning," a swarthy Neanderthal taunted.

"I have already had that privilege," Alex said evenly. "She is mine in *every way* but on paper, Colin."

Colin drew his pistol and leveled the gun at Alexander's head. "Drop that gun at your side or I will tell my men that they may have a turn at my bonny-bride when I am done with her." He drew his stallion closer to Alexander's mare.

"You would not dare."

"Want to find out? I am losing my patience with you."

Alex released the revolver. It hit the ground with a thud.

Colin snickered. "Smart man. I do hate spoiled goods, but I guess I should thank you. Now I can fuck her as hard as I want once, I claim her as my own!"

Alexander launched from his mount and hit Colin so hard that both men went catapulting backward over the side of Colin's horse. A shot rang out. Alex heard it connect with one of Colin's men.

Alex scrambled to right himself amongst the whipping tails and dust being kicked up by the frightened horses. He fell on Colin and proceeded to pummel him. A horse assisted him when, in its frenzied attempt to escape, its hoof landed Colin a hard kick to the ribs. Alex searched the ground for his gun. His hands mercifully landed on the handle, and he jumped to his feet.

Through the chaos, Alex heard the steely slice of an arrow cutting the cool night air. He looked up just in time to see it embed itself in one of the rider's throat.

A chainmail fist hit Alex hard in the back of his head and his eyes lost focus. He spun, trying to locate his new attacker. Alex drew his pistol and blindly shot. Someone kicked his knees out from under him.

He hit the ground hard just as Colin's ruddy face lunged at him. They rolled, resuming their brawl amongst the dirt, arrows, and trampling horse hooves.

Another arrow sailed through the air and connected with the last standing man's thigh. Alex heard footsteps, but he could not tell if they were retreating or advancing. He hoped they were retreating.

Colin twisted beneath him as he fought to get leverage. Alex wildly smashed his fist into the Irishman's face. He swung again and McGreggor's head rolled back, unconscious.

A thick arm wrapped around Alexander's middle, dragging him off Colin's now limp body.

Alex flailed his arms to free himself from his new attacker, but the man only tossed him to the side like a sack of flour.

He scrambled, finding his feet and quickly righting himself in preparation for the next fight.

A familiar, grinning face stared back at him.

"Time to go, old chap."

GREYLAND WATCHED in terror as the clergyman's body hit the stone floor with a resounding thud. The hulking giant that had snapped the old man's neck took two long strides toward her. She pulled the pistol from her gown and held it out straight, arms shaking. The beast of a man only sneered through bloodshot eyes and brown teeth. In one arching motion, he swung his arm up faster than her eyes could follow and sent the gun flying.

She turned to run but only got a few feet before he grabbed her by the back of the hair and yanked her hard against his chest, crushing the breath from her lungs. The smell of ale and unwashed body assaulted her nose.

"There be but two ways we do this," he slurred, and turned her roughly to face him.

She struggled in his vice-like grip. He only held her tighter. Greyland was sure her wrist would break.

He moved his lips to hers. "Maybe we have a sampling before I deliver ye to me laird."

She thrashed about even harder as he tried to reach her lips with his. "Hold still, ye wen—"

A bullet came through his forehead, splattering chunks of bone, blood, and brain-matter all over Greyland's face.

The man stared at her with dead eyes before falling forward and knocking her to the ground.

She screamed again and struggled to heave the massive weight off her. From her pinned position, she noticed a second Irishman locked in battle with a man by the door.

She rolled the body to the side and scrambled to her feet just in time to see a third mountainous man charging her. Greyland skirted to the right, narrowly avoiding her new attacker. He succeeded on his second swipe and snatched her to him as she attempted to retrieve the dagger.

He drew back a massive fist, but before he could deliver the punishing blow, something low to the ground, dark and fast moved behind him. Greyland twisted in his grasp and ducked right as he swung and connected only with air.

A streak of black fur was all her eyes had time to register before Malikite tore open the man's throat.

He fell, gurgling on the floor, razor-sharp teeth slashing at his face.

Greyland turned away from the sight, as the stench of death filled her nostrils.

She doubled over and retched.

The sound of someone hitting a wall had her quickly back on her feet. To her horror, the smaller brown-haired man that had come to her rescue was losing his battle against the Irishman with the knife.

Without thought, Greyland unsheathed the dagger Alex had given her and flew at the barbarian. The blade connected with bone. He whirled around, eyes blazing.

"Down!" yelled the brown-haired man.

Greyland dropped to the floor just as a bullet exploded through the Irishman's chest.

ADRENALINE AND MALICE coursed a river of acid through Alexander's veins. He fought to calm the rage still warring in his body. He wanted to keep hitting Colin McGreggor until there was nothing left of his face.

But that was not going to happen. Not here. Not tonight. He kept his sights trained on Thomas, who was currently evaluating him like one might a rabid dog.

"Alex?" his best friend ventured cautiously.

Alex ran the back of his hand roughly over his wet mouth. "So, you are not a mirage."

Alex flicked the blood from his hand and pivoted slowly, taking in the aftermath. The dust was still settling. Men were dead. Perkin and Edward were working quickly to restrain one of Colin's brethren. Another man lay moaning, an arrow notched clean through his thigh. Horses were scattered; some could still be heard galloping away. If mayhem had a visual, this would be it.

"How many times must I save your ass?'"

Alex turned back to his best friend. He still could not believe he had lived through it. His eyes met Thomas'.

"Greyland!" The memory of Colin stating he would not honor sanctuary dragged Alex forcefully out of whatever fog his head was still recovering from. "She is still in danger. The village!"

He scanned the horses. The smart mare had bolted when he had left her back. Alex made for one of the remaining steeds.

Thomas grabbed hold of Alex by the shoulder. "Not without me."

Alex regarded him with a silent understanding and made a quick search of the ground for the revolver. He found it and tucked it into his jacket before swinging up into the saddle. Thomas retrieved his horse and did the same.

Edward's head snapped to attention. "What are you waiting on? For the love of God, *go*!"

Perkin glanced up, a look of unnerving calmness residing in his icy blue orbs. "We will be right behind you."

Alex knew without a shadow of a doubt who had loosed those arrows.

Edward was a fighter, like himself.

Perkin was a natural born killer.

GREYLAND SHOOK as she fought her exhausted limbs' desire to remain where she had fallen. The metallic stench of blood curled around her, suffocating with its hot, humid cloak. She managed enough strength to command Malikite to *"go"* when he padded up to her side, licking his kill from his fangs. She knew any minute the villagers would come running and she did not want the half-breed to get speared by a pitchfork. The dog bolted over the bodies and out the church doors.

Two arms encircled her waist, assisting her to her feet. She looked up into her savior's concerned gaze.

"Are you hurt?" The man removed a handkerchief from his pocket and began tenderly wiping the blood from her face.

She blinked and did a double-take. Alexander's eyes looked back at her, yet the rest of the man's features were softer compared to her fiancé's rugged face. This man's eyes also held an unfettered kindness, something her dark lord kept shielded away from the general public.

"I am fine..."

The village folk came barreling through the church doors, armed and ready.

The stranger pulled her closer to him. "These men attacked and killed the clergyman and were attempting to do the same to this young woman who was seeking sanctuary!" He had to shout to be heard over the crowd.

A shrieking woman rushed forward to cradle the clergyman's lifeless body in her arms. Greyland recognized her as the kind, old lady who had admitted her entrance into the church just minutes before the old man's brutal death. She had left Greyland to talk with her husband while she had gone to warm some tea.

"Let me through!" A voice bellowed out from the thick of onlookers. Greyland's eyes shot up to see Alexander. Bloodied, but alive.

His stare tethered to hers: rage, relief, and unbridled fear emanating from her fiancé.

"My God..." he pushed through the throng of villagers. "Are you hurt?"

"No." She felt hot tears running down her cheeks as she started to rush forward, but a protective hand shot out and held her in place.

Alexander eyed the hand on her wrist, his whole body growing taut, like a bow string ready to snap. His stealthy gaze followed the stranger's arm up to his face, as if noticing the man at her side for the first time.

"Henry."

Greyland felt her rescuer become apprehensively still.

"Alexander."

She quickly looked from Alex to the younger man beside her as realization sunk in.

His brother!

Alexander's penetrating glare bore down on the man as if the burning embers in his eyes might shoot flames on command. But Henry stood firm and pushed Greyland behind him.

"He saved me!" She managed to get out from behind the man's broad shoulders, though she was not exactly sure which brother needed to be assured of that fact.

Alexander halted in his already advancing tracks. "Is this true?"

"Yes." Greyland ducked down and around Henry and leaped into Alexander's arms, burying her face in his chest.

She was not surprised when she heard Thomas' baritone, not far behind Alex, take control of the townspeople. He ordered some of the men to dig graves and carry out the bodies and other men to ride out of town and assist on the road.

The earl then instructed a few town women to start cleaning the chapel before telling a young man to ride out and inform the local lord's manor that he would be having guests—both in his house, and in his dungeon.

ALEXANDER HUGGED Greyland to him tightly, bowing his head to kiss the top of her head as he whispered assuring words into her hair. But his eyes never strayed from Henry's.

Alex had imagined many times what he would do and say when he met his brother again. How many sleepless nights had passed with him thinking about Henry and how he had surely killed their father? Henry had been feuding with the Duke of Ravenswood. He had taken money from their father's Man of Affairs and run. The duke had disowned him.

All that coupled with the deeply seeded fact that Alex had hated Henry since the day he was born. It all made sense that Henry would be the one to murder their father. No one else would have dared. No one else had a motive. No one else hated the Duke of Ravenswood more...

Except for Colin McGreggor.

Alex had been so blinded by his continued disapproval of his brother that he had not seen clearly; he had been wrong. Henry had not shot their father...the McGreggors had.

Now, standing before Alex was the very man, he had vowed to run through just days ago. The same man who had just saved Greyland's life.

Someone yelled that one of the Irishmen's throats had been ripped out. Alex looked around at the overturned room. Sure enough, a man laid in a puddle of his own blood, his jugular clearly missing.

His sights fell back on his brother.

"I might have had a little help from your dog, and the lady," Henry said, by way of an explanation.

Alex slowly peeled Greyland from his chest and placed one gentle finger on her chin. "Did you scream for help, alerting Henry to your plight?" Her translucent sea-green eyes salted with tears. "Oh, darling." Alex squeezed her back against his chest. "You did what you needed to survive."

She sniffled into his jacket sleeve. "I stabbed him through the neck with your dagger."

Alexander stood, stunned, absorbing the confession.

The edge of Henry's mouth turned up. "I should have known you would not be satisfied with a typical wife."

Alex soothed down Greyland's hair. "No, I do not suppose so."

Greyland's head suddenly snapped up. "Alex! Did you kill Colin? Is he still out there?"

"There is nothing to fear from him anymore," he asserted. "You are safe."

She softened again into his embrace. Alex inclined his head to his brother. "I owe you much, starting with an apology."

Henry said nothing at first, seemingly weighing his words. Finally, after a long silence, he replied, "I accept your apology, brother. There is much I must say to you, but for now I believe our time would be best spent getting your lovely lady to a proper residence."

"Agreed." Alex turned to Thomas when the earl stepped up beside him. "Will you take Greyland to Lord Humphrey's manor?"

"Right away."

"Make sure she has every comfort she requires," Alex added. "I will join you there with her brothers once I have seen to everything back on the road."

Greyland jerked her head at the mention of Perkin and Edward, worry foreshadowing her eyes anew.

"They are hale," Alex hurried. "Seems we all had guardian angels on our shoulders tonight." He kissed her forehead. "Now, please do not fight me on this. Go with Thomas. I will meet you there shortly," he added in a tone he hoped brokered no debate.

To his surprise, she held her tongue and allowed the earl to lead her away from the horrific scene.

Alexander refocused his attention on his Henry. The once thin lad had filled out since he last saw him. But somewhere deep inside, Alex also knew this was the first time he was really *seeing* his younger brother. A feeling of shame crept up inside him. He had never given the boy a chance. Henry was not to blame for his birth, no more than Alex had been to blame for his mother's death.

As he stood staring into his own eyes—his father's eyes—Alexander suddenly felt an odd sense of calm. All his years of angry resentment seemed a burden greatly lessened. Odd how the dark paved a way for the light.

X

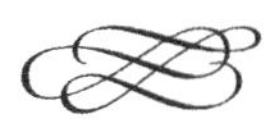

Laughter echoed through the manor's halls as Greyland hastened past the escorting servant and into the dining room. To her delight, she found Edward, Perkin, Thomas, Henry, Alex, and a middle-aged man she guessed to be the lord of the house. They all stood abruptly. Perkin and Edward rushed to her.

Edward boldly pushed Perkin aside and scooped his sister into his arms, swinging her around as he had done when they were kids.

Perkin narrowed an irritated scowl on his younger brother but waited for him to set her down. He then wrapped her in a hug of his own making. "I am so glad you are safe. Did you get some sleep?"

Greyland took a moment to enjoy his comforting touch and familiar scent. "Yes, a little."

Perkin gently released her.

A feast lay on the table behind him. For a man that had been awakened in the middle of the night and forced to entertain on a moment's notice, the residing lord sure did not disappoint his guests.

Alexander smiled down as he took his turn embracing her. "I did not want to wake you. You needed the rest."

He then turned his head toward their host, Lord Humphrey. "Thank you for getting her settled so quickly last night."

Lord Humphrey smiled at Greyland. "But of course. Were the accommodations to your liking?'

"I must confess, I think I was asleep before my head could sink into the pillow," Greyland replied. "Thank you."

"I only wish your arrival had come under better circumstances." Lord Humphrey reclaimed his seat. Everyone else followed suit. "Such a nasty ordeal you had to endure. I am glad you were able to apprehend the dastardly fellows."

Greyland turned her head sharply to Alex. He only told her they had been dealt with. As soon as she left the church with Thomas, her body and mind had all but given out. She was glad she was riding with the earl, for Greyland was not sure she would have remained upright on her own. She had fallen asleep against his chest before they were even out of the village, waking only when they arrived at Lord Humphrey's.

From there, everything leading up to slumber was a bit foggy. Lord Humphrey had been overseeing the dungeon preparations when she and Thomas had arrived, so his butler had escorted her to a ready bedchamber. She had no idea how long she had slept but when her eyes opened, a thin hue of tangerine had bathed her room, indicating the dawning day.

Alex, cleverly following where her mind had traveled, filled in the missing space of time. "Thomas and your brothers captured all of what remained of Colin's men. They are in the dungeon awaiting the Bow Street Runners. We have sent word to The Queen as well. She will be informed of all that has transpired."

"All hale The Queen!" Thomas shouted, clearly a good way into his cups.

Greyland could not fault him for that. She raised her glass.

Edward, not far behind Thomas in celebration, rose from the table and loudly clinked his glass to the earl's. "Here, here!"

The others joined in with sounds of chairs pushing back and crystal ringing out as high-spirited praise was passed around the table. Greyland smiled, but remained seated, taking a moment to reflect on the events of the past twelve hours while the men rejoiced in their victory.

Last night, and all its many horrors, was over. The Queen was being notified. Her soldiers would be arriving to take the prisoners back to the Tower of London. *They were all safe.* Colin McGreggor was no longer a threat. It was as if it had been a bad dream.

Except, it had not been a mere dream, something one could simply wake from and dismiss.

Earlier, after being shown to her chambers, Greyland had submerged herself in a hot bath. Then watched with pensive vision as the water turned a pale pink from the dead knight's blood. The last traces of the man's life washed down the drain, but the solemn stench of death still clung to her senses. She knew an invisible and haunting scar had formed from the trauma; a scar that would remain unseen on her soul from this day forth.

From across the table, a hand reached out and took hers. She looked up into Henry's eyes. They were reading her unspoken thoughts with a look of genuine concern. Alex, newly reseated beside her, visibly tensed.

Greyland cast her eyes quizzically in Alexander's direction when his hand found her thigh under the table. Where was this possessiveness coming from, she wondered? *Henry was his brother.* She made a mental note to discuss this with him at a later time.

For now, she turned her attention back to Henry, who withdrew his hand from hers as if he had sensed better of the action. "No woman should have to witness man's vengeful wrath. I am sorry you had to endure such."

Perkin, ever observant, chimed in. "Henry has filled us in on exactly what transpired in the church." He nodded in Henry's direction. "I am forever in his debt for him coming to your aid."

Her brother's eyes turned dark, and the room took on a more somber note as they all collectively reflected. "I do not want to think what would have happened if he had not been there." Perkin's voice had turned to ice.

"Let us not forget that she saved me as well," Henry added, forcing the conversation back into a more positive light. "And Malikite earned his share of table scraps for the rest of his life."

"Malikite...where is he? Did he find us?" Greyland asked, suddenly worried anew.

"He is out in the stable," Alex confirmed. "He showed up while you were sleeping."

Greyland breathed a sigh of relief. Turning back to Henry, she asked, "How did you find yourself in the church? Just when I thought I was done for, you appeared?"

Henry lowered his eyes, obviously uncomfortable with the praise, and the question. He took a long sip of his wine. "It is really a simple story of just being in the right place at the right time. From the tavern's window, I saw you enter the church doors. Then moments later, I saw the Irishmen enter...ah, rather by force. I was halfway up the steps when I heard a scream."

He tipped his head to the left and grinned, "The rest, as we say, is history."

"A toast to Malikite!" Thomas called out.

A resounding laugh echoed out around the room, followed by more wine served and more retelling of the past night's events. Greyland felt her own nerves relaxing as she sipped from her glass and listened to the men pat themselves on the back.

The levity continued until a footman arrived to inform Lord Humphrey that the guards, he summoned from the neighboring village, had arrived.

Greyland stood and excused herself from the table as the conversation turned to exporting the prisoners. Alex swiveled his head in her direction with a questioning look in his eyes.

"I would like to lay down for a little while longer," she said. "I am still fairly exhausted."

She leaned down and kissed him on the cheek. Alex smiled and nodded his consent. "I will come to check in on you in a bit."

Greyland gave a quick curtsy to the other guest before retreating down the hall. She was not being dishonest, she told herself. She was indeed going to bed. She just needed to see to one last thing for herself before she did.

PERKIN RELAXED his left hip into the edge of the windowsill and beckoned Alex to the far side of the room. "I am dying to know something, Alexander."

"Yes?"

"Last night, right before your fisticuffs with Colin McGreggor, the man pulled a gun on you rather unexpectedly."

Alex raised his eyebrows, feigning a lack of memory in an attempt to stall the conversation. He had not known at the time that Greyland's brothers and Thomas were hiding in the tree line. Had they heard every word he had said about having already taken Greyland's virginity?

"It was all such a blur," Alex said. "The man was belligerent in his bride lust. Our conversation accelerated quite quickly once he began describing the things he wished to do to her."

"And yet," Perkin's said, his focus sharpening, "it was *his* gun that got the most agitated, not yours?"

Alex knew this was a losing battle. "Perkin, you know how much I love your sister, and in my eyes, she is already my wife. We just need a church to seal the binding." Alex hoped Perkin's fists were not nearly as hard as Edward's, though he knew he deserved it.

Perkin, to his credit, had an exceptional card face. Better than anyone Alex had ever seen, with the exception of Richard Kingston.

"In your eyes?" Perkin repeated.

"Yes."

"Tell me, Alex. What side of your face hurts the most from your brawl last night?"

Alex exhaled. "If you are going to hit me, I would prefer it to be my right side."

Perkin's eyes cut sharply to the window just as Alex was preparing for the blow. "Where did Greyland say she was going?" Concern edged into his normally tempered voice.

"Her bedchamber… Why?" Alex pivoted to peer out the window.

"Edward!" Perkin barked out across the room.

Alexander scanned Lord Humphrey's courtyard. As expected, the guards had already loaded up the prisoners to take to London. The Irishmen stood locked in two large cages set on wheels behind a horse. And then he saw what had obviously caught Perkin's eye.

"Bloody hell! She would not dare."

Both men bolted as Perkin cursed, "Of course she would!"

GREYLAND GLARED into the heated eyes of her once intended. She was able to discern who Colin McGreggor was the moment she spied him lounging against the iron bars of his rolling prison like a bored prince. He might have been attractive, if not for all the blood crusting his face and the swelling of both his eyes and lips.

He sat in his cage with another surly-looking Irishman. Both men raked her up and down with their lustful eyes as she approached. "Well, well, you are a beauty. Are ye sure you do not want to go with me and live like The Queen you are?" Colin cooed. "I could make you very happy."

"Never." She stood her ground. "I do not desire to be a queen and I already have a true love."

"Then why did you traipse all the way down here? Away from your…*true love*." He emphasized the last two words with the flutter of his eyelashes.

His mocking proved effective in provoking her. If there was one thing Greyland detested, it was being made to feel like a foolish girl; too unaccustomed to the world around her to differentiate myth from fact. But that was exactly what he wanted. *To push her.* Colin McGreggor was a mean man, used to getting what he wanted through manipulation, brute-force, and riding the back of his family name. He was not the first man she had met like this, and he would not be the last.

Greyland looked him straight in the eyes. "I wanted to look into the eyes of my enemy and take the measure of you. And I wanted you to see me. So, you will fully understand what you can never have, by heart or by force, should you ever fall to such immeasurable folly again."

The future Irish laird's laugh was abrupt and guttural, but it lasted a touch too long. *She had stumped him.* "She even speaks like a goddamn queen!" he roared to the other prisoner.

Colin then turned back to Greyland, fully recovered. "Oh, trust me, I have seen you well. And my only enemy will be the ones that harbor you from me. You are going to be mine. By heart, or by force." He grinned and reached his hands through the bars. "Now, why don't you give me a goodbye kiss before I go?"

Greyland stepped back from the grasp and collided with a wall. Before she could contemplate where the wall had come from, a hand grabbed her by the wrist, and she was spun in place.

Greyland stared up into the stormy eyes of her one true love. Colin suddenly looked like a puppy by comparison.

Drat!

Perkin roared at the guards to be off from somewhere nearby. Her brother sounded as livid as Alex looked, but it was very clear which one of them now thought she was his to protect.

Before she could mutter a word, Alexander turned on his heels, forcing her to keep pace with his long strides, he marched back to the manor. She had to take two steps to his every one, lest he be dragging her. His hold on her showed no mercy as they made their way across the courtyard and through the manor's main doors.

Making a left, then a right, they arrived at Lord Humphrey's library. Alexander flung open the doors, terrifying an unsuspecting servant dusting off books.

"Out!" he ordered.

The man clambered past them.

Alex issued a final command before pushing Greyland into the room. "Make sure no one comes anywhere near this room." With that, he slammed the doors closed.

"Alexander, I do not think my brothers would care to find us unaccompanied together in a room," Greyland reasoned. "We are not yet married in the eyes of God."

Alex did not answer. He just stood, deathly absent of words, facing the double doors. The sound of the lock turning was the only sound.

"Your brothers should be the least of your concerns, dear wife."

Greyland felt a shiver crawl over her skin. *Dear Lord, he was mad.* She suddenly felt like an errant child. "I believe you might be overreacting just a tad."

He faced her and closed the distance between them before she could even consider an escape.

"You lied to me!"

"I...I just changed my mind. I did not lie." She tried to stand her ground, but the intensity of his stare drove her to retreat a step.

He matched it.

Suddenly the back of her legs connected with the back of the sofa, pinning her in place.

"Please." The word came out like a plea. It was hard to breathe with his form stealing all the light and air from the room.

Alex glowered down at her. "Please, what? Please let you go back out there? Where Colin might be able to get his hands around your pretty little neck and snap it? Or please, do not do it myself?"

Greyland's breath hitched in her throat. She had never seen him so enraged.

"Both, I suppose."

He turned away and stalked the length of the room.

Fresh oxygen filled her nostrils, and she greedily took it in. Her limbs warred between wanting to collapse right where she stood and needing to reach out to him.

She should calm him somehow. He was a man that needed to be in control, and she had tested that by doing only as she pleased. She should say something, do something, to pacify the raging beast.

No sooner did the thought enter her mind, he turned, moving swiftly back across the room to stand in front of the sofa. He took a seat. "Come here."

Greyland blinked at his quick change of pace. Maybe he was ready to see reason. *Good.*

She walked around the sofa to stand in front of him. "I am glad you have come to the conclusion we should discuss this matter in a more civilized fashion and—"

He snapped his hand out and grabbed her, dragging her effortlessly over his knee.

"What are you doing?" She squirmed and fought for solid ground. "Have you gone mad!"

"Something someone should have done a long time ago. And yes, I am quite mad at the moment." He lifted her skirts, exposing her thin undergarments. "My hands are in need of striking something, so it might as well be your stubborn, beautiful bottom."

"Alexander! You cannot! You would not! You said you would never hurt me."

The flat of his hand came down with a sting.

"Ouch!"

"I should have better clarified the definition of hurt. This is not what I consider hurting you. Making you as uncomfortable as you just made me, perhaps, but not hurting you."

He rubbed the spot where his hand had slapped. Then to her dread, he pulled the material of her unmentionables down. She had just enough time to take a large breath before his hand smacked the other bare cheek.

She yelped.

Alexander slowly began to massage the sensitive imprint, and something strange shifted within the mood of the room.

With his fingers he traced tiny circles around her backside and then down her thighs, soothing her tender skin from the punishment.

She tingled with raw anticipation as goosebumps prickle her legs.

He leaned over her and whispered, "Now, that was not so bad, was it?"

"Alexander, let me up this instant." Greyland squirmed in his hold, not willing to concede her defeat. Yet, at the same time, she had a very real and clear understanding that this game was just getting started.

To her shock, some perverse part of her wanted to see how it would play out.

ALEXANDER SMILED at the writhing vixen in his lap. "Just one more, and you will get your reward."

Before she could protest, he swatted her bottom again and watched the marks rise to the surface. He moved his hands down to the apex of her thighs, allowing his eager fingers to find the heavenly warmth they craved. She inhaled sharply as he gently parted her delicate folds then moaned ever so quietly.

It was all the encouragement he needed. He lifted her to her feet and watched the blush move from her bottom to her face. Alex sat there, drinking her in before taking her hands in his.

He tugged her back down to meet his eyes at his seated level and kissed her softly. "This is what you do to me." He moved her hand to the bulge in his pants. "Even when I have resigned myself to stay mad at you. Now, please lie down."

"In here? That is not very proper."

He smirked, enjoying her bemusement. "My dear, I think we passed proper a while back."

She worried her bottom lip but did as instructed and sat back down. She reclined back against the cushions.

"Roll over." Alex knew his tone held absolutely no room for refusal and that suited him just fine. He enjoyed being the one in control. He just never expected to have such a motivating participant. "I want another good look at that round little bottom of yours."

She obeyed, turning over so that her stomach lay flat on the sofa.

Alex stood and removed his pants, tossing them to the floor. He leaned over and lifted her skirts, exposing her delectable flesh, still rosy from his handprint. His hands moved between her knees and pushed them apart.

Never taking his eyes off her profile, he climbed onto the sofa behind her. His erection was so hard he wondered how long he could last. She did something to him that he had never experienced before. He craved her like a hopeless drunk needed a drink.

Placing both hands on the curve of her slender waist, he pulled her ass into the air. Then, with more control than he thought possible—slid deep inside her.

She tightened around him. He held very still. Slowly, he felt her muscles relax, beginning to adjust to his girth. He gently rocked back and forth, his pulse increasing with every stroke.

She joined in his rhythm after a few long strokes. He increased the pace, driving deeper each time. She was so slick. So eager. He could not last much longer. His hips pistoned, her bottom bouncing with each thrust. He looked down and watched his engorged shaft glistening, and then disappearing as he buried himself to the hilt within her.

Alex felt his body taking over, seizing control of any ability to hold back or slow down. Punishingly, his body slammed into hers. She screamed out as her climax overtook her and he was done for. With one last furious thrust and a blinding oath to God, he filled her completely with his hot seed, claiming her body as his.

He bent over and laid his chest lightly atop her back, both their breathing coming out as hard, ragged gasps.

"I did not hurt you, did I?" he managed.

"No," she panted. "That was...needed."

Alexander kissed the side of her mouth. "Do not ever do anything that stupid again. And do not try and deceive me, Greyland. Understood?"

She nodded her head against the sofa cushion. "I just needed to see his face."

She started to move but he pushed his hips down, forcing her to stay put. "If you want to do something, all you have to do is ask. I would have taken you to see him. Under my supervision."

She hesitated. "I did not think you would approve."

"I would not have." He released his hold over her by sliding out of her warmth and pushing to his knees. "But you should put more trust in me."

He stood and extended his arm down to help her up. "It is a requirement from now on."

She rolled onto her back and accepted his hand. "I will. I am sorry." Her bottom lip trembled, and a tear slid from her eye.

What anger remained dissolved as a flood of guilt rushed over him. He had been so mad. He must have scared her to death. Alex mentally kicked himself for it.

"Do not cry. No tears here." He pulled her to her feet. "Not now that we better understand each other." He hushed her with a kiss, pulling back only to whisper against her ear. "I love you."

He might never forgive himself if she did not understand his need to keep her safe. He could not defend his overpowering decision to punish her with a spanking. It seemed the only rational option to control his blinding anger at the time. She had been so careless, and then so antagonistically stubborn.

Likewise, Alex would not feel an ounce of guilt for branding her as his just now. There had been something primal and completely intoxicating about taking zero precautions against getting her with child. In fact, the idea made his cock stir to life anew.

"I love you, Greyland," he repeated.

"I love you, too."

"We need to get back to the others before they think I might have killed you."

Her lips curled at the edges. "It is an emotion they can relate to, I am afraid."

"It is a problem that ends here," he said firmly. "Next time, I will have to spank you harder." He felt a grin manifest on his lips at the prospect.

To his delight, Greyland flushed and looked up shyly through her long lashes. She was not opposed to the idea, either. Blessed be the day this woman had trampled her horse bareback into his world.

XI

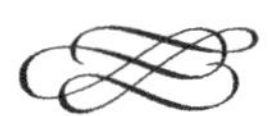

Greyland was sore. She insisted on riding her mare, that Samson had found grazing in a village garden, earlier that morning when their caravan had departed. However, only thirty minutes in, she quickly realized her folly. She could endure the bouncing no longer. Alexander, having told her as much before they left, smiled triumphantly, and helped her into the carriage.

Lord, always right.

She should have known that intense marital relations, near-death experiences, and being bent over an irate lover's knee might wear a person out. She felt her cheeks heat once again at the memory.

Greyland had not been sure she could face their traveling party when she had woken from her short nap. She could not shake the feeling that they all *knew*… Surely someone in Lord Humphrey's household had heard them and told the tale. It would take no time at all getting passed around the servants table, and then everyone's personal staff would know. Samson would know! They all could know by now! *Did they?*

She could not be certain, but she had taken her midday meal in her room, and mentally scolded herself for being a bloody coward. It was a massive manor house; surely her embarrassment was getting the better of her.

Greyland had held fast to that last probability and walked with her head held high to the carriage, acting as if nothing whatsoever had invoked her fiancé's wrath earlier that morning. No one said a thing, but they avoided eye contact for the first hour. She told herself it was all due to Alex pulling her angrily from the courtyard. They probably assumed he simply scolded her after that in the library.

Nevertheless, she had to keep reminding herself, as she watched the five viral men riding alongside the carriage, that only one of them knew exactly what had taken place behind those closed doors in Lord Humphrey's library. Surely, she was not the first woman to endure a blistering lecture from their spouse.

Blistering being the operative word.

Greyland sighed, her thoughts shifting to wander back through time. So much had changed in the past week. She taught The Queen of England to dance. Met and fallen in love. Been drugged. Uncovered a family secret of substantial importance. Run from a disgruntled Irish laird's son hell-bent on marriage and taking over the country. Lost her virginity—thankfully not to said Irish laird's son. Aided in killing a man, *and,* while she was keeping a running tally, been indoctrinated into a wanton world of hedonistic desires awoken and fueled by the man she going to spend the rest of her life with.

A fairly typical English debut. She suddenly had to repress a laugh. Maybe she was going a little crazy. It was just all a little much when you put it together as she had just done. What on earth was her life trying to do to her? Was this some grand duchess test? Master stabbing a man through the neck, and you earn your societal bon ton title?

Her mood grew suddenly somber as images of the previous night's events assaulted her mind anew. Of all the memories, this was the one plaguing her. Greyland shook her head, trying to cast off the encroaching shadows of fear and the suffocating stench of death that still followed her. She shuddered. She had killed a man! Well, *assisted* in killing a man. *Would she go to Hell for that?*

She pulled back the curtains of the carriage a little more and glanced at the riders. All the men out there had endured some form of the same horrific scene and they all seemed decidedly unfazed. She felt foolish at her squeamish resolve. Did men simply not flinch when met with the choice of 'fight or flight'? Was it nothing for them to take a life that threatened theirs?

Greyland learned a long time ago that, try as she might, she would never be able to understand men. That did not stop her from wanting to be like them; to have their emotional courage and physical strength. She often played a game with herself in which she tried to imagine herself as other people. To put herself in their shoes. Greyland closed her eyes to do so now.

She thought about Perkin's courage first. He was the hardest of the Kingston men to read. She had deduced, at the wise old age of five, that if she could learn to think like him, she would be just fine.

How would Perkin feel after taking a life?

With her eyes sealed shut, she took herself back to the night in the church. The sound of Malikite tearing out the Irishman's throat, the smell of copper as the blood met with fresh air and turned acidic in its decay, the feel of the muscle ripping and parting as the blade she wielded tore with savage teeth through the man's thick neck.

Greyland exhaled slowly and allowed the unpleasant sensations to wash over her once again. This time, thinking as Perkin might, she did not feel the sick bile rising in her throat. Instead, she replayed the actions and understood them. She had acted to save her life.

She opened her eyes and peered again at the men riding outside her carriage. These men fought, not for themselves, but for her. A new understanding and respect emerged. She would have done the same. Greyland would have done anything to protect her brothers and Alexander.

She almost jumped out of her seat as a new realization washed over her. That was why Alex had been so mad last night! Her life meant more to him than his own. Why had she been so blind as to not see it? Greyland placed herself back in the small chapel once more and this time observed the horrific colors of death with different eyes. *Alexander's.*

Suddenly, she felt...nothing. Nothing at all of killing, if killing was meant to protect the people she loved. Courage and survival replaced fear.

A quiet resolve settled within her heart. Greyland leaned back against the cushions and embraced the new knowledge, drawing comfort in the understanding.

Her mother's poem made sense now. *She was to be tested.* She was destined to continue, to learn from the world around her and seek wisdom from the silent strength of the ones she loved.

Always dancing, singing, and sharing with the world for the problems of the day would be mere skipping stones in the river of her life tomorrow.

"It is magical!" Greyland exclaimed, her eyes fixed straight ahead.

"It is yours, my lady." Alex smiled. This was just the start of all the wonders he would provide. Next would be the wedding of her dreams. She deserved the world, and he would move heaven and hell to make sure she had it.

Greyland had insisted she ride the remainder of the trip on horseback to better take in the scenery. Alexander willingly obliged, since he knew it was not too far and he secretly wanted to etch into his memory her first reaction to his ancestral home.

He watched as her gaze climbed hungrily past the sea of welcoming wildflowers laid out before them like a lush carpet and came to a rest on the majestic medieval castle that rose formidably from the rich English soil. The near impregnable structure had been constructed around the thirteenth century and had remained in the Hamilton family since Queen Elizabeth gifted it to his forebearers.

Just beyond Greenshire Castle, the ocean undulated. Its deep blue hue changing to a sea-green as it drew inland, then reached with foamy fingers to tickle the soft sand of the beach. It was the most magical place in England.

Alexander barely had time to register the glint of mirth that lit in her eyes before Greyland called out: "Race you!" And she was off.

Alexander urged his stallion into a gallop after her. A roar of laughter escaped from his lungs. It felt good. He heard the rest of their traveling party whip their steeds into competitive pursuit.

Battle cries lifted in the wind as they stormed the castle. Henry's mount started to pass. With a snort and a familiar pinning back of his ears, Alex felt Socrates up the ante from beneath him. He smirked. The beast liked a good rivalry as much as his rider did. Socrates snaked his strong noble head to the right, challenging his opponent.

Alexander waved a friendly goodbye to his brother and left him in the dust. He trained his sights on the perfect, round derriere poised high in the air in front of him.

ONCE INSIDE THE RAMPARTS, everyone dismounted and turned their horses over to the stable hands. Greyland stood awestruck by the enormity of the great stone walls. She had seen many such structures in her travels, but there was something otherworldly about this one. She dragged her eyes away from the castles towering battlements to find Alexander studying her closely.

She grinned as he sauntered over and lifted her without effort into his arms.

"I must carry you over the threshold."

Greyland giggled. "Of course. But perhaps I could meet the staff first. Atop my own two feet."

"Very well." Alex sat her back down and wagged a playful scolding finger at her. "These practical suggestions. I will have no more of them."

Greyland laughed and turned to the line of newly formed and curious faces waiting to greet them. One by one, the household of Greenshire Castle made their introductions. Greyland, smiling, embraced them all in some fashion. She hugged the women and extended her hand to the men. A young groom, no older than twelve, did not know quite what to do with her extended hand so she had patted his shoulder, saving him any embarrassment.

A rotund, jolly woman named Annie rounded out the house of fourteen active staff. A little girl, with shy eyes and blonde curls, peeked around her skirts.

Greyland's heart swelled with excitement, and she dropped low, making herself as close to eye level as she could with the little darling. Big, saucer-sized blue eyes goggled out at her. The little nymph could be no older than five, Greyland surmised.

"And who might this lovely princess be?" she asked.

The girl turned bright red and gifted Greyland with a smile of pure delight.

"This is Annabelle, my lady," Annie spoke for the child. "We took her in last month. Thanks to His Grace, she has found a home here."

The girl bashfully pulled the maid's apron over her face. "She is a big help around the kitchen, but she has yet to let us hear that beautiful voice we know she must have. She hasn't spoken a word."

Greyland held out her hand to the child. "Miss Annabelle, would you do me the honor of showing me to my chamber?"

The girl looked up to Annie for approval and when granted permission, took Greyland's hand and excitedly led her toward one of two imposing staircases that circled up to the castle's main doors.

"I will be right along," Alex assured from behind them.

Annabelle guided Greyland through the massive doors, up the solid stone staircase, and to the most beautiful bedroom she had ever seen.

The room had been expertly made ready and was filled to the

brim with fresh cut flowers. Greyland's hand fluttered to her mouth as she took in the feminine additions that had been made especially for her arrival. Alex had arranged all of this. *For her.* Her eyes grew misty.

The child wordlessly patted the edge of the bed. Greyland smiled and pushed back the tears of joy. "It is a bed fit for a queen."

The child beamed as if Greyland had answered her exactly. And indeed, Greyland mused, it was a bed like no other. It likely had been a queens at one point in this castle's illustrious history. A four-poster bed with meticulous wood-working detail carved into the headboard took up the middle of the room. A canopy of gauze curtains draped around the frame. It blew gently in the ocean breeze, wafting in from the open window.

"This has to be the best room in the house," Greyland concluded.

Annie entered behind them. "Ah, my lady. It is only equal to His Grace's master chamber, through that door." She pointed. "His Grace wanted your room to be filled with flowers. In fact, he sent a message stating he wished you to have them every day for the rest of your days." Annie smiled a tender, knowing smile.

"He did?" Greyland thought that if a heart could burst from love, hers just needed a needle.

"I must confess, none of us ever thought he would marry at all, much less be so head-over-heels in love with his intended." Annie continued to smile at Greyland as if the new lady of the house had single-handedly dispersed a coastal storm. "It is so good to have you here, my lady. Greenshire has been too long without a lady of the house." Annie summoned Annabelle to her side. "I hope you will be happy here," she said as they made for the door. "I have waited a long time for this glorious day."

Greyland smiled, humbled by the older woman's praise. "I am so very happy to be here. Thank you."

"I will leave you to get settled in then. Just ring that bell-pull if you are in need of anything." She motioned to a rope on the left side of the giant bed.

Greyland stopped her, curiosity doing what it always did, getting the better of her. "Annie? One last thing. How is it that Annabelle came to live here?"

Annie nodded to the child. "Why don't you go see if Cook has his pastries ready for Her Grace."

The little girl sprang into action and darted down the hall.

Annie smiled from the hallway, watching her go and turned back to face Greyland. "The child's mother was traveling through the village and took ill. The poor woman died within a fortnight and the little darling had no one to take her in. We wrote to His Grace, and he graciously gave permission for her to live in the castle. As I mentioned, she has not spoken, but I believe with time she will." Annie suddenly looked anxious. "I hope this arrangement meets with your approval?"

"Of course," Greyland said, nodding her head vigorously while still processing the little girl's horrible misfortune. "Of course it does. I love children and look forward to seeing her daily." She paused, not wanting to overstep her boundaries in a house that was run as well as a palace. "If you can spare her on occasion, perhaps Annabelle could spend some of her time with me. Learning Latin and other things?"

The older woman smiled, and her eyes shone with honest gratitude. "That would be most wonderful." Annie lowered her head and backed on out of the doorway. "Thank you, Your Grace."

No sooner had she left did Alex materialize, as if from thin air, looking as devilish as ever. He leaned leisurely against the door jam. "Is everything to your liking?"

His ocean-blue gaze was direct, holding her eyes as he waited patiently for her answer. She would never tire of the way he looked at her, a mixture of studious concentration, curiosity, and unabashed wonderment.

Like she hung the stars in the nighttime of his life, and for the life of him he could not figure out how.

Greyland launched herself into his arms. "Yes, my wonderful husband!"

He chuckled. "A title I cannot wait to have on paper. What say we have it in four days' time?"

"Oh, yes, yes, yes! Then may I share your room with you?" She delivered kisses to every inch of his neck and chin and then tugged on his neatly tied cravat, encouraging him to lower his mouth. He willingly obliged, lowering his lips to hers.

God, she loved the way he tasted. She surrendered to the stimulations humming through her veins and bit down on his lower lip. He moaned, and she withdrew just enough to ask again. "Please say it will be soon?"

"But of course. This current arrangement is only for the benefit of your reputation, although I believe Perkin already knows I have corrupted you." Alex grinned. "He has just not been afforded the time needed to beat me senseless."

Greyland gasped, suddenly worried about what exactly her older brother might do if he knew. "No. He would not dare. I will talk to him."

Alexander placed his hands on her shoulders pulling her back enough to look into her eyes. "You will do no such thing. I will talk to him tonight and ask that he not mess me up too badly before the big day."

"As you wish," she said, resigning the matter and stroked her hands down the front of his trousers, loving how just her touch could produce a quiver from a man of his size and strength. He closed his eyes and his inhaled deeply.

"But you better remain handsome for my wedding," she teased.

AFTER GREYLAND HAD SHOWN Alex her delicious appreciation of their new home, they joined the others for a tour of the estate. Perkin remained glued to Alexander's side, quizzing him on all matters of engineering and architectural merits regarding the castle, while

Greyland and Edward raced ahead like children in a candy store, calling out with delight every time they came to a new room.

Thomas, the big child himself, joined them in their hunt and thundered through doors ahead of them as their jubilant guide. Their excitement was contagious and even Henry got swept up in the spirit of the moment, showing them the hidden passageways he played in as a child.

Alexander took the lead when they arrived at two large oak doors. Behind them lay what had originally been used as the castle's Chamber Hall. He would be the first to show Greyland this particular conversion. He opened the doors slowly, for effect, then stepped aside.

All the Kingston mouths fell agape. Even the normally calm Perkin let a murmur of appreciation roll from his controlled tongue.

Greyland inhaled and then ran headlong into the ballroom. Large, ornately carved pillars dominated the white marble floors. Candelabras lined the walls, illuminating beautiful Greek-inspired murals. Above them, a giant crystal chandelier hung as if suspended by only the night. For indeed, by all appearance's sake, the only perceivable ceiling was the sky.

The dome-shaped glass ceiling that encapsulated the whole ballroom was an architectural marvel and one Alexander was quite proud of. Greyland stood beneath its grandeur and stared up. Alexander and the others moved to do the same. Alexander reached her and slipped his arms around her waist.

"Will this do for practicing our wedding dance?"

She leaned back into his embrace. "It is the most beautiful ballroom I have ever seen!" She suddenly spun around to look up at him, anticipation shining in her eyes. "Can we start now?"

Alex smiled. He would always be the voice of reason with his little spit-fire bride, a fact he thoroughly loved. She was his other half. She kept him invigorated, excited, and full of adventure. He would have to keep her grounded. Together they made a perfect whole. Together they were indomitable.

"Let us eat and relax," he said and tapped her nose. "We can start first thing tomorrow after I show you the grounds."

. . .

ALEXANDER WOKE and reached out for Greyland but found only her kitten, Sir George, snuggled up where Greyland should have been. His betrothed had once again charmed him into sharing her bed before their vows.

He rose quickly and retrieved his clothes from his adjoining chamber. Alex smiled fondly in remembrance of the evening spent with the Kingston brothers, Thomas and Henry.

Perkin had not disfigured his face as expected for taking Greyland's virtue before the wedding, but he did offer a friendly threat. "Do not disappoint me again." Alex would not have expected anything less.

They both agreed not to tell Edward. Alexander always thought Perkin to be the more dominant brother, but apparently Edward's bond with his sister was unchallenged and frighteningly lethal when provoked. Perkin had shared a few stories from their past growing up in New Orleans. Through them, Alex gained a greater understanding and respect for the younger Kingston brother.

His conversations with Henry were the most rewarding. Alex had shared a cheroot with him as they took a stroll across the grounds. He apologized again, they consumed too much brandy and laughed into the wee hours of the morning.

Alex's head began to ache as he descended the stairs in search of his soon-to-be wife. *Entirely too much brandy.*

He stopped and asked a servant coming up the stairs as to Greyland's whereabouts.

"She is in the kitchen," replied the maid with a prankish grin.

"That is most curious."

"You might have a look, Your Grace," the servant suggested.

Alex pinched the bridge of his nose, mumbled his understanding, and continued down the stairs. By the sixth step, the most intoxicating smell filled his nostrils.

Suddenly starving, he followed the beckoning aroma through a pair of doors and found his true love wearing an apron and covered in flour. She was furiously whisking the contents of a bowl while his head chef, along with the little girl and three other kitchen aids, looked on expectantly.

Alex stepped back before he could be noticed.

"Now I add the eggs." She demonstrated by cracking them into a bowl. "Oh, Pierre...flip the flapjacks." Greyland gestured with her adorable nose, also covered in flour, to a pan on the stove. Pierre hurried over to assist.

Flapjacks?

Alex continued to watch avidly as Greyland explained to his snooty French chef how to make the perfect Southern breakfast. Pierre, obviously smitten, *naturally*, with the new lady of the house seemed eager to learn.

If the perfect Southern breakfast lived up to the amazing scent it produced, then Alex was a luckier man than he already thought himself to be. A smile tugged at the corners of his mouth.

Another serving maid entered behind him and ran right into Alexander's back.

She squeaked, dropping a tray of glasses. They crashed to the floor, shattering into a million tiny shards on the unforgiving stone.

"I am so sorry, Your Grace!" she stammered, scrambling to retrieve the debris.

"It was my fault. Let me help," Alexander insisted.

He bent to help but Annie rushed in and shooed him off.

Alexander straightened and turned to find Greyland and his kitchen staff gaping at him.

Before anyone could speak, Edward wandered in, yawning. "Ah, flapjacks. My favorite."

He sauntered across the large kitchen and opened the wood-burning stove, allowing even more delicious smells to enter the room. "And do my eyes deceive me?" Edward closed the stove and looked over to his sister. "Buttermilk biscuits?"

Greyland swatted his hand as he reached for one. "Do not dare! They are still hot, silly. I thought we should expose Alex, Thomas, and Henry to—"

"The perfect Southern breakfast," Alex supplied the rest.

"I hope you do not mind," Greyland said. "I love to cook. It is an overlooked art form." She shared an understanding head nod with Pierre.

"Not at all." Alex patted his stomach, surprising himself by the action. *Edward Kingston must be rubbing off on him.* "How much longer until it is done?"

"Just a few minutes." Greyland tiptoed over to Alex and pressed her lips against his cheek, leaving a dusting of flour he was sure, on his skin.

The maids grabbed trays and platters and ushered the men out of the kitchen while the little girl hurried to help by untying Greyland's apron strings.

"Go sit with His Grace, my lady," Annie encouraged.

Edward, Alex, and Greyland made their way into the dining room. To Alex's astonishment, the other guests were already in attendance, all seated and taking their pleasures around the table. Perkin was kicked back and reading the paper. Thomas was on what appeared to be his third apple, and Henry was pouring a cup of steaming coffee.

"Good morning," Alexander addressed the room and took a seat across from Edward.

The staff rushed about, placing platters of food on the table. Annie commanded the servants in the way she always had, with a quiet control and piercing round eyes. Once everything was to her liking and she had convinced Greyland to be seated, she hustled the staff out, leaving the guests to their fare.

"I will take two!" Thomas said, reaching for the warm biscuits.

From the smile on Greyland's face, Alex could tell she was thoroughly pleased with herself.

Greyland said, "I was thinking a house party would be nice since we are asking half of London to come to our wedding. We have more than enough space."

"What a bloody good idea," Thomas said between bites. "Especially if that means more biscuits."

"Only if you invite that lovely sister of Lord Ashlown's." Edward wagged a brow, teasing Perkin. "I do believe she has eyes for me."

Everyone chuckled, but Alex stiffened at the thought of having to play nice with Lord Ashlown.

"What do you think?" Greyland had placed a hand on his knee.

"How can I deny you anything?" he replied, and to his dread, realized that he truly meant it. "We will have Samson write out the invitations."

Greyland all but shimmered with joy. *Until she did not.* A sudden frown marred her beautiful face as she considered something.

"What is it dear?" Alex inquired.

"Just make sure he leaves out that horrible Lady Chatsworth and Jeremy Lovingston."

"They will not be receiving any invitation," Alex confirmed. "They will be at the top of the list of not welcomes, and they will be tossed on their arses if they dare set foot on my land."

"So," Henry ventured, "who wants to fill me in on this bit of gossip?"

"I will tell you all about it on our morning ride." Edward pushed his chair away from the table and stretched.

"I will stay behind and help Samson with the invitations and make sure he knows exactly who is, and who is not, welcome. Plus," Thomas asserted, leaning in to snag yet another biscuit, "this is where all the food is."

THE GROUP of riders followed the tree-lined path before turning east into the rising sun. As they made their way down the dirt road leading to the beach, they passed three cottages Alexander owned. The riding party stopped at each home for introductions between Greyland and the tenants, and for Alex to obtain brief updates on annual crop production.

All three families were surprised and overjoyed when Greyland invited them to the wedding. She knew her soon-to-be-husband had been taken aback by her impromptu invitations, but he had hidden his shock well. He was becoming quite good at not dropping his jaw every time she broke the molds of societal norms without so much as a proper warning.

Greyland smiled over at him as he veered Socrates into the meadow she had asked about the night before. She had stood staring from her eastward facing window at its sprawling views for the better part of an hour before bed. This rolling meadow was the last visual trace of land one could see from Greenshire Castle before the ocean beckoned the eyes out to sea.

"The road takes you right to the beach, but the meadow holds the best prospect," Alex explained.

Greyland noted his smiles came easier since they had arrived at the castle.

Lord Overprotective was relaxing.

They meandered through the freshly shorn grass until they were standing on the edge of a cliff that separated the meadow from the sand below.

"Oh, Alex!" Greyland gasped, her eyes drinking in the white-capped sea. "This is the spot."

His gaze enveloped her like a wool shawl.

"Is it?"

She turned her head quickly to him and found a knowing smile on his beautiful lips. He had read her thoughts. Her eyes began to fill with tears. All her dreams were coming true.

"It is," she said. "I know a church wedding is what is expected, but this place is magical. Can you not just feel it deep within your bones? Surely there can be no better place to pledge our love."

Greyland took a quick breath and continued to prattle on. "Afterward, we can regroup in the ballroom and dance the night away."

She swung down from her horse and skipped out into the grass, turning in tiny circles. She threw her head back and squealed into the cool ocean winds.

She heard Alexander chuckle right before he caught her by the waist and lifted her into the air. "A dusk wedding it shall be."

He spun her in his arms and then lowered her into a kiss, completely ignoring the others.

Someone cleared their throat.

Perkin?

Greyland pulled back slightly, suddenly aware of their audience, but Alex did not release her from his hold.

"I will get the vicar set to deliver the ceremony next Saturday at dusk then?" Henry asked from atop his horse.

Greyland nodded rosily. "That would be wonderful."

Henry smiled. "Consider it done." He turned to the others. "Who wants to ride into town with me?"

"I do," Both Perkin and Edward answered in unison, reversing their steeds back to the road. Greyland giggled and looked back up into Alex's blazing eyes. He grinned down at her.

"Looks like I have you all to myself now."

She pushed him backward. "Then you better not waste it." She laughed when he pretended to fall and landed on a bed of clovers.

Alexander licked his lips, his hands going straight to his belt. "Oh, I shan't."

GREYLAND MADE her way to the library to get to work. The guests would be arriving in two days, and she still had many arrangements to make. In hindsight, perhaps she should not have insisted she do everything on her own without help. It had definitely been a rash decision that she was regretting now. So worried about placing further burdens on the staff, Greyland had taken them all on herself, not accounting for the adjustment time needed to comprehend the staggering amount of work that went into 'being a duchess'. A beginner's mistake that she would not make in the future.

A castle did not run itself after all, and Greyland was determined to be the best duchess that ever lived. She had taken to her new responsibilities like a duck to water; a Southern analogy that had given her English fiancé great mirth. *Well,* aside from the whole ordeal of arranging a house party around one's own wedding, but who was she to focus on the negative.

That minor detail aside, Greyland had been an excellent student, dogging Alex's every waking step and asking for explicit details regarding everything from summer crops to tenant Christmas presents, and she had not stopped there. Greyland had visited the tenants and discussed their personal concerns, met with the town's vicar about holiday festivities and village morale, and insisted on a school.

When Alexander suggested that perhaps she slow down, Greyland, never one to be deterred and knowing that men usually got hesitant where money was involved, had gone through the estate ledger books to locate the funds for such expenses. She then proudly outlined where the corners could be cut, allowing for all her community projects to be explored. Alex only laughed and conceded defeat, encouraging her to change as many things as she saw fit—provided she continued his midday dance lessons.

And that was just the start of it.

Having fallen helplessly in love with little Annabelle, despite Alexander's warnings not to get too attached, Greyland set herself with the personal task of teaching the child to dance and ride. Besides, asking her not to become smitten with the wide-eyed child was simply a pointless request.

Greyland stopped short on the landing, pulled forcefully out of her wool-gathering when she heard the sound of something, or someone, in distress.

Turning around quickly, she headed toward the kitchen, pausing only when she pushed through the doors to find Annie rocking a whimpering Annabelle in her arms. Both jumped at the sudden sight of the lady of the house.

Annabelle sniffled and wiggled free of Annie's embrace, running right to Greyland, and throwing her arms around her legs.

"I am so sorry, Your Grace," Annie apologized profusely. "I hope we did not wake you?"

"Not at all. I was on my way to the library," Greyland put her hand on the back of Annabella's head, stroking her soft curls. "What are the tears for, sweet child?" she coaxed. "Did you have a bad dream?"

Annabelle lifted her little cherub cheeks and nodded. The sight of her wobbling chin and red-rimmed blue eyes nearly caused Greyland tears of her own.

"She has them every night, my lady," Annie explained. "I tried to comfort her back to sleep, but tonight's dream seems to have been worse. So, I brought her with me to start work early."

Greyland bent at the waist and picked up the child. "You have too much on your hands, Annie. I will take Annabelle and try to console her."

"Oh no, Your Grace, I could not ask that of you. I can manage. After all, I am the one who insisted we take her in."

"It is my pleasure." Greyland turned before the woman could protest any further. "And Annie…" she stopped and looked back over her shoulder, "I am glad you insisted."

Greyland left Annie in the kitchen and headed to the library with Annabelle clinging to her like a little monkey.

The room was lined with built-in bookshelves from the floor to an impressive, second-level ceiling. Greyland went right to *King Arthur*. The two had started it yesterday and Annabelle was hooked.

Greyland plucked the book from the shelf and sat down with her reading companion in her lap. Annabelle wiped the last tear from her cheek with the back of her chubby hand. Greyland opened to the worn novel to the marked page they had left off on and watched as the detailed illustrations of a white knight and a fair maiden worked their magic on the child.

Greyland felt a relaxed smile form on her lips. A smile that was pulled forth from an unfamiliar place in her heart. She could identify it as love, but there was something more to it than any love she had known before. *Motherhood?*

Alexander's words echoed in her head as she began to read the words written on the aged yellow paper.

Do not get too attached.

They had talked about it at length. Alex would post inquiries about town and have his Man of Affairs begin the search for any possible remaining family members. His biggest concern was that Greyland might grow too interested in the child, just to then have a relative show up and take her away.

Greyland easily understood that fear, for it was mounting daily. She also knew Alex had, likewise, developed a soft spot for the little girl. He had lost his mother when he was about the same age, so he surely understood the little girl's plight. Greyland's heart broke for them both. The world could be so unfair and cruel.

Greyland repositioned Annabelle in her lap and continued reading the story, but her mind was elsewhere. She could not stop thinking about what having a child of her own would be like.

If her monthly course did not arrive in a couple of days, she might be getting that wish sooner than expected.

Thanks to Lord Virile.

XII

Alexander opened the doors and found both Greyland and Annabelle fast asleep in one of the oversized chairs, just where the cook told him they would be. He stood there quietly, not wanting to disturb them just yet.

Annabelle had a twirled lock of Greyland's hair wrapped in her fingers. The child had obviously fallen into slumber while caressing it. Greyland's arms encircled the little girl, encasing her in a protective hold that even sleep could not shake. They made a lovely pair. Annabelle's buttercup blonde curls contrasted beautifully with Greyland's midnight mane.

Movement beyond the window interrupted Alex's quiet admiration.

A carriage was approaching at a rather fast clip. Instant suspicion niggled the back of his mind. The guests were not scheduled to arrive until tomorrow. Alex could not tell for certain yet, but it appeared to have The Queen's crest on the door.

He left the girls to greet the carriage.

As he passed the dining room, Perkin and Henry emerged wordlessly and flanked him. He must not be the only one being needled by doubt.

The carriage rolled to a stop and out climbed an always striking, but somewhat weary, Richard Kingston, followed by Lord Ashlown. A vein in Alexander's neck throbbed with irritation.

Lord Ashlown merely eyed him with the same nonchalant, couldn't-care-less look he always held. The look had the same effect on Alex that it always did; a sudden desire to plant his fist in the other lord's nose. At least they were consistent in their hatred for one another.

Richard made quick to amend the awkward silence that was settling around them all like a fog. "I will not waste time on pleasantries. Colin and his men escaped on the road," he informed them matter-of-factly.

"Christ!" Henry exclaimed.

"We will talk inside." Alexander turned.

No one wasted time taking offense to the duke's discourteous instruction. Instead, they followed him into the castle and directly to the study.

ALEXANDER OFFERED the most basic of introductions once they were all inside the room. "This is my brother, Henry."

"Very nice to make your acquaintance. I have heard many complimentary words spoken of you from your father over the years," Richard said, taking a seat.

Henry tipped his head and smiled, accepting the kind words but recognizing now was not the time for diverting off the more serious topic at hand. They all followed Richard's lead and took their seats around the room. All except Perkin, who positioned himself by the window.

Alexander had never asked the tallest Kingston if he had been in the military. If not, the man's instincts were either a natural gift from God, or an inherited gene from his royal ancestors. If Alex ever fancied invading a small country, Perkin Kingston would be the man he would want at his right side.

Richard turned his head and set his serious, aristocratic grey eyes pointedly on Alexander. "As you are aware, I spoke immediately with The Queen after you departed London. She in turn called Lord Melbrooke and I into a private meeting. Seems there was some confusion...you might say. Between The Queen and Lord Melbrooke concerning our family."

That might explain Melbrooke's absence and Ashlown's presence, Alex quickly assessed. If Melbrooke's high-reaching claws had anything to do with his father's death, he would strangle the man and deal with The Queen's wrath later. At this point, she may very well thank him, if Melbrooke, *the rat,* had used sensitive information against her friends.

Richard continued. "After we cleared up the matter concerning our illustrious ancestors," he paused, seemingly, arranging his thoughts and considering his next words carefully.

Nothing good ever followed a pause like that.

"Alexander, before we get to the threat the McGreggor's pose, there is another piece to this puzzle I must explain. We have been upturning stone upon stone, and it is painfully obvious that Derrick has been using his knowledge of our family and our past against us, and..." Richard regarded Alex carefully, "I am even sorrier to say, against you."

Alexander, to everyone's surprise, *including his own,* did not immediately react. He did not move or speak at all. He simply held the older man's gaze, digesting the words.

Alexander lifted his hand. Samson turned toward the room's sideboard table, reading the gesture, and moving quickly to fulfill the silent request. The loyal servant worked quickly. He topped the glass off just at the brim and delivered the drink to Alexander's waiting palm. He then returned deftly to the bar and began pouring four more.

Still, Alex said nothing. He thought about his uncle, a man he never really knew; *the man next in line for his title.* That last thought repeated in his head. How could he have been so blind? Derrick was jealous and spiteful. He was also dangerous.

After all, he was family.

Lord Ashlown's even tone broke the dead calm. "Your uncle led Lord Melbrooke and I to believe the worst about the Kingston's return to London. Derrick ran straight to Lord Melbrooke the moment Richard set foot on English soil. Your uncle was eager to advance his standing with the Crown. The Queen explained the true situation to us after you left London. However, unbeknownst to her, I had already had him followed the eve of your engagement party."

Lord Ashlown accepted his glass from Samson. "That next morning, he and Lady Chatsworth went straight to his house just outside the city. Guess who arrived right before them?" He sat back in his chair, crossing one ankle over the other knee. "Colin McGreggor and his henchmen, of course."

Perkin swore an oath under his breath that promised some form of medieval torture and stalked across the room to the brandy decanter, as if it was his intended victim. Samson had the good sense to step aside and allow him to pour his own glass.

Alexander tipped up his glass and drained the ruby-colored liquor in one swallow. Samson retrieved the crystal and refilled it.

"That posturing little shit!" Perkin's normally smooth voice was laced with acid. It turned everyone's head. "If he has been behind all this torment, I will gut him and feed his insides to the bloody hounds!"

Henry went a shade paler, Alexander's previous speculation just dawning on him. "Could he have been behind our father's murder?"

"There is really only one reasonable answer to these events." Lord Ashlown said. "The only one standing in the way of Derrick taking the title of Duke—"

"Was our father." Alex finished the other lord's sentence. "And now...me."

"He intended to keep Greyland from you," Richard said. "That would mean one less possible heir in his way, which is why we think he worked with Lady Chatsworth and Lord Lovingston to drug her the night of the mask. When that did not work, he turned to the only people left who, likewise, had a reason to keep the two of you apart."

"I searched for Lord Lovingston to question him, but he has completely disappeared," Lord Ashlown admitted. "Even his twin knows nothing of where he might have gone."

Alex lifted his cold unnerving stare to Lord Ashlown. "And pray tell, why should I believe you? You yourself were after Greyland from the start. How do I know you are not involved?"

"Lord Melbrooke sent me to lure her away. He wanted me to keep an eye on the Kingston family. That was right after Derrick first told us of their lucrative lineage and the obvious problem that could come from it."

Dalton turned his hands, palm sides up. "After meeting her, I confess, who would not be charmed. But you were quicker, it appears."

Alex tightened his hand around the crystal. "Let us not forget that fact."

Any other man would have been unnerved by Alex's clipped tone, but his old rival simply took a sip from his glass.

Richard shifted forward in his chair. "The Queen has given us her protection, but the McGreggors will want their own justice to be served. They are a fiercely prideful clan. After the wedding, I intend to travel to Ireland and try my best at damage control."

Perkin's head snapped around to stare at his father. "What are you thinking? They will cut you down before you can utter the first words."

"I see no other option. I will not live in fear of their revenge, and this is my fight, after all." The look on Richard's face left little room for debate. "In the meantime, I do not think they will try anything during the festivities here, but I have asked for reinforcements from The Queen's guard."

"Her men should arrive in the next hour." Richard stood. "Where is Greyland? I do not want to alarm her, but she needs a guard posted with her at all times until the ceremony is over."

"Absolutely," Perkin quickly concurred. "I will get her."

"I will kill him," Alexander pledged, his tone so low and flat that it barely resonated as a sound to his own ears. It was really more of a silent omen than a statement. A threat shared between his personal vendetta and the air.

Seconds later, *or had it been minutes,* Alex's anger shifted targets as thoughts of dismembering Derrick flitted across his mind.

Perkin burst back into the room. "She has gone riding with Edward. The groom is saddling our horses."

GREYLAND ANCHORED the bowstring to her chin. She was one breath short of overthinking her mark. That would cost her the contest. With studied control, she released and watched as the arrow hit the desired knot on the tree trunk. "Yes!"

"Very good, Grey, but I was pointing to the mark just above that one." Edward offered her a lopsided grin.

"You were not!" Greyland gifted him with an unladylike punch to his left arm.

"Ouch!"

Greyland laughed and did her best victory dance. In truth, they had tied, but the joy she felt at finally getting that close to besting him was too much to contain. She beamed up at her brother before plopping down in the tall grass.

"I am so happy, Edward."

He joined her, stretching out long, like a cat in the midday sun. "I imagine you are." He put both hands behind his head and stared up at the sun. "You are getting very good. For a girl."

"Ha, ha. You are very funny. But I was speaking in general."

Greyland did as he did and laid back against the soft earth. It was a beautiful day with white cotton clouds dotting the expansive blue sky. They laid there in contemplative silence, just as they had done as children. Greyland closed her eyes and savored the moment, locking it away in her memory under the things she loved most.

"Are you fine with everything that has happened?" she ventured after a few minutes had passed.

Despite the easy nature she and her brother shared every time they were together, Greyland needed them to be serious for a moment. She wanted to make sure he understood and was content with her decision to marry Alex.

"It is not going to be the same without you in the house," he admitted and rolled his head to look at her. "Who will keep me in check?"

Greyland grinned. "That is a question that does not need answering. You should be more worried about when Perkin leaves the nest. That will be a day you should fear."

She giggled as one of Edward's brows lifted unnaturally high with mock disdain.

"And what if I am the next to go? I am starting to think this whole marriage thing..." He waved his hands in a large, animated circle for emphasis, "might not be such a horrid notion."

Greyland's mouth formed a dramatic O shape. "Why Edward, I am astonished. Is there an unlucky lady I do not know about in need of a challenge?"

Edward's eyes danced with mischief and his lips curled into the lazy, charming grin both brothers were known for. "Perhaps."

Greyland propped up on one elbow and pinned her brother with inquisitive eyes. "Who?"

"I am not telling. You shall have to figure it out when the guests arrive."

"She will be attending? Shall we put a wager on my ability to figure it out?"

"But of course. I wager—"

Thunderous galloping sliced the words right off his tongue.

So much for a private conversation.

Greyland huffed and sat up. Shielding her eyes from the sun, she turned and twisted towards the sound of the intrusion. Two horses were just topping the hill. Alexander and Henry bore down on them.

Something was not right.

"Something is amiss," Edward echoed her thoughts as he shot to his feet.

Greyland squinted toward the horizon as she quickly took her brothers' offered hand and pulled to her feet. Sure enough, as Alex drew closer, she could see the concern etched on his handsome face; almost feel the tension that rode between his shoulder blades.

Greyland's heart began to pound out the same tempo as the approaching horse hooves.

What had happened?

As the horses slowed. She and Edward hung mute, waiting for one of the two riders to speak. Neither did. Instead, Alex shoved off Socrates and marched decidedly toward them.

Towards her.

His long strides were confident and commanding. She sensed various emotions warring inside him.

When he finally did address them, his words came out clipped and stern. "You need to return to the castle."

She nodded her head, unsure how to proceed, but decidedly sure that opposition was not the best option.

Compliantly, she turned to fetch her mare. Edward was already two steps ahead of her in doing so, but before he could reach the horse Alex sailed by them both.

He stormed right past her brother and snatched the reins that had been allowed to rest on the ground while they took their leisure.

"Alexander!" Greyland exclaimed.

Edward took a controlled step back, yet the look in his eyes was anything but submissive.

Greyland hurried forward, feeling a surge of protectiveness for her brother. She reached for her mare's reins. "I can fetch her myself."

Alexander did not let go. Greyland's initial concern re-categorizing sharply to anger.

"What is all of this untoward commotion about?" she demanded, tightening her grip on the leather in an attempt to take control of her horse.

He did not release the reins over to her.

She tugged, her pulse quickening. "Answer me!"

"Greyland." Edward's voice held an undeniable warning, which only served to irritate her more. Why did everyone have to do as the Duke of Ravenswood said? *Even when the insufferable man was not saying a damn thing!*

Alex locked his hard gaze on her.

She yanked the reins again. This time the mare threw back her head and snorted.

Alexander's eyes narrowed.

He opened his hand wide in an obvious show of letting her take possession of the horse, but his eyes stayed focused on hers.

"This...commotion," he said, stabbing the words, "has to do with McGreggor escaping. And you leaving the castle without nary a word to me as to your whereabouts."

Concern and anger. Both feelings, right on the heels of one another, raged once again in Greyland. She pursed her lips. "You really need to improve upon your communication skills."

"And you should show more respect for your future husband."

"By acting the part of a dog that does not leave its yard?" She stomped her foot.

"By not rolling around in the grass with another man for everyone to see!"

She slapped him. *Hard.*

A covey of quail took flight from a nearby bush, but not a solitary muscle twitched on her intended's face.

"Your father is at the house," Alexander stated, his voice as even as a river-stone turned in the current for years.

He walked past her.

Greyland began to shake, but she gritted her teeth and stood tall.

Damn him! Damn him and his stupid male pride.

She stood there, as if rooted in the earth, until she heard a nicker, followed by the sounds of a horse galloping away.

"Greyland?" Edward ventured hesitantly.

"Was he right?"

"Greyland, no!" Her brother rushed toward her.

She held up a stilling hand. *No,* she would not take pity. If she went into Edward's arms now, she would crumble. *She would not do it.* She would not fall apart after she had acted so assuredly. *She was not wrong.*

The sound of another horse walking across the grass alerted Greyland to the fact that Henry had not departed with his brother.

She angrily wiped a tear off her cheek.

"He did not mean it," Henry said from behind her. "He is just scared."

Greyland scoffed and turned to face him. "Funny how he wields that emotion like a sword."

He offered her a sympathetic half-grin. "He is not good with feelings, in general."

She shook her head, grateful for his understanding. "I have noticed."

Had these two brothers really been sired by the same man?

Henry seemed so compassionate and understanding, sensing when something needed to be handled with care, while his brother chose to go straight for the jugular in full brutish lord affect.

"We really should hurry back," Edward said with unusual practicality. "A storm is heading our way."

Greyland looked up at the sky. Sure enough, dark clouds were rolling in, advancing off the ocean at a rather considerable pace. She wanted to laugh out loud. Even the weather was influenced by her Dark Duke.

"Thank God." Richard Kingston walked quickly down the corridor to greet them.

"Daddy," Greyland rushed into his arms. "I am so glad you are here."

Alex felt like a jackass. The news of Colin's escape had just come as such a shock. It had knocked him down a peg. That, coupled with the bone-chilling fear that tore through him when he realized Greyland was not on the premises, had sent utter terror coursing through him. It had felt like he was reliving the night they were intercepted on the road all over again.

Powerless...

That one word summed up everything. Power and control were everything that Alex strived for and adhered to his entire life. Ever since his mother had died, anyway. He had constructed a wall around his emotions, and that wall was made of supreme jurisdiction over his environment.

When he and Henry had crested the hill to behold his intended stretched out in the tall grass with another man, Alexander's blood had all but ignited in his veins.

Granted—that man had turned out to be her brother—but the feeling lingered despite his attempts to curb it. She was right; he really needed to learn to control his emotions. Alex was so afraid of losing her that he was treating her like something fragile that needed to be watched closely, like a mother might hover over a wobbly toddler.

He cringed inwardly. Greyland was everything to him. And by her own words, she felt like a dog that could not be trusted out of the yard.

God, how he wished those words, spoken out of anger, back into his stupid mouth. He had deserved her wrath, and then some. He needed to make this right. *Quickly.* He was a better man than this. She deserved a better man than what he had just demonstrated to her out in that field.

"Samson, please have someone bring tea to the main parlor," Alex said when it became clear the guests were all loitering in the main entry, waiting on his instructions.

Everyone acknowledged his directions with nods before heading toward the parlor. Everyone except his lovely bride-to-be. She kept herself tucked under her father's arm; eyes averted from Alex's.

His heart broke in two. He had to amend this. *And he would.* But something told him dragging her aside right now would be another mistake. She was hurting, and as much as it killed him that she was seeking solace in the familiar, rather than him, he had to let her have that time. Plus, it would do him good to tamp down his immediate reaction to *'fix this'* by inserting himself into her path. Not everything in life could be corrected with sheer, indomitable will.

Or so he was learning.

AN HOUR later and everyone was well-informed regarding the current McGreggor fiasco, and all the men were well into their cups. The mood had lightened considerably, aided largely by the spirits. That, and the comfort of knowing it would take Colin time to regroup. The future laird was likely on his way back to Ireland as they spoke. As for Derrick, he would not dare to come here. Especially, not with half of London set to descend on Greenshire Castle for the wedding of the season. For the moment, they were all safe.

Alex looked over at Greyland for what had to be the hundredth time. She had relaxed considerably since her return to the castle, even engaging him in conversation as she did everyone else. To the outside world, nothing seemed amiss between them. Alex had not acted a fool, and Greyland had not struck him in anger for it.

He ventured a glance at Edward. *Correction.* Her brother had not forgotten. Edward reclined back indolently in his chair, his movements coming with the same practiced ease everyone expected of him. But his eyes said something completely different when they looked at Alex. He had lost the man's trust and the youngest Kingston son was not going to let him forget it anytime soon.

That only left his own brother among the witnesses to Alexander's absolute failure. He looked at Henry. His brother was a much better actor. He laughed and conversed now with Richard as if they had known each other for years.

Alex fixed his eyes back on Greyland. Something had shifted in her present mood. Two faint lines pinched between her brows and her lips pursed slightly. He knew that look well. An idea had just taken root.

She shifted in her seat, arching her back and tilting her long neck to the side. The move drew an appreciable hesitation in the conversations being had by his brother, who was becoming much too smitten with his fiancée, and Lord Ashlown, who had always wanted her.

Alex could not fault them. Greyland moved in the most feminine of ways. A practiced Courtesan could spend a lifetime perfecting the skill and never have it come as natural. What was even more attractive about her subtle gestures—the lilt of her chin, rolling of her fingers, and rotation of her ankles—was that she had no earthly concept the power it had over men. She simply came by her womanly charms in the most earnest of ways. In a world where women either tried too hard to gain a man's attention, or prudishly not at all, it was a most coveted trait.

Greyland suddenly rose from her seat, prompting all the men to rise with her.

"Please..." She smiled warmly, encouraging them to reclaim their seats. "I just need to move about a little."

She made her way to the bar. Samson all but jumped in front of her as she reached for the brandy. "Please allow me, my lady."

She inclined her head in assent. "By all means. But please, do not dilute it."

Samson looked over to Alex. Alex nodded and the drink was

poured, no water added, and offered to the lady of the house. Greyland, not showing even the slightest annoyance with her request needing approval, smiled, and walked to the window.

"Darling, is it not a little early for such a drink?" Richard's voice rose over the others.

"All of you have had several," she replied logically. "Are my nerves considered more solid than those of you big, strong men?"

"You do have a point," her father said, sighing in agreement. "Today is a rather taxing exception to an otherwise normal Thursday."

"At least step back from the window." Perkin pointed out just as a bolt of lightning illuminated the stormy sky behind her. "I know you're frightened, but I assure you, we will—"

Greyland swiveled her head and glared at her brother, which had the effect of cutting him off like the heel of a hand jabbed between the eyes. A look of daring determination burned within her eyes. "I am not frightened in the least. I have been face-to-face with death now, and I have a good understanding of what emotions such an encounter produces. I, for one, am not scared. I am bloody-well mad!"

She crossed her arms, beverage held confidently atop them as she looked down the thin ridge of her nose. "If anyone tries to hurt my loved ones, or anyone in this household, for that matter, I will take great pleasure in finishing them myself!"

Silence enveloped the room. She did not sound like an overly indulged child putting on an act. She did not sound like an old maid lecturing as if God himself was standing right behind her.

She sounded like a Queen.

Alexander saw Lord Ashlown's jaw go slack. Alex smirked. The pompous lord might have expected such words from Perkin earlier, but he definitely did not expect such a heartfelt declaration from this fragile beauty.

Outwardly fragile, he mentally corrected.

Alex felt something akin to pride bloom in his heart.

A second thunderous bolt of crackling lightning rattled the windowpanes. Victory speech aside, *she was still too damn close to that window.* Alex stood.

She might possess more strength in her little toe than most men did in their whole bodies, but she was still his. And she still needed his protection.

Alex moved to her side and placed a hand on the small of her back. Without a word, he steered her away from the glass.

"If you will excuse us," he addressed the room. "I have a few things I need to discuss with my bride-to-be."

XIII

Greyland's palms began to sweat with anticipation as he calmly but firmly steered her out of the parlor and through the house. She trailed behind him as they made their way up the stairs wordlessly, her hand still securely in his. Only the faces of passing servants confirmed their master was not scowling, for they all nodded and smiled. Of course, *would one give away their intentions if they were about to commit murder?* She wondered.

He had been so…*amicable*…since returning to the castle. Considering that was not a word ever associated with her fiancé she had good reason to be suspicious. Of course, there was also the itsy-bitsy fact she had slapped him in broad daylight in front of his brother, and hers…

Greyland might not be the most perceptive person, but she wagered that striking a man such as Alexander Hamilton might bode unwell for the dunce that dared. Yes, upon further consideration, she was fairly certain his intentions were to kill her now.

Once inside his bedroom chamber, he released her and closed and locked the door. Greyland held her breath, preparing herself for whatever storm was about to descend upon her. He slowly turned to face her, his eyes shrouded under prominent brow bones and tousled hair that fell freely across his forehead.

He leaned back against the door. "We need to talk."

The lack of inflection in his voice did nothing to comfort her but talking was better than her first suspicion. Greyland mustered her bravest, most pragmatic disposition and dove right in.

"I have offended you with my actions and for that, I am sorry. I understand if you wish to call off the wedding. I am sure we could be off by daybreak. Provided the storm clears."

He stood there, motionless, staring at her. "Is that what you want, Greyland?"

"It does not matter what I want if I am disappointing to you. If I bring you strife and shame." The words tore at her throat. They cut her to the bone. Like death knocking on the door to her heart. If his next words confirmed all this, she would die.

"Is that what you think?" He pushed from the door and stood to his full height. "That you bring me shame?"

Greyland could take no more, her resolve was crumbling around her feet with every word cast out. "It is what you said." Her eyes found the patterns of the rug. "That I was laying with another man..." her voice faded down to barely a whisper, "for all to see."

"Greyland."

It was the last thing she heard before the sound of her own racking sobs overtook her trembling lips and poured from her lungs. Her shoulders shook and tears flooded her cheeks, rolling faster than her hands could catch. She did not bother. It was too late. Every doubt she had ever suffered, every fear she would ever have, raced like wild horses across her heart.

Her legs started to cave to the floor just as strong arms scooped her up. "Shhh..." He pressed his lips to the side of her head. "Greyland, listen," he implored.

"I cannot," she managed to squeak out through cresting waves of hitched breathing. "I cannot hear you."

He was moving now, carrying her across the room. She felt her weight settled onto his lap as he sat down on the bed. He said nothing, just let her cry. Pressed solidly against his chest, he rocked her gently to the rhythmic sound of the falling rain.

Minutes passed. Maybe more. Maybe less. Eventually, the onslaught of emotions began to subside into a mindless absolution. Whatever was to happen would happen. There was no longer a right and wrong between them. Fate now held the cards.

"I am sorry," she said.

"No." Alexander adjusted her just enough so that one of his hands could cup her chin and level her gaze up to his. "I am the one that should be apologizing to you. You did nothing wrong. I overreacted. I was out of turn." He kissed her forehead. "I could never be ashamed of you."

He tilted his head and kissed tenderly just under her jaw, then his lips roamed up to hover above hers. "You are everything to me. I love you more than I could have ever imagined loving another human being." He kissed the corner of her mouth and pulled back just a little. "Can you ever forgive me? I will do whatever it takes to right this wrong."

Greyland breathed in his scent, a heady mix that reminded her of worn leather and sweet grass. She leaned in, needing more of it.

"I forgive you," she heard herself whisper against his warm skin.

He covered her mouth with his, effectively reading her mind and understanding better than she did, what she was craving.

Greyland kissed him like he was the air she required to live, her tongue deepening the kiss. He let her take control, devouring him as she needed. She climbed her body up and over his as her hands raked through his hair.

His hands were moving up her skirts now. She pushed him back against the bed, following him down. Both of his hands pushed under her pantalets and palmed her bare bottom. He squeezed his fingers into her flesh.

She kissed him again, moaning into his mouth as their breath became one. She pulled back, taking his bottom lip between her teeth and stretching it just enough. The result caused him to moan and instantly grow harder between her legs.

Greyland leaned into his neck, her words no louder than the rain gently rapping the window outside. "I think you deserve a spanking, my lord."

His breathing all but stopped.

She sucked his earlobe into her mouth.

He shivered.

She was going to enjoy this very much.

GREYLAND RAN for the newly arrived carriage in which Bella alit from. Alex watched as his betrothed lift her skirts all the way to her knees for better speed. His jaw tightened predictably when he noticed Lord Ashlowns admiring the sight. Even Henry was transfixed.

He looked past his brother—that he had never wanted to punch more—to find Richard grinning, almost knowingly over at him. Alex quickly surmised the look to be one of relief; relief that the order of protection had now passed hands from father to spouse.

After Greyland released Bella from the hug, Thomas swooped in and lifted his bride-to-be off the ground. Bella laughed and then promptly demanded the earl release her so she could continue her greetings.

Alexander's focus quickly changed when Greyland, unaware that anyone was looking, bent over to remove a stone from the bottom of her slipper. Her perfectly round bottom lifted skyward provoked the most *stirring* memories of the afternoon spent in Lord Humphrey's study. Alex suddenly felt the need to reposition his jacket.

He dared to look about the yard discreetly. Not a soul was even remotely aware of where his thoughts had digressed to, as they were all transfixed on his fiancée.

Alex cursed under his breath as he moved to her side. He wound his arm around her tiny waist and bent his head to whisper, "You give me great inspiration in that position, my dear."

She looked at him innocently. He smirked and her eyes widened comprehensively. "Alexander Hamilton!" she admonished quietly before leaning in with a conspiratorial grin. "Just say when."

She swiveled, as if ready to make for the house, and in doing so, allowed her hand to brush across the front of his trousers. She smiled confidently when he shuddered. "I am all yours, Your Grace."

"Yes," he growled low in his throat. "You are all mine. So please take care. I would hate to have to hit my own brother."

Greyland feigned a scowl. "Do not dare, Lord Ravenswood. You are running out of family members that do not wish you dead."

He chuckled. "There is that."

Bella glided by then, seizing Greyland as she passed. "Lady time," she excused. "See you gentlemen shortly."

Bella ferociously patted the cushion on the settee in Greyland's chamber, motioning for her to sit. The gleam in her twinkling amber eyes promised a deluge of questions. Greyland had missed her friend greatly and was glad to have another woman around, but she was not sure how ready she was for recounting every detail of their trip out of London.

"Well?" Bella's voice thrilled.

"Well..." Greyland looked out the window. "Is this estate not just breathtaking?"

Bella raised one perfectly manicured eyebrow. "Yes, beautiful, amazing, so on and so on. You know what I really want to know."

"Why, whatever do you mean?" Greyland flashed a coy smile.

Bella wagged a knowing finger at her. "Oh, pish posh, missy. Out with it. I know you are no longer an innocent."

"Bella!" Greyland gasped, utterly shocked. That shock trotted away as quickly as it had ridden in. She leaned close to Bella, suddenly worried. "Can you tell?"

Her friend grinned. "No. Other than the way you two regard one another." Bella inched forward. "Do not worry, nothing is written across your face. Though your true love looks wound tighter than a coil." Her eyes danced. "Whatever have you done to that man?"

Greyland felt the heat rising in her cheeks. "I suppose nothing that he has not experienced before."

Bella pursed her lips. "I have known Alexander Hamilton for years since we were children. I have never seen him look the way he did when I stepped out of that carriage today."

"Truly?"

Bella nodded. "Truly. Now," she said reasonably, "tell me how it was?"

Greyland clasped her friend's hands, giddy excitement taking over. "Oh Bella, it is like..." Her eyes flitted up, trying to pinpoint the right words. "It is quite..." She looked back at Bella. "Magical."

Bella exhaled dramatically. "Oh, sweet merciful God." She laughed. "I was so afraid it was overrated. On the woman's end of events, anyway."

Greyland nodded adamantly. "Oh, I believe it is kept a well-guarded secret on purpose. So young debutantes shy away from the deed. But it is most tantalizing."

"Does it hurt?"

Greyland blushed again, thinking of all the ways Alex had already taken her. "The first time is uncomfortable for only a moment, but then..."

Greyland flopped back against the cushions, dragging Bella, giggling, with her. "It is something you begin to crave deep in your belly and all over your skin." She gazed up at the ceiling, pausing briefly for a more thorough examination of her thoughts on the subject matter. "I fully understand why it turns men into cads."

She looked over at Bella, grinning ear-to-ear beside her on the sofa. "I really want to become a cad now."

They both erupted into a fit of giggles.

THE LAST OF the guests had arrived and been shown to their rooms. They were now either wandering the grounds or still tucked away in their guest quarters getting ready for the evening's festivities. Alexander buttoned a button on the sleeve of his shirt as he observed the gardens below from his upstairs dressing room window.

He spied Edward escorting two pretty debutantes across the lawn and felt himself grin. *Your turn at the races,* he thought and chuckled. It was about time some other man took over the title of most desired catch amongst the bon ton.

Alex rolled his neck. For once it was not tight leading into a night like tonight. He closed his eyes and welcomed the absence of tension, all due to his bewitching young fiancée that had liberated him from the clutches of every rung-climbing female in England. He was officially off the market, and he could not be happier for it.

The new Kingston men were now the center of attention and Alex could understand why. Both of Greyland's brothers were distinguished and debonair, per society's standards. Edward was charismatic and easy-going, with an underlying hint of carefully concealed danger. The latter part always attracted the ladies. Perkin, on the other hand, was both elegant and commanding. Two traits hard to find encompassed in one individual. People were drawn to both brothers like moths to a flame.

Even Richard Kingston was in high demand, it seemed. Widows and plotting mothers alike had their eyes set on the regal older gentleman. It was evident where both younger Kingston men had gleaned their striking features. The only difference was in the eyes. Perkin and Edward's were a deep shade of slate-blue, whereas Richard's were the most unusual grey, almost the color of a dove's wing.

His betrothed must have inherited her striking green color from their mother. Perhaps one day soon, he would have a child of his own to inherit those eyes.

The unexpected thought caught him off-guard. In the past, he had never entertained the idea of children, other than to solidify the family bloodline. They had ranked no further up in the concerns of his mind than the maintenance on a carriage might; a possession a man needed only because it was practical.

Alex turned from the window. The idea had considerably more merit now that he had managed to make a love match. In fact, he found the notion rather appealing. Especially the idea of making them.

Alex smiled on that most desirable thought and made his way out of his dressing room. *Where was his lady love?*

He took the stairs and headed down the main corridor toward the ballroom. He was certain where she could be found. No doubt making sure everything was in order for the ball.

Alex rounded the last corner, entered the main foyer and stopped mid-stride when the sound of soft sniffling caught his ear. He looked around for the source. *Nothing.*

The soft whimpering sound drifted out again, and this time he pinpointed the source. Alex bent down and looked under the large round table in the center of the room. A pair of blue eyes, the color of robin's eggs, stared back at him.

"Ah, what do we have here?" Alex smiled and made his stature as demure as he could. "Did you get lost, sweetie?"

Annabelle shook her head and buried her face back into her knees.

"Are you scared of all the people?" he asked perseveringly.

She peeked up through a mop of blonde hair and nodded.

"Will you allow me to protect you?" Alex reached out a hand. She considered him carefully. "I could use your help finding Lady Greyland. I do not want her to be scared either."

A look of concern darted across her huge blue orbs and Alex immediately felt a pang of guilt for causing her anymore worry, but he needed to redirect her energy. He recalled using similar tactics on Henry when he was small. Sometimes the only way to correct a situation was to reshape it to look completely different.

And it worked. The child reached out and placed her hand in Alex's proffered one. He slowly coaxed her out. As soon as her head cleared the tabletop, she launched herself into his arms.

Alex remained on bended knee. Her little shoulders shook, and she buried her head into the lapels of his jacket. "Oh sweetling," he soothed. "No one is going to hurt you here. You are safe."

He had no idea what to do. He felt completely out of his element. If she had been a boy, it would seem plausible to give a short lecture about overcoming fears, and knights fighting dragons, and whatnot.

But she was not a boy. She was a tiny, scared little girl. Something strange tugged at his heartstrings.

He stood, Annabelle still clinging to him for dear life. "Where should we start looking for the lady of the house?"

Annabelle rolled her little head to the side and pointed a chubby finger in the direction of the ballroom.

"Ah, how clever you are, Annabelle," Alex praised and started walking toward the ballroom.

He looked down as they walked and could see that the tears had started to dry on her cheeks and her eyes had grown intently focused on the direction they were now moving. This was progress.

She wiggled a little in his arms as she tried to crane her head around more. "Would you like to walk?" Alex offered. "Maybe you could escort me into the ballroom?"

She wordlessly nodded and he carefully sat her down. She put her little hand in his and began pulling him on. Alex's heart wrenched a little tighter as her previous fear seemed to wash completely away, replaced by a newfound excitement.

She was practically dragging him by the time they stepped foot inside the ballroom. Annabelle's eyes scoured the room. Greyland was not in here. The little girl turned her face up to him and her chin trembled precariously. She was about to cry again.

"I am sure she just stepped out and will be right back," he rushed to distract her. "Will you show me the waltz while we wait? Greyland said you were getting so good."

She looked around tentatively.

Alex held out his hand to her.

Her eyes fixated on it.

"I could really use the help."

She regarded him again before a gleam of determination danced across her eyes and she stepped forward and accepted his hand.

Annabelle let him lead her forward as she lifted her arms, as wide as she possibly could, demonstrating her newfound dance-frame. Alex could barely stifle the chuckle that threatened. He quickly shut his mouth. He knew she would not appreciate him laughing while she was trying so hard to be serious.

Instead, he went with the one thing he knew all ladies liked to hear. "Why, Lady Annabelle, Lady Greyland has taught you well."

Annabelle smiled but kept her serious focus straight ahead. Alex lowered down as best he could and began leading her through a few basic patterns in the waltz. He was actually shocked at how much the little lass had learned in just a few days.

Feeling like it was a good time to propose more spontaneity, Alex asked, "Ready to go faster?"

She nodded eagerly, so he scooped her up and began twirling her around the room.

She squealed out in delight. Alex turned even faster. Her smile widened and she threw her head back, letting the wind lift her hair to stand on end.

Alex slowly brought them to a stop and placed her on the ground, making sure she was steady before letting go of her. "Ah!" He lifted a finger. "I forgot one last move!"

She beamed up at him and nodded her approval.

"We cannot have a proper dance without..." He reached for her, turned her twice in a tight circle and then dropped her into a theatrical dip. "One of these."

This sent Annabelle into another fit of giggles.

Applause cut through the ballroom, quieting both their laughter.

Before Alex could even straighten, Annabelle had wiggled out of dance-frame and was running as fast as she could across the ballroom.

"Very well done," Greyland clapped once more and then lowered down to catch Annabelle, now bounding into her arms. "There may be hope for Lord Ravenswood yet." She tossed him a teasing smile.

"She is almost as good a teacher as her mentor." Alex grinned.

Greyland hugged the child tightly and gave her a kiss on the top of the head. She released the little girl and stood back up. "Now, Annabelle, go and fetch yourself a sweet from the kitchen. Cook has just made some fresh for you." Greyland smiled over the child's head. "I have promised my future husband his own dance."

From his concealment behind a rather large potted palm on the far side of the ballroom, Derrick watched the little girl scamper through the grand entrance and disappear down the hall.

"May I have this dance?" His nephew bowed and extended his arm towards the Kingston wench.

"I would be honored." She curtsied then allowed Alex to escort her to the middle of the room. Derrick wanted to gag.

How bloody romantic.

Derrick could feel a white-hot jealousy unlike any he had ever known begin to claw at his skin when they began to move around the space.

How dare his spoiled nephew get all of this?

His eyes darted around the room, mentally cataloging every

expensive and excessive detail that screamed wealth and power. The sheer opulence of this place defined his family's name and position in this country.

And it should be *his*.

He should be holding her. This house party should have been summoned for *his* wedding. *He* should be the master of this house. *He* should be the duke!

Derrick's eyes glared on as the couple finished their dance with a flurry of pivots and one last overindulgent dip.

His nephew lowered his lips to Lady Kingston's.

Derrick could kill him now. Stab him right between the shoulder blades when he least expected it.

Do not be a fool!

There were too many possible eyes milling about, and Derrick had worked too hard to be throttled by impulse now. His hands balled into fists as the loving couple broke their embrace and walked out of the ballroom, hand in hand.

He slid out from behind the plant and made haste toward the servant's entrance. There was more than one way to skin a cat.

Derrick snuck down the narrow hallway that would eventually lead to the back courtyards. He had seen all he needed to see. Now he could put action to plan. He just had to make it back out of the castle unseen.

A door opened a little further down the passageway and a maid stepped into his path. Derrick quickly lowered his head and slouched his shoulders, in hopes his stolen servant's garb would allow him to pass unnoticed.

Keeping his eyes averted, they passed one another, but before he could draw a breath of relief… "You there," she called out. "Where are you going? Are you not needed in the stable?"

Derrick slowly turned around and flashed the maid a winning smile. "Yes, I wuz just gettin' that way. Had to fetch an order for me lord."

He made a deliberate scan of her person, looking her up and down more closely before allowing his smile to narrow into an approving leer. "Unless you have a better need of me?"

The woman blushed, unaccustomed to the blatancy of his words. She bobbed her head awkwardly and turned, all superiority in her rank flitting away as she quickly fled down the hallway.

Derrick took a moment to appreciate how her hips swayed as she scurried off. Nothing like a good combination of fear and seduction.

He turned, pulling his height back to his birthright's noble stature, and strolled onward to the stable. A plan etched itself beautifully in his head. He knew exactly what he needed to do next. He would have to wait, but only a short while.

XIV

Greyland traced her fingers over the gold beveled script of the renowned dress maker's signature, stamped boldly on the outside of the ivory trunk. It had arrived, via one of The Queen's personal footmen less than a half-hour earlier. Greyland had been so excited she nearly ran from the sitting parlor where she had been entertaining the other ladies over high tea.

She took a deep breath and lifted the lid. Her hand flew to her mouth. Greyland allowed her other trembling hand to slowly lower to the dresses' delicate material, marveling at the coolness of the snow-white fabric. Her wedding dress.

It was perfect!

Her skin prickled with excitement. It had been cut and designed exactly for her by The Queen's own designer before they had departed London. And now it was here.

Greyland gathered the courage to gingerly lift the gown out of the trunk. A tear sprang to her eye as she thought of all that had transpired in her life over the past month. The world had shifted on its axis and, she had held on.

This dress represented her journey. It had been commissioned right after her father had agreed to Alexander's request for her hand in marriage. It would now be worn to solidify her vows to him.

She carefully laid the gown across her bed and picked up the note at the bottom of the truck.

My Dear Lady Kingston,

I could start this letter off by offering words of comfort for all that you have been made to suffer at the hands of over-reaching men, but I will not. I get the feeling you are not the sort of woman that needs words to right wrongs. Instead, I write to offer you congratulations on your new journey into marriage and to inform you that those that wished you harm will be dealt with by The Crown of England.

Secondly, as a token of my affection for your family, I wish to give back your family's rightful place in society.

Richard Kingston will henceforth reclaim the title, Duke of York.

Perkin Kingston is from this day forward, Earl of Dessmark.

Edward Kingston will, from this day forward, be granted the title, Earl of Wellington.

All ancestral lands and holdings have been transferred into their possession, as well as Westingham Castle, the original home of your line.

I hope that these small contributions can ease some of the strife your family has been made to endure over the years.

Lastly, my dear Greyland, know that you and your family will continue to have the full weight of the Crown behind you. I cannot change the past wrongs, but hopefully, we can forge a new future together.

Forever, your Queen and friend,
Queen Victoria

GREYLAND'S HANDS shook with gratitude as she folded the letter. After centuries in the shadows, her family would finally be welcomed back to the stations they deserved. They could all start a new life here in England. Greyland was not the only one with a promising and steadfast future now. The Queen had made sure that they would all be recognized.

A giddiness hummed through her body. *Did they know yet?* Her father and brothers would be thrilled with the news.

"Have I told you today how lucky I am?" Alexander's sensuous voice caressed the stillness of the room.

Greyland quickly moved in front of the dress, shielding it from view. "Alexander! Do not move a muscle."

He canted his head curiously. "Not exactly the response I expected."

"Turn around." She pointed her finger down and rotated it, as if that was direction enough. "You cannot see my dress."

He chuckled and did as asked, turning toward the door.

Greyland quickly put the dress neatly back into the traveling trunk. "You can turn back around now."

He did, grinning. "Can I have my answer now?"

"But of course, my handsome lord," she smiled. "You have told me at least a hundred times how blessed you are. To my account, that is a hundred times shy of your daily quota," she teased.

"Then let me increase that number by saying it again. Greyland, I love you, and will love you for the rest of my days. I am the most fortunate man alive."

He advanced upon her, cupping her face in his hands, and raising her mouth to his. "You are mine. To have and to hold, forever."

"Hmph!" came Annie's, not so subtle, introduction into the room.

They ended the kiss, but Alex kept Greyland locked in his arms. "She will not need assistance with her dress, Annie."

He smiled down into Greyland's eyes as a blush crept across her cheeks.

"Yes, Your Grace," the maid said.

Although Alex's solid wall of a chest blocked Greyland's view of Annie, she could just imagine the steam rising from the older woman's cheeks. Greyland playfully pushed at his chest, rebukingly. He cocked his head, in that desirable fashion she loved, and silently mouthed the word, "What?"

"Please shut the door on your way out."

"Yes, Your Grace," Annie replied.

After the door closed behind them, Greyland pushed up onto her tiptoes and kissed the rakish grin on Alex's face. "You are horrible! That poor woman probably lives in fear of coming around a corner and finding us in some compromising position."

"She should knock. Now let us get you into this dress," he said as he reached around her for the lid to the trunk.

"Do not dare, Alexander Hamilton!" Greyland swatted his hand. "It is bad luck to see the bride's dress before the wedding. You know full well it is not the one I am wearing tonight."

"Oh, fine." He settled both hands on her waist and pulled her hard against him.

She reached up and tapped the tip of his perfect nose. "We would hate to break with tradition and whatnot."

"Ah, yes. You and I do love to follow the rules." He grinned wickedly and then averted his eyes on something behind her.

"How about that one?" She followed his line of sight to the exquisite gown hanging in the corner.

Her dress for tonight's ball was another masterpiece. It was a dark shade of amethyst satin and had a black velvet floral overlay that began just under the bust. The velvet grew in size and design as it made its way down the dress to take over the entire bottom of the skirt.

"Do you like it?" she asked.

"It is nearly as perfect as the body it is about to don." His eyes darkened. "Turn around."

Greyland did as told and turned, lifting her hair so that he could have free access to the buttons that lined her back. She had grown accustomed to this ritual of him always being the one to dress and undress her. Her day dress hit the floor. Alex scooped it up and laid it gingerly on the bed before walking across the room to where her ball gown hung. She would never get tired of the way the man filled out a pair of trousers and a waistcoat.

He retrieved the evening gown, strode back to Greyland, and lowered it for her to step into. "I have been thinking a lot about children," Alex said as he lifted the dress up the front of her body, adjusting it over her shoulders.

"Oh?"

"What would you say to adopting Annabelle?"

Greyland's heart tightened in her chest. "Yes! Oh, do you really mean it? Yes! Yes! Yes!"

A tear ran down her cheek and Alex rose to capture it with his finger.

"Ah darling, to be so strong and brave, you are so beautifully tender and feminine." He wrapped her in his arms and kissed the top of her head. "I will have the proper papers drawn up tomorrow. I had not planned on mentioning it until after the ball."

"Oh Alex," she was not sure what to say. How to put into words all she felt at this moment. How much she loved him and the many sacrifices he had made for her and her family.

"I know I am not the most disciplined of ladies."

Blast it!

She took a deep, shuddering breath, dismally aware that she was about to cry. *Again.*

"And you seem to find me crying rather much as of late, but I promise..."

He placed a finger on her mouth. "Shhhhh. I will have no talk of what is expected of a proper lady. And as I said, I find it extremely appealing that you are driven by emotion. Gives me something to protect." He slid his thumb over the seam of her lips. "You remind me of water, Greyland. Soothing and dangerous, like a drug slipped effortlessly into my veins. You are my soul." He smiled down at her.

She beamed up at him. "How did I ever get so lucky as to find you? You have made me the happiest woman on earth. I love you with all my heart, Alexander Hamilton."

"Destiny," Alex added as he moved to the back of her dress and began to fasten the buttons. "And, your brothers choosing the right pub, of course." He chuckled.

Greyland whirled in place and kissed him hard, then drew back just enough to whisper. "Destiny, huh?"

She painted more kisses down his jaw, rendering him silent as her hands moved to his trousers. He rasped out a low oath as she freed his length.

She lowered to her knees before him and pushed his pants over his hips, doffing them to the floor. "Let me show you, and destiny, my gratitude then."

"How much longer do we have to stay here?" The woman's whiny voice grated on his ear canals like a rake across cobblestones.

Derrick felt a dull pressure building around the perimeter of his forehead, the same headache he always had when in Lady Chatsworth's presence. He was not sure how much longer he could be near her without placing his hands around her neck and squeezing until the prattling noise ceased to babble from her throat.

His silence elicited a foot stomp right beside his chair. He slid his eyes from the fire up to her tiresome scowl. He reminded himself, for about the twentieth time tonight, that he needed this woman. At least for tonight. Tomorrow he could kill her.

"We have been over this, love," he reminded her tersely. "Tonight, you will have your revenge on Lady Kingston and tomorrow, my nephew will be all yours."

Derrick plastered on a tight smile. "Now, lift your skirts and ride me like a stallion."

She narrowed her eyes. "Why should I?"

"Because it is all part of the plan." He unbuttoned his pants. "And you are a greedy whore."

Lady Chatsworth made to strike him, but he grabbed her wrist and yanked her down to his eye level. "Giddy up."

She glared at him. He released her wrist and grinned.

She stepped back, reached under her dress hemline and removed her pantalets, then stepped back up to his chair and started to lift her skirts. "Not so fast," he stopped her. "I am not ready yet."

She reluctantly leaned forward. Freeing him from his pants, she began working him over.

Derrick closed his eyes and pictured Greyland Kingston. It would be her ministering to him soon enough. His plan would be set in motion tonight. He would soon have the title of Duke of Ravenswood, and when he did, she would be forced to take him instead.

Lady Chatsworth, albeit annoying, was a brilliant pawn in his plan. All he had had to do was convince her she would marry his nephew once they got Greyland out of the way. But that was just the beginning of his plan. Sure, she would be gravely disappointed and mad when he killed her heart's desire, but he could really not care less.

Derrick cracked his eyes open when she took her hands off him and began to climb up onto the chair. "Other way, dear." Her brows pinched together. "I am trying to picture you as someone else," he said as plainly as one might address a toddler.

"Why you…" Her features contorted unpleasantly. "Wretched man."

"Careful," he warned. "Turn around."

She pushed off the chair, spun, faced the fire, and began to hike up her skirts.

Derrick licked his lips as her ass was made visible. It was, after all, her best feature. He imagined Miss Kingston's delectable ass was just as sweet. He could not wait to find out.

He put both hands on Lady Chatsworth's hips before she could speak again and ruin his illusion and forced her down onto his ready length.

Her surprised yelp was the first welcomed sound he had heard in hours.

XV

Greyland was beyond happy that her maid, Elise, had finally arrived. Elise was the only one who could make sense of her out-of-control curls. Greyland had been told since childhood that her ringlets were a gift from God—at least that's what everyone said—but God had a twisted sense of humor. No fashionable hairstyle could be artfully maintained with such unruly hair.

Elise eyed her opponent with raw determination, as if sizing up how best to slay a dragon. This brought a smile to Greyland's lips. She had missed Elise so. Both her and their family's longtime butler, Ocman, had arrived earlier that day. Greyland felt everything was complete now. She had everyone around her whom she cared deeply for.

"Ah-ha!" Elise exclaimed triumphantly. "I have just the thing." She opened a drawer and began to dig through a pile of loose fabric intended for garment repairs. She clapped when she found a lovely swatch of black lace.

"I thought we were torturing my head, not making a dress?"

"Oh, you just wait, Miss Greyland, I have plans." She dove back into her work with confident hands.

Ten minutes later, Elise took a calculated step back and exhaled. She motioned for Greyland to turn and face the mirror.

"Oh, Elise, you have done it again. It is beautiful!"

Elise had gathered the mass of hair high in the back and selected specific curls to be released. She had then pinned the swatch of lace to the top of Greyland's head and wound the loose curls through the lace eyelets. The effect made her hair and the lace appear as if they were one intricate work of art. It was the perfect complement to the dress that followed a similar aesthetic with how the black velvet encased the bottom of her amethyst dress.

Greyland stood and twirled for Elise.

A slow applause came from the doorway.

"My, you are a vision," Perkin said.

Greyland smiled. "So, you approve?"

"Indeed, I very much do." Her brother smiled in return. "Are you sure Alexander deserves you?"

"I do not." Alex rounded the doorframe and patted Perkin's shoulder. "But every day I plan on dreaming up new ways to prove my worth."

Both men stood in thoughtful observation for a long moment.

Greyland looked to Perkin and saw a proud older brother who was surely contemplating the gravity of not having her trailing his every move any longer, while Alex's look was one of unyielding love and desire.

Her heart soared with love for them both. "You two better say something." Her fingers fluttered in front of her eyes, trying to halt the threatening tears. "Elise will kill you if you make me cry and ruin this blush."

As if rehearsed, Elise waved a hairbrush at them. A resounding laugh broke the spell.

"We shan't have that," Perkin concurred.

"Come now." Alex walked to her and offered her his arm. "The world is downstairs waiting to see the most beautiful woman in all of the land."

THE BALLROOM BUZZED WITH ACTIVITY. Men in their dark coats and light trousers contrasted beautifully with the array of colorful gowns ranging in hues of the deepest crimson to the palest green. Alexander observed them all below as they moved about like a tapestry come to life.

Greyland's arm squeezed tighter to his as they began their descent down the stairs. Alex drew her in tighter to his side, reassuringly. She was surprisingly shy entering large crowds, which was interesting considering how opposite she was in every other aspect of life. Still, he found it endearing.

Who was he kidding? He found everything about his bride-to-be endearing. From her fiery headstrong determination to the innocent way she picked at her lips when she was worried.

The crowd noticed them and one by one, their heads lifted. Alex would not delude himself with thinking they watched him; he knew every eye in that ballroom was fixated solely on the beauty at his side. She just had that magical appeal about her.

Now, Alex would grant himself one accolade. Together they made a marvelous team. He could also, unfortunately, understand why so many had sought to undermine their union. But they had failed. *She was his.* And he would do everything in his power to keep her safe.

They took the last step together and as expected, the crowd descended upon them. Greyland smiled reassuringly and released his hand as a group of twittering ladies swept her away. Perkin nodded briefly and proceeded to the library where a group of distinguished lords were no doubt discussing some new act The Queen was about to dispense.

Alex turned his attention to his own host duties and shook Lord Anderson's hand when he tottered over. After a few more pleasantries had been delivered, Alex walked to the edge of the ballroom and did something he seldom did. *He observed.*

To his own astonishment, he did not feel the slightest bit inclined to head straight to the parlor for refuge. Alex did not scan the room for predatory matrons, and he most certainly cared nothing for searching out a lover for the night. It was as if a weight had been lifted from his shoulders. For the first time in his adult life, he could simply take in the evening without the constant reminder that everyone wanted something from him.

On that blessed note, Alex turned his attention to where Greyland had ended up across the room. Her upswept curls shined beneath the glow of the chandelier. She tipped back her head in laughter, exposing her delicate throat. He wanted to be the jeweled necklace adorning that sweet patch of skin. She tilted her head and smiled sweetly to a young dandy who had just entered the throng of admirers. Alex rolled his eyes but resisted the urge to walk over and position himself at her side. He had made a promise to temper his over-protective nature and he intended to keep it. *Even if it killed him.*

He spotted Thomas and Bella and was just about to join them when a familiar voice, on the other side of the stone pillar Alex was leaning against, caught his attention.

"My God, she is the most beautiful woman I believe I have ever seen!" Lord Melbrooke was saying to someone.

"I have only known one other as lovely," Richard Kingston replied. "Her mother."

Alex stopped short and took a step back. He wanted to hear what both men had to say. Melbrooke had arrived earlier that day and professed his remorseful apologies to Alexander and the Kingston's for doubting them and their intentions to the Crown. In an attempt to keep with the peacefulness of the day, Alex had admitted him.

"You are truly a family blessed," Melbrooke continued, but the tenor of his voice read false.

Bitterness, Alex conjectured.

His instincts had always been on high alert around The Queen's head advisor. There was something too ambitious about the man for Alexander's liking, something he simply did not trust.

"Indeed, we are," Richard responded. If he had picked up on the insincere clip to Melbrooke's sentiment, Greyland's father surely did not convey it through his own words. "If you will excuse me, I must go and greet my daughter."

Alex continued to hang back as Richard strolled through the crowd toward Greyland. Melbrooke headed off to the other end of the ballroom. He would need to keep an eye on that one. There was not a shred of doubt as to why Melbrooke had traveled here today and begged forgiveness for the slight he had dealt the Kingston's. The man was simply keeping his friends close and his enemies closer.

GREYLAND DANCED the first waltz with Alex and then danced with each of her brothers and her father. Perkin danced the first Viennese waltz, so Edward demanded that another one be played that evening. He had Lord Ashlown's younger sister to impress, Greyland surmised.

Jessica, a pretty little thing with the same moss green eyes as her older brother, seemed completely enamored with Edward. Greyland squeezed Edward's hand as he spun her out for a final exiting turn. She was happy for him.

Now, if only Perkin could find the right girl. She scanned the crowd for her oldest brother, tapping the edge of her closed fan against her chin. She found him on the dance floor, bathed in admiring gazes from the onlooking crowd. Greyland smiled. Perkin was the epitome of regality as he twirled a blushing lady through a fast country dance.

She looked around the room for Alex next but caught the movement of a fast-moving serving girl out of the corner of her eye instead. Bobbing through the crowd with a look of controlled panic in her eyes, the girl made a beeline straight for Greyland. It was Betty from the kitchen staff. *What was she doing out here?* Annie would skin her alive if she caught her out of her station and in the ballroom. Greyland felt the hairs on the back of her arms lift.

Something was wrong.

Betty thrust out a letter. "Me lady, pardon me. This just came for you. The messenger said it was a matter of life and death and that I must place it in your hands directly." The girl wrung her hands in her apron.

Greyland took the envelope and quickly broke the seal.

Lady Greyland,

I have something of yours that I believe you will want back. She is the loveliest child I have ever seen. It is a pity she is mute. If you do care for the child as I suspect, meet me at the small hunting cabin in the woods, overlooking the ocean. Tell no one and come alone. There is a horse waiting for you by a tree just off the west wing. If you betray this request, I shall be forced to turn the child's blonde curls to red...

Greyland tried to school her expression. She folded the paper with trembling hands and looked the serving girl squarely in the eyes. "Tell no one of this letter or that I have received anything. Understand?"

The girl's eyes shot across the room with uncertainty. "But...me lady—"

"Not a word to anyone. Now, I relieve you of your duties for the night and request you take yourself to bed."

"Yes, me lady." The girl's eyes studied the crowded floor once more as she turned and hurried out of the ballroom.

Greyland looked around herself. Bella was fast approaching with two glasses of champagne. She forced her breathing to slow and tried to smile.

"Here you are." Bella handed her the sparkling beverage.

Greyland took the glass, but not before Bella's keen eyes saw the tremble of her hands.

"Are you feeling all right?" Bella asked, worry replacing her mirth.

"Yes. I just remembered I left no orders for when Malikite should be released from the kennels tonight." Greyland handed her glass to a passing server. "I will relay the message to the gamekeeper and be right back."

"Surely I can get a servant to see to—"

"Truth be told," Greyland said, cutting her off, "a moment of fresh air will be a Godsend."

She patted her best friend's hand assuredly. "I will be right back."

Before Bella could protest or offer assistance, Greyland started moving toward the servant's entrance.

She could hear nothing but the hammering of her own heart as she ran down the long hall that connected the kitchen to the ballroom. Once inside the bustling kitchen, her eyes darted about frantically. She immediately located a knife by the stove and moved to retrieve it.

"My lady, can I get something for you?" Annie asked.

"No." Greyland paused midstride. "I just wanted to make sure dinner was set to be served after the last waltz."

"Why, yes. We are right on schedule. I just have to..." She glanced back toward the ice chest, remembering something, and that was all the distraction Greyland needed.

She pushed a large pot of soup off the stove. The loud crash brought half the kitchen staff racing.

"Oh no!" Annie rushed forward to aid her. "My lady, did it get on you?" The older woman's eyes scanned her dress before bending to examine Greyland's feet.

"I am all right," she said, stepping away before Annie could see that indeed her ankle had been burned in the splash. "I am so sorry," Greyland apologized over the chaos erupting around her. "It must be the champagne. I should get some air."

Annie reluctantly turned her attention back to the overturned pot as Greyland continued to back up to the door.

Greyland glanced once more around the kitchen. Everyone was busy attending to her mess. Her eyes landed again on the knife.

She swiped it and darted out the door.

SHE FOUND the horse where the note said it would be. Greyland quickly removed her gloves, wrapped them around the blade's sharp edge, and shoved the knife into her tight bodice. Then she lifted herself into the saddle. She was blind with fear. Who could threaten a little child? Her mind slammed back to the night in the church.

Colin...

She could not think straight. All she knew was that she must save Annabelle, and if that meant walking into a trap, so be it. She was prepared to spare the child's life at the cost to her own. At least her family would know where to look for her. *If it was Colin.* It had to be! Who else could be so vile?

Greyland breathed in the chilled night air and kicked the horse into a gallop. She hoped Alex would understand and that she would be around later to explain it to him.

She heard a lone howl pierce the black night, followed by a thunderclap echoing off somewhere over the ocean.

She rode low as she entered the woods.

The howl drew nearer. Her horse's ears pricked higher, and its nostrils flared with unease.

Malikite! He must have gotten out somehow.

The realization gave her courage. She spurred the horse on.

ALEXANDER SEARCHED the ballroom for Greyland. *Where had she gone?* He spied Bella and made his way over to her. "Have you seen Greyland?" he asked, interrupting her conversation with the Viscount Shawson.

"She left the ballroom a few minutes ago."

"She left?"

Bella looked a bit taken aback by his tone. "She said she must relay a message to the gamekeeper, about when to release your dog."

Alexander's skin prickled. "That makes no sense. I told her I had taken care of that an hour ago." His breathing suddenly increased.

"Perhaps we should go find her?" Bella suggested, catching the urgency of the concern.

"I am going to the gamekeeper."

Perkin joined Alexander as he stormed out of the ballroom. "What is wrong?" he asked, matching Alexander's insistent pace.

"Greyland has left, and the excuse she gave Bella does not add up. I am going to the kennels. Where she was said to have gone."

"The kennels? What does she need in there?"

"Nothing."

Rain greeted them as they opened the massive double front doors.

Before they could take two steps, a stable boy raced toward them. "Your Grace, a man gave me a note to give to you." He handed Alexander the paper.

"When?" Alex wasted no time tearing the seal.

"About a half-hour ago. He told me not to bother you during the party." The boy looked suddenly doubtful. "He said it was of no urgent matter and to give it to you when you came outside. I have been watching the front doors ever since, Your Grace."

Alexander's heart stopped beating. The ink had already begun to bleed from the rain, but the message was clear.

I AM TAKING back what is mine.

McGreggor

ALEX ANGRILY THRUST the paper at Perkin, who scanned it quickly and then crumpled it in his fist. "It is not him."

"I know." Alex turned back abruptly. "The script is my uncle's handwriting."

GREYLAND PUSHED the wet hair from her face as she studied the hunting cabin and its surroundings. She had tied the horse to a tree, far enough away that it would not shy off when the wolf moved in. So far, Malikite had kept to the dense woods and out of sight, but she could feel his eyes on her.

Greyland tried to conjure up some of the half-breed's courage as the rain painted tiny rivers down her cheeks. Light spilled from the cabin's front door. She was thankful for the cover of night. The door opened wider as she advanced, and a lone figure stepped out onto the planked porch.

A woman!

"So glad you could join us," Lady Chatsworth called out.

Greyland froze. A sick, raw fear pulsed through her blood.

"Very glad indeed, little lamb." The masculine voice came from directly behind her.

Derrick.

Greyland shuddered as he placed a hand on her back and pushed her steadily toward the steps and a maniacal looking Lady Chatsworth.

"Where is she?" Greyland demanded.

"Why, the little brat is right here." Lady Chatsworth moved to the side to reveal Annabelle, shivering with fright.

Greyland bolted for the child.

Lady Chatsworth quickly pushed Annabelle back and threw all her weight into Greyland as she charged up the cabin steps. Annabelle screamed. Greyland, unable to avoid the shove, collided with the railing but caught herself before she could topple over the edge. She whirled on the older woman, rage replacing her previous fear.

Greyland took one solid step forward, and doing just as her brothers had taught her, drew back her fist and punched Lady Chatsworth right in the nose.

The blonde reeled backward, her arms flailing wildly as she tried in vain to prevent her fall. She bounced down the remaining steps and landed on her ass at the bottom. Her hand flew to her bloody nose, and she gasped, glaring at Greyland from where she lay sprawled. Unfortunately, she did not stay down long.

The older woman trudged to her feet and charged.

Derrick grabbed her, effectively halting her attack. "Ladies, ladies...this is most improper."

"I will see you hanged!" Greyland spat.

The mirth in Derrick's eyes chilled at once. "Better watch that tone in the presence of children." He marched slowly up the stairs.

Greyland stepped in front of Annabelle.

Derrick stopped one step below where Greyland stood. They were eye to eye. He leaned in. "I will deal with that mouth later when we are alone."

Be it the cold seeping into her bones from the soaking rain or the actual threat, Greyland visibly shivered. Derrick caught the reaction, like a spider pleased with a snared fly, and grinned. Capitalizing on his power, he made a deliberate show of looking over her wet clothing before licking his lips.

"I do not see what Alexander sees in her. She is so plain," Lady Chatsworth said smugly, still wiping the blood as it dripped from her swelling nose. "After a night with me, Alexander will completely forget about her."

"Is that what this is all about?" Greyland hissed.

"Why, yes," Derrick replied.

Greyland reached behind her back for a sobbing Annabelle. The little girl pressed herself into the back of Greyland's skirts, trying to hide.

"This way, both Lady Chatsworth and I get what we want. She gets my nephew and his title. And I get you."

He paused to enjoy her discomfort. "See, Alexander has always gotten everything, and now it is my turn to make him miserable. I can think of no better way than taking from him what he wants most in this world."

Greyland felt her stomach roll over. "He will come for me. He will find me, and he will kill you!"

Derrick smiled. "Ah, yes…about that. He is going to believe you died. You see, Lady Chatsworth is going to proclaim that she was on her way to plead her innocence at Greenshire Castle when, through the driving rain, she saw a small child being thrown into the raging river by murderous looking mercenaries wearing the McGreggor crest. She will then say her cowardly footman jumped from her carriage and fled into the woods when one of the men started their way. From there, she will go on and on, in dramatic female fashion, about how terrified she was."

He rolled his wrist. "She will end this heart-wrenching tale by saying she was able to escape, only because of a sudden commotion back at the water's edge. The McGreggor thug turned back to see what it was just as, to her greatest shock, you burst from the bushes. I am sure you can guess what happened next. You threw yourself into the water after the child and Lady Chatsworth ran as fast as she could to the castle for help." Derrick cocked his head to one side. "Are you keeping up with all this, little lamb?"

He did not give her a chance to reply, not that she could. "They will all mourn you and the orphan, giving me time to take you to France and make you, my wife. We will return in a few years, and by that time Alexander will have married Lady Chatsworth, and you will belong to me." Derrick laughed cruelly. "It is brilliant, you see. I will have broken his heart twice: once when he learns your fate, dying the same way his mother did—you know he still blames himself for that—and then again when he sees you on my arm."

Greyland looked from Derrick to Lady Chatsworth. The woman grinned savagely. Apparently, killing a child to secure a title was no problem at all for her. She had definitely lost her mind.

Greyland searched Derrick's eyes next and saw something different. He had been planning this for a long time. He was not crazy; he was ruthless and wicked.

She had to play this just right.

Why had he divulged his plan to her? Did he really think she would willingly leave Alex, kidnapped or not, and agree to marry him? Did he plan on locking her away so she would not escape? There had to be more. Derrick knew Alex would not accept Lady Chatsworth as a replacement. *No,* he was leading the crazy woman in the only direction she wanted to go. But he had other plans, besides just wounding Alexander. Greyland was sure Derrick planned to kill him.

She winced as the reality of it all punched her right in the solar plexus. Greyland fought back the desire to retrieve her knife and stab Derrick through the heart. He would be on her before she could even get to it. She had to think fast.

Lady Chatsworth was muttering something now. Greyland's mind raced. Annabelle squeezed tighter to the back of her legs.

"Give me the damn brat!" Lady Chatsworth moved directly in front of her.

Greyland stepped back, taking Annabelle with her. "You will have to kill me first."

"That is a lovely idea."

"Now, now." Derrick stepped between the two women. "Let me deal with her." He looked from Greyland to Lady Chatsworth. "I promise to give her a good thrashing." Derrick fixated his perverse stare on Greyland again. "Do you really want the child to watch you die?" He tutted. "I think not."

He turned, snatched Lady Chatsworth forcibly by the elbow, and dragged her off the porch. "I will give you a minute to say your goodbyes to the child."

Greyland bent down and spoke quickly and quietly to the whimpering little girl. "When you get to the carriage, scream, hit, punch and then run to the castle and get help." She saw the terror in the child's eyes. "Malikite will protect you. He is waiting in the woods. Do not look back—just run."

Greyland knew she was right. The dog had grown loyal to the little girl in the last week. He had stayed glued to her side like a shadow all around the castle grounds. He would protect her just as he had protected Greyland in the church.

"Time is up," Derrick said, yanking Greyland up unexpectedly, and pushing Annabelle down the steps. Thankfully the five-year-old managed to stay on her feet through her rough descent.

Lady Chatsworth grabbed hold of the teetering child and started dragging her away. Greyland felt hot tears rolling down her cheeks. She angrily swiped them away before the little girl could see. Annabelle looked back pleadingly with her eyes. Greyland gave her a firm nod.

Derrick stepped in front of Greyland, cutting off her view of the outside world, and pushed her through the cabin's front door.

SOMETHING SHIFTED in Derrick's eyes the moment the door slammed shut behind him. He stalked toward Greyland. She stepped back, but not fast enough.

Derrick caught her wrist and pulled her to him. "Now to see what all the fuss is about." He forced her around and started undoing the buttons at the back of her dress. Beads of sweat broke out on her forehead and her palms grew damp with fear. She had to be strong—at least long enough for Annabelle to get farther away.

"Why do you need to kill him?" She needed to keep Derrick talking.

He stilled at his task. "How very perceptive you are." Greyland felt the heat from his breath on her neck when he leaned in. "I want to be a Duke, of course."

Greyland shuddered when something wet and warm licked up the back of her neck. "I do not want to talk about Alexander now, though." He ripped her dress open.

She gasped and jumped away, using her arms to clutch the torn material to her breasts. It was a natural instinct, and one she hoped would conceal the knife she had just caught with her left hand as the dress had begun to fall.

Derrick's smile was poisonous as he raked her over with his eyes. "I will tell you only once to do as I say. Now, come here and give me my reward."

Greyland brandished the weapon just as he advanced. He froze in his tracks and laughed. "Really? A kitchen knife? That is almost cute, but I will not afford you even the one mistake. Now you must be punished."

He took one more step toward her. She swung the blade and connected with his arm. He cursed, his lips pulling back from his teeth. Before she had time to brace herself, he backhanded her so hard her vision doubled, and she crashed into a side table.

He was on her then, throwing her to the bed. She scrambled for the other side on her hands and knees, but he jumped on her, pinning her down. All the air left her lungs as his weight crushed her face into the mattress.

He flipped her under him and held her hands above her head. "Tisk, tisk. Now, you have forced me to be the bad man."

She spat into his face, earning herself another hard smack to the cheek. This time she tasted blood.

"*Bitch!* Time to see what all the men in London have been killing themselves over. I wonder if you taste as good as you look?" He reached down and bit her nipple hard. She screamed and bucked beneath him.

"That is the spirit, little lamb. I love it when they put up a fight." Derrick restrained both her hands in one of his while his free hand yanked up her skirts. She was no match for him—he was just too strong.

A wave of panic raged through her veins, and she fought with all her might. Derrick smiled at her futile attempts while he fumbled with his trouser buttons. Greyland closed her eyes and felt tears burn her cheeks as she prepared her body for his invasion.

Just as he freed himself from his pants, a woman's ear-piercing scream from outside shot through the night. Blood-curdling snarls followed. Derrick's head jerked to the door.

After what seemed like a lifetime, he slowly turned his face back to Greyland. "When we resume this," he hissed, pushing up and off her, "I will not be nearly as gentle."

ALEXANDER HEARD the death cry pierce through the storm as lightning split the sky. Perkin spun his mount to face him. "It came from over there." The eldest Kingston's intense eyes narrowed in on the woods that lined the cliffs.

Alexander did not answer. Instead, he brought Socrates around in a tight circle and bolted in the direction of the old hunting cabin. Henry and Perkin followed. The rain angrily bit into Alexander's face, but he only felt a sick fear drumming inside his head. Someone had just been killed! By the sound of it, a woman, and she had perished in a most gruesome way.

They were no more than twenty meters from the tree line when a small child burst from the underbrush. She was looking over her shoulder and did not see the three riders approaching. Nor could she hear them over the pelting rain.

The three men had to draw their reins up tight to stop the child from being trampled. She whipped her blonde head around and cried out as she toppled backward. Socrates reared in protest.

Alexander was off the stallion before the beast could put all four hooves in contact with the ground again. He dropped to his knees in the mud and scooped Annabelle into his arms. "Hush, hush…I am here."

She looked into his eyes and then began to wail against his chest.

"Where is Greyland?" He had to almost yell now to be heard through the driving wind and rain.

She pointed a shaky little finger in the direction from which she had come. "Bad man!"

Alexander's brain barely registered that the child had just spoken for the first time since she had come to live at his estate.

Henry was beside him now, prying the child from Alexander's arms and lifting her up into his own. "*Go!*"

Alex wasted no time. He swung back onto Socrates and kicked him into a gallop. He heard Perkin just a pace behind him, pushing his steed to match Socrates' gait. Alex had no idea what they would find. He had heard the cry—they all had—and it brokered no debate for whether the victim had lived.

DERRICK JERKED Greyland from the bed and hauled her to the cabin door. She dug her heels in and clawed at him with her free hand. He slammed her into the wall so hard she nearly lost consciousness.

"Stop fighting or I will kill you!" he grabbed hold of her jaw with one hand, his fingers digging punishingly into her cheeks, and forced her face up to meet his eyes. "Understand?"

His face was a blur, but the meaning hit its mark. He released her and she fell forward, her body giving out, against him. He hoisted her up and tossed her over his shoulder with a curse and marched out into the storm.

The muddy earth and Derrick's backside were all Greyland could see until she was thrust over the back of a horse, face down like a sack of flour. She did not recall seeing the animal when she arrived so it must have been tied out back.

"Sit up!" He barked.

Greyland gathered enough of her muddled wits to realize her dress had slipped the rest of the way down and was now around her ankles. She managed enough strength to kick it all the way off and hoisted herself up to sit astride the saddle. Her thin, rain-soaked shift was now the only thing she had left. Derrick snatched the reins free from a post and climbed up behind her, kicking the horse into action.

It was freezing now, and her body ached with every jostling stride the steed took. She forced her mind from its pain-filled haze by sheer will, enough to notice that Derrick was taking the road that would pass over the river. It might be her only saving grace.

ALEXANDER AND PERKIN were almost to the cabin when Malikite sprang from a low ridge. Socrates calmed immediately, but Perkin was not so lucky and was thrown from his mount. The dog lunged for the blond man, but Alex shouted a halting command.

The half-breed stopped as recognition seemingly set in. Perkin scrambled to his feet, breathing hard. Something caught his eye and he went deathly still.

"What is it?" Alex's voice trailed off as his eyes followed the trajectory of Perkin's stare.

Socrates was prancing nervously now that he had caught the scent. *Fresh blood.* Alex forced his unwilling eyes to look at the carnage beneath the tree.

"It's not her!" Instant relief flooded over him. The woman had blonde hair. "It is Lady Chatsworth."

Perkin regained control of his horse but eyed Malikite with trepidation as he slowly moved both him and his steed away from the wolf and its kill.

"Malikite was protecting Annabelle," Alex stated as realization set in. "That means Greyland is still out there somewhere." He looked around wildly. "Derrick still has her."

Perkin swung back into his saddle. "Then let us go get the bastard."

Greyland's head was on fire, but she pushed beyond the pain to formulate a plan. Through the rain and blood, she could now make out the bridge. A flutter of hope sailed through her mind. If she flung herself into the water, she might stand a chance of out-swimming him.

As the bridge came into focus, her heart dropped. The past two days of storms had caused the river to swell over its banks. There was no way she could survive in that. She was just about to give up hope when she saw, out of her peripheral, a lone rider advancing. She squinted her eyes trying to focus. A black steed.

Edward!

Derrick must have seen him too for he spurred his mount faster, but the beast seemed to be going lame. Greyland held on a little tighter to the saddle, wrapping her fingers beneath its pommel, as they galloped onto the bridge. The last thing she wanted now was to fall into the flooded river and be swallowed up. Alex could not lose the only two women he had ever loved to the same waters.

Suddenly, Derrick yanked back hard on the reins and Greyland went lurching forward. He snatched her back before she was sent careening over the horse's withers. He whirled the winded steed around to face Edward and drew his pistol, aiming it dead center at her brother's chest.

Greyland heard herself scream just as two more riders came out of the woods.

DERRICK TURNED the gun and pressed it to Greyland's temple. Edward, who had made no sign of stopping when the pistol had been trained on him, now halted abruptly. For a long moment, no one said anything. Alexander ground his teeth, noticing that the fiend had rid her of her dress.

Derrick seemed to read Alex's thoughts. A smile took hold of his face as he spoke. "I will make a trade…her life for yours, dear nephew."

"Done!" Alexander said and jumped down from his horse.

"Well, come and get her." Derrick's smile widened as he slipped off his saddle, dragging Greyland forcefully with him.

"No!" she screamed, but Alex continued with steady, purposeful strides.

Alexander felt the power of the river raging underneath the bridge as he made his way onto it. A million sleepless nights thundered through his head, like demons ascending from hell. He was now close enough to see that Greyland's lips were swollen and bloody and there was a cruel gash on her brow.

"Release her!" He growled.

Derrick's hooded eyes danced with mirth. "Gladly, dear nephew."

Before Alex could draw his next breath, Derrick shoved Greyland over the railing and into the deadly waters.

A gunshot exploded into the night.

Alex thought for a moment that he felt fire festering deep into his arm, but the chill of the river dissolved the pain.

THE CURRENT WAS LIKE A LIVING, breathing monster attempting to consume her. Just as she thought she might break the surface, the relentless beast would again pull her back down into its murky depths.

Large objects were slamming into her body, adding to the water's madness. The debris caught up in her shift and clawed down her body. *Bony fingers dragging her down to hell.* Greyland swam with all she had, fighting immeasurable odds.

All of a sudden, she broke free. She gulped a frantic breath of air before she was yanked back under, into the swirling darkness. She felt the freezing water forcing its way into her lungs.

Alexander...

Panic wracked her body as the cold wrapped her in its deadly embrace. She could not move. Her mind watched in horror as her limbs grew numb and gave up. The dark smothered out all light. *All hope.*

Alex...

Alexander fought with everything he had. He fought with his anger, he fought with his body, and he fought with his heart. Then he saw her head pop up out of the vicious current. Hope propelled him on and he swam hard to reach her. Like he had done a million times in his dreams.

But unlike those haunting dreams, one factor had changed. He was no longer a child. This time, he had strength on his side.

Alex dove down. He could not see her, but he connected something threadlike and soft...*hair!* He swam deeper until he was able to grab her arm and pull her to him.

When he broke the surface, he saw a man's figure racing along the shore. *Perkin*! He just had to get Greyland closer. A tree limb crashed into his ribs and a crack of bone sounded within his chest. *Just one more push.*

He felt someone grasp his shoulders and haul them both out.

Greyland lay lifeless as Perkin began his attempts to resuscitate her on the muddy riverbank. Alexander held her hands and pleaded with her. All he heard was the deep, desperate drumming of his heart and the river roaring for its robbed sacrifice. She was cold. *Deadly cold.*

He screamed at her to wake up.

Perkin pounded on her tiny chest.

Someone tried to pull him back.

Alex struck out, sending whomever it was falling backward.

She coughed.

The life-giving sound was music to Alexander's ears. She coughed again and water sputtered from the corners of her mouth. Perkin rolled her to her side and a wave of river water poured out of her lungs.

Alex felt hot tears streaming down his face, mixing with the freezing rain as he dragged her tiny body into his arms. Someone was shouting from behind them now. Greyland began to convulse. Alex hauled her body closer to his own, squeezing her to his chest for warmth.

"We have to get back inside, quickly," Perkin said. He stared hard at Alex. "I need to take her from you." Alex felt his head shake out *no,* but he knew Perkin was right.

"My body is warmer," Perkin said. He swept her up and out of Alexander's arms.

Alex did not remember the ride home. He did not remember the looks of horror on the ladies' faces as he ran headlong into the castle's front door and up the stairs. His brain could not recall anything except the moment Derrick shoved Greyland off the bridge. Her body being snatched up and carried under by the violent and ravenous currents of the angry river.

The image replayed over and over in his weary mind as he stared at her now. Three maids were working tirelessly in a flurry of activity. They had wrapped Greyland's body in hot blankets and were now placing smoking bricks between the goose-down comforter and mattress of the bed.

Perkin worriedly paced the floor, an ashen pallor to his face.

Alex looked pleadingly at the doctor who had been dragged from the village. "If we can get her temperature up, we have a chance," the man said. "Your Grace, you are bleeding." He motioned a serving woman to tend to Alex.

Alex waved her off when she rushed to his side.

"I believe she will want you alive when she wakes up, Your Grace," he added.

The physician's logical reasoning took shape. Alex relented and drew up a chair beside Greyland's bed so the woman could work on cleansing his arm. He did not feel a thing. He realized he would never feel anything ever again if Greyland did not pull through this. He would die along with her.

He heard the maid attending him gasp. "He has been shot!"

The doctor came over and took her place, investigating his arm. Alex did not look. He did not inquire. Did not utter a sound. He kept his eyes fixated on his sleeping beauty. If she would just open those luminous green pools and meet his gaze once more. She looked so frail…so far away from the room. Alex encased her hand in his and bent his head in silent prayer as the doctor took a needle and thread to his wound.

"You are lucky it went clean through," he said.

A serving boy burst into the room a second later. "You must come quickly. Mr. Kingston is in need."

Perkin and Alexander's sights crashed into one another.

"Take care of her," Perkin ordered before bolting from the room.

Alexander's head spun with a sudden realization. *Edward…* He had last seen him on the bridge, just before Alex dove into the river after Greyland. Had he taken on Derrick single-handedly?

The strong smell of the ointment permeated Alex's nostrils as the doctor interrupted his thoughts. "I must attend to Mr. Kingston now. I will be back in when I am done with his wounds."

The doctor's words wedged their way into Alexander's mind and his head snapped up. "Go, quickly!" Alex commanded.

The doctor hastily quit the room. The three maids followed, leaving Alex alone with Greyland. He buried his face in her arm and let the tears build until they ran freely from his tortured eyes. "I am so sorry. This is my fault. Please do not leave me."

Alex knew the moment the door creaked open that Richard had arrived. The pain emanating from Greyland's father matched his own. It filled the room. Alex turned his face to the other man.

"I have someone who I believe can help." Richard glanced down. Alex followed the older man's eyes. Malikite was standing beside him. "His body temperature is much higher than ours. It should elevate hers. If you lie on one side of her and Malikite lies on the other, I think the effect will double."

Alex wasted no time calling the animal up and onto the bed. Malikite seemed to acknowledge his new role as nursemaid and snuggled up close to Greyland.

"How is Edward?"

Richard's solemn expression said everything Alexander needed to know, "He is in grave danger. If they cannot stop the bleeding..." His voice crumbled into a barely audible murmur. "Pray for both my children."

Alex nodded wordlessly. The two men regarded each other for a long moment before Alex spoke. "Is Derrick...?"

"He is dead," Richard said. Then turned and closed the door behind him.

SUFFOCATING HANDS GRIPPED HER THROAT. She tried to scream but could not. Her hands clawed at the unknown assailant. She felt her ribs being crushed as she broke the surface of the water. Her vision blurred around the edges. All she could make out, through the fog that enveloped her, was a dim golden hue burning faintly like a candle on the far side of a vast and dark room.

Then she felt something wet touch her hand.

Greyland forced her mind to focus on the warm golden light, letting it cast off the tunnel of black surrounding her. Shapes began to emerge out of the haze. *Specifically,* a wolf's shape.

Malikite.

He was staring her right in the eyes with those piercing yellow orbs of his. *Her candle in the dark.*

Greyland forced her mind further from its dreamlike state. She was in her room. Malikite was in her bed with her.

A sudden and sharp pain shot through her sides. She winced. What was the squeezing sensation? She looked down and found large arms wrapped around her tightly.

Alex?

Before she could roll over to confirm, a pleading moan reverberated out from behind her.

She pushed out of the vise-like hold and turned to find him locked in what appeared to be his own strangling nightmare.

"Alex! Wake up!" She shook him until his eyes flew open.

He lunged for her, drawing her to his chest, one arm around her waist and one cradling her head. "Thank God!"

She tried to look into his eyes, but his hand held her head firmly against his body. As if he were afraid to let her go. Greyland could feel the wild tempo of his heart hammering against her ear. She began to weep silently for his obvious pain.

He pulled back, just enough, so that he could stare into her eyes, worriedly. "Do not cry, darling. Everything is good now. You are safe. Annabelle's safe. Edward's safe. And Derrick is dead," he rushed to console her.

Greyland's mind scrambled to keep up. She searched his eyes. "Where are they? What happened to Edward?"

"Annabelle is sleeping down the hall, with Annie hovering over her like a hawk. Edward is recovering from his wounds. He killed Derrick. However, during that fight he was stabbed, but the doctor was able to stop the bleeding. He has already asked for a comely nursemaid to attend to his every need." Alex grinned slowly, as if the muscles of his cheeks were trying to remember how to shape the simple action. "If that does not tell you he will be just fine, I do not know what will."

Greyland laughed, and then grimaced when her body protested the action. Alex's smile vanished as he considered her battered face more closely. He softly traced his finger up the outline of her jaw, stopping when he reached her cheekbone. "Greyland, Derrick did not—"

"No, he was about to, but my plan with your dog prevented him the chance." Greyland reached around behind her and patted

Malikite's head. "I knew this good boy would protect Annabelle. She did as I instructed and screamed when Lady Chatsworth took her out of the cabin. They had planned on killing her and staging my death so that Derrick could steal me away and marry me before returning to kill you. Of course, he kept that last part from his accomplice, and she believed she could have you once you accepted my fate."

Alex did not speak for several heartbeats. "I am so sorry I did not reach you sooner." His brows drew together tightly and a muscle in his jaw twitched.

"Oh, Alex, do not blame yourself. I got an anonymous note saying that whoever had Annabelle would kill her if I did not come alone."

Greyland reached up and cupped Alex's jaw in an effort to soothe the tension residing there. "I am just sorry I walked into his trap. I really thought it was Colin and that you would know where to find me. I could not let anything hurt her. You must understand." Her voice wavered, on the verge of a new set of tears.

She was stunned to see his blue eyes grow glassy. "I thought I had lost you. When he shoved you into the river…my world stopped."

She moved up and kissed his jaw, his lips, and his eyelids, tasting the salt. "You saved me." Her voice shook as she moved back to look into his eyes. "Your mother would be proud."

"Greyland." He said softly, her name coming out scarcely louder than a whisper. "You are my everything."

Greyland took a deep breath before the words rushed out. "Will you please get the blasted Vicar in this room right now? We can give everyone the big production in a week."

Alex regarded her for a moment. "Are you certain? The gossip hounds will run amok."

She grinned and pressed her lips against his. "Alex, I want you to do a quick review of everything that has transpired in the past six weeks and tell me if you honestly think I care."

He tilted his head and flashed her that wicked, scandalous smile. "You are absolutely right."

He jumped up from the bed, with seemingly no effort at all, and pulled on the bell-rope. Greyland's eyes landed on the bandage wrapped around his arm. "Alex, your arm!"

Alex smiled as he donned a shirt. "Tis merely a flesh wound." He leaned over the bed and kissed her forehead. "One I would take ten times over for you."

Samson arrived mere seconds later when Alex had just finished pulling on his trousers.

"Ah, Samson, I have need of Vicar Thomson." He glanced over his shoulder at Greyland. "Please tell Richard, Perkin, Thomas, Bella, and Henry to meet us in Edward's room when he arrives. And please give my regards to the rest of the guests and send them home. I am sure they will understand."

"Yes, Your Grace. Most have already departed," Samson said before giving Greyland his full attention. "How are you feeling, my lady?"

"Much better. Thank you." Greyland smiled.

"Have a feast prepared for our remaining family and friends. Spare no expense." Alex continued, clearly glad to have a task at hand that did not involve watching Greyland cling perilously to life.

"Yes, Your Grace. Anything else?"

"That will be all."

When the door closed, Alex sat back down on the bed. "Within an hour, you will be a duchess. Is it acceptable that we wed in your brother's chambers? He cannot move from the bed for at least a week. Doctor's orders. And I daresay, I will not want to face him later, if he finds out we did not include him." He reached out and ran a lazy finger down the bridge of her nose.

"I think that is a wonderful plan." Greyland agreed. "Just us, and our closest friends and family. That is all I ever desired anyway."

She pushed up to a seated position. Alex reached out and dragged her gingerly into his embrace. He cupped the back of her head gently with his hand and rested his chin atop her hair. After a long moment, he breathed out a sigh that spoke volumes. They had been through so much, and yet, they still fit together perfectly. With Greyland tucked into his protective embrace. Two pieces of a puzzle that made up a whole.

Greyland felt her cheeks lift into a content smile. She could stay this way forever, snuggled against his chest, intoxicated by his amazing scent and shielded by his indomitable strength. Her Dark Duke. The most stubborn, handsome, romantic, caring man she had ever met. The man she had bared her soul to and the man that had likewise, turned his life upside down to accommodate her. The man that would be the father of her children. The man that would give her Christmas trees…*and stillness*.

Greyland looked up into his penetrating blue eyes. "Do you still believe all of this was destiny?"

Alex lowered his head, his mouth hovering just above her lips before whispering, "I believe it more this day than ever before." He kissed her slowly, as soft as the beating wings of a butterfly.

He pulled back slightly, his thumb replacing his lips to caress the seam out her mouth. "My life was created with one purpose, Greyland. To find you. *My* destiny."

XVI

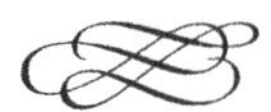

"Please say you will never tire of me, love?" Alex said.

"Alex...or should I now call you, Lord Ravenous? You have nothing to worry about."

They laughed, their voices blending as one. A knock sounded. "Yes?" Alex called out, his tone clipped with annoyance.

"Lord and Lady Kennington are newly arrived," Annie answered.

"Thank you, Annie." He smiled rakishly down at Greyland, still pinned beneath him on their bed. "Please supply our guests with lemon cakes. Lots of lemon cakes," he added loudly, then lowered his voice back to a more conversational level. "We know how voracious Bella's appetite has become now that she is with child."

"Yes, Your Grace, of course." Annie could be heard quickly scurrying off down the hall.

Alex kissed Greyland's forehead then rolled to the side and pushed to a sitting position on the edge of the bed.

He grinned over his shoulder when the bed shifted behind him and Greyland leaned in to softly trace the tattoo on his shoulder. Edward, Perkin, and Alex had all gotten one last month from a Chinaman who had been passing through London.

Edward had found the tiny old man and insisted the three go and get symbolic tattoos. It had taken a few too many rounds at White's before Alex and Perkin had agreed, but there they all sat the next morning, hungover and taking their turns getting stabbed repeatedly with a tiny needle.

Both the brothers had chosen their family's ancient crest, the White Rose. Alex also selected the White Rose but added his family's crest, the dragon. The old Chinaman drew Alexander's ancestral crest first and then artfully wrapped a delicate rose stem around the stoic dragon. Together the two symbols complimented each other beautifully and made for a striking representation of the two families. The dragon and the white rose, together as one, as both had been for over three hundred years. Now joined together in blood by his and Greyland's union in marriage.

"You still like it?" he asked.

"I love it."

"Good." He stood, reaching out a hand to her. She grinned up at him and placed her hand in his. Alex pulled her effortlessly from the bed. "Now, let us go see how big your best friend has gotten in the last month. I am sure she is dying to see how much Annabelle and little Tristan have grown."

He loved how Greyland's smile widened with unabashed joy at the mention of their children. She had blessed him with their first son six months ago and the little boy was already growing like a weed. His hair was thick with brown curls and his eyes were jade green, just as Alex had hoped they would be. He was a pretty baby and Alex knew he would grow into a handsome man.

Annabelle had bloomed under Greyland and Alex's love. Their little girl now talked from sunup until sundown when Greyland would tuck her into bed and tell her bedtime stories. Annabelle loved her new baby brother beyond belief. She constantly asked to hold him. And to both her parents' relief, she seemed to have no memory of that horrible night last year.

The Queen's men had arrested the McGreggor Laird and forced him to sign a document of peace with England and the Kingston's. The Queen then banned both father and son from ever returning to

English soil, in exchange for them being allowed to keep their heads.

The Queen's generosity with the Kingston family had also continued. She honored Richard with many more holdings, and it was widely known that he was now her closest confidant. She relied on him in all matters of state.

Perkin had also risen like a shining star in the Kingdom. He held a very high seat in Parliament and worked closely with his father and The Queen.

Edward had spent the better part of a year abroad but hastily returned from Italy for the birth of Greyland's and Alex's first-born. He was currently enjoying the London season in excess, alongside Henry.

Perkin was too wrapped up in matters of state to socialize with the ton very often. This left Edward as the most sought-after lord in England. Edward took to his role of self-indulgent rake with little to no effort at all and seemed to be enjoying his carefree bachelor lifestyle in abundance. Alex knew Richard pressed both brothers consistently to take a wife, but Perkin insisted he was too busy, while Edward insisted he had too many mistresses.

Alex also knew that Edward still secretly nursed a broken heart after the sudden death of Lord Ashlown's sister, Jessica. She had taken to the sweats and died within a week. Edward had been devastated. He had planned on asking for her hand after a three-week courtship, but she passed away from the illness before he could propose. He had left to tour Italy and Greece right after the service.

The middle Kingston was doing his best now to mask any painful memories with an excess of brandy, gaming, and women. Alex, Perkin, and Richard, all welcomed him back without judgment. They understood his way of healing and knew in time he would settle down and put aside the demons that haunted his past.

Alex turned his attention back to his lovely wife and helped her into her day dress. As his hands worked to button the back of her gown, he could not help but bend down and kiss the nape of her slender neck.

“Alex,” she playfully warned.

He ran his fingers up her spine and marveled at the tiny gooseflesh that lifted to the surface of her skin.

“We have guests, Bella and Thomas would…”

He bent and took her earlobe between his teeth. She moaned. Alex began undoing the previous work he had just started. “What is ten more minutes?”

“My lord,” she intoned in that breathless, sensual way that meant Alex had succeeded in winning her over. “I daresay they will be just fine with the lemon cakes.”

She turned and pushed him onto the bed.

To Be Continued...

PREVIEW

Please enjoy a sample of Book Two, Under His Guidance. Available now at all online retailers!

Edwards's story

London 1839

Edward swirled the brandy in his glass as the last tinges of daylight filtered through the branches on the great oak tree. The encroaching night snaked in from the western shore of the lake, its smooth, feathery mist leading the way. A crisp breeze, with a hickory smoke breath from a nearby fire, caught a falling leaf and danced it gracefully down to land beside his black polished boots. The delicate foliage added to the symphony of colors he had been admiring, each leaf singing with their own individual voice. Brilliant golden tenors and sensuous burgundy baritones all lent a song, as another beautiful autumn day came to an end.

Too bad he had missed it all, sleeping off the previous night's bender. Edward sighed. He really should take his brother's advice and try to rise at a more appropriate hour.

He shook off the unpleasant thought like a chill. He had no idea how Perkin stayed so… damn perfect. Alas, such a lifestyle was not for him; Edward Kingston was far from perfect.

Besides, there was limitless enjoyment reaped in the skilled art of being bad. On that thought, he rapped his walking stick on the ground. A grin etched the corners of his mouth as he turned abruptly, eager to start his affair with the night.

Out of the corner of his eye he saw Henry take a long drag off his cheroot before discarding it on the ground. The two began their silent trek back up to the manor. No words were needed between them. It was time to begin the hunt for the next great scandal.

They matched strides twenty paces down the lane like a pair of stalking lions. As they drew near the house, a carriage appeared. A footman hopped down from the rolling transport and opened the door before the carriage wheels could make their final rotation. Both gentlemen climbed inside.

Henry tapped the roof and the sleek black rig pulled away. "What shall it be first? Dinner, cards, and women. Or the races to start? Followed by dinner, cards and dancing."

He lounged back in the seat across from Edward and stretched his arms behind his head, lacing his fingers together at the base of his skull. "The order matters not to me as long as the end result remains the same. A few lovely ladies, gifted with questionable morals, draped across our arms?"

Edward could feel the corners of his mouth pulling upwards. "I fancy both options." He smiled. "The night is young and as we know, full of delights."

Punishing hands groping at her. A pungent liquor-soaked tongue stabbing around inside her mouth. Vile threats spitting poison into her ears.

Morgan jolted awake, choking on the dryness of her throat. Her eyes darted around the carriage in a frantic effort to re-familiarize herself with the surroundings. Her heart pounded heavy in her chest and her skin crawled, as if a spider had unfurled itself in her hand.

She shook her head, forcing away the lingering imagery of her much-too-vivid nightmare. She was safe. In a carriage bound for London. *He was not here.*

Her mother and maid were still asleep on the other side of the carriage. Morgan exhaled slowly, not wishing to alert them to her personal hell. The last thing she wanted was to bring anymore worry to them. Her mother had been through enough after losing Morgan's father, having to hastily remarry, and then being forced to live with the life that followed those tragic set of events.

Morgan's stepfather, the Earl of Vistmont, had seemed agreeable at first. Having recently lost his own spouse, the two were a logical match. But the honeymoon was short lived. The earl's well-meaning concern and practical protectiveness over his new bride turned dark and twisted with alarming succession. Before the ink had barely time to dry on their marriage license, the earl's domineering ways increased to the point of physical violence.

Morgan watched her mother resting peacefully across from her. It pained her deeply to think that her only repose would, forever forward, be solely found in the confines of her sleep. Life was not fair.

And unfortunately, the strongest usually gave all. As her mother was now doing for Morgan. Bumping along in a carriage, on a rutted out old road, freedom bound.

Luckily for Morgan, the earl had not laid a finger on her. That was exactly how her mother intended it to stay. The countess had written to her sister, the Duchess Vandicamp, and implored her to invite them to the city, where Morgan could be "educated on some of the finer skill-sets befitting a lady".

Her dear aunt had graciously accepted, practically beside herself with the prospect of indoctrinating a new debutante into the lucrative world of London's elite bon ton. Morgan hoped the Duchess would not be disappointed when she alit from their dilapidated old carriage.

Morgan glanced at the empty seat to her right. The fabric was threadbare and had an odor that could best be described as cat piss—

though she knew it was likely comprised of various stenches—all of which a young lady should know nothing of. At least the compartment was in better shape than the outside of the carriage. The transport looked like it had fared poorly in more than a few races and might have even been submerged at one point in time.

Morgan cringed as she considered what a truly note-worthy entrance they would be making on Governors Square. Just another way her stepfather could inflict shame on her mother. The earl had agreed, reluctantly, to allowing Morgan a turn at London, but there was no way he would allow them the use of one of his finer rigs to get there. Those he saved for entertaining his whores.

Morgan rolled her eyes. At least she would be free of the earl's dreaded household. She resigned herself to think no more of the vile man. Her stepfather was not worthy of her time, or attention. Besides, there was plenty more pressing matters to contemplate.

Foremost, she had much to learn before the season got underway. Once she became engrossed in her education, Morgan would make sure she applied those lessons to all aspects of social obligation. By chance, she might be successful in finding a gentleman that would think her agreeable.

Morgan felt herself nod, affirmatively. Any arrangement would be better than the life she was leaving behind. She would appreciate her winter away—not just from her unpredictable stepfather, but from his horrible offspring as well. *Roderick.*

A familiar chill crystalized across her skin like ice over a pond. She pulled her shawl up tighter around her shoulders. Despite her resolve to look only to the future, her thoughts dragged her backwards yet again…to her stepbrother. Or as she referred to him, the devil incarnate.

Throughout the first year of their parents' marriage, Roderick had merely taunted Morgan with nasty, degrading snips here and there. Everything from her simple country upbringing to the way she held a teacup. Apparently, she had hands like a man and the grace of a butcher. He had also taken great pleasure in encouraging his boorish friends to do the same. There was not a day gone by that she hadn't been made to feel inadequate in her home.

However, it had not stopped there. Roderick's torment only intensified when her body dramatically changed over the course of one summer, from lanky teenager to voluptuous woman. Her upbringing ceased to matter much now. Her stepbrother suddenly seemed to seek her out everywhere she went, his jeers becoming even more perverse, filling her ears with all sorts of sexual Innuendoes every chance he was afforded.

If her maid, Bertrice, had not interrupted them the night before they left for London…Morgan knew he would have made good on his threat to show her *just what* her body was made for. "To give pleasure to men," he had rasped, after having dragged her into the kitchen pantry and pinned her against the wall.

She had been truly terrified for the first time in her life but did not tell a soul, save Bertrice, who had witnessed the abuse first-hand. Her loyal maid had reluctantly sworn secrecy, and Morgan had spent the rest of that night in two vastly different states of mind. One half in tears, feeling utterly helpless, and the other half wanting to fight, vowing to be the best deduced debutante London had ever laid eyes on. The latter, however, was her only ticket out. For if she ever did return to her stepfathers' residence, her honor, and thus her life, would be over.

All would be fine, she reminded herself for the millionth time, if she could get to London and quickly secure a husband. That was about her only hope. Apart from running away to America.

Morgan rested her head against the seat back. There was no way she could survive in America. She was no more suited for living on her own than she was suited to be the Queen of England. She sighed. No, she was trapped smack dab between two vastly different worlds. Not born an aristocrat, and not born a farmer. She would have to go with her most obvious choice of escape…marriage.

To accomplish that she would need to take her studies at the duchesses very seriously, for she was severely lacking in some of the finer skills expected of a lady. Her needlepoint was subpar, her musical talents were mediocre at best, and her dancing was deplorable. She required desperate help. Thankfully, her aunt had already hired instructors. Morgan could embark on her education as soon as they arrived in London.

At least she was pretty. Or rather, that is what her mother and Bertrice claimed. Roderick's friends had confirmed this ideology when they raked her over with hungry, roving eyes. As disconcerting as it was, Morgan assumed that at least the feeling of being basically undressed by a man's gaze meant one was not altogether unappealing.

Still, she was not the ideal bon ton beauty. As her stepbrother had crudely pointed out. She had the body of a 'doxy' and no 'proper' London gentlemen would find her desirable as a wife.

She knew she was unfashionably curvy for being only eighteen years old. Morgan did not know what a paramour's body looked like, but she suspected the rogue knew what he was talking about.

Morgan continued to mentally tick off her physical attributes and failures. She was of medium height, with good skin, but her fiery auburn hair was just as unfashionable as her overly developed figure. She looked *too* Scottish, another of Roderick's claims. Her shapely legs were probably her best feature, but she could not exactly flaunt those about town. All in all, Morgan suspected she was average—much like her lot in life.

She looked out the window and was pulled sharply from her reverie. The first glimpses of the city were coming into view. Her mouth fell open. This was nothing like her little village town.

Morgan was immediately captivated with the bustling landscape. People darted everywhere, moving in and out of the impressive stone buildings that seemed to grow right out of the ground, as though they had been rooted in the soil for centuries.

As the carriage ambled along, the practical and more rudimentary exteriors began to give way to newer, more artistic detail, each delicate carving of the craftsman's tool telling of the fortune that had gone into the beautiful homes. Extravagant entry ways now stared down at them like imposing guard dogs questioning their intrusion and silently judging their worth. It was both intimidating, and exquisite.

The coach hit a bump, jostling Bertrice and her mother from their slumber. "Oh, Mother!" Morgan exclaimed. "You can practically feel the city breathing, can you not? It is as if every individual heartbeat on these streets is joining together to make up one gigantic beast." She clapped her gloved hands enthusiastically. "This city, London, is where I am meant to be."

She looked back at the two older women, sitting speechless across from her, and smiled. "This beast of a city is our savior!"

ABOUT STACY VON HAEGERT

Stacy grew up in Nashville, Tennessee, daughter of a singer-songwriter and an equestrian enthusiast. When she was not tagging along with her father into music city staples like the Blue Bird or riding her mother's Arabians at breakneck speeds over the Tennessee countryside, she was writing short stories and poems. She is obsessed with old houses, good literature, and boogie boarding.

Her passion for words grew and in 2013, Stacy released her first book, 'Under his Protection,' that raced up Amazon's charts landing at #2 in the US and #1 in the UK.

Stacy currently lives in historic downtown Franklin TN where she writes by day and teaches ballroom dance in the evenings.

Don't forget to stalk me on social media!

Made in the USA
Las Vegas, NV
19 April 2024